BREAKOUT

HOLLYS BOOK RACK

Michael Gear

Price: $ 3.50

The area's only
Trading Bookstore

Over 60,000 Used Titles!
All at ½ Price!

Hours:
Mon-Fri 10am-7pm
Sat 10am-6pm
Closed Sundays

1408 Lexington Avenue
Mansfield, Ohio

www.hollysbookrack.com

This book is dedicated to my friend, Mark Seger,
who has given his life to the youth of Dublin, Ireland.

Your dedication and prayers are bringing about a
God "breakout" beyond anything you dream
or imagine.

OTHER BOOKS IN THE
EXTREME FICTION SERIES

Book 1: *Point Blank*
Book 3: *Real*

BREAKOUT

MARK A. REMPEL

THOMAS NELSON PUBLISHERS®
Nashville

A Division of Thomas Nelson, Inc.
www.ThomasNelson.com

Copyright © 2002 by Mark A. Rempel

All rights reserved. Written permission must be secured from the publisher to use or reproduce any part of this book, except for brief quotations in critical reviews or articles.

Published in Nashville, Tennessee, by Thomas Nelson, Inc.

Scripture quotations are from THE NEW KING JAMES VERSION. Copyright © 1979, 1980, 1982, Thomas Nelson, Inc., Publishers.

Library of Congress Cataloging-in-Publication Data

Rempel, Mark A.
 Breakout / Mark Rempel.
  p. cm.—(Extreme fiction series ; bk. 2)
 Summary: A year after a tragic shooting at Lincoln High, Taylor finds his prayers answered when a dramatic spiritual awakening occurs among the students and begins to spread throughout the country and the world.
 ISBN 0-7852-6547-3 (pbk. : alk. paper)
 1. Christian life—Fiction. 2. High schools—Fiction. I. Title.
PZ7.R2838 Br 2002
[Fic]—dc21   2002003474

Printed in the United States of America

02 03 04 05 06 QWB 5 4 3 2 1

CHAPTER 1

SETH ANDERSON DROVE LIKE A MANIAC into the parking lot of Lincoln High School. It was half past noon and he was late. He slid into an empty parking stall, slammed on the brakes, and jumped out of the car before the vehicle was fully in park. Seth grabbed the two cheeseburgers in a fast-food paper bag from the front seat while shutting the door. His new Etnies tapped on the pavement in a quick pace as he headed for the Lincoln High lunchroom door. Seth grabbed the handle, stepping inside.

"I need a pass," remarked Mrs. Huey, his former guidance counselor, in a grave voice before she recognized his face. "Oh, Seth, how are you?" she continued, now sounding more pleasant.

"Great," he said in a rush. "I don't have time to sign in. Will you cover me?"

Mrs. Huey thought about it for a moment and then responded. "Sure, Seth. Anything for you."

"Thanks, Mrs. Huey," he said back, running down the hallway. "I owe you one."

"How about one of those cheeseburgers?"

Seth reached in the bag and threw one down the hall in her direction. It landed on the floor in front of her feet, dumping the hamburger patty out on the floor. "Sorry!" he screamed, keeping a consistent pace.

"Hey, Seth!" shouted a friendly voice from somewhere in the crowded hallway.

"Seth, what are you doing here?" said another.

"Nice shoes, Sethboy!" an underclassman noted.

"Thanks," Seth replied, glancing down at his feet. A few weeks of overtime at his job had paid off. Retail work at a local sporting goods store wasn't his favorite pick for a job, but he worked consistent hours and the pay wasn't bad. He'd been saving for these shoes for months now.

After car insurance, gas, a car payment, first-semester books and clothing of course, it hadn't been an easy road saving for shoes. But he insisted on having them, and Liz would have liked them.

"Coming through," he shouted, pushing the library door open as hard as he could. He tucked the one cheeseburger left in the brown paper bag under his shirt, smiling at Mrs. Levy, Lincoln's stone age librarian. Seth kept thinking she was going to retire, but every year she seemed to pull through. He glanced through the main floor crowded with books, newspapers, magazines, and a few study centers that were really uncomfortable molded-plastic chairs at Formica tables. He noticed a light on in one of the rooms along the back wall.

"That's gotta be him," he whispered to himself.

Seth walked briskly through the American History section, never once realizing that he was part of American history himself. It had been sixteen months, seven days, and ten hours since his name had been printed across the headlines of almost every newspaper in America. Not to mention getting his face on the covers of *Time* and *Newsweek*. Then, there had been the interview with *People* magazine, the *New York Times*, and the *National Enquirer*. He was surprised at how true the story had come out once the tabloid got ahold of it. Probably his favorite moment, though, was the hour-long chat that had been arranged for him through America Online. In just sixty minutes, more than one hundred thousand questions were e-mailed to him. Not to mention an audience of over one million listeners. He loved sharing the message of hope he had received through the entire nightmare. But several months ago all the media attention seemed to dissipate. The only coverage had been the one-year-anniversary broadcast CNN had done live on the day that marked the shooting. Since then, Seth was just an ordinary guy again. Today, he was an ordinary guy with new Etnies on.

"Taylor," he said, stepping into the small study room.

"Finally!" Taylor Shepperd remarked, taking a bite from the apple he took out of a brown paper bag. "Watch out, if Mrs. Levy catches us eating in here she'll wig out. I'll get stuck in detention again."

"So this is a secret lunch meeting you called then" Seth joked back, shutting the door.

"Kind of. Thanks for coming, dude."

"Hey, you're the student council president. You call, I come."

"Well, you're still a hero around here. You always will be. In fact, we can eat our lunch because Levy will give us a break when she sees I'm with you," he said, dumping a smashed sandwich inside a plastic bag onto the table.

"So how's the year going?" Seth asked, taking a bite out of the cold burger in his hands.

Taylor paused. His short blond hair, blue eyes, and medium muscular frame gave him the all-American look that made him one of the most popular guys in the school. "I guess all right."

"You don't sound too sure of yourself."

"I don't know. Man, I wish you were on campus every day like you were last year. It's like everyone has put the past sixteen months out of their minds. People want to forget about everything that happened around here."

"Is that all bad? I mean, there isn't a day that goes by that I don't want to."

"I guess not, but I don't feel like it's over."

Seth's eyes shot up. He set down the last part of the cheeseburger and stopped chewing.

"What? Did somebody threaten the school again?"

"No, no, not like that. I mean, I don't think God is done using this thing. I think He's just begun."

"You're confusing me."

"Sorry. I just think something big is going to happen on our campus. What happened to you and the rest of the school got us thinking. And for a while, it changed us. But there is more, I know it. That's not enough. God wants this entire school to go after Him like you have."

"Well, I'm not perfect. God knows that."

"So do I, Anderson." They smiled at each other. "So our FCA has grown a little. So a few kids are more vocal about what they believe. Sixteen people didn't die just for that."

"I believe that, too."

"I wish more people would. It's like people forget their visions so quickly. You said something in your graduation speech I'll never forget. 'Our triumph is going to change the world.' I don't know if our triumph is still even changing the school. Our school, Seth. Yours and mine."

"What are you getting at?"

"Priorities. Why do our priorities change so quick? Do God's? But who am I arguing with? I mean it's not just our school, but our culture. There is so much more than what we've seen."

There was a pause. Taylor stared into the distance.

"So, what are you thinking?"

"It's big, Seth. Really big. Like a nation big."

Both of them were quiet for a moment.

Taylor continued. "I've been praying like crazy lately, Seth. I can't sleep. I can't eat. I just want to see something happen. I want to see the students in this school changed."

"But there has been change, Taylor."

"I know. But you think they're not still drinking on the weekends? Or having sex? I had some kid in my philosophy class totally admit he had been experimenting with some really weird sexual thoughts lately. He got a lot of the ideas off the Internet. My class just accepted it like it didn't matter." He paused. "But it does matter. It all matters. I keep thinking, *What else will it take?* So all I can think of to do is pray."

Seth finished off the cheeseburger, staring into the fake wood-grain pattern glued onto the Formica table.

"I figured I would talk to you about it. Because I don't know if I can go into that lunchroom again and pray over my food, expecting a miracle and never seeing it." He paused, then glanced at his watch. "I've got five minutes before history starts."

"Yeah, well, Taylor—," Seth started before his friend cut him off.

"Listen, Anderson, I know you're busy with your pre-law classes and your dream to bring justice to schools around this country and everything—"

"How'd you know that was my dream?"

"I watch *20/20*, too." Taylor laughed. "But I'm talking about this school. Our school. Right here. The place where it all happened. Building an entirely new west wing on this place isn't going to change what needs to happen first. This is something only God can do."

"So what do you want me to do?"

Taylor glanced at his watch again. "Pray. Just pray."

"I do. Every day for this place."

"Then pray harder. Something has got to happen, Seth. Something."

Taylor grabbed his red backpack and stepped out of the room. The door shut, leaving Seth in the silence. Sometimes he hated silence. That was when he seemed to hear the gunshots echoing from the past the loudest.

A few students walked by laughing and talking wildly. Seth noticed a new pair of Etnies on one of the students. He looked down at his shoes, realizing how much a part of this school he would always be. He had been busy lately trying to rebuild his life like everyone else. After all, he had always dreamed of being a lawyer. And now, being labeled as the central figure in America's worst school shooting only gave him more fuel to study and fight for the laws of this land. He was desperate to never allow what had happened to him happen to anyone else. "This is a good cause. I'm busy for a great reason," he debated with himself. "But," he whispered, "good causes don't save lives. Prayer does." Seth bowed his head and started to pray. Until now an act of man had been the defining moment in Seth's life. He was now ready for an act of God to define it.

Mrs. Levy marched through the History section to reprimand whoever was talking so loud in Room Two. She reached for the door handle, noticing it was Seth Anderson through the glass window. He was alone, and alone she would leave him. Mrs. Levy turned around and headed back through the shelves of books. Little did she know she was about to touch American history again.

CHAPTER 2

TAYLOR SHEPPERD GRABBED a green lunch tray and stepped back into the lunch line. He read the sign posted on the wall above the silverware cart.

Wednesday, October 11.
Goulash. Mashed potatoes. Roll. Butter. Green beans.

"Great," he said to a younger student standing behind him. "It's starch day. Can't forget those carbs, eh?" he said, hitting the student on the shoulder. "And goulash. What the heck is goulash, anyway? And the word *goul*? Sounds like something scary, you know?"

"Whatever you say," the student remarked back nervously. Standing next to Taylor was a big deal to the younger freshman. "Hey, I voted for you," he said with a squeak in his voice.

"Really? Thanks. I'm sure I needed that vote in the recount."

"Close race."

"Sure was," Taylor said back, lifting his tray. A wet scoop of beef and noodles slopped down onto the main compartment of his plate. He smiled at the lady with the hair net. She smiled back, her two front gold teeth sparkling in the fluorescent light. "Mmm good," he said sarcastically under his breath.

The walk to his normal eating spot was short. The lunch table was full today. Not to mention the sound in the lunchroom. The noise seemed to be unbearably high. This Friday was Lincoln's first football game of the season. After last year's loss in the state finals, comeback was on everybody's mind. "Maybe that's what everyone is talking about," he said to himself.

"Hey Taylor," Kimberly Le said, winking at him. "I saved a spot for you."

"Thanks," he said, sitting down. "You're welcome to try this delicious 'ghostlosh' with me."

"Ghostlosh?" she said, smiling. Her crush on him was obvious.

"Yeah, 'ghostlosh,' because it comes back to haunt you. I'll probably be on the toilet all night."

"Thanks, Shepperd, you just ruined my lunch."

"How come you're eating on campus this year? Seniors don't have to, you know?" Kimberly asked, hoping she was the reason he was there.

"Oh, I love you juniors so much that I can't bear to be without you," he said sarcastically.

"Right. You're full of it, Shepperd," Matt Forrester said from across the table.

"Full of what? Wait, don't say it! Virgin ears, virgin ears!" Taylor remarked quickly.

Everyone laughed.

He glanced around the lunchroom. The very reason he was staying through lunch this year was what he would do next. Taylor bowed his head to pray.

"Hey," Matt cut in before Taylor could start, "can you tell whoever you pray to that I'm desperate to pass that history pop quiz today? I may need some brain help."

Taylor lifted his head. "Forrester, you need all the help you can get." He bowed his head again, first praying for his food, then his school as he had done hundreds of times before. That's why he was here. He committed at the beginning of his junior year to pray every day at the lunch table for his school. All through last year, and now this year. He could feel the stares around him as usual, but prayed silently. Today longer than normal. Taylor tried to lift his head after saying a formal "Amen," but he couldn't. His head felt like it weighed eighty pounds. He tried again. Something inside gave him a feeling to keep praying. He said a few short words again then lifted his head. It was a struggle, but he managed to lift it to where it had been before. He opened his eyes. The lunchroom was unusually quiet. So quiet you could hear a pin drop, or a noodle from a pile of goulash for that matter. Taylor glanced back and forth, then back and forth again. Something had changed during the sixty seconds of prayer. What, he couldn't put his finger on. He heard sniffling, then faint cries. Somebody was crying.

"Kimberly?" he whispered.

Kimberly's dark hair flowed over the table. Her head was facedown.

Oh my God! Taylor thought. *There's been a shooting. She's been shot!* Taylor breathed in a deep breath to shout, and then stopped, noticing Kimberly's face as it rose from the table. He noticed her tears weren't of fear or pain, but they looked as if they were tears of . . . remorse.

Taylor looked at her, confused. He looked around the lunchroom, confused. Kimberly wasn't the only one crying. The sounds of hearts breaking were coming from all over. Taylor hadn't heard cries like this since the memorial service for the sixteen lives lost. But this was different. These cries, these tears, felt very different.

"What is going on?" whispered Taylor in shock. Then he remembered his prayer. He said it again quietly to himself. "Oh God, bring this school to its knees. Oh God, I'm desperate. Bring this stinkin' lunchroom to repentance!" He closed his eyes, then opened them again. Could this prayer really be coming true?

Matt stared deeply into Taylor's eyes just a few feet across from him. "God, Shepperd, I need Him. I need God. Lead me to God." Matt collapsed with his face in his hands onto the table. "I need God!" he sobbed.

Taylor took a deep breath. He needed Him, too.

CHAPTER 3

LENNY JOHNSON ORDERED A DIET COKE and a Chicago-style hot dog with extra kraut. The small Chicago-based doghouse was a popular stop across from Kennedy Junior High on the outer edge of the east side of Harlem. He glanced at his watch while sitting in a booth by the window, staring at the school. No movement. Just a few security guards drinking coffee, standing outside the old brick building. Security on the grounds of most Harlem schools had been beefed up after the Lincoln tragedy. Not just in this tough neighborhood of New York City, but all over the country.

"Diet Coke and Chicago with extra kraut," hollered a man from behind the busy counter. Lenny stood and retrieved his food. It had been a typical Monday for him. He had spent a few hours at the church answering several phone calls, then headed over to the restaurant to meet with six students who prayed once a week for a breakthrough within the neighborhoods of Harlem. Lenny had fought hard to have the prayer meeting on campus, but the busyness of the class schedule only gave him an early morning spot. He had been working with teenagers long enough to know the answer. Early morning wasn't an option for a thirteen-year-old. So he settled for a lunch meeting once a week. It was routine now. By the time he had ordered his hot dog every week, the students who normally met him would have retrieved their special permission permits and been escorted by a security guard to the lunch diner. Today was out of routine. Lenny took a sip of the soda, glancing at his watch again. He wondered where everyone was.

Harlem hadn't been the easiest place to pastor. He and his wife, Clarise, had moved out here just a year ago from the suburbs of Detroit. They had left the position of their dreams to follow after a vision for young lives in New York City. The change had been difficult. And the honeymoon of moving to America's largest city was over. Lenny took the final bite of his hot dog and started his ritual battle with disappointment.

Why am I doing this? he thought to himself. *Why are we praying for a community that never changes?* He thought about the three thirteen-year-olds who had been shot to death in a drug deal that went bad the night before. One of the students had visited the small youth group he had been pastoring for eight months now. They hadn't had many visitors, but he had been one of them. *Why?* a voice echoed between both ears. *Why? I should just go back to Detroit. Or anywhere, for that matter. Maybe somewhere simple, like Alaska. No, that wouldn't work. I'd probably be the only black man there.* He chuckled to himself.

"Lenny. Pastor Lenny!" a rushed voice said in his direction.

Lenny turned, noticing Alison Clarbridge out of the corner of his eye. She had been the most faithful out of the small band of students that met him every week.

"Lenny, did you hear?" she said, running to his table.

"Hear what?" he remarked with frustration. "I've been waiting here for over a half hour. Thought you guys forgot."

Alison tried to catch her breath. "No, it's just that, something happened during an assembly this morning. They showed some video about the big school shooting last year. And something happened during the assembly. We can't get kids to stop crying. There are a whole bunch lying on the floor crying out for, for God." She tried to relax her breathing. "That's where I've been. We don't know what to do."

Lenny put down his cup in shock. The prayers of one of the students the week before ran through his mind rapidly. "Oh God, break Harlem. Start with my school."

"They sent me for you. The principal wants to talk to you. He doesn't know what to do. Lenny, the kids won't leave the auditorium. Can you help?"

CHAPTER 4

"Ms. Harrison, we have a problem."

Marjorie Harrison, Washington Junior High principal, put down the paperwork she had been working on diligently and looked up at her faithful secretary of five years. "Problem?" she repeated, her long dark hair cascading down over the shoulders of her gray suit. She removed her black-plastic square frames, setting them on a pile of paperwork.

Problems? Marjorie was used to them. Every school principal deals with problems, right? In her eyes, dealing with problems came with the job. Schools have problems, she reasoned with her staff constantly. The goal was to work through them.

"This is an unusual one, though."

Marjorie smiled. Unusual? She had seen her fill of unusual problems. Being the first female principal in the small Roanoke, Virginia, school district brought many obstacles her way. But she was tough.

Tough enough to stand up to a community that didn't always welcome her opinion. "What could be that unusual, Kendra? We've seen it all, right?" She smiled warmly.

"Just come with me. I can't explain it. I'll have to show you."

The two women left Marjorie's big office, heading out of the administration wing toward a small classroom located next to the library.

"Uh, it's been going on since about 7:45 this morning. You know that Bible Club we okayed last month to meet before school?"

"Uh-huh," Marjorie responded.

"Well, I don't know how to explain it. I'm wondering if it is a cover for some kind of cult or drug ring. Whatever it is, the behavior is what I meant by 'unusual.'"

"Behavior?"

The two women turned the hallway corner. The entrance to the library doors was in view.

Next door, a small group of students and teachers were huddled in a circle looking through the glass-paneled door.

"These students won't leave. Some of them are lying on the floor. Donald Rutherland's daughter is crying uncontrollably. And the leader, Jim Smith, is singing songs with a guitar. Marjorie, honestly, it reminds me of when I went to Woodstock in high school. Something so out of the ordinary I can't explain it. I just can't explain it."

The group of students and teachers parted the group so Marjorie could get a front-row glance.

What she saw even she couldn't believe.

Over in a corner amid some moved desks was a student dancing and jumping. She recognized his face. Peter Olmstead. Marjorie had suspended him earlier in the year for selling crack on campus. She wondered if he had been smoking it again. On the ground next to him was Mandy Forsythe. Both of her parents had died in a devastating car wreck nine months earlier. She had been on so much medication to deal with the pain of the loss that she had been put in several special education classes just for extreme personal attention. Her eyes were closed. The look of peace on her face transcended any pain that had been there before. One student was praying loudly with his face in his hands; several others were crying what seemed to be tears of joy. The odd thing Marjorie noticed was that although every person was not reacting in the same way, the small group of students all had a look of concrete peace.

"Excuse me," Marjorie said, slipping by a girl who was talking to a friend about how weird everything looked.

"Are they in trouble?" another student asked as Marjorie reached for the door handle.

"I don't know," she responded, confused. "But what I do know is that we are going to get to the bottom of this."

CHAPTER 5

THE SUN TRICKLED DOWN onto Sean Rassmusin's shoulders as he waited for the Los Angeles Public Transit bus to pick him up. The east side of the city wasn't the worst part of town, but also not the best. Sean glanced at his watch. He didn't want to be late again. The manager at the fast-food restaurant would be upset. His family needed the money. Sean's income was the only money they had coming in right now. His parents had both recently been laid off from their jobs. The entire family had moved everything they owned three years ago from Mexico City. Sean, now a junior, didn't mind working. If it meant he was helping his family, then it was the right thing to do. And he wanted to do the right thing.

Beads of sweat were dripping down, exiting from the scalp of his jet black hair across the brown skin of his forehead. He wiped the sweat away with his shirt sleeve, looking for a place he could shade himself from the hot sun. His brown eyes squinted in several directions only to reflect a sea of people dealing with the daily grind of life like everyone else. His saggy khakis and Nike tennis shoes were a part of the uniform he had to wear on the job. He never put on his greasy polyester shirt until he got to the fast-food restaurant.

The small church he and his family attended had been experiencing a real spiritual awakening over the past month. People he never thought would change were changing. It felt like a spark had been lit in their church that was turning into a roaring flame. Unexplained salvations. Miraculous signs and wonders. And then there were his peers. The church was suddenly full of them. Young lives that were striving to get their hearts right. On some nights there were more young adults in the congregation than any other age-group. Three gang lords had accepted God into their hearts just days before. Something was definitely going on.

Traffic was heavy as usual for this time of the day. Horns were blaring, people were hollering curse words out their windows, and the smell of exhaust was strong. The stench of urine made it evident that somebody had slept under the bench recently. A cardboard box just feet away from the bench housed an old man sitting and begging for coins. Litter decorated every corner it could find a place to hide. Paper cups, bottles, and even a McDonald's wrapper blew by in the hot wind, reminding Sean that a night of flipping burgers was close at hand. "Excuse me. Do you know what time it is?" a pregnant woman asked sitting on the bench next to him. Her small frame and big belly gave away that her baby was due soon. Her white tank top seemed extra large on her, draping over the elastic-waste denim shorts she wore.

"Uh, 4:30," he replied.

She started to fan herself in the heat with a newspaper she had picked up off the bench before sitting down. Sean noticed that one of her arms was stiff. She carried it, tucking it neatly against her side, holding the handle of a paper shopping bag. She noticed Sean was staring. "Don't worry, I won't hurt you. It's just an arm."

Sean paused, evaluating the safety of asking another question. "How, uh, did it happen?"

The woman wiped her brow with a Kleenex. "Shortly after I got pregnant, I had a stroke. It paralyzed my left arm. But they say my baby is fine."

She wiped her brow again. "Sure is hot out here. It makes me kind of dizzy."

"Yeah, it is hot," he replied. "You gonna be okay?"

"Oh, I'll be fine. If you're gonna live in Los Angeles you've got to be okay with the heat."

"No, I mean your arm. Is there anything they can do for it?"

"No, not now," she said, patting her stomach. "Not until this little guy gets here."

Sean remembered a girl at his church last week who had been healed. It's not that he didn't believe in healing, but nothing like that had ever happened. This girl had come into their church during a youth service. She couldn't breathe easily. Every breath she took sounded painful and took a huge effort. A group of students had gathered around her and prayed. It wasn't long after they had started that Seth noticed her breathing wasn't shallow anymore. He stepped back from the circle and started to cry. It didn't seem possible. Moments later she stood up and he knew she was healed. He asked her again last night at church if she was well. Her smile said it all. He turned back, looking the woman square in the eye.

"So I was wondering, have you ever prayed before?"

"Sure. Who hasn't? Didn't work. But I'm not mad. I just don't understand."

Sean's stomach was knotting up. "I forgot to introduce myself. My name is Sean." He glanced at his watch again. Time, there wasn't much time. He looked back up. "I was wondering, um, I just feel like I should pray for you. Would you let me pray for you?"

CHAPTER 6

MARIA GAVE THE CAMERAMAN a "not ready" sign with her hands. She hadn't done a field report in a while. She had been the News 4 lead female anchor for more than a year now, taking the position a few months after Janet Theisen had left. Her glamorous job as a lead anchor had polished her skills and given her a new look. Maria enjoyed being the "top dog" rather than just another reporter in the business. She now understood why Janet had loved her position so much. But her interest and heart for Lincoln got her out of the studio today. She wanted to be the one to lead the live report from the high school campus. The red light on top of the camera started to blink.

"This is Maria Severson, reporting live for News 4 once again on the Lincoln High School campus. History is happening again at the Chandler, Arizona, school. There is no glass shattered, bullets dodged, or death today. In fact, it seems as though the opposite is taking place."

The camera panned off Maria and moved over to the cafeteria windows reflecting the sun.

"We have recently received word that inside those windows in the Lincoln High School cafeteria odd behavior has taken over. Some two hundred students, since around twelve noon, have been stuck in the cafeteria. But this time there is no gunman to keep them there, just their own wills. Some of them are crying, some are praying, one girl was begging for God to forgive her. It seems as though some kind of spiritual awakening has taken over this part of the school. Faculty members have tried to stop it but to no avail. They can't seem to get the students out of the lunchroom. Senior class president Taylor Shepperd seems to be leading the spontaneous meeting by praying and speaking. I have a faculty member with me, history teacher Joe Ellison. Joe, tell me, in your opinion, what is going on inside?"

The camera moved to capture Joe's confused reflection. His fat tie and black horn-rimmed glasses were a staple around Lincoln and gave him a geeky appearance that most of the students knew him by. "Uh," he said, mesmerized by the camera, "uh, I don't know what is going on in there. I walked into the lunchroom. And there was this presence, some kind of presence. Some of my students were crying, some were talking and praying together. I don't know. Odd—it was very odd."

The camera quickly focused on Maria. "Thank you, Mr. Ellison. He is a history teacher at Lincoln High School where we are reporting another odd occurrence in a school that has seen so much tragedy."

"Maria," a deep voice bellowed through her earpiece.

"Yes, John," she said back at the camera.

"Does this seem to be tied to the shooting in any way? Perhaps cult-related?"

"No, John, I don't think it is. If anything, there seems to be such a positive atmosphere here that it feels very different from the day of the shooting."

Maria hadn't forgotten that day. A small scar on her cheek was there every day to remind her. Covered in makeup, plastic surgery couldn't fully remove the cut she had received when she fell on a piece of glass after a blast blew out an upper window while she was reporting. The feeling that day on Lincoln's campus made her sick when she thought about it. But today, the feeling was very different. Although it was unexplainable, it wasn't making her afraid. Reports from inside the school say it is life-changing."

"Unexplainable," he said back in a superficial voice.

"Yes, it is, John, very unexplainable. A few parents and area religious leaders have gathered outside the school waiting to see what the next move from the administration will be. I have with me a local youth pastor, Trevor Clark."

The camera director pointed at a second camera with a blinking red light that focused on Trevor's long face.

"Tell me, Reverend Clark, how do you explain this?"

Trevor paused, then spoke with confidence. "I don't know how to explain it. The only thing I can come up with is that we are seeing a modern-day move of God. It makes sense that He would use a place of such tragedy to bring such an awakening."

"Awakening?"

"Yes, for too long the church, believers in Christ, have been 'asleep,' so to say. And today, God chose to use a student, or a group of them, to do something only He could be in control of."

"Reverend Clark, how does something like this start?"

Trevor stared into the camera. "Prayer. Only through prayer."

"So what you're saying is that somebody inside, a student we'll say, isn't coaxing others to act in such strange ways?"

"No. This could only happen as an act of God. I believe this has been coming for a long time. God is going to use this school to change the world."

Maria was personally interested now, but professionally out of time. "Yes, this school will be heard of again. Thanks, Reverend Clark. Thank you."

CHAPTER 7

THE MUSIC COMING FROM THE CLUB outside Sydney, Australia's art district could be heard several streets over. Inside, the temperature was up and the bodies were hot, dancing and drinking the night away. The music emanated loudly from the live band playing center stage. The pulse of the bass could be felt on the tabletops around the nightclub. Hands were pounding on the bar to the beat. Electronic laser lights were blinking on and off so fast they were nauseating unless you were moving on the dance floor. The stench resembled that of a mixed drink made with more alcohol than drink mix.

Ryan Clarabough lifted the bottle of beer in his hand to his mouth, drinking down the last few drops. He slammed the bottle on the counter to the beat. His feet tapped along to the music, but that was as far as they would go. He wasn't much of a dancer. Especially now that he was immersed in the culture. Australians were very energetic and physical dancers; Ryan was not. He glanced at his watch, wondering what his mother and father were doing back in Chandler at that very hour.

"Hey, can I get another beer?" he shouted over the band. The bartender looked at him, confused. Ryan pointed at the bottle. The bartender signaled a nod back.

Australia hadn't been the change he had dreamed of. Getting out of Phoenix and away from Lincoln was all he could think about after his sister was shot. Down Under seemed to be the answer since it was far away and he didn't have to learn a totally new language. Besides, the day of Liz's funeral he had promised himself that if the opportunity came he would get as far away from Lincoln High as he could. Not to mention the fact that he secretly desired to run away from God. After all, He was to blame, right? Bernice and Mark Clarabough weren't too happy about him going that far away but knew it might be just what Ryan needed. They took their life savings, Liz's college fund, and sent their son away to the famous Sydney Harbor Art School to finish his college education. The tuition was high, but if it would help Ryan to grasp his dreams, it was worth it.

Ryan grasped another bottle. He was starting to feel light-headed now. On nights like this he was thankful he lived just a few blocks from the downtown campus. He glanced at his watch, wondering again what his parents were up to.

CHAPTER 8

MARK AND BERNICE stood quietly outside Lincoln's lunchroom doors. Mark put his arm around his wife. The school brought back too many memories. Today, though, that was changing. Something was changing, and what was happening inside those doors was a big part of it.

"How long have they been in there?" she asked Mark, looking at the clock hanging on the wall in the hallway.

Mark glanced at his watch. "I don't know, maybe ten, eleven hours." He yawned, signaling the lateness of the day.

"Do you think they'll come out?"

"Well, if they don't, a large number of parents are about ready to go in."

Another news truck rolled into the parking lot. Mark glanced at it out of the hallway windows. He ran his fingers through his hair. It felt like it was happening again. This time, though, there would be news headlines that would not follow death, but life.

Bernice noticed the principal, Don Whitiker, signal her to come over to him. He trusted the Claraboughs more than any parents he had ever worked with before.

Bernice followed the hand sign with Mark close behind.

"Listen, Bernice, we've got a real crisis here. I've got more angry parents and faculty members than I know how to deal with. Can you go in and try to talk to Taylor? Maybe you can talk some sense into him."

The attention surrounding what had started during lunch was rising. Parents and faculty waited outside the exit doors, peering in occasionally to see if the status had changed. Students with friends inside waited, leaning against the brick structure, impatient with the work God seemed to be doing.

Mark spoke up. "What do you think, Don?"

"Boy, I don't know. I mean, I've canceled school before to send the basketball team off to the state championships. We closed school when the air conditioners broke down last year, but I've never closed school before because of an act of something, God or whatever you want to call it. I just don't know if I can do it again tomorrow."

"But Don, look at what's happening here. A year and a half ago dead bodies lay inside that cafeteria. Tonight, students that want to make their lives right with God are lying in there. How can you argue with that?" Bernice said warmly.

"I know. I know. I just don't understand."

"I'll try to talk with Taylor. Besides, I'd like to see Seth. He came over earlier, right?"

"Yes. He talked to a few newspeople and then went in and got lost—in there."

"We'll try not to," Mark said reassuringly.

Mark and Bernice stepped inside the quiet cafeteria. What was normally a place for talking loudly had become a sanctuary. A student standing on a lunch table was leading some songs with a guitar while several dozen others sang with him. Some were on the ground praying, kneeling beside the collapsible tables. A few individuals had their Bibles open and were journaling their thoughts on the day. Bernice noticed Taylor praying with someone in a corner and grabbed Mark's hand to follow her. Sacred; it was a school cafeteria and yet, it felt sacred. Taylor finished up, noticing Mark and Bernice coming toward him quietly.

"Taylor," Bernice whispered, "can we talk to you?"

"Sure. Let's go out here," he replied with reverence.

Taylor led them out of the cafeteria through a set of double doors to an entry area located at the east exit of the school. He leaned up against the wall, resting his head on the brick. The dark rings under his eyes told Bernice he was tired.

"How are you holding up?" she responded in a warm, caring voice.

Taylor closed his eyes. "I don't know. I mean, great. This is great. This is incredible." He looked at Bernice eye to eye. "Is this real?"

Bernice and Mark exchanged glances. "It's real, Taylor," Mark said. "As real as it gets. You've got over two hundred students in there who are experiencing something they never have before. You've got angry parents who want their kids home. The police have been called in. The media is here again. Yes, this is real."

"All I did," he mumbled, "all I did was pray. I bowed my head at lunch and prayed." The prayer he prayed earlier that day shot through his mind like a random bullet.

Dear God,

Here I am again, in the middle of this lunchroom, praying for the friends around me who need You. Today I feel unusually discouraged. But with Your strength, I'll do this again. Lord, awaken my school. Awaken my city. God, awaken this world to their need for You. Oh, yeah, and bless this disgusting goulash. Man, I love You. Thanks for encouraging me . . . Wait, God, things seem really quiet . . . Amen . . .

"All I asked God for was to awaken our school."

Mark smiled. "Well, something woke up."

"I wish Liz could have been here," Taylor responded, staring at the ground.

"Oh, she is," Bernice said, "she's here. I see her in the eyes of the kids in that lunchroom. She prayed for this you know."

"I know," Taylor said. His eyes started to water. "I've been in there all day, just longing after Him. Confessing my sins, praying for my friends, praying for myself. I just can't get enough of Him, you guys. I don't know what to do."

Seth noticed the three of them talking between

the doors. He stepped into the entryway with them quietly.

"Do you think we should tell everyone to go home?"

"Taylor, I think at this point, that might be the right thing to do. Maybe we could schedule a meeting with the student body in the morning if we talk to Mr. Whitiker. Have a few of the students share some testimonies. Let them talk to each other."

"I would be willing to help, Taylor," Seth said with genuine sincerity.

Taylor wiped a tear from his cheek. "Okay. I think that would be the right thing to do. I'm just afraid it will all stop once we leave. Tomorrow everyone will come back to school and act like it never happened."

"I know what you mean," Seth spoke up again. "What is it going to take for us to truly change? God has given us so many opportunities. And then this?"

"Trust the Spirit of God," Bernice insisted. "If He started it, then let Him finish it. I'm choosing to believe what has started today is only the beginning. Who knows? This could impact our entire world."

Seth thought of Liz for a moment. She had always talked about impacting the world with her testimony. Now, her prayers would really be answered.

Don Whitiker busted through the doors harshly. He was out of breath. "Mark, Bernice, Taylor . . . I've got a parent who wants to speak to you out here. He's ang—"

Before he could get the full word out, an angry Jake Forrester slammed open the double doors. His buzz cut, navy blue suit coat, and white pants made him resemble an angry naval officer trying to take charge of a disgruntled situation. "I can't believe this, Shepperd. What do you think you're doing here?"

Taylor stepped back until he felt the brick wall behind him.

"I can't get my son out of there. He says he wants to be with God. What is going on here? And you, Whitiker, this should have been stopped hours ago. This is a violation of the law, for crying out loud."

"Now, Jake," Don reasoned.

"Give me a break! If you don't shut down what's going on in there right now, I will make such a stinkin' scene that the police will have no other choice. You hear me?"

"Mr. Forrester," Seth tried, "you just don't understand—"

"And you," Jake replied, pointing in Seth's face. "I've been meaning to tell you you're full of nothing. That entire graduation speech you spilled was a violation of the law. And this—I don't want your cult crap in my home. Stop it now!"

Mark stepped forward. "C'mon, Jake, let's step out here and talk about this, you and me."

"I don't need you or anybody to talk to me about this. I can see it with my own eyes. This is not a church—"

Bernice reached out her hand, placing it on Jake's shoulder. "And that's the beauty of this entire what-ever you want to call it. It happened outside our churches.

These kids experienced something more real about God here than they ever could within the four walls of a church."

Jake shrugged her hand away. "You people. You're all crazy, all of you. This isn't the end. This will never happen again on this campus."

"What? Think about what you're saying, Jake," Mark said, boiling with frustration. "Do you want another student to bring a gun on this campus to blow away the little we have left? Don't you get it, Jake? We are dealing with the anger here. God is moving to release all of the pain that is hidden deep within the hearts of those students in there."

"Listen, Mark," Jake fired back, "I'm sorry about your daughter, but I'm not about to allow my son to believe all the crap you and your bunch of Christians say is true. If God is real then He would have stopped the killing of the fourteen innocent lives."

"Do think we haven't asked God that?" Bernice responded. "Every night of our lives? But what good is it to be mad at God?"

"It does a lot of good. It keeps Him away from me. Now stop this thing, or I'm going to talk to Lieutenant Nielson and get the whole bunch of you arrested!"

Jake stomped through the double doors. The breeze of his departure blew through the area like a tornado wind in a small Kansas town. Mark and Don raised their eyebrows at one another. Bernice put her arm around Seth then reached out for Taylor, looking deep into his eyes.

"Don't think your prayer was a mistake for one minute. Not one. You hear me?"

Taylor nodded back. His face was whiter than a starched sheet.

"We really need to do something," Don commented. "Or Jake will. I know it."

The five of them experienced a long pause before making a decision. The quiet seemed to make everybody reflect on the events of the day.

"C'mon, Taylor, I'll help," Seth said confidently. "Let's go in there and pray for everyone. Then we can encourage them to go home and get some sleep. Mr. Whitiker, can we do an assembly first thing in the morning?"

"We are going to have to do something to address this," Whitiker reasoned.

"Don," Mark suggested, "why don't you let it be student-run. That way it's fair for everyone. Maybe brief the faculty first thing. It's not like they haven't been through confusion before. Then let the students go."

"We'll see. Guys, can you shut this thing down?"

Seth spoke up quickly. "I don't think we can shut it down, Mr. Whitiker. It's God's. But, if it will help, I'll try to get everyone home."

"Good. I'll go make an announcement to the parents waiting outside," Whitiker said, walking away briskly.

Seth put his arm around Taylor's shoulders. "Let's go, dude." Both boys walked slowly through the double doors.

Mark and Bernice stared into one another's eyes.

"Are you thinking the same thing I am?"

"I think so," replied Mark.

"Ryan," they whispered together.

"I wish he could have been here," Bernice said, placing her head on Mark's shoulder. "I wish he could have been here."

"Me, too."

CHAPTER 9

RYAN SET ANOTHER BEER on the bar. His mind was foggy now, and he liked it that way.

"You all right, mate?" a voice said next to him.

"Fine."

"You American?"

"Sure."

"Where from?"

Ryan looked up. A young blonde with rich blue eyes stared into his. Noticing her appearance, he cleared his throat, combing his fingers through his hair.

"Uh, Arizona."

"Southwest, right?"

"Yes, actually Phoenix."

"Phoenix? Really? I love Phoenix."

"You've been there?"

"Long time ago. But I watched the news like crazy when that school shooting took place there last year." She paused, then continued, "It's beautiful there."

Ryan stared down at the empty beer he was holding.

"Tragic, eh?"

"What?"

"That shooting. I can't imagine it. What bloody fool could?"

Ryan didn't respond. He wanted to get up right then and leave. How could Lincoln have followed him all the way Down Under?

"Did you live close to it? The shooting?"

Ryan didn't respond. He wanted to turn and slap her face.

"Sorry, did you hear me?"

"Loud and clear," he mumbled under his breath then speaking up. "Uh, no. I didn't live there then. Sorry."

"Oh, just wondered. My name is Jackie." She stuck out her hand to shake his. Ryan didn't respond warmly. His eyes caught the images that were moving on the television above the bar. The bartender was trying to turn up the volume.

The television flashed a picture of the front of Lincoln High School, then back to a news reporter.

Ryan sat up straight, rubbing his eyes.

"Hey, mate, how do you turn this up?" the bartender yelled to a cocktail waitress. "Some bloody report about something that happened at that school they shot all those kids at in the States."

An image of Lincoln's campus appeared panning over the building.

"Hey," Ryan screamed out, "can you turn it up?" He stood up with a jolt, knocking his beer bottle on the floor. It smashed into several sharp pieces. "I said, 'Can you turn it up?'"

CHAPTER 10

MARJORIE STEPPED INSIDE the small room like a woman with a mission. Kendra, her loyal secretary, followed close behind. The room was warm and stuffy. A few voices could be heard whispering, praying for a hunger to know God. Jim stopped playing his guitar when she stepped toward him. A few students noticed her, but most of them were grasping the presence of God they were sensing.

"Jim, can I talk to you over here for a moment?" she said tightfisted, teeth clenched.

"Sure. Yes," he replied, setting down his guitar.

Another girl kept singing even though Jim had stopped playing.

Marjorie led him over to an empty corner. Kendra followed close behind.

"Jim," she whispered with authority, "what is going on here?"

Jim looked around the room. "I don't know. I just came in this morning, got the room opened, led this Bible study, prayed at the end, and then *bang*, 'this' happened."

Marjorie paused. She wanted a mature answer. "What do you mean by 'this'?"

Jim and Marjorie looked around the room again.

Kendra couldn't look. She felt uncomfortable so she stared at the floor.

"I don't know exactly," Jim replied truthfully.

Marjorie's whispers were starting to sound like steel now. She resented being put in the position of being at odds with the Bible study. "What do you mean 'you don't know'? You are a responsible student, and in charge of the Bible study. I've never had trouble with you. You're on the dean's list, and the most intelligent answer you can give me is that you don't know? I'm not buying it, Jim. Do you understand?"

"Uh, Mrs. Harrison. Sometimes you just can't explain what God is doing. He just does it."

"What do you define as 'it' then?" she replied with a sarcastic tone. Marjorie was getting fed up with his answers.

"This," he responded and looked around the room, throwing up his hands. "I've tried to get them to classes, but nobody wants to go. They keep saying how hungry for God they are. How do you argue with that? God and all. You try it," Jim said sincerely.

"Well," she said, stepping closer, sternly speaking directly into his face, "you can't argue with the law. May I remind you that this is not a church. You can have the first fifty minutes of the day, as can any other club for that matter. But not an entire school day. Is this some kind of game? Are you all trying to skip your—?" Her voice was breaking now. She softened for a moment then toughened up.

"No, ma'am," Jim tried to explain respectfully, "not at all. It's just that we want God more than anything. Is there anything wrong with that?"

Marjorie took a deep breath, digging her heels into the carpet. She was going to have to use her authority to make something happen. "Well, you all have classes to go to. So you need to end whatever is going on, Jim, and then get back to your classes. I'll only ask you once. Then I'll write up each and every one of you."

"Excuse me, Mrs. Harrison, if I may ask, can you try to get them to go?"

Marjorie cleared her throat and pushed Jim aside. "All right, students," she said, snapping her fingers like the master of ceremonies at a show. Her force was strong, alarming Jim and making Kendra very uncomfortable. The snapping wasn't working. Marjorie resorted to clapping her hands; still no response. Her face flushed red and a large vein popped up in the middle of her forehead. She tried to cover up what was really going on inside. After a deep breath she lifted her head as if she were going into serious battle. A battle she was determined not to lose. "It's time to get to class! No more games here! Do you hear me, no more games! This is not accept—"

Jim noticed a tear falling down her cheek.

"Acceptable. Did any of you hear me?" She repeated several times, then stopped yelling and covered her face with her hands.

Kendra stared at Marjorie uneasily. "Marjorie?"

she said, worried. It wasn't often she saw her boss come unglued.

"Mrs. Harrison, you all right?" Jim asked, confused.

There was a long pause. Most of the students in the small room had her attention. "Uh, no, no I'm not. I don't know how to say this but, after coming in here—" The tears were like a thunderstorm now. "I, I, uh, I realize that I need God, too."

CHAPTER 11

ALISON PUSHED THE BUTTON to cross the busy Harlem street.

"So, explain this again?" Lenny asked her. There were butterflies in his stomach. He didn't know if what she had explained was true or if this entire scenario was one big dream.

"Well, every week we have an assembly, right?"

"Uh-huh."

"And this week they couldn't get a speaker in, so they showed us this video about the Lincoln shooting. Cut right to the core. Some kid whose life was saved—"

"Seth Anderson?" he commented back. The light turned and the walk signal came on.

Alison thought for a second as they crossed the street. "Yes, maybe. Anyway, the FCA group got ahold of this video and got Principal Mulligan to show it. And this guy, Seth or whoever, starts to talk about the shooting and how his life was changed because of it. Then, after it gets over, like, a student, Tim Waelti, stands up and starts confessing all this stuff he had done lately."

"Really?" Lenny commented with shock. He blinked his eyes, wondering if he would wake up from this dream. Things couldn't be that overwhelming, could they? Besides, he reasoned, kids always stretch a story.

"Yes," Alison continued, "and then a few more students did the same. Some of my friends started crying. I prayed—the only thing I could do."

"And?" he said, anxious for more.

They reached the sidewalk leading up to the run-down institution.

"Then Principal Mulligan sent me for you. I don't know if he knows what to do. He's pretty nervous."

An understandable position for a school administrator in the present political climate, thought Lenny, opening the heavy glass-and-steel door for Alison. She walked in first, explaining to the security guard what she had been asked to do. The guard spoke into his radio and within seconds they were heading toward the auditorium.

"So, what are you going to do?"

Lenny thought for a moment. "I don't know, Alison. It's up to God on this one. I'm at a loss."

And so was the auditorium. Lenny opened the door with a squeak. What he saw almost put him into shock. Basketball jocks were weeping. Cheerleaders were kneeling. A few students were walking and praying. A group of teachers were standing in the back talking quietly, trying to get some answers. Another student in a black leather jacket and expensive high-top basketball shoes took the microphone.

"Uh, I just want to say that my mom was killed when I was two by some gang lords in east Harlem.

They shot her up. And, ever since, I've hated them for doing that to her. She was my only mama." The young man paused, collecting himself then continuing. "But today, for the first time, I just have this feeling inside telling me I've got to forgive."

A few students listening clapped as loud as they could.

"I forgive you, whoever you are."

Lenny closed his mouth, as it had been hanging open. That same kid had just returned from juvenile detention for attempted murder as a minor.

"Lenny," said a concerned voice next to him as another student grabbed the microphone. Mr. Mulligan reached out to shake Lenny's hand.

"Thanks for inviting me in, sir. It's an honor to witness this."

"Well, maybe, but I need to know what's going on here. What are we witnessing? Is this just a bunch of built-up youthful frustration at what these students experience every day?"

Lenny rubbed the goatee on his chin.

"You see, Lenny, the First Amendment does not keep religion out of schools, but it says religion must come in a way that protects the rights of all the kids, protecting them from the government either suppressing or promoting any one particular religion."

Lenny looked out at the student body. "But just look at this. These kids don't care about what church is represented here. How did this happen again?"

"Well," he whispered, "the Fellowship of Christian

Athletes convinced me to show a short documentary on what happened at Lincoln High School last year. I thought it would be a good tool to talk about the violence we see every day here and how to deal with it. We showed it, and one of our students stood up to share his perspective. Now look."

Stretched out on the stage of the auditorium was a line of more than thirty students, waiting to share thoughts with their peers.

"Some of these students have been sharing intense, even emotional confessions about life and the pain they have suffered. I don't know if I can stop it. My question is, should I stop it? In over thirty years of administration in Harlem schools I have never seen this sort of thing."

Lenny smiled to himself. He couldn't believe his eyes either. A girl was now sharing her story into the microphone. Her tears reflected the pain she had been through from birth. A friend held on to the handles of her wheelchair tightly. The students listened to her describe what it was like to be made fun of her entire life.

Mulligan continued. "I've, dismissed them all to lunch. No one will leave. What do we do? Do you have any suggestions? I knew you were meeting with a few students over the lunch hour today, and before calling the superintendent I thought I would call on you."

Lenny sighed. He crossed his arms and turned toward Mulligan, looking him right in the eyes. "Don't stop it."

"What?" Mulligan said, hoping for a tamer, more reasoned perspective.

"Don't stop it. Let it go. God's not finished yet. In fact, He's just beginning."

CHAPTER 12

"Hey, you got a newspaper around here?" Ryan screamed, unable to hear the news reporter over the music flowing down from the dance floor.

The bartender ignored the request. "Idiot," Ryan said under his breath.

"I think I saw a *Sydney Times* machine outside," Jackie responded, trying to help.

"Oh, uh, thanks . . . ," Ryan said, racking his brain trying to remember her name.

"Jackie. It's Jackie."

Ryan reached into his pocket, grabbing at the few pieces of change that were there. He hopped off his bar stool and almost ran toward the entrance.

"Hey, wait . . . ," Jackie called out.

Ryan ignored her, pushing past the club entrance doors. The music faded immediately as he stepped out of the building. He looked for the newspaper machine Jackie had told him about.

"Gotcha," he whispered, locating the machine a few feet down. "C'mon!" he hollered, slamming his fist on the machine window. Inside there was not even one newspaper to be found. Ryan looked across the downtown street. A small coffee shop was nearby. He wondered if there would be a paper there.

His feet tapped across the wet pavement. The smell of coffee filled the air as he crossed the busy street. It made Ryan nauseous. He burped up some beer, swallowing it back down.

Inside, the cafe seemed empty. He sat down at a table with a littered newspaper on it.

"Can I help you, sir?"

"Uh, is this today's paper?"

"I think. Check the date. Should be," the waitress commented in a thick Australian accent.

"Coffee?"

Ryan checked the date. It matched the present day.

"Uh, sure. Just a cup." He had no intention of drinking it. Beer, yes; coffee, never.

Whatever he had to do to stay he would do. He turned the pages of the newspaper with frustrated intensity.

"Looking for something in particular?" the waitress asked, dropping off a fresh cup of java in a white china cup and matching saucer.

"Uh, yes, I'm from the States. Arizona. Something happened at a school there today. Same school as the shooting last year," he said, still leafing through the paper, but hoping that she knew something.

"Shooting? Another one?" she responded. Apparently, she didn't.

"I don't know. That's what I want to find out."

"Haven't heard a thing. I hope not. What's this world coming to?"

Ryan hoped she would leave him alone.

"International news. Back of the first section," she informed him before heading back to the counter.

Ryan licked his index finger, turning as fast as he could.

"C'mon, what do you need, a map to read this thing?" he asked, irritated at the unwieldy complexity of the local paper. There, his eyes fell on the back page of section one. He scanned the headlines and found the treasure. He read the headline . . .

AWAKENING PUTS LINCOLN IN THE NEWS AGAIN

"Awakening?" he said out loud to himself. His eyes kept reading.

CHANDLER, Arizona (Worldpress)—American history is happening once again at Lincoln High School, located in the suburban East Valley city of Chandler, Arizona. This time, though, history is not being made through death, but in an event that many are calling an "awakening."

"I just can't believe it, I can't!" said Mrs. Huey, a guidance counselor at Lincoln. "It's just like something has come in and changed these students. I cannot explain it. One moment they were eating lunch, and next they were crying and praying."

Reports from inside the school indicated that senior student body president Taylor Shepperd has been leading the student body in this spiritual "awakening" since it started around noon yesterday.

"I bowed my head to pray for my lunch," Shepperd told reporters, "and when I stopped praying somebody across the table from me asked me how to get to God. Then someone else did. Before I knew it, I was on the lunch table looking into their faces."

Although the faculty questioned the "spiritual awakening," students in the cafeteria would not leave, wanting to stay until it was over. What is being described as one of the strangest moments in modern school history is something that many thought may be related to the massacre, or a vigil to talk to the dead.

"We were worried that this had something to do with the shooting," Principal Don Whitiker said to reporters outside Lincoln's main entrance late yesterday afternoon, "but now I understand this does not. As far as we can tell, the students are saying they want nothing else than to have a 'relationship with God.'"

As of late yesterday evening, around 200 students still remained inside the cafeteria doors at their own will. Many are praying, singing, and talking about their newfound need to have "a relationship with God." Although many parents and faculty are skeptical about the awakening, this seems to be a peaceful event.

"This is just what this community needed," says Arizona Senator John Philipps. "The scars are still there. Maybe this is a way of dealing with them."

Not everyone is happy, though. Several dozen parents have been protesting outside the school, arguing the need to respect the separation of church and state. Jake Forrester, parent of senior Matt Forrester, doesn't agree with what he is seeing. "I cannot believe that they have not stopped this. This goes against every right in the book. I am angry with the school, Principal Whitiker, and the students. They are pushing this on their peers. I knew this was going to happen. They let Anderson go too far when this entire situation hit the fan. Now look at where we are," Forrester said, referring to senior shooting survivor Seth Anderson.

Although Forrester has been inside to retrieve his son several times, he came back out without him due to his son's desire to stay in what he calls "the presence of God".

Whatever it is, Lincoln is once again in the news.

The school is off-limits to the press. Only parents and faculty are allowed inside the newly remodeled building.

Correspondent William Shriver with Mary Schuster and Worldpress contributed to this article. Copyright Worldpress Syndicated. Used by permission.

He stared at the article.

"Did you find what you were lookin' for, mate?"

Ryan nodded his head. Words couldn't describe his feelings.

CHAPTER 13

THE MOUNTAINS OUTSIDE THE CITY of Dublin were covered with a green canvas that proclaimed new life had grown again. The inner-city courts of Dublin didn't mirror the same. Inbetween the old ivy-covered buildings and the newer structures reaching for the sky, Fatima Mansions provided shelter for those who couldn't afford better. Mansions? Not quite, but the inner-city apartment structure was a home to heroin addicts, prostitutes, and the many other characters you could find on Dublin's rougher side. Fatima Mansions wasn't the county's ideal place to live. You didn't live here if you didn't have to. The rent was cheap, the heat worked, and at least it was a community to live in— even if it wasn't something out of an American television show. For Dirk Shannigan it was home. At least for now. His medium frame, short legs, red hair, freckles, and big smile gave away the Irish heritage that flowed in his family's bloodline. His boyish good looks made him a favorite with all the younger girls in the neighborhood.

It had been two and a half years since he had been on American soil. He was born in Ireland, but had grown up in the States. Now back after a twenty-year absence, he wanted to see this country close to his heart changed. He dreamed of being the Saint Patrick of the twenty-first century. But at the pace he was going, Dirk figured grabbing a "saint" position was far from ever happening. He was busy just trying to keep the kids down the hall from buying bad dope from the seedy dealers who preyed on communities like Fatima. What brought him here was his heart. To see his generation find purpose for their wasted lives was his dream. He often wondered why the steps to a dream took so long to come true.

"Good mornin', Mrs. O'Riley," he said in as much of an Irish accent as he could imitate. Living in the States all those years made it hard for him not to seem American. Although his citizenship was in America, his heart was in Ireland.

"Good mornin' to you, son," she said back. "Have you seen my son?"

"Didn't come home last night?"

"No, some of the kids say he was last seen with that troublemaker of a boy, Marshall. Can't keep him away from that bad influence."

"If I see him, I'll tell him he'd better get home or he'll get battered." They both laughed, trying to hide the pain of the truth.

"Battered? I just want to keep him alive. Keep workin' on him, Dirk."

"I will. And of course, I know God will, too."

"I hope," she said, turning the key and heading into her small flat.

Dirk was on his daily prayer walk. For two years

he had circled the complex every day, praying for the deliverance of the human souls inside the cement walls. He buttoned the top button on his jacket. It was starting to rain. Although he didn't consider himself a missionary, that was the job description the American church that sent him across the sea had given him. The small work he was a part of definitely needed some help. But he was here for the millennial generation. Their young lives captured his spirit.

"Hey, born-again boy," a young Irish voice screamed from an open window, "pray for my mother. She is very sick."

Dirk smiled and waved. "You know I will. I expect to hear a report of her healing in the morning."

The window shut, leaving Dirk to focus on his prayers.

"Dear Lord," he whispered, "what will it take?" He surveyed the landscape. A man huddled under a stairwell with an old sleeping bag. A young girl running through the streets begging for a few pennies to buy some bread. A lad puncturing his arm with a syringe full of heroin in a dark alley.

Dirk closed his eyes. "When?" he pressed. "When?"

The fall sprinkles turned into a downpour. Wet, cold, and soaked, Dirk took shelter in a nearby cathedral. Dark and cold, it was used as a community center now. The church had dwindled and died a few years ago. For a moment, Dirk's imagination toyed with the idea of it being open again. Full of lives. Full of the miracles Dublin was desperate for.

He stepped inside, dripping with the residue of rain. The drops echoed as they fell from his wool overcoat.

Dirk's steps were loud and clumsy as he moved through the dark sanctuary, now a community meeting room. He sat close to where the altar may have been in decades past. Where people came to grieve and lament over the daily choices they had made.

He looked up. A colorful cross, scenes from the Bible, and symbols of the sacraments could still be seen in the stained-glass windows that surrounded the room.

"Oh God," he said, disappointed that he had to come in because of the rain, "I pray for Dublin. We need a miracle in Dublin. Send us a miracle . . . "

Dirk stopped thinking for a moment. The sound of another body breathing gave evidence he wasn't alone.

"Hello?" he said, trying out his new and improved Irish accent.

Dirk stood quietly, trying to hear the breathing again.

A loud scream stunned his ears and brought his feet up off the floor. The cursing caught him off guard. In the faint light he scanned the area from where the voice was coming.

"Hello? Are you hurt?"

"Go to hell and leave me alone. Unless you got a stash of heroin somewhere on you, don't come near me."

Dirk knew what was happening. He had seen it hundreds of times before. Users who couldn't get their fix would literally crumple up to die until they could find another hit. Sometimes they would just lie in the streets. Dirk still couldn't find him.

"I don't have any heroin, but I have a warm wool coat you can have if you are cold."

There was silence. Then breathing, heavy breaths being taken.

"Are you all right?"

"What do you think? Do I sound like a chirping bird in the park? I haven't had a hit in twenty-four. The best thing you could do for me is to get me some gear. I'm hurting real bad."

Dirk wrestled with what to say. Even two years on the streets of Dublin hadn't prepared him for this kind of opportunity.

"Sorry, lad, can't do that. But what I can do is offer you some friendship." Dirk's eyes were adjusting now. He could faintly see the outline of a body lying in a damp corner.

"I don't need a friend. I need a dealer. You're neither."

Dirk stepped over his way. Every step seemed to reek of the miracle he had just prayed for. "Can I sit with you for a few moments?"

"It's your life."

"True. Same to you. How long have you been here?"

"What do you think? Out of all the things the good Lord could have sent me, He puts a fool here," the deep, raspy voice echoed between the walls.

Dirk was now standing over the body in the darkness. The lad reminded him of how a body is laid out at a crime scene before they take it away, leaving a chalk outline to mark where it was. He knelt down, feeling a shoulder; the stench from the body nearly took his breath away. Dirk noticed the man's hair seemed matted. "You really should take my coat, you know. You're shaking."

"Well, it's not because I'm cold."

A flash of light broke through the storm clouds outside the cathedral, shining through a stained-glass window formed of a beautiful picture of Saint Patrick. Dirk noticed the bruises on his arm and the yellowish tone of his skin before it went dark again.

"You won't want to come much closer. I'm positive, you know."

A lie to get Dirk to leave? The truth? Who knows? The fact was Dirk really didn't care. Nothing could keep him from caring for this young man.

"What?"

Lightning flashed again. Dirk could clearly see the filth on his face, and a few of his teeth seemed to be missing. And his breath—Dirk thought it was the worst he had ever smelled.

"HIV."

Both guys were quiet again. The rain could be heard tattooing the rooftop.

"You're not the first I've met, and you sure won't be the last, lad," Dirk said with confidence, sitting next to the young man without a face.

"Can you just let me lie in peace now?" the voice said with irritation.

"Nope. There's no peace in here."

"There should be; this place is an old church, right? Isn't that where you go to find peace?"

"No."

"You sure you're not a dealer?"

They both laughed, especially Dirk.

"Peace isn't about one certain church, but it can only be found in the reason for that church."

"You're talking nonsense now."

"It's Christ, my friend. A friendship with Christ."

A flash of lightning lit up the room again. An unrolled newspaper lay there with two soiled syringes on top of it. Under the needles Dirk noticed the headline.

FROM MURDER TO MIRACLE: AMERICA'S LINCOLN HIGH MAKING HISTORY AGAIN

A miracle. Dirk needed a miracle. He had yet to see one person believe in the peace he had shared about so often on the streets. Two and a half years of wondering, watching, and waiting.

"If I gave you a chance to find a miracle, would you?"

"Does it come with a needle at the end of it?" the voice gasped.

"No needles. Just love."

"What miracle could that be?"

Fear gripped Dirk's heart. What if this miracle never happened? He had been obedient in his faith but also disappointed. He wanted something to happen in his time frame, rather than waiting on God's. His hands were sweaty as he tried to choke out his response. Dirk paused again. Then, clearing his throat, he whispered it loud enough for his new friend to hear. "You," he replied. "That miracle is you."

CHAPTER 14

THE AUDITORIUM AT LINCOLN had not been built to hold the two thousand–plus students that packed themselves inside like sardines. Faculty, parents, and students filled every possible space inside the fifteen-hundred-capacity performing arts center. Fire codes were ignored; hot, dry air was tolerated; and every person listened intently. It wasn't a morning filled with idle chatter or sleepy students; the occupants wanted to know what was happening to the students in their school. The meeting was closed to the newspapers, radio, and television. Even CNN couldn't pry their way into the hotbox.

Whitiker stepped onto the stage. The room was silent except for a few clusters of whispers that could be heard from students trying to remember things about the events of the previous day. Don sounded as if he were walking through an empty cave as he stepped directly in front of the microphone on the platform. "I have spent over an hour this morning briefing the faculty about the occurrence we experienced here yesterday," Principal Whitiker began. "It is after great consideration that this morning's meeting with the student body of Lincoln High will be student-led. That means all of you must listen. Not to a forty-seven-year-old man, but to those you are closest to in this room, your peers. We are not afraid of what happened yesterday. Although we are dealing with a complicated situation, thank God we are not dealing with violence again. Even so, yesterday can only be explained by those who were there, and that was over two hundred of you. We will end this morning's meeting when we feel that we have adequately addressed the situation. Together, we will sense when that is. Otherwise, because of the sensitivity of the subject, unless there is an emergency, or you plan on wetting your pants, we ask you to stay in this room, and do not comment to the press until the assembly is over." A few students laughed at Whitiker's comments about using the rest room. "Am I clear? I have asked a former student, Seth Anderson, to open with a few words. Please give him your full attention."

Seth had his eyes closed. He had been praying intensely in the front row. Taylor tapped him on the shoulder after Whitiker's introduction. Seth knew it was time to go. He stepped onto the stage, grasping the microphone from Whitiker. Instead of the thundering applause he had become accustomed to as a survivor of the massacre, there was only silence. The microphone squealed loudly when he started to speak into it. The student body gasped, breaking the tension.

"Fellow students of Lincoln High, I'm sure you're wondering why I am here. It's not like I haven't talked and thought about this school every day of my life for the last few years. Whether I wanted it or not, it has made me who I am. And who I am today did not just happen. But the pain of what I faced with you a year and a half ago has molded me. I believe what happened yesterday goes back to what only a few other schools in this nation would understand."

He stopped, clearing his throat. "Taylor Shepperd and I were talking just a few days ago about what we longed to see happen on our campus. Not only did we desire to stop violence and bring peace, but we also hoped that some of us would change. It having took a gun pointed to my head to make that decision, and I pray it doesn't take that for you. Taylor and I talked about the effect our school had on the entire nation. I believe that started yesterday. But we can only affect others to the degree that we have been affected. Yesterday can't be pushed on any of you, but if you simply believe, it can change you."

He stopped, staring at the stage floor for a moment then looked up at the student body with fire in his eyes. Seth's voice tightened and he stood straight up. The students read his body language, listenening intently.

"Okay, let's cut the crap. Forget the speeches. We've heard a lot of them over the past year. Something happened here yesterday that I can't explain. But we had better listen to it closely, because I don't want to miss what it could do for our nation, our world. This isn't about us. It's not just about you and me; this is about God. He is using us. Now, we can either be used, or forget about it and go on just like we've done with the shooting."

He set the microphone on the ground and walked off. The room stopped. It was almost as if everyone inside the auditorium had quit breathing. Seth had broken through the "God" barrier. Everyone who had been at the heart of yesterday's awakening was aware of that, but nobody knew how to say it. The pathway had now been forged by his honesty and genuine spirit. Seth found his place next to Taylor in the front row. He covered his face with his hands, feeling like a failure. He didn't know if his words had pierced hearts as he had hoped they would.

The next two minutes were some of the most uncomfortable most in that room had faced. No one wanted to say Seth was right, even though they all knew it.

A young woman with long black hair and long black nails stood up, breaking the silence. Every eye was on her. Her thick high heels echoed inside the room when she stepped on the hollow stage floor. She knelt down to get the microphone as graciously as she could, even though her black spaghetti shirt showed off more than it should have.

She tried to speak, but the tears started before her words could. "I, I was in the lunchroom yesterday. You know, just eating like any other day." She paused again. "And then, something hit me, like a huge shoe that got thrown at my head. I can't explain it, but all I could think about was God." The faucet in her eyes turned on again. "And I'm not into God. I have been involved with Wicca for two years now. I'd been preparing for the past six months to be a witch."

A few students chuckled.

"I didn't want anything to do with God. And today I woke up with such a, a . . . I don't know how to explain it, but on the inside, I don't know, I just want to know about this whole God thing. Nobody preached at me, nobody pushed me, and all I know is that I don't want to be a witch anymore."

She set the microphone on the stage with a thud. A few students clapped. The silence began again. This time two students started walking toward the stage. The first to reach the stage was a teen who, despite his young appearance, introduced himself as a senior in the school.

"Jackson Mannington, senior. I don't like microphones. But I want to say something to all of us who have grown up in church, but really don't believe what we know. God told me something yesterday in that lunchroom. He told me that we were the ones who were lost. Lost because we've been spoiled with the truth without believing it. I . . . I," he continued, starting to weep, "I feel so bad that I know all the Bible stories, but I've never known the God who authored them. I think about, about all the years I have wasted. Yester-day, all I wanted to do was know God. Deeper and deeper."

He broke down so hard that he had to hand the microphone to the girl standing behind him. She took it gently, stepping up to the front of the stage. Her long golden hair flowed over her shoulders.

"I don't know what happened yesterday. I wasn't in the cafeteria, but some of my friends who were there are not the same today. Kim, Elizabeth, and Matt. I don't know what has happened, but if your change is real, then this God is real."

She set the microphone on the floor and hopped off the front of the stage. The honesty that was transparent was scary for some, and yet fulfilling for others. The line for the microphone was starting to grow. Those who had shared already blazed the way for the student body to talk. Communication was starting to flow. More than ten students followed the pathway to the stage, hoping to encourage their fellow classmates with a word of truth. One of those students, Matt Forrester, tried to hide himself in the line. His testimony was worth the entire assembly. Just yesterday morning he had been smoking a joint be-fore school. Some students had clung to God for strength after the shooting. Matt wasn't one of them. The influence of his father had always been strong. He was the kind of student that was going to show the world he could make it on his own. And he did, with great success. His testimony would change others and he knew it. That's why he couldn't stay glued to his seat. Unbeknownst to most in the room, Jake Forrester snuck into the sound booth in the back of the auditorium.

"Where do I start?" Matt said into the microphone. Some of the faculty sat up to listen. He was a student whose name seemed to make its way into the teachers' lounge on a weekly basis. "The only reason I am up here is because I couldn't stay down there. And it wasn't because my butt was getting sore." The student body laughed. "It was because yesterday during lunch I heard a voice. I know this sounds like I'm crazy, but I'm sitting there eating that goulash crap and Taylor prays over his lunch like he does every day. And I hear this voice say, 'Get to Me. You need to get to Me. Don't waste any more time. Call out My name.' And I remember saying to myself, 'Who the heck are You?' And, the voice came back and said, 'Your Father.'"

The auditorium was quiet again. Matt was making Lincoln history. Every school has one student you think will never change. The faculty couldn't wait to see him leave, the students knew he was the key to every party on the weekends, and the girls understood he was a magnet that could draw anything he wanted out of them.

"I know I've basically been a jerk around this school. And I'm not saying it's all going to change overnight. But if I don't stand up here and tell you what happened, then I know and so do you that nothing will change. I found a new friend in Taylor. He said he would help me. So, I'm not the same. Okay?"

A few girls in the left-central section clapped and screamed as if he were a famous rock star promising change. Jake stared at the stage from the booth. He wanted to holler at his son as loud as he could. His son had just embarrassed himself in front of twenty-five hundred of his friends. Jake shook his head. With every step Matt took back to his seat, Jake seemed to boil with more and more anger. He slammed his fist on the light board as he headed out the door and down the stairs on a crash course for the stage. There was no way his boy wasn't going to hear from his father. "This entire institution will hear from me," he said with anger, stepping down onto the auditorium's main floor. Jake pushed a few students aside on his trip to the stage. Although the line was long, his black wing tips tapped right up to a student with the microphone. He pulled it from the young girl's hands. A loud squeal of feedback caused everyone to jump and notice he was there.

The squeal caught Whitiker's attention. He turned his head, realizing that Forrester had just taken the platform. "Oh my God!" he whispered. It wouldn't be long before he was on the stage with him.

CHAPTER 15

THE YOUNG GIRL GESTURED for a ride in the gentleman's car before she climbed into the front seat. He handed her a wad of cash before driving away. Sevilla waved at her friend in the car, who was in no position to wave back. The deal had already begun.

She stared down at her new shoes. She loved the color red. Sevilla reached in her purse, taking out a bottle of cheap perfume. She sprayed it on herself when she felt unclean. It had been a busy day and it was only the afternoon. An entire night lay ahead, not to mention that it was Friday. Weekends always brought thousands of visitors to Bangkok's red-light district. They were good business days but hard on the body.

Bangkok was a busy city. A cross between the technologies of the twenty-first century, yet alive with the traditions of the past. Only in such a city could village huts sit alongside steel skyscrapers that stretched toward the sky. Clouds of hot, blowing dust gave the skyline a constant cloudy look. Even so, this city was home to many who could see the dirt and still call it home.

Sevilla sighed, leaning up against the brick wall behind her. Her name had been passed down through her family. Her grandmother was the last one to bear it. It meant "giving heart."

Sevilla's boss would be around any minute to make sure she was staying consistent with hourly tricks with whoever would buy her. But until she saw him she would rest. A man drove up in a car, rolling down the window.

"You for sale?"

Sevilla slipped the sweet perfume back in her purse. "Not right now."

"What? Did you not hear me? I want to buy you for an hour."

She took a compact out of her purse, applying some foundation to her face. "I told you, I'm not open."

The man revved his engine. "Double. I'll pay you double."

"I don't care what you pay, I'm on a break. Can't you see that?"

"All I can see is that I want you for an hour."

Sevilla closed her compact, shoving it into her purse next to her perfume. "Triple."

The man tightened his grip on the steering wheel. His eyes looked deep into hers. "Triple then."

She reached for the door handle, climbing inside the faded vehicle. It wasn't new by any means, and neither was the driver. An older man, his tie and wedding band gave her the clue he was visiting the city for the weekend. He was one of hundreds she would meet over the next few days. Men away from their villages, children, and wives, but most of all, away from responsibility.

The man held out a wad of cash. She counted it, took it, then stuffed it into her front pocket. Sevilla wondered how many women he had been with before. He gave her exactly the right amount, tripled. He must have known what a woman cost on the streets of Bangkok. The underworld of prostitution was a big moneymaker in the Asian city. It had been for decades. As a young girl, Sevilla had dreamed of leaving the tiny little village for the capital city. Raised by a single mother, Sevilla had longed for the love of a father. She had found it sleeping around with the men of the village. It was an easy way to get the quick fix of affection she longed for. Degrading, yes, but if you did it enough times it became addictive.

In an effort to give her daughter a new chance, her mother had traded dirt roads for paved streets. She had hoped the move to Bangkok would help her daughter. Two years later, the hurt was bigger than both had imagined. Sevilla quit school, left home, and found a friend on the streets that introduced her to Sawat, her "boss." It was good money, an adventurous living, and it temporarily filled a hole in her heart.

"How long have you been doing this?"

Sevilla was taken aback by his question. Most men never said a word.

"I have two years' experience in Bangkok. But I've been with men since I was eleven. So I am very experienced."

"Really. That's an awfully long time for such a young girl."

"Not really. I still have my entire life to live."

"You do?" commented the driver. "Do you think you'll ever be able to quit?"

Sevilla had never thought about that. She was satisfied living life day-to-day, hour-to-hour, and partner-to-partner. "I don't know. I hope so."

"So do I, for your sake."

Sevilla clutched her purse tightly. Things were starting to feel awkward. She looked around the interior of the car. It was worn from the sun, and dirty from the dust. A few Styrofoam cups littered the floor with dried coffee rings on the inside. She glanced at the rearview mirror, taking note of a Bible verse on a note card taped to it. She frowned. *That seems odd,* she thought.

They drove a few more miles in silence.

"Where are you taking me?"

"You'll see."

"No, really. Where are we going?"

"It's my hour, right? I paid triple."

He was right. Sevilla had done some strange things for more cash. But today something felt different. She unzipped her purse again and dug to the bottom. She pulled out a picture of her mother. The photograph was worn, ragged, and faded, but she could still make out her mother's sweet grin, eyes of grace, and beautiful smile.

"Who's the picture of?" the man asked.

"My mother."

"Does she live in Bangkok?"

"East side."

"What's her name?"

Sevilla was feeling angry now. "Look, I don't indulge my lovers with any personal information. This is strictly about one thing, sex. So let's pull over and get this over with. I'm already going to have to pay for a bus ticket back to the district."

"I'll pay it. Sorry for asking."

Most of the men Sevilla had been with she classified with the pigs. She remembered seeing them in the village she lived in as a little girl. Why would this one have some manners? The old car hummed along until it turned down a dirt road. Sevilla noticed the reflection of Bangkok's skyline in the mirror on her side of the car. She hadn't been this far out of the city since she had moved there.

"You only have a half hour left."

"I know, I know. Remember, it's my money. Let me spend it in whatever way I want."

Sevilla felt the wad of cash in her pocket. She would pay double to Sawat and keep a little for herself. That meant a good dinner tonight. She smiled. Only a half hour left and she would be free.

The car pulled into a dirty parking lot. A brick building stood there. A cloud of dust blew past the tinted windows. Sevilla wondered what was happening inside.

"Is this it?" she said, staring at the building in confusion. *I've done some weird things,* she thought, *but this one tops it off as one of the weirdest.*

"Yes, my friend. This is it. Remember, I still have a half hour. After that, I will personally drive you back to the street I took you from."

Sevilla frowned. "That's okay; I'll take the bus." This entire situation seemed very strange to her. Not only did the man pay triple her hourly amount, but he had taken her so far out of the city that a ticket back would cost a good portion of what she had made.

The man parked the car and got out. Sevilla followed. A hot wind blew on her face and through her black, shiny hair.

"Let's go. I have much to show you in less than thirty minutes."

Now things were starting to feel the same. Sevilla felt comfort in the routine of what she knew to do. "Is this place some kind of motel?"

The man hesitated. "Nope, no motel. I look at this place more as a hospital."

Sevilla stopped. "Hospital? Listen, this sounds way too weird."

"Not that kind of hospital. This kind." The man put his hand over his chest. "This is a hospital for the heart."

CHAPTER 16

MARJORIE HARRISON shut her townhouse door with a slam. The front inside walls of the newly built two-story structure shook. A picture she had recently hung fell to the floor, shattering glass across the tile entryway.

"Oh, great," she said in anger, ignoring the glass she crunched over on the floor. "What else?"

She dropped a few letters and some junk mail on a nearby table. Her briefcase found its home on a plush chair by the couch, and instead of hanging her slick tan overcoat in the closet, she chose an easier route by bundling it up into a ball and tossing it on the floor. The house was decorated with a few modern furniture pieces resembling something out of an IKEA furniture catalog. It wasn't easy finding modern-looking home decorating pieces in this conservative East Coast environment. Marjorie kept her home neat, clean, and in control. She wondered why life seemed to feel the opposite, especially on this particular day.

She opened the refrigerator, pulling out a soda. Collapsing on the couch, she decided her mind could use some mental baby-sitting before she dealt with the situation the day had thrown her. She tried to find some network news and distract herself with problems other than her own. She reached for the remote, not clicking fast enough. A student talking about God caught her eye, but it was too late. She had passed by the channel.

"What channel was that?" she whispered, thumbing the remote back. "C'mon," she sighed.

The young blond boy's face filled the screen. His name flashed on the bottom of the television.

Taylor Shepperd, senior at Lincoln High

"Well," he said in a shaky voice, "all I remember is bowing my head to pray over my lunch. When I was done, something was different. The students around me were crying, crying out for God."

Marjorie sat up. She wasn't relaxing anymore. She set the can of soda on the table where her feet were resting.

"This strange event happened at a place that has become synonymous with American tragedy. But, the horror of the past seems to be gone for a day. Even so, not everyone is happy. Dozens of parents are protesting in anger. Whatever the case may be, it is happening in the shadow of America's worst school tragedy. This has been Wendy Rhead for Channel 7."

Marjorie clicked the off button. She sat in silence with her mouth open. It was almost like somebody grabbed her heart from inside the television and took it to Chandler, Arizona. She knew exactly how those at Lincoln, especially those in authority, must feel. Her feet hit the floor, heading for the closet door. She had been keeping a scrapbook of newspaper clippings and articles of newsworthy items that pertained to other schools around the nation. Marjorie grasped the binding of the book and started to flip through the pages. One headline after another . . .

SCHOOL BOMB THREAT ENDS IN PEACE

HIGH SCHOOL LUNCHES FULL OF FAT

GANG ACTIVITY INCREASING IN INNER-CITY SCHOOLS

PRIVATE SCHOOL ABORTIONS ON THE RISE

She flipped furiously as far back as she could. The headline she was searching for caught her eye.

LINCOLN HIGH ONE YEAR LATER: REMEMBERING THE GRIEF

Her eyes continued on . . .

LINCOLN ONE YEAR LATER:
Remembering the Grief

CHANDLER, Arizona (Worldpress)—On May 17, two students stood up in their senior philosophy class, took several loaded weapons from their backpacks, and at approximately 11:32 A.M. started nonchalantly firing shots at their fellow students. Forty-five minutes later, a school lay in destruction and 16 were dead.

One year later, a community and nation shocked by the rampage are still trying to come to terms with pain and anguish that haunts the mind and asks the question "Why?"

To mark the one-year anniversary of the suburban Phoenix massacre, there has been a week-long series of events. Private ceremonies, prayer meetings, grief counseling, and many candles lit for Lincoln students. Many students have even taken part in all-night vigils to remember their friends and family who died in the shootings.

"I feel like it happened yesterday," said surviving former student Karissa Dalton. "I was there in the classroom. If it hadn't been for my teacher, Mr. Danielson, I would never have had the courage to climb out that window. Sometimes I have to play my music really loud to drown out the gunshots that I keep hearing."

Other students, like Taylor Shepperd, believe the entire situation could change the school, perhaps the country. "This thing hurt us bad. But I think God wants to do something in our school and country like we've never seen before. My friends didn't die in vain, but through their deaths I believe we can find true meaning to life."

Many are leaving the Phoenix area for the day, despite police efforts to increase security at Lincoln and in Chandler.

"Most people I've talked to," says fellow student Matt Forrester, "say they're getting out of here. They want to get as far away from this place as possible, especially the ones who were actually there. I mean, John ran right past me that day. I will never forget seeing his gun in my face. I'm alive today because he tripped and lost his balance. I know that I'm not going to be here on the anniversary."

"There's a lot of fear in people still," says Don Whitiker, the principal of Lincoln High School. "I think we are all afraid. But we are facing this together. Nobody is alone. Although school is canceled on the anniversary day, not one person in this community won't be thinking about those who are not with us anymore."

At a nearby Chandler park, located in the heart of the community, thousands are bringing flowers and handwritten notes. A public remembrance service and candlelight vigil led by community youth pastor Trevor Clark is planned.

Arizona Governor Jane Hull planned to lead a public service at the capitol building in downtown Phoenix, including a statewide moment of silence at exactly 11:32 A.M., the time the shooting began.

One of the few survivors from the philosophy class who gained national recognition, Seth Anderson, will be speaking to the student body in an assembly the following morning. "This has affected all of us. I will never be the same. My relationship with God is the only thing that has brought me through everything. This community will one day be known for its triumph. I just know it."

Seth publicly acknowledged his Christian beliefs shortly before one of the killers was shot down by his accomplice, who seconds later shot himself in the head.

"All we can do is offer hope," Pastor Clark says. "It was the darkest moment in American history."

The school itself remains off-limits to the public.

Correspondent Carrie Mantei and Worldpress contributed to this article. Copyright World-press Syndicated.

Marjorie closed the scrapbook and collapsed on the couch again. Yes, this was the same school. But why now? Almost two years away from the tragic anniversary date, why would a spiritual awakening like this happen now? The questions kept coming. So many that she almost forgot what had happened at her school earlier that day.

Ring!

The phone startled her. She sighed, picking up the cordless phone on the table next to the couch.

"Hello?"

"Ms. Harrison?"

"Uh, yes, this is. Can I ask who is calling?" she tried to say back politely.

"It's Connely."

"I'm sorry, Mr. Connely, your name isn't familiar to me. Is there something I can do for you?"

"Yes, there is. I'm sorry to bother you this evening, but I need you to come down and meet with a group of us at the school if you could."

Marjorie was feeling very unguarded. So unguarded she responded back defensively. A tone not associated with her character very often.

"Meet? At Washington? Why? I am the principal there, you know."

"Exactly. You'll be able to help us clear up the problem immediately."

"Problem?" she said back innocently. "What problem? Is somebody hurt?"

"No, no. I am the legal representative for the school district you are employed with. It seems there was a violation of a law today in your school." He cleared his throat. "That happened under your jurisdiction."

Marjorie tried to calm down. Her hands were starting to shake. "Law? Who violated the law?"

"Why don't you just come down and we can talk about it."

"Why don't you just tell me what is going on here."

"Please, Ms. Harrison, calm down. You are not in trouble. We just need to find out the whole story."

"I'm still out in the cold here, Mr. Connely, or whatever your name is. What are you talking about?"

"I'm talking about the spiritual 'awakening' you allowed on your campus today. I have several teachers, parents, and school board members who are very upset at your actions. I'm not coming against you, they are. There may be a lawsuit at stake here. That is why I am involved. It's my job to keep this school out of court. So, if you wouldn't mind coming down here and apologizing for your actions today, we may be able to smooth this one over. Now, is that informative enough?"

Marjorie was silent. She didn't have a response except to drop the phone into her lap.

"Hello?" Mr. Connely's voice echoed from the receiver.

She put the phone back up to her ear. "Uh, sure. I'll be there shortly. As soon as I can."

"Good. I will let them know you're coming."

"Them?" she said with hesitation. "Mr. Connely, I'm not on trial here. I don't need a jury."

"Fine, fine. Just come."

Click.

Marjorie's heart started to beat at a rapid pace. Not because of the meeting she was going to, but more from the meeting she had come from. Her life had been touched today on Washington's campus. So touched that she felt like a new person after Jim had prayed for her. She and several other students couldn't stop crying out for God.

"How am I going to explain that?" she whispered to herself, slipping back into her high heels and heading out the door. "Well, God," she said politely, grasping her keys. "It's been nice knowing You for a few hours. Sorry to have to ask so quick, but HELP!"

And help she would get. Her new platinum VW Bug traveled at a snail's pace down Virginia's County Highway 5. A rose Jim had given her bounced joyfully in the flower holder. It lost a few petals when she turned off on the exit that would lead her into the heart of Roanoke. Most days she couldn't wait to get to Washington Junior High. Tonight, she was dreading it. A sign welcomed her into Roanoke, Virginia—the friendliest "little" city in the world. "Friendly?" she sighed. "We'll see how true that is."

Roanoke was a nice place to live. It was safe, comfortable, and small. Although the city was growing, the census bureau had recently counted only thirty-five thousand residents. Even so, Roanoke had a nice-size mall, two high schools, three junior highs, and a Super Wal-Mart to top it off. It was everything most people needed to survive. But in Marjorie's eyes, the town felt small. Her position as junior high principal had been a source of heated debate among the city council members. Despite her valued education at Harvard and a master's degree in education, a woman running a school crossed ethical lines with many of Roanoke's chief political players. Even so, her hard work had changed Washington. So much that it was voted the top junior high in Virginia last year. One school board member cited that it hadn't been Marjorie's efforts that had gotten it there, but the fine students the city of Roanoke had filled it with. Needless to say, her actions today would only make it easier for her opponents to question her leadership.

"It would be easy to back down," she reasoned with herself. "All I have to do is apologize, tighten the grip on the Bible Club, and things will go back to normal."

Normal? Marjorie pondered that thought for a moment. *What is normal after today?* She knew the battle wasn't going to be that easy. Did she know enough about what she had gotten into to put up a fight?

She turned down Maple Street just a few miles from the entrance to Washington. Her stomach started to tie itself in a knot. There wasn't much in life that made her nervous. But for some reason, she had a funny feeling about this meeting. Meetings never seemed to scare her, even when she was meeting with an angry parent or a disillusioned student. This time, though, Marjorie was the center of discussion at the meeting. That is what made her nervous.

The Volkswagen purred into the parking lot and into the stall that posted a sign with her name on it. Marjorie rested her head on the rubber steering wheel. "Oh God," she prayed, "I don't really know You, but what I do know is that I need You. Strength—can You please give me strength?"

She reached for her door handle, busting open the door before stepping out onto the pavement. A line from Jim's prayer for her ran through her mind.

Lord, I pray this commitment Ms. Harrison is making to You today is real. If she would be tested on that realness, give her whatever she needs to make it true. Not only for our school, but for our nation.

"Nation?" she whispered. "I plan on taking care of this tonight."

Her steps were heavy as she headed toward the office doors. Normally, the office looked dark and uninviting at night, but tonight it glowed with life.

"Hello," Mr. Connely greeted her as she entered the building. He stuck out his hand. She reached back with hers.

"Hello. Marjorie Harrison."

"Yes, yes, I know. I've seen your picture circulate around our office."

"Really, now. What else am I in trouble for?" she tried to kid back.

"No trouble. We were all proud that Washington was chosen as one of Virginia's best."

"*The* best."

"Yes, you're right," he responded awkwardly, then stared out the window for a moment. "Listen, why don't I brief you for a moment before we go on in."

Marjorie wasn't liking his tone. In fact, she didn't like the way he seemed to act. Instead of protecting her rights as a school administrator, she sensed his desire was to keep the school "off the hook." Marjorie knew that meant she was suddenly in a war where she could be disposed of in order to win the battle. She looked at him again. He reminded her of a few nerds she had gone to school with. His greased hair and tight blue suit echoed his passion to study law more than fashion.

"Now, understand, Ms. Harrison, that you are walking into a bees' nest. Because of the sensitivity of the issue of church and state, you have a number of angry people in there who want an explanation."

"What if I can't give them one that will satisfy?"

"Try."

Marjorie sighed. Connely continued, starting to move slowly down the corridor.

"I have made them aware of their rights, as well as yours in running this institution."

"Mr. Connely, this is not an institution; this is a school, full of students I have really dedicated my life to. I have a master's degree from Harvard. Honestly, I could be making a lot more money somewhere else on this side of the country. Instead, I chose Washington because I believe that every small-town school deserves a chance. I am here every day fighting to give that chance to every student on this campus. My actions are a result of fighting for every group, club, or student for that matter. Regardless of my personal opinion."

"That is where the problem lies. This action today did involve you personally, correct?"

Marjorie hesitated. "Should I call a lawyer before I answer that?"

"Darling, I am your lawyer."

"No, you represent the school's interests, not my own."

"Then let me continue. The conflict today resides in the fact that you were involved with the religious club's actions for over two hours."

Marjorie closed her eyes. *Two hours?* she thought. *It didn't seem like two hours.*

"According to your secretary, you were lying on the carpet, and I quote, 'crying out to God,' end quote."

"Who told you that?"

Marjorie glanced through the glass that lent a view of the front office desks. Kendra's purse was there. She felt betrayed, and anger was starting to burn inside her heart.

"No names," continued Mr. Connely, "just a remark we want to know the truth about. Is that correct?"

Marjorie could feel it. Although her heels weren't stuck in the mud, they felt like they were. Tonight's meeting was going to go nowhere. She knew it and so did Connely.

"I think I would like to speak to a personal legal representative before I answer any more of your questions."

Mr. Connely smiled with a plastic grin. "Now, Marjorie, I believe we can settle this issue rather quickly. You love your job. I enjoy mine. We are all on the same team, right?"

"That's what Brutus said to Caesar," she said back with a hint of sarcasm. She was feeling very alone right now.

Mr. Connely opened his jacket. "No knives here." He laughed. "C'mon," he said, opening the glass door for her.

Marjorie tried to move her heels, but the imaginary mud had taken over again. This time, it felt more like quicksand. "I, I guess. But I will not hesitate to leave and get legal counsel if I sense anything funny going on."

Entering the office wing didn't feel as friendly as it normally did every morning she was there during the week. Connely led her to the conference room. The door was shut, but the light glowing from under it signaled life. Mr. Connely opened it with a squeak. Marjorie adjusted her eyes from the dark hallway. Twenty-five sets of eyes stared back. She took a deep breath.

"Have a seat, Principal Harrison," Connely said in a dry tone, letting Marjorie know he had now become her opponent.

The room was as quiet as a cold Nebraska night. Marjorie set her briefcase on the table and slid into a brown leather chair. She looked around to see who was there—a few teachers; her assistant principal, Daniel Webster; her seemingly loyal secretary, Kendra; and a group of parents that reminded her of the crew fighting for Virginia's death penalty.

"Gentlemen, ladies, I am sure you all know Ms. Harrison. She has been a principal here for three years now. And she was present at today's event."

Marjorie felt like a dartboard. The eyes of her co-workers and peers were starting to pierce the heart inside her.

"Mr. Connely, excuse me for interrupting," said Wanita Hill with a thick West Virginian accent, "I've got a baby-sitter at home. Why don't we just get to the heart of the matter."

Mr. Connely nodded. Mrs. Hill continued, sounding like a Southern belle gone mad.

"Now, pardon me, Ms. Harrison, but when my son came home and reported to me what happened on this campus today, I couldn't help but think that all of this has really hit the fan."

The tense atmosphere stepped up a notch.

"Ms. Harrison, what these parents and teachers want to know is, in your own words, what exactly happened today?," said Connely.

Wanita cut in. "I'm sure you're aware of our nation's policy on the separation of church and state. If I wanted my son to go to a private, religious institution, I would have sent him there."

Marjorie was tired of the word *institution*. It made Washington Junior High feel like a hospital or a prison.

"From what we've gathered from Kendra, your secretary who was with you at the time, a group of students were having a Bible Club before school hours. The club was given permission to last throughout the day—"

Marjorie could wait no longer. "Mr. Connely, parents, faculty members, and Kendra—loyal secretary of five years, I did not get wind of the club until around the noon hour. Kendra notified me there was a disturbance and I left immediately to take care of it. That is my job, you know. To seek out and take care of disturbances that may harm my students."

Wanita rolled her eyes.

"When I got to the room they were meeting in, I went inside. What happened there I can't quite explain. I've been trying to ever since I left. But in no way was it putting into danger the rights of any of our students or faculty. In fact, it was doing the opposite. What those students were engaging in was bringing life."

"In what way does a religious practice bring life?" Mrs. Samone, a parent of an eighth-grade student, chimed in.

Marjorie felt a shadow of defense. "This wasn't some type of religious routine movement, but there was a sense that something genuine was happening among the students."

"What do you define as 'genuine' then?" harped John Harding, a volunteer assistant coach for the school's football team.

"Excuse me, but do you understand where these students are? The lack of genuine experiences they have actually had in life? John, you're with the students just about every day. Do you understand what kind of homes some of them come from? The pain of divorce, the poverty, the racism?"

"So," Wanita cut in, "you give them anything that feels good? Ms. Harrison, may I inform you that what you are describing is what I define as a cult."

Marjorie had reached the point of no return. She tried to control her anger. "Then if you've got all the answers and come from such a perfect home, why was your son on the floor crying, and I quote, 'I need God,' today?"

The imaginary ammunition was coming out. The room started to stir.

"Everyone. EVERYONE!" Mr. Connely said in a raised voice. "Now, let's be civil here. Ms. Harrison, all we want to hear you say is that you are sorry, and that you will not allow this on our campus again."

A number of heads nodded in agreement.

"I guess what I'm after," one of the school's art teachers commented, "is how involved you are, Marjorie. It's one thing to let these kids go through an experience like this, because kids will be kids. I was one once. I experimented with a lot of things, as did all of you. But if these students see you contributing to the behavior, then you become a figure for them to follow."

Marjorie rolled her tongue around inside her mouth. She was trying to keep any words from coming out. She collected her thoughts as quickly as she could. Thinking fast was part of what she did every day a few doors down.

Sorry. I'll just say I'm sorry, she reasoned in thought, *then this whole thing will be over. That would be the politically correct thing to do, right? But*, another voice shouted, *that would shut down and confirm that what happened today was just one big emotional experience.* She thought of Jim, Mandy, and many other students' lives that were touched today. This decision wouldn't affect her, but it would affect them. *Besides everyone else, what about what happened to me? Did this God I prayed to really touch my life?*

"Ms. Harrison, we don't want to know what you want personally, but as far as Washington goes, that is the answer we are after. Remember, your answer not only affects our school, but more important, our community."

Political garbage, Marjorie hollered inside her head. *All you care about is yourself. You could care less about this community. What you care about is your position in it.*

The room was quiet. Wanita sighed, signaling the need for Marjorie's answer. A simple "no" would make it all go away. She looked into the eyes of those there. Away, she wanted them all to go away.

"Yes."

"Yes, what?" Mr. Connely replied, surprised. "Yes to what?"

"Yes, I would allow it. I believe that it is in the best interest of our students at Washington."

Wanita gasped. Marjorie continued.

"The last time I looked, my name was still on my door: Ms. Marjorie Harrison. Principal. That position is not yours, but mine. Until that changes, I will do what is in the best interest of the students at Washington Junior High, including your son, Mrs. Hill. I care about them. I care that they find meaning in their lives. The God who was presented to them today is all about meaning. It's all about life. Our campus needs it. That's where my interest lies. I hope that is where yours does, too. Now, if you'll excuse me, I've got to prep myself for another day of being the principal of this school. Thank you."

CHAPTER 17

MARJORIE TURNED ON THE LIGHT inside her office. It was early, yet she felt as though she had worked an entire day. An early administration meeting that morning had been tense. Last night's meeting had become the talk, not only at the school, but at the coffee and donut shops all over town. The talking was stirring up controversy like a sugar packet into a black cup of coffee.

Her phone buzzed. Kendra's voice interrupted the stillness.

"Marjorie?"

"Yes," she said warmly, trying to deal with the animosity and betrayal she felt.

"*Roanoke Times* is on the phone. Line 2. Do you want to talk to them?"

Marjorie stood stunned for a moment. "Did you say '*Roanoke Times*'? Like in newspaper *Times*?"

"Yes, it's a reporter from the *Times*."

Oh God, help us here, I'm not ready for this. "Take a message. Tell them I just walked in the door."

Marjorie sat down at her desk. She sank into her big, comfortable leather chair. It was too early for this. Normal morning routine had Marjorie dealing with a broken copier, substitute teachers, late buses, and the general hustle and bustle the first part of the day brings. She was starting to understand how deep this was getting. Marjorie had a feeling it was just the beginning. She wondered how she had ever gotten into this mess. Her eye caught a paperback Bible lying on the end of her desk with a note attached to it.

> *Thought you might need this to make your decision real. Your students are behind you.*
> *Sincerely,*
> *Jim Smith*
>
> P.S. Go to page 668.

"A Bible?" she said to herself. She hadn't thumbed through one of these since she was a child. Her idea of a Bible had been a big, fat bunch of papers wrapped in black leather. She turned to the page marked 668. A few red lines under some script led her eyes to a verse.

> *We are hard-pressed on every side, yet not crushed; we are perplexed, but not in despair; persecuted, but not forsaken; struck down, but not destroyed.*

She closed her eyes. That was just what she needed to hear. A knock on the door brought reality back.
"Yes."
"It's Kendra. I really need to see you."
Marjorie wondered if she wanted to apologize for her confession to Mr. Connely and the group of onlookers last night. "Sure, come in."

Kendra was holding a legal pad bearing a few scribbled notes when she sat down in a soft, velvet chair in front of Marjorie's desk. "I don't know how to say this, but we have a problem again today."

Marjorie rolled her eyes. "Problem? Wasn't the paper enough of one? What, did the networks call, too?"

Kendra didn't respond.

"What—what is it?"

"We have a group of students who are . . . uh . . . experiencing whatever you want to call it again."

"What? But they only have Bible Club once a week. Yesterday was their day."

"Well, from what I gathered from a few students, Jim and a group came early today to pray for the school. They met in the back of the auditorium," she continued reading from her scribbles, "supposedly not to make a scene, and more and more kids just kept coming in. Last I heard, about 150 students are in there praying, or whatever they do."

Marjorie sighed loudly. She glanced at the clock. "And, I suppose with all those students missing for the first ten minutes of our day, a few teachers noticed."

"Yes, and"—she stopped—"and—"

"And what?" Marjorie said, cutting her off, nervous now to hear Kendra's response.

"And a faculty member called one of the local news affiliates. They just arrived and started filming the kids that are in the auditorium."

Marjorie stood up. "Oh my God, why doesn't somebody tell me these things are going on?"

Kendra stood with her. "I just got word."

Marjorie headed for the door. "Who was it, Kendra; who called?"

Kendra paused, trying to use her legal pad as a buffer. "Was it one of the faculty members?"

"It wasn't just one, but several. Mr. Connely was here this morning. He organized a meeting with them, and had a part in the decision to make some calls."

Marjorie was beside herself. "But he's a lawyer. He doesn't want bad press for the school!" She paused, then spoke softly to herself. "Unless he wants to get rid of somebody as much as everyone else does."

Kendra looked up for a response. Marjorie was already gone.

CHAPTER 18

"STOP THIS! Stop all of it!"

The abrupt words and tone caught Lincoln's student body off guard. The spirit of freedom and release, prevalent in the theater that morning, started to slip away.

"Listen to yourselves. Have any of you honestly listened to yourselves? I don't believe a single word of it. It is all a pile of crap. I'm embarrassed for my family, my community, and my school district. This is NOT, I repeat, NOT A CHURCH."

"That's the point!" a student yelled out three rows from the front.

"Shut up. I mean, be quiet. All of you, hear me out. What's happening this morning is a violation of the law. Yes, the law established by the Supreme Court justices of our nation."

Principal Whitiker ran toward the stage. His feet couldn't carry him there fast enough. It didn't matter. The students had already taken matters into their own hands.

"Boo!" Several of the seniors stood up and bellowed out toward Mr. Forrester.

"Sit down!" another yelled.

A few teachers stood, hoping to cast a shadow of control through the antsy crowd. Mumbling was coming from everywhere. A few pieces of crumpled-up paper landed on the stage at Jake's feet. He just ignored them and kept talking.

A feisty brunette stood up in the back. "Don't you tell us what we can and cannot do. If we want to experience this, then let us. Tell me, where were you the day the shooting began? I know where I was." She pulled up her sleeve to display the scar.

"You're not understanding me clearly," Jake responded.

"I hear you loud and clear," she continued in anger. "If this God they are talking about could have changed our school so this would have never happened, then we should have let Him in a long time ago. Where's your scar?"

She sat down. A few more insults were hurled. Things were starting to look like an episode on the *Jerry Springer* show. Mr. Whitiker stepped onto the stage and tried to grab the microphone from Jake.

"Fine," Jake yelled on borrowed time, "I may not be able to stop this here, right now, today. But I will in court. You can count on that. This school is a public school and I will fight to keep it that way . . ."

The students were so loud that Jake's words were drowned out. He dropped the microphone with an overwhelming thud, jumped off the stage, and marched up the aisle. Matt stood to follow him out, but stopped when his father walked past without the slightest recognition of his son standing there.

"Go to hell, all of you!" Jake yelled, slamming the door as he left.

CHAPTER 19

SEAN WAS STARTING TO SWEAT profusely. Not because of the heat, but because of the fear he felt from his recent proposition to the pregnant woman sitting next to him.

"Prayer?" she commented with a snicker, "Why pray? What, do I look like a saint or something? I can barely get myself out of bed every day."

"Does your husband pray?"

She snickered. "Husband? I ain't got no husband. My man left me the minute he found out I was pregnant. I don't know what I would have done without my mother. Boy, it's hot."

The woman paused, wiping the sweat off her brow. "But, come to think of it, she does pray. Goes to Mass a few times a week. She keeps tellin' me God is going to touch me. Right. God don't got no time for me."

Sean knew it was true. He could feel it. God did want to touch her. But He wanted to do it through Sean. Inside a battle raged. Half of him wanted to pray, half of him wanted to catch the next bus no matter where it was headed. He stood up, trying to relieve some of the stress he was feeling. Sean noticed a bus heading in their direction. He may have missed his opportunity, and he wasn't sure how he felt about it.

"This one yours?"

The woman shaded her eyes with her hand. The smell of diesel fuel filled the air. Oprah smiled from a poster printed on the side of the bus. Her eyes fixed on the blinking sign above the driver. "Nah, it's going north. I'm east."

Sean let out a deep sigh. More time—he had been given more time. He continued to fidget. The questions were starting to pile up in his mind. *God move at a bus stop in this part of Los Angeles? God move in Los Angeles, period? God use me, but I'm only a kid?* Besides, he had only seen one person healed in his life. A stroke? How could God heal the aftereffects of a stroke? *Nope. Can't do it.* He didn't doubt that God could do such an awesome miracle; he just doubted if God would. And foolish—Sean hated looking foolish. Looking cool was a part of who he was. *What will people say driving by? What if a cop stops me from praying! Nope, next time.* His eyes focused on the woman's left arm. *What if there isn't a next time?*

Sean cleared his throat. "Your arm," he said, standing and pacing in back of the bench like a madman. The woman was starting to notice that his behavior was somewhat strange. "Is that the only part of your body that was damaged?"

"Well, what does it look like? Doc said I was some kind of miracle." She laughed obnoxiously. "Some people get put six feet under with a stroke. Me? I just got a dead arm. Still got a brain, I think." She laughed again. "But I sure do get tired. Ain't as strong as I used to be. I hate bein' fragile. Can't do as much. They almost fired me for it. But they don't got enough people to work third shift." She took out a cigarette and lit it, blowing a swirl of smoke in Sean's direction. "This little guy just needs a little love, that's all." She patted her tummy again.

"So," Sean said nervously, "what do you do? You know, for a job and all."

She laughed again while blowing out a puff of smoke through her chapped lips. "You really want to know, eh? It's not very exciting." Her smile revealed the left-front tooth that was missing.

"No, tell me."

"Manufacturing. I'm on the line. I die-cast screws."

"Really?" The question came out before he even had thought it through. "Isn't that hard work for a woman expecting a baby?"

She laughed out loud. "Well, ain't you the first person I've met to show some sympathy!" She laughed obnoxiously again. "Good pay. Benefits. What more could I ask for? Beats flippin' burgers."

Sean looked down at his shoes. He was hoping she wouldn't ask him what he did at his job. He noticed another bus in the distance. It turned left at the light a few streets up. *JUST DO IT!* he screamed to himself, silently, though. He was cool, after all. "Listen, I, ah, um," he mumbled, wiping the sweat off his face, "would you—"

"You trying to pick me up or something?" she said sarcastically, then smiled to herself. "Now that hasn't happened in a while. Not many guys attracted to a dead arm. Besides, you're a little young to be hittin' on a lady my age." The wrinkles around her eyes gave away her age like the rings inside a tree.

Sean's eyes were like silver dollars. He couldn't tell if she was serious or teasing. "Pick up? No way." It wasn't supposed to go this way. "I mean, it's not that you aren't pretty and all. No. I want to pray. Would you really let me pray for you?"

Things were quiet for a few moments. All that could be heard was the busyness of Los Angeles. Cars driving, horns blaring, people talking.

The woman pondered the idea then came up with an answer. "Sure. Why not?" she said, snorting a smile. "Gosh, I thought you were just kidding." She glanced at her watch. "Darn, the 4:45 is already a minute late."

He sat down next to her. "Can I hold your hand?"

"Which one?"

Sean felt awkward. "Um, both."

She guided over her dead hand and then grasped his hand with the other.

"I've never really done this before. You can close your eyes if you want, but if you don't want to do that it's cool. It might look too weird."

"Weird? What's weird? People are already lookin' at me? What's a few more, right?"

Sean closed his eyes. He was ready now. For the first time in his life he was taking the risk of breaking out of his own comfort zone.

CHAPTER 20

MARJORIE PRESSED THE CHERRY COKE button. A loud roll signaled the aluminum can was on its way down. The soft drink landed with a thud. The noise startled Marjorie. She was nervous. The school board was meeting in less than five minutes to decide the fate of her job, not to mention the move of God that seemed to be sweeping across the small campus. The morning it had started had just been the beginning. Now, weeks later, outbreaks were happening daily. The student Bible Club was meeting over the lunch hour. Early morning prayer meetings were happening in several classrooms around the campus, led by a few teachers, local youth pastors, and students; but most were led by students. These students were leading one another into a relationship with Christ on a daily basis, whether it was in front of the lockers or over a hockey game in gym class. Drugs, bottles of Jack Daniel's, pornographic magazines, cigarettes, and many other items were left outside the office door with notes like this taped to them . . .

God is moving. This is keeping me from going there.

A note scribbled on the outside of a box of condoms found on the office counter reflected the desire to change:

I'm tired of having sex with my girlfriend. I'll try to stop.

Although many of Lincoln's faculty tried to stop the spiritual movement, nothing could hold back the flame in many of the students' hearts. The change in the student body was starting to cast a polarizing effect on the faculty. They were dumbfounded, wondering how so many of their very own students could have changed. The inevitable was upon them. Either they would change, too, or become an opponent to the winds of change.

Roanoke was in a stir. Not only had the papers gotten ahold of it, so had the local television stations. One local news show scheduled a nightly report on the events transpiring each day at the school. Arguments were heating up. You couldn't eat in a restaurant without overhearing some conversation about the separation between church and state. A verbal war between two mothers had taken place at the registers of the local Wal-Mart. The heat was on and Marjorie could feel it.

She opened the can of soda. It seemed to echo an "ahhh" back at her, a reminder of how she longed to have this entire ordeal over with. But this time in her life had been a time of strength in her relationship with God. Never before had she relied on Him to pull her through her daily routine. She was either putting out fires on the school grounds or encouraging them to stay burning. Although she seemed to be threatened on a daily basis regarding her job, the nameplate still hung on her door: Marjorie A. Harrison, Principal. She kept herself busy by staying in the middle of the school's day-to-day events. At first she had tried to control or at least help direct the breakouts around the campus, but she soon stopped. There was no way to schedule how God was going to move on the campus that particular day. The more the teachers seemed to crack down, the more God's Spirit seemed to spark up. Students were in her office on a daily basis talking about how their lives had been changed. Not at a church, not at a concert, not at a conference, but on the grounds of her school. This was something nobody had ever experienced before, not only in Roanoke, but also in Virginia. She liked it that way.

Marjorie's legal pad was full of notes. She sat quietly in a seat, watching the school board conduct business as usual. But this wasn't just any ordinary meeting. This particular monthly happening had been highly publicized. The room was standing room only and there was even a crowd hoping to see something as they stood and waited outside.

"I think we have passed the lunch menu item. We will no longer serve the chicken nugget items that are full of fat, but we will serve leaner portions of chicken breast, precooked and grilled. Agreed? All in favor, say 'Aye.'"

It was unanimous; Roanoke would soon cash in its chicken nuggets for leaner pieces of meat.

"Next order of business," Mr. Cromer, the school board president, said in a deep, rich voice.

Wanita Hill stood up. "I believe that is me," she whined in a domineering voice.

Marjorie took a sip from her can of soda and prepared herself for Wanita's speech.

"Mr. Cromer, elected school board officials, friends and Roanoke family—"

"Just get to the point, Mrs. Hill," Cromer came back in a strong tone. He couldn't wait for this order of business to be over.

"Well, as most of you know, something extremely controversial and peculiar has been happening on the campus of Washington Junior High."

"I am aware of that," Cromer said, hoping to speed her along.

"Well, then you know that strange behavior, students publicly 'following God' and other forms of religious activity, are happening on the junior high campus. Some students are even being forced to participate in this ridiculous behavior. Again, I remind you, on a public school campus."

"Yes, Mrs. Hill, we have all read the newspapers and seen it on the news. What do you propose we do?"

"Stop the activity. That's all we are asking." A group of militant parents and a few students stood behind her, agreeing.

Marjorie rolled her eyes.

"How do you propose we do that? From what I understand, faculty members are closing down the activity whenever they see it. What else do you want us to do?"

Wanita's face flushed red. "Mr. Cromer, from your tone of voice it sounds to me like you agree with what is happening." She was pushing for a confrontation.

He sighed loudly, his face flushing back a deeper shade of red. "I never said that. I don't agree with it. I know how to stop an epidemic of chicken pox or an outbreak of lice, but this is not something I can just give some medicine to and make it go away. From what I understand, Washington is dealing with this on a daily basis. Again, what do you propose?"

She paused, then darted her eyes and pointed her right index finger at Marjorie. "Get rid of her."

The crowd stirred.

Marjorie kicked her can of soda over, trying to keep the spill as small as possible.

"Well, now, Mrs. Hill, that is something we just can't decide at a school board meeting. It's easy to decide the fate of chicken nuggets, but somebody's job? That is another matter. We would need to consult legal counsel and then make a decision about termination."

"She is the problem here. She is encouraging this behavior. Ask the faculty and students. They'll tell you. Pardon me, Mr. Cromer, but this is a matter that needs to be dealt with."

"I wish she would just leave," Marjorie whispered to herself. Several parents started to protest, agreeing with Wanita. Her fan club seemed to be much larger than Marjorie's. Jim Smith and his parents sat close to her. If it hadn't been for the constant support of students like him, she would have left the position a long time ago. But for students like Jim, this was worth fighting for.

"Why don't we hear from Ms. Harrison? Is the principal here?"

Marjorie stood, pulling her skirt down as far as she could. She felt at home with a roomful of students but a little intimidated with a roomful of hostile parents.

"There you are, Principal Harrison. Can you clear this up for us?" Mr. Connely sat close to the front. He glared back at her, hoping she would say the politically correct words that would stop this mess.

"I'll do what I can, Mr. Cromer. It has never been my intention to push or pressure anybody to believe a certain way—"

"That's a pile of—," Mrs. Hill shouted.

"Wanita"—Cromer pounded the table with his fist—"enough."

She sat back down.

"A number of weeks ago, when this all started, I had every intention of shutting it all down. I am fully aware of the representation of the First Amendment in a public school. But when I saw the incredible effect it had on our student body, I didn't want it to stop. Every form of rebellious behavior has declined at our school. Words used to curse have been exchanged for words that encourage. What students used to call the smokers' corner is now called the Christian corner. Many of the same students that used to smoke pot before school now meet there to pray. Think of it in whatever way you want, Mr. Cromer, but whether you agree with it or not, our school has changed."

The crowd behind Wanita Hill started to get unruly. She stood up with a jump. "Mr. Cromer, ask her, ask her!"

Mr. Cromer pounded his fist again to quiet the crowd and stop Mrs. Hill from interrupting. "All of you; Wanita, please! For goodness' sake, ask her what?"

"Ask her if she believes!"

Mr. Cromer was silent for a moment. He cleared his throat and stared at Marjorie. "I guess that's the question they want answered here. Ms. Harrison, do you share the same beliefs as the students who have been pushing this 'God' movement?"

Marjorie looked down at Jim, who was sitting next to her. He smiled at her, nodding his head. She knew he was right. To deny it now might save her job, but to proclaim the truth would encourage the student body that Jesus was the answer. She looked back into Mr. Cromer's eyes. "Yes, I believe."

The room came unglued. The parents and students on Marjorie's side were standing and arguing with the majority, who were hurling insults and spewing words of anger on Wanita Hill's side.

Mr. Cromer stood up. The other school board members were silent, shocked at the behavior of those in their community.

Wanita got on top of her chair. "What? Are you going to allow prayer in our schools again, too?"

Marjorie sat down. She didn't want the spotlight anymore.

"People, people, quiet. Quiet!" Mr. Cromer hollered. Finally, Joan Cravitz, school board secretary, put two fingers in her mouth and whistled as loud as she could. The crowd stopped their shouting abruptly.

"My goodness," he said, like a parent to an overstimulated child, "settle down. Settle down! I didn't realize the tension this was causing in our community. Ms. Harrison," Cromer said back in Marjorie's direction, "this is the question I've been thinking through this evening. If you share the same belief as many of the students involved in this movement, don't you think the example you lead and direct is biased in some way? How can it not be?"

Before Marjorie stood up, a student two rows in back of her did. The room gasped. Wanita's mouth opened, reminding Marjorie of the entrance of a dark cave.

"Mr. Cromer, can I say something?" the young man said bravely.

Mr. Cromer looked at the board members seated with him. A few nodded their heads. "Why not? I don't think anything you could say would add to the chaos of this meeting. What is your name and what school do you attend?"

"Washington Junior High. My name is Kyle Hill, Wanita's son."

Now Mr. Cromer's mouth looked like a cave. "Proceed," he finally said.

"Kyle, sit down," his mother bellowed.

Ignoring her Kyle said, "Many of us have changed since this thing started. Consider me—I've been taking crystal meth for a year now. I was addicted. Sometimes I wouldn't sleep for days. I had to have it. And that morning it all started, I went into this Bible Club to hide out because I had just taken a hit before school. Who would suspect it; I was there, right? Well, God totally gets ahold of me, and I haven't used drugs since. Explain that," he said in his mother's direction.

A few parents in the room stared in shock at Wanita, who was caught with a grim expression on her face.

"I didn't know, I didn't know," she said to them defensively, shrugging her shoulders.

The room started to wind up again.

CHAPTER 21

EVERYONE WHO LIVED IN FATIMA MANSIONS knew something was different. Curtis O'Riley was a new person. Not only had his best friend, Frank Marshall, lost someone to drink a few pints of Guinness with, but O'Riley's recent change hit Marshall hard financially. Curtis had always been his biggest client. Not everyone living in the Mansions would buy that much heroin at one time. O'Riley had been buying it like candy. Now he wasn't touching it. He hadn't put a needle to his arm in over two weeks.

A knock on Mrs. O'Riley's door startled the single mother while making a cup of tea. She opened the door just a crack to see who was there. She was used to screening knocks at the door because of Curtis's seedy friends who often stopped by.

"Who's there?"

"Just me, Mrs. O'Riley. Dirk Shannigan."

The door was now open wide. "Oh, Dirk, come in, come in. It's nice opening up and seeing your face."

"Your son here?"

"He's still asleep. Let me get him." She shut the door behind them, welcoming Dirk into her simple, small flat. The sun was shining in through a small window in the kitchen, spilling light across the linoleum floor.

"It's not the most beautiful place, but it's home."

"That's all most of us need, just a home."

"Right you are. Can I get you a cup of tea?"

Dirk looked at his watch. "Sure. I haven't had my morning cupper yet."

"You know the Irish. Tea is better than water. The kettle is always on the boil in this house."

They both laughed. She poured the steaming tea into a white china cup with a matching saucer that had a blue ring painted on it.

Dirk loved stepping inside the O'Rileys' flat. Most homes were drab and dark, but Kate O'Riley had worked hard to fill the flat with the vibrant colors of life. The yellow walls smelled of fresh paint despite the musty fragrance that was emitted when you sat on the old, dark brown leather couch. A beat-up fabric chair and matching ottoman sat in the corner with a few patches of matting sticking out from the corners. Bright green and yellow pillows accented the chair and couch along with a stained-glass lamp that had a few panes missing from the back side. A bright ray of light illuminated the spackling on the wall. Pictures of her father, a potato farmer from the northern part of the island, hung on the walls like a scrapbook, revealing the pain and progress from the past to the present. Mrs. O'Riley kept things neat and tidy, reminding Dirk that home wasn't about the location of where you live, but the heart of what you live.

"Lovely day, wouldn't you say?"

"Very lovely."

"Sit with me for a moment, Dirk. I want to talk to you about the brilliant change in my son."

Dirk sat at the undersized aluminum table. He frequently sat with Mrs. O'Riley at this table talking about her son and just life for that matter. He wrapped his hands around the hot cup.

"I got to be honest with you, Dirk. Sometimes I don't know what to do regarding all this fuss over the change in Curtis. He's different, you know."

Dirk felt confident about the changes he had seen in her son's life. "I'm sure it has to be pretty overwhelming."

"Overwhelming! Overwhelming is not having to pick up any more dirty needles around his room. They were getting more rampant than the dirty clothes." She took two spoons of sugar from a bowl sitting at the center of the table and stirred them into her tea. "Do you think it will last?"

"I do."

"Why do you say that?"

Dirk scratched his chin. "In all my years of life, I have never seen somebody change so quickly after accepting Christ to be Lord of their life. Never. He's a miracle, Mrs. O'Riley."

Tears squeezed out of her wrinkled eyes. The stress of life had given her the appearance of being on the other side of the mountain of middle age. She wiped her tears away with the apron she was wearing. "Oh, I just wish his father could have been here to see the change. He died, you know, trying to find Curtis. Some hoodlums stabbed him to death and took his wallet just a few blocks from here."

"I remember hearing the story."

"That's right, you hadn't moved here yet."

"I think it happened during a time I was visiting. I remember the news making it a big deal."

"His dad, John, was used as an example of the violence that has crept up in the last few years." She got up to pour herself another cup. "I think most of the people around here are still scared of Curtis. They still don't see the light."

"It takes time, though."

"Oh, I know, but I just don't want people to think he's going to hurt them or steal money. That's not our Curtis anymore."

"Mrs. O'Riley, I think God really wants to use your son."

Her smile said a thousand words. "Oh, I think He already has."

"No, I don't think you understand. I believe God may use Curtis to change this nation."

Mrs. O'Riley was stunned for a moment. "Dirk, what do you mean by that?" she continued, sitting down again. She believed in her son with her entire heart, but change a nation? She was reluctant to believe that an O'Riley could be capable of that.

"Well, I've been praying for our nation in ways I can't describe. Moments before I found Dirk in the abandoned cathedral I had been praying for God to send Ireland a miracle. That miracle was your son a few minutes later."

"Are you sure it's just not a coincidence?"

"Was Saint Patrick a coincidence?"

"But, Saint Patrick? Dirk, he's only a boy. I'm just happy he's not taking drugs anymore."

"Keep your eyes on God, Mrs. O'Riley. He is going to do something. He's already started to break out around this nation by saving your son."

"Yes, Dirk, I believe He has."

"I have an idea. Do you think he would be willing to share about what has happened at the Fatima Mansions meeting tonight?"

She thought for a second, then replied, "I don't know, Dirk. You know how he hates attention and crowds. Fatima knows what's happened anyway. He's been the talk of the flats. That may have to be enough."

"There is so much more. Will you help me?"

"Help? How can I help?"

"Just get him to that meeting. That's all I ask."

"Dirk, what do you have up your sleeve?" Mrs. O'Riley said with a small grin. She tipped her head closer to Dirk's, not wanting to miss a word of Dirk's answer.

"A plan. A brilliant plan."

"After all you've done for my son, I'll do whatever you ask. He'll be at the meeting."

"Good," he said, finishing his cup of tea. "Then I'll see you tonight."

"Tonight," she replied with excitement. She didn't know what God was up to, but if it involved her son she was more than willing to comply.

"Has Curtis," Dirk started to say with hesitation, "has Curtis told you anything about himself?"

Mrs. O'Riley stirred her tea again, staring into the swirl that her spoon had begun. "If it's what I think you're referring to, yes, he has told me." The tone of the conversation suddenly turned from hope to a deafening note of despair.

"Has he seen a doctor?"

"No, not yet. It's just been good enough to have him at home."

Dirk grabbed her hand and held it. He was ready to make a risky statement. His stomach tightened and his teeth were somewhat clenched. "What if God healed your son, fully?"

Mrs. O'Riley shook her head. "Don't go filling my head with ideas. I've got to face this, and so does he, fair and square."

"Do you believe?"

"I tell you what, Dirk. I believe in anything after seeing his life changed. Besides, I thought he'd be dead by now because of all the drugs. If God heals him, brilliant. If He doesn't, I get him longer than I initially thought."

CHAPTER 22

RYAN SET THE NEWSPAPER on the counter, exchanging it for the hot cup of coffee that sat in front of him. The warm liquid flowed down his throat, healing the chill he had been left with since he'd finished reading about the breakout at Lincoln. He desperately wished he could have been there.

"You all right, mate?" a waiter said to him passing by, noticing the tear that was trickling down his check.

"Yeah, fine," he reassured him, wiping away the water stain on his face.

Fine? An easy answer he knew to use when he didn't want to face the truth. The fact was that he wasn't fine and he knew it. Things were far from fine. The article regarding Lincoln only confirmed that. Sydney had been a tough time in his life. Instead of using the city to study his passion for art, he was using it to run away from the past year of pain. He missed Liz and couldn't understand how a God of love could have taken her away, especially so tragically and mindlessly. "Why?" he asked himself often. But the answers never came. Only other escapes did. Clubbing, drinking, and the women he had used were his way of dealing with the issue. And Lincoln? Tonight had been the first time since he had moved here that he admitted even living close to Chandler.

He reread the article three times until the last drop of coffee was gone from the cup. He set it on the saucer with a clank. He closed his eyes, slowly uttering the first prayer he had prayed since Liz's funeral.

God, are You even there? he said without uttering a word from his lips. The only answer was the ambient sound of coffee being served to a few late-night drunks who stopped in after their nightly trip down "club alley." *I don't really know what to say, except that, that I feel so far from You. So lost. Look at me. I'm here in Sydney and I don't even know why.*

He opened his eyes for a moment to reassure himself that he was alone. Since the tear, the waitress did not bother him.

I guess what I'm trying to say is that I'm, I'm sorry. Very sorry. You can be mad at me, but please, oh God, please forgive me. Why Liz, God, why? Why me? How could You ever turn this whole thing into anything good?

He opened his eyes and stared at the article, reading the headline over and over again.

AWAKENING HAPPENS AT LINCOLN

He closed his eyes again. His face started to flush red. God was talking to him, revealing His love for him. Giving him purpose despite what the circumstances seemed to reflect. Then, like a bolt of lightning, a thought flashed inside him. A thought that changed his eyes, his demeanor, and his perspective on life.

"Another cup?" the waitress said softly.

"No, no thanks. What time you get off?"

"We close in about ten minutes."

"Good. You know where the club is down the street to the left?"

"Sure do."

"Come there when you're off. Something is going to happen that God wants you to see."

The waitress paused. She was interested. There was something about the way Ryan responded to her. "Something bad?"

"No, something so good it goes beyond any words you or I could say."

She poured a pot of coffee down the drain then responded, "All right, I'll try."

"Please, try hard. You're going to hear about it in the news around the world. It would be a tragedy for you to be so close and miss it."

"All . . . all right. I will try."

"Good. See you there."

"You, too."

The waitress watched Ryan sail out the door like a boat on a rough sea. His words brought fear and interest to her. She glanced at her watch. Soon she would understand his thoughts.

Ryan bolted out of the shop, crossed the street, and moved with a mission toward the entrance of the club. The steps he took were long and confident. He could hear the music thumping outside its doors. At times he felt like he was dragging cement blocks behind him, but his feet wouldn't let up. His flesh didn't want him to reach the entrance doors, but his heart fought to keep his focus on getting there. A few steps away from entering the club a drunken man bumped into him.

"Sorry, mate," he said with a laugh.

Ryan stared at him for a moment, then looked away. His concentration had broken, and now he was questioning whether he should go through with what he'd promised himself he would do. With less than an hour before it closed, a few stragglers held the door open for Ryan before entering themselves. He stopped suddenly before following the drifters inside. He closed his eyes for a moment. *I don't exactly know what I'm doing here, God. But, if You'll give me the courage here, I'll do it.*

Ryan stepped in, swallowing hard. He knew what he needed to do. Jackie, still sitting at the bar, caught his eye. She motioned him to come back to the seat she had been holding for him. He moved through the crowded area over to where the night's events had all begun.

"Say, did you find what you were looking for?" she said kindly.

He pulled the bar stool out, sitting down. "Yes."

"Did you find out if there was another shooting?"

He paused, then responded, "Something bigger. Much bigger."

A look of terror raced across her face. "Oh my God."

"Yes, it is something only God can do. And so is this. Wish me well."

Jackie looked at him without comprehending. "Are you feeling all right? Is there something I can do? This must be very hard for you to accept."

"That's the problem; I haven't accepted it. I've been running. I can't run anymore."

She took a cigarette from her purse and lit it. "Run from what?" she said after a drag.

"From this . . ."

Ryan ran out onto the dance floor. His force caused a few drunken dancers to fall onto the ground. Jackie watched him jump onto the stage and stand directly in front of the band. She took another puff from her cigarette and stood up.

The lead singer had just finished bellowing out a note to the dance rhythm when Ryan grasped the microphone from his hands. The music kept moving for a few moments, then stopped, spilling only silence onto the dance floor. Bodies became still; the individual Ryan knocked down stood up. A quiet hush fell over the bar where just seconds before laughing and joking had been heard.

"Oh my God," Jackie whispered to herself. She thought Ryan was going to pull out a gun and start shooting. After all, he wasn't a stranger to violence, she reasoned.

The waitress from the coffee shop stepped through

the door. Her attention immediately went to the dance floor. She recognized the man on the stage.

"Say, mate, what are you doing?" cried out a voice from behind the drum kit.

An uncomfortable hush fell over the club. Not a word was said. Lips were locked tightly shut. The only set that moved was behind the microphone. Ryan cleared his throat and began to speak.

"You don't know my name, and you won't recognize my face. But I have a message for you. A message for all of you tonight."

The club had never witnessed such a quiet moment. Jackie didn't even finish her cigarette for fear the sound of her blowing smoke from her lungs would be heard. She smashed the half cigarette in an ashtray on a table in front of where she was standing.

"My God, look at our lives. Look at us. God never intended it to be this way. I have one question for you tonight," he continued in his thick, American accent. "Why are you here?"

He expected to hear a few heckles and jeers but was confronted with only silence. "I know why I'm here. Running—I've been running." Tears filled his eyes, adding to the reality of his words.

"My sister was shot in the chest at Lincoln High School in Chandler, Arizona, over a year ago because of her faith. Because she loved God. And here I stand tonight, hating Him because of what happened to Liz. I ask you, Why are you here? I came in tonight to run again. Drink a few beers, dance with the beat, and get lost running from my pain. But I want to face it. I want to embrace it. And I want to come back to the God who understands it better than I ever will. And, I was wondering tonight, maybe some of you would want to come with me."

Jackie started to weep. Something she hadn't done in years, since her father left this earth in an automobile accident that she never quite recovered from.

The waitress standing in the doorway dropped her coat on the floor, falling to her knees. The lead singer standing next to Ryan fell to the ground, hiding his face.

Cries, tears, and a spirit of brokenness fell across the dance establishment like a thick blanket covers you on a cold, snowy night.

"He wants you to come home to Him," Ryan continued. "All you have to do is ask. Ask this God that created you. If you want to do this with me, cry out to Him. FOR GOD'S SAKE, CRY OUT TO HIM."

Ryan broke. He fell to his knees, leaning his face to the ground. His cries spilled the pain and torment he had been stuffing away since Liz's death. The questions, the anger, the bitterness, were all being released in one of Sydney's busiest dance and bar establishments.

Even the owner lay on the beer-covered floor in back of the bar, speaking out to a God he had never uttered a single word to.

Jackie pulled her skirt down below her knees as she gently knelt to the floor. She leaned her head against the bar stool, not sure what was happening, but knowing it was the most genuine feeling she had ever felt.

The Spirit of God loomed through the club like the thick fog that hung over Sydney Harbor. No more words were spoken. The only words uttered were hunger pains that were far from a cry for food, but for God's Spirit. God was moving. Ryan felt it. Jackie knew it. The waitress from the coffee shop responded to it.

A woman walking by peered through the glass doors where the club's bouncer usually stood and noticed the odd behavior. He was sitting on the floor, leaning his head against a wall, tears of release streaming down his face. She reached for her cell phone inside a coat pocket. She dialed the number with passion.

"Hello, get John. Quickly. I can't tell you, just get me John." She paused, waiting for a familiar voice. "John. Sorry to wake you. But you won't believe this. I was walking home from the concert tonight, through the club district in the Harbor, and something is happening at Lucky's that I can't explain. The people inside are on the floor crying, thinking, and praying. John, I think they are praying. Can you come down here? Please come down here. I think God is moving."

She lifted her eyebrows as she listened to his response. "I know it's a dance club, John. That's why I called you. I sense the Spirit here more than I ever have, even at church. I know it sounds crazy, but come. Please come."

She folded the flip phone, placing it back into her coat pocket. Grasping the door handle, she reverently slipped inside. Just a few steps beyond the door, she was on her knees like almost everyone else.

A newspaper fell on Pastor John Henson's porch shortly before the sun rose. Darlene, his wife, stepped outside, hoping it would make the time go faster as she waited for her husband to come home. After a call from his secretary late in the night, he left reassuring his wife that something odd had definitely been happening downtown. She brought the newspaper in and set it next to the empty cup and saucer on the kitchen table. A bell signaled a pot of morning coffee was ready to help her face the day. She filled the cup with the hot, muddy liquid. The chair squeaked on the tile floor when she pulled it out. Sitting down, she relaxed for a moment. It had been a hard night. Darlene was tense, worried about John and the district down in the Harbor. It had been known for its wild clubs and bars that promised great fun and a needed diversion for those wanting to get away from the truth of life. "A move of God?" She laughed to herself. Darlene took a sip and opened the paper. The coffee spattered out of her mouth across the front-page headline.

ACT OF GOD HAPPENS IN SYDNEY BAR

She wiped the coffee dripping from her chin, shook off the newspaper, and continued on.

SYDNEY, Australia (Worldpress)—Odd behavior was the talk on the street in the early hours of the morning in Sydney's club and saloon district today. The occurrence took place at Lucky's

Dance Club, a popular nightspot for "twenty-something" singles located on the Harbor's east side. At approximately 12:00 midnight, during the peak hours of the club's business, with over 200 customers in attendance, a young American art student got up on stage and started to speak to the inebriated crowd. Within minutes, most of those in attendance were on their knees crying out for a "God." Even the club's owner, Lance Dooley, was lying facedown behind the bar on the beer-stained floor.

"I don't know what happened. Something hit us that I can't describe. This young American started to speak to us about where we were in life. And it made sense to me. Logical sense. I just responded to what was asked. I decided to get my life right."

The odd spiritual "awakening" is one of many happening, not only in Australia, but as news sources are saying, around the world. Several school campuses in the United States of America are also experiencing similar movements. Many are confused, perplexed, and overwhelmed by these "awakenings." Church leaders are scrambling in Sydney, trying to handle the event. Dooley says that he is opening the club tonight void of dancing and liquor. He is proposing that a pastor from the community lead some kind of explanation and service. Pastor John Henson . . .

Darlene spit out some more coffee. This time she blurred the article so much she almost couldn't finish it.

. . . has been asked to lead a meeting tonight starting at 7:00 P.M. Many churches and religious organizations are criticizing him for his desire to lead the service at the club. Ryan Clarabough, the young American that spoke up at the scene, is scheduled to say a few words tonight. He is the brother of one of the victims murdered last year at the school shooting located in Chandler, Arizona, in the United States.

The phone startled Darlene away from the newspaper. She tried to regain her composure to answer the call.

"Hello?"

"Darlene, it's John."

"Thank God, are you all right?"

"I'm great!"

"I just read the headlines. Do you realize you are in the headlines?"

"Darlene, get the house ready."

"For what? What are you talking about, John?"

"I'm bringing over a group of them."

"Who?"

"A group of young people that were in the bar last night. They have so many questions! Ryan Clarabough is with me."

"Ryan who?" Darlene said back, confused.

"The boy from America. He wants to help us with this."

"This what?"

"This awakening, Darlene. There has been a 'breakout.'"

"Breakout?"

"Of God's presence like I've never seen. Darlene, it's what we've been praying for."

Darlene was silent, overwhelmed at the thought of God breaking out so strongly. It's not that she didn't want it to happen; she just remembered all the nights talking over a cup of tea about how awesome it would be if, and when, God would move His hand like a raging fire.

"Coffee. I'll put a pot on," she finally replied.

CHAPTER 23

ROANOKE WAS OUT OF CONTROL. Not only had the media sensationalized the spiritual "awakening" that happened on the campus of the city's own Washington Junior High, but the parents in the community had created their own daily chatter and train of comments. Phones were ringing, mothers were meeting in coffee shops, fathers were talking at the offices in closed-door discussions, and teachers were filing reports and complaints to the district on a daily basis. The most mature group of individuals in the stirring, surprisingly, had been the students. For the first time in the city's history, denominations were coming together, youth pastors were meeting, and unity was building. Store-owners put posters in their windows announcing the campaign slogan "LET THEM BELIEVE," which referred to the students who had been impacted deeply on Washington's campus. Other shop owners tacked up opposing slogans like "IT'S THE LAW: Separation of Church and State," and "Let Our Schools Be What They Are . . . SCHOOLS." Tension was high. And the awakenings had spread to some of the other schools in the district. Students who desired to see God move on their campuses felt free to share about the God they believed in.

Marjorie had never dreamed things would escalate

to this point. In fact, she was rather shocked. Although the nameplate on her door hadn't been taken from her, the adversity she experienced kept her thinking about trading in her job for something less controversial.

"It's at the state level now," she said to her mother on the phone in her office. "Mama, I don't understand it all. They still haven't cornered what the argument is exactly about. I know there is a group of parents statewide who are fighting for some kind of bill that, if passed, would stop any kind of act of God on campus and basically fire any district employee who encourages that kind of activity on campus. Mmhmm, I know. It's crazy. I'm crazy. But I called to ask you to pray. I have a meeting with the school district this afternoon. They may ask me to step down from my job. Yes, I know they can't do that, but in theory they can. If I am endangering my student body in any way I can be removed from my position."

Kendra buzzed in.

"Just a minute, Mom. Yes?"

"You have a phone call from another principal on line 3. Do you want to take it?"

Marjorie paused. "Can you tell them I'm talking to my mother long-distance?"

"Sure."

Marjorie turned her attention back to the conversation with her mother. "Sorry, Mom. Every day now I have school officials from all over the state asking me questions."

Kendra buzzed back, irritating Marjorie. "Yes?"

"Do you know a Principal Whitiker from Lincoln High School in Chandler, Arizona?"

Marjorie picked up a pen and tapped it on the desk. "Chandler, Chandler," she said to herself. Then it hit her like a barrel of rocks. "Kendra, yes, I'll talk to him. Hold on." She set down the pen calmly. "Mom, it's the principal from Lincoln High School in Phoenix. Remember? The shooting last year. Yes, I'll call you later. Bye."

Marjorie picked up the pen again and began clicking it nervously. She pushed the flashing button signaling line 3 was holding. "Ah, hello?"

"Hello. Principal Harrison?"

"Yes, this is she."

"Hello, my name is Donald Whitiker. Principal at Lincoln High School in Chandler."

"Yes, good morning. I have seen you on the news before."

"Unfortunately, yes. Not a part of my job that I planned for."

Marjorie breathed in deeply, then exhaled. "Yes, I'm sorry about all the tragedy. I don't know what I would have done in that situation."

"Thank you. I did the best I could. Listen, I got your number from a friend who said that he was watching a news program yesterday that reported your school was experiencing some of the same things we have been as of late."

Marjorie felt overjoyed. Finally, somebody who understood. "Really?"

"Yes. We have had several of these spiritual 'awakenings' happen on our campus. The community is in an uproar about it even though it has dramatically changed our student body. Are you experiencing anything similar?"

"Yes," she replied with excitement, "we are. We truly are. In fact, a group of parents are lobbying that the state pass a bill to stop these acts of God. Separation of church and state. You know, I'm sure."

"Yes, I do. I think what we have going for us, unfortunately, is that the city and state have been very understanding because of the shooting. If it is a part of healing the scars then I think they want to see it continue to some extent. The press don't seem to be snatching it as much, though, because there has already been so much publicity."

"Well, we are taking some of it for you," she said comically. "The press is having a field day with it here. I'm so proud of our students. They have handled it like champs, unlike some of their parents."

"I fully understand. I was just calling to encourage you and to let you know we are here to support you in any way we can. We are behind you no matter how far this situation goes. It's all about the students."

"That it is."

"I want you to call me to talk if you ever need a friend. And a number of our students would like to talk to your students, or even your community if that would help. We have faced our own hardship and want to pass on the strength. In fact, I have a student here who would like to say hello."

Marjorie could hear the phone being fumbled from one hand to another.

"Hello, Ms. Harrison?"

"That's me. Who is this?"

"Taylor Shepperd."

"Taylor, I read about you in the newspaper."

"Really? Out there? Man, I thought I was just in community news."

"Well, it's a small world, you know."

"Listen, Ms. Harrison, if I can do anything for you, let me know."

Marjorie's eyes lit up. "Taylor, I do have one thing."

"What?" he replied.

"The student who was leading the Bible study when things broke here, Jim Smith. He could use an encouraging word from someone who has been through something similar. Can I give you his number?"

"Cool, I'll call the dude," Taylor said. Marjorie gave him the information. "Oh, Ms. Harrison, I've got one more person here who wants to say hi."

Marjorie wondered who else would want to talk to her. She hoped it wasn't a media spy trying to get in on a good story using personal contacts. "Sure, put him on."

Again, the phone was jostled. She could hear laughter and then a loud bang giving evidence the phone had been dropped.

"Sorry, Ms. Harrison, this is Seth Anderson."

Her eyes started to water. She knew that name, that face, and his story. "Seth, what an honor."

"No, the honor is to speak with you. You must be a woman of courage."

His comments were like soft rain on a parched field. "I try."

"Well, keep it up. We have been praying for you here like crazy. Really. Every day, in fact. God is moving in our nation. Our world. And just think, you are a huge part of that. Don't give up!"

A tear fell on her wooden desktop. She wiped it away with her hand. "I won't."

The thought was overwhelming to her. To think that she was talking to one of the survivors of the worst school shooting in American history.

"Well, if you need anything, let me know. I'd come out to see you in a heartbeat."

"Aren't you in college?"

"I decided to take the semester off. My former school needs me."

"And they are so lucky to have you."

"Well, Mr. Whitiker is waving at me. I guess that means I have to go, right, Donald?" She could hear them laughing.

"Thanks for calling."

"Keep up the faith."

"Oh, I am. It may be new, but not lost."

"Cool. Bye."

"Bye."

The dial tone signaled that her friends from Chandler were gone. Just for now, not for good. She set down the phone, glancing at her watch. "Oh no, my meeting!" she hollered at herself. Marjorie collected her coat, briefcase, and legal pad of notes. On the way out she stopped to stare at the name plate that hung on her door for just a moment. *This all has been worth it. I know it. My life has been changed because of it. That is proof enough,* she thought to herself. *Whatever happens, happens.* She walked past Kendra, smiling while pushing some of her long hair behind her ears. "I'll be back shortly."

Kendra smiled superficially. Marjorie's risk made her uncomfortable. She wished she could be as bold as her boss was. "Bye."

CHAPTER 24

"Dear Lord," Sean prayed as genuinely as he could in the middle of the busy intersection in east Los Angeles. "You see this arm. And You see my faith. And I ask, in the name of Jesus, that You would be merciful to heal it despite the fear I feel in praying for it. God, I'm sorry if this prayer sounds dumb, but I really want to see You move. I can't do this, the doctors can't do this, but You can. I thank You for healing my friend Brooke at youth group the other night, and I pray that You would heal this lady I am sitting with here." He paused, not knowing what else to say. "Amen."

Both of them kept their eyes closed for a moment, then opened them, staring at each other. She spoke first.

"Thank you, young man. I'm grateful for your courage."

Out of the corner of Sean's eye he saw her bus roll up. It rumbled loudly next to them.

"Well, I've got to go. This one's mine. I hope it's air-conditioned," she said, wiping her brow.

Sean stood up with her. He shook the hand that seemed to work. "Yes, thanks," he said awkwardly. "Maybe I'll see you here again."

"Maybe," she replied, walking toward the bus.

Sean stared at his shoes for a moment, then looked up. The woman grabbed the handle next to the door to lift herself up on the first step. His eyes focused on the arm and the hand holding on to the handle. "Your arm!" he screamed out. "Your arm!"

The woman noticed it, too. She turned to say something back but the door shut too quickly. Sean ran up to the windows, lifting, waving, and pointing his hand representing her own. She sat down in front of a window, waving with the hand that was dead just a moment ago.

"It's alive! Your hand is alive!" he screamed as the bus started to move away from where he was standing.

She mouthed a genuine "Thank you" before her face was too far away to make out what she was saying.

Sean started jumping in the middle of the Los Angeles street. This was too good to be true. God had broken through.

"You won't believe it," he said to a passing older lady carrying a bag of groceries in her arms, "God just healed a woman's arm. And He did it through me. Me!"

She smiled at him fearfully.

"I can't believe it. He used me. It's not like I'm some faith healer or anything."

The woman's eyes were like saucers. She tried to walk away.

"No, really. It happened. I've got to tell you about it. You see, I was really scared. I mean, I've never asked God to use me until a girl at my youth group was healed. Say, can I carry your groceries for you?"

Flipping hamburgers would have to wait. There was too much to tell. Sean grabbed the grocery bag out of her arms.

"So," he continued, "this lady sits down next to me . . ."

CHAPTER 25

MARJORIE DROVE INTO the parking lot of the county school district office, north on Highway 75 outside Roanoke. She opened the door only to feel a cold, fall wind blow against her cheeks. Climbing out of the car, she could see her breath rising like a mist and disappearing into the air every time she breathed. She grabbed her briefcase, stuffing her legal pad and cell phone into a side pocket before she shut her door.

Beep!

Marjorie unpacked her phone, noticing that she had a message to retrieve. She glanced at her watch—she had a minute to spare. She dialed in her voicemail number and then her password. The message clicked on.

"Ms. Harrison, this is Jim Smith and a whole bunch of students!"

Marjorie could hear a crowd scream when Jim acknowledged they were there.

"We know you have an important meeting or something and we wanted to call and let you know that we are behind you, right guys?" More screaming and shouting. "So don't be afraid. All right? Cool. We think you're the best, all right?" The screaming got so loud she pulled the phone away from her ear for a moment. She smiled. "Bye!"

This really is about the students, she thought to herself. *Thank You, God, for giving me such an awesome group. I couldn't do this without them.* Marjorie shoved the cell phone back into her pocket as she headed toward the office door.

Inside, the building felt gloomy to Marjorie. She had only been here one other time—when the district had hired her shortly after she graduated from Harvard. She didn't remember it feeling so depressing. *Shouldn't school districts be places of life?* Marjorie wondered to herself again.

She met Mr. Connely in the lobby. He was dressed in a dark blue suit, white shirt, and gray tie. *Gloomy,* Marjorie concluded in her head, *not to mention a tightwad.*

"Hello, Marjorie," he said, his words sounding very plastic.

"Hello," she said back with a forced smile.

"Right on time. Efficient as always."

"I try."

"Here we are again, I guess. Waiting for another meeting to start."

Marjorie didn't feel like making small talk. "That's what it looks like. Are they ready to start?"

"I believe so. Why don't we go in. Best to you, Marjorie."

Her heart sank. *Best to you?* she said back inside her head. *What does that mean?*

The boardroom inside the district office was sterile and uncompromisingly plain. Six school board members, along with Mr. Connely and Charles Deets, the district superintendent, sat down with Marjorie when she took her seat at the end of the long oak table.

"It's an honor to have you here, Ms. Harrison," said Mr. Cromer, Roanoke district school board president. "We have all taken time off work to make this meeting happen. It is of utmost importance that we make a decision regarding the events at Washington Junior High School. We hope you feel the same way."

"Yes, I do."

"Good, good. Then why don't we get started. Water, anyone?" Mr. Cromer asked, pouring himself some water into a clear glass in front of him. He took a sip in the silence before continuing, "Ms. Harrison, I have asked Professor Deets, our school district superintendent, to help us with this meeting. Have you two ever met?"

Marjorie remembered shaking his hand a few times over the past several years. "Yes, we have met."

He reached his hand across the table and she reached back. "Good to meet you again."

"The same."

"Well," Cromer replied, "why don't we get started. Charles?"

"Marjorie, you have done an impeccable job leading Washington Junior High these past five years. Your record is clean, not to mention the award your school received last year after being voted the best school in the state as far as academics go. My hat is off to you. I wish all our schools had the kind of leadership you have presented."

"Thank you, I think," she said, feeling like a lamb being led to the slaughter.

"Do you have any thoughts on the events of the last month?"

Marjorie was quiet for a moment. The last month? There was no way to describe the emotions, trials and feelings associated with what seemed beyond her control. "No, I really don't know how to respond."

"Let me help you. Would you say that you are proud? Scared? Excited? Any of those words describe your thoughts?"

"Well, I, uh, don't know how to take the past month and label it with a one-word response. I think we all know that this goes way beyond me or all of you. Something has happened here that I can't deny."

"We aren't asking you to."

"Then why am I here? If I have done such an excellent job where I was placed, why the interrogation?"

"This is not interrogation," Connely spoke up. "It has to do with everyone's rights."

"Even mine?" she barked back at him.

"Even yours."

"These events at your school have created a lot of news in our city, state, and now our nation. The wind is blowing this thing everywhere it can."

"I never intended that," she replied.

"Neither did we," he said. "But there has to be some kind of end to it or we are looking at a legal case that could cost our district money we don't have."

The room got uncomfortably quiet again.

"So this is about money?" she questioned.

"In some ways, but more than dollars we have to look at rights, the rights of every student at your school. Do you think these outbreaks are giving people a right to choose God?"

"Mr. Deets, choosing a relationship with God is all about freedom. The students at my school have been given a choice. That is the problem. Parents, faculty, even you don't like the choice they have made. When a student chooses to follow God his life changes. It makes the world we live in a little bit more uncomfortable. It creates, shall we say, controversy. Believing in something we can't see. And isn't that why we are here, over controversy rather than the students?"

"Well—"

"Look, since prayer was taken out of schools in 1963, we have seen a noticeable change in student behavior and academic studies." She took a few sheets of paper out of her briefcase and set them in the middle of the table. "Look at the stats over the last thirty years. I thought it was a fluke, too. That was, until I noticed what God was doing in some of Washington's toughest students. When we took God out of our schools we lost control of them."

Mr. Connely picked up the papers, scanning them as quickly as he could.

"God has changed our school, Mr. Deets. All the

evidence is there. Listen to the students; they will tell you. If you want to go back to the old Washington, then that is your choice. But I want to move forward. There are so many hurting kids who walk the hallways of our districts every day. Washington is just one of thousands searching for the answer. What I'm saying to you here is that we found it this year. I found it."

"How do you know that, Ms. Harrison?"

"Come with me to school tomorrow. Look at all of you. When was the last time you got on a campus to know what was going on inside? Do you understand how many kids are on serious drugs like Ecstasy and crystal methamphetamine? Do you know how many of our own students—and I remind you these are junior high students—are having sex with not just one partner, but several? I used to think the only way to stop all this was by offering programs or bringing in guest speakers. That is, until I found the truth. Jesus Christ is the only answer for our 'institutions.' I'm not out to fight with you here. I'm after students' rights, too. Including the right to live life to its fullest."

Not an eye moved from her. A few board members cleared their throats, but the looks cut like a thousand knives. Marjorie finished pouring herself a cup of water.

"Well," Mr. Deets finally remarked, "I think we may need a few minutes to talk about this."

"Excuse my question, but what exactly are we deciding today?" she said, taking another sip.

Mr. Connely spoke up. "In the best interest of the

district, we are deciding whether or not to replace your position."

"Oh, I thought you already had," Marjorie said with fire in her eyes.

"No, no, Ms. Harrison," Connely said artificially. "Why don't you step out and give us a few minutes."

Marjorie collected herself, picked up the sheets of paper sitting in front of Mr. Connely, and grabbed her briefcase as she headed for the door. She turned before closing it. "If I may, I beg you to do what's best for the students. Think of them, not me. They are the most important part of this entire breakout. God cared enough about our students in Roanoke to move among them. Shouldn't we respect that?"

The door shut. Nobody made a sound until Mr. Cromer poured himself another glass of water. His mouth was dry and so was everyone else's sitting inside the room.

"Well," Deets said firmly, "we have a decision to make . . ."

Marjorie's high heels clicked down the hallway. They echoed in the emptiness of the building. Even so, Marjorie's heart wasn't empty anymore. Nothing could echo there. Despite the fact that she might be out of a job in a few moments, her heart couldn't have been more full. She wasn't angry and bitter at Deets, Cromer, or even Connely. *What good would that have done,* she reasoned. Her heart was full of the miracle of God. He had changed her life, and she would never be the same.

Marjorie heard the humming sound of a soda machine coming from a vacant break room. She pulled a dollar bill from her wallet, placing it into the slot marked for bills. A Diet Coke dropped down into her hands. She unscrewed the cap. Coke shot everywhere. Marjorie tried to put the cap back on as quickly as she could, but the pressure inside was causing the liquid to squirt with greater power. She dropped the bottle onto the floor, stepping away from it. The Coke sprayed its final contents. She looked down at her new suit. Splotches of wet, brown stains were everywhere. "Oh, great," she responded with frustration.

"Need some help there?" a voice muttered from the doorway.

She turned to find an older man dressed in a flannel shirt and dirty khakis standing there, staring her way.

"Oh, sure, I guess," Marjorie said, embarrassed. There was soda dripping from her hands and down her legs.

"I've got a few clean rags here in my cart." He reached around the corner of the doorway and came back with two bleached white cotton towels. "There you go," he said, handing her the cloths.

"Thank you; really, I'm quite embarrassed."

"You never can tell about those soda bottles. Sometimes they come out fighting you. It's almost like they are waiting and preying on you."

"I sure didn't expect this," she said, wiping down her arms, legs, and new gray suit.

The old man brought in a mop. He picked up the

empty bottle and started wiping up the mess. Marjorie felt awkward, not knowing what to do.

"You look like a very important person. I haven't seen you in the offices around here."

"Well, I'm not from this particular office. I do work in the school system, though."

"Teacher—you're a teacher," he said warmly. "My wife was a teacher. She retired a few years ago. Taught first grade for twenty-five years."

"Really. How wonderful. It's hard to find a dedicated teacher like that."

"Yep. Same school, same district. She passed on last year."

Marjorie reached down to wipe off her shoes. "Oh, I'm sorry. She sounds like a wonderful woman, though."

"She was. And still is, in my mind. My granddaughter really misses her."

"Granddaughter? How old?"

"Seventh grade."

"Really. Can I ask what school?"

He walked out for a moment to ring out the mop, then came back in, slopping it around again. "Washington Junior."

Marjorie's eyebrows wrinkled. "Good school, I hear."

"Good?" he questioned back. Marjorie was ready for a verbal lashing.

"That place has changed her life, not to mention my own. I only wish Avendale was here to see it."

"How do you mean?"

"Haven't you heard? Who hasn't? This office has been buzzing about it for over a month. I've seen it all. I get to throw away the garbage, you know. Good golly, there have been agendas, memos, and closed-door meetings. You name it."

"What's all the fuss about?"

"Oh, there was some kind of spiritual awakening on the Washington campus. Bunch of kids got their lives changed. My Avendale, she prayed for that to happen for over twenty-five years. And it happened because of her prayers. My granddaughter gave her life to Christ over at the school. Changed her completely."

"Really. That is incredible."

"Words are useless. It's purely a miracle. I've been a janitor in this district longer than my wife was a teacher. And I tell you, I've seen it all. But nothing like this. It's good to see God moving on our campuses again. Ain't no bureaucratic political hogwash that can stop Him. I'm glad He finally found a school He could break through to. In fact, my hat's off to that principal over there. She's taken a lot of cow dung to keep this thing continuing. Avendale would have been proud to meet her."

Marjorie smiled. "Well, I'm sure that principal would have loved meeting your wife. All this wouldn't have happened if it weren't for teachers like her, praying for so long that a move like this would happen."

"Ah, sure it would. God's gonna do more of it. He

just uses us to help Him get it there." The mop soaked up the final spots on the floor.

"Well, it sure has been good talking to you. I'm going to head to the ladies' room to try to wash the remaining Diet Coke off myself. I've got a meeting to finish."

The old man stepped out of the room, placing the mop into its bucket. Marjorie's heels clicked down the hall.

"Say," he hollered after her, "if you meet the principal, you tell her what I said."

"Oh, I will," she said, turning back.

"Say, what school did you say you were from?"

"Washington. What's your granddaughter's name?"

"Madison. Madison Landoll. What's your name again so I can tell her to look for you."

"Marjorie Harrison," she said back quietly. "I'll look for Madison," she replied again as she disappeared into the bathroom.

"Marjorie Harrison. I'll try not to forget that. Goodbye," he yelled up the empty hallway, but Marjorie was already gone. She now understood more than ever the role she played, not only in Washington's history, but the spiritual history of every student on her roster.

CHAPTER 26

FATIMA MANSIONS WASN'T THE EASIEST PLACE to live on the southwestern outskirts of Dublin, nor was it an easy place to hold a local meeting for those who lived within its borders.

The monthly meeting was sponsored by the Dublin Corporation, the city's council, and was supposed to be an informative meeting for those who lived in the poverty-stricken crime area. A few city elders were there, as well as the lord mayor. Most of the time the evening turned into a verbal bashing between those who lived in the area and those who lived far from it in their expensive high-rise apartments.

The mood was especially bright this evening. A few local musicians provided music in the dungy basement located in an apartment complex. They played their fiddles together, trying to create a surreal environment for those who attended. Drinks and chips, paid for by the lord mayor, who was seeking reelection this spring, were served by a few of his personal secretaries.

Dirk arrived shortly before the meeting started. The moldy walls smelled musty to him. The room was packed to capacity. Every folding chair that could be sat on had somebody sitting in it. A few latecomers were standing in the back with Dirk. As far as he could tell, no Mrs. O'Riley, and most important, no Curtis. Dirk wondered why the meeting seemed to be so full. Most individuals in the community despised the meetings because of the politics involved in the city government. The poor and needy were a growing demographic for the city of Dublin, and the lord mayor's office didn't know what to do about it. So, serving chips and drinks was used to help ease the pain.

"Excuse me, if you don't mind my asking, but is there something special going on tonight? This seems like an awful lot of people for this type of meeting," he said to a nearby bystander leaning against the back wall.

"I heard there was going to be a special guest here this evening," he said in an Irish whisper.

"Really? Who would that be—lord mayor?"

"No, I heard it was Curtis O'Riley."

Dirk just about lost the fish and chips he had devoured for supper. "Curtis O'Riley?"

"Yes; you know, the drug dealer. I guess he changed. His mother told me to come and hear about it."

"She did, eh? Good ol' Mrs. O'Riley," he said. Dirk reasoned she must have made her way through the neighborhood, telling anyone who would listen. But there was still no sign of Curtis or his mother.

The meeting began on Irish time, thirty minutes late. After last meeting's notes had been discussed, a special presentation was made regarding the new AIDS community center to be built in the heart of Fatima Mansions. The current site the center was operating out of was a vacant storefront that had been used for several different Irish pubs in the past few years until a fire nearly destroyed the entire structure. Although it smelled like smoke, most of those who came for food, shelter, and medical assistance didn't mind. At least it was help, and that was all they needed.

"All who agree say aye," the man leading the group replied to the audience.

"Aye!" came back with an electric response.

Dirk looked around as they moved to the next order of business. The room continued to fill. Not only were there no more chairs to sit on or walls to lean against, but there was purely no more room to even snugly fit another Irishman. The room buzzed with a synergy never seen before at a community meeting. Several of the regulars didn't know how to respond. Suddenly, the entire community had become a captive audience. Meetings usually lasted less than an hour, but the town's elders were taking extra time, enjoying adding all the meeting protocol they were supposed to use on an ongoing basis.

"Next agenda item," board member John O'Malley hollered.

"I think that is it, unless we have any questions from those attending tonight," the secretary said.

O'Malley took a deep breath. "Any other items, speak up now, or drown them out in a pint of Guinness later."

The crowd seemed restless. No hands were raised. No shouts were heard. Everyone was waiting for the unknown guest of honor to arrive.

Without a glamorous entrance, Mrs. O'Riley pushed her way through the crowd, confused at the amount of faces she recognized there. *I just mentioned it to a few people,* she thought to herself. Curtis followed closely behind her. He portrayed an even more confused appearance. Little did he realize the mob that had assembled was there to see him.

"Mrs. O'Riley is here!" someone yelled. Another voice followed. Gasps, excitement, and a defiant tone filled the air. Dirk tried to signal his friends, but there were too many people to see his hands waving in the air. The crowd was mumbling the O'Riley name so much that John O'Malley thought the sweet, older woman must have had an innocent question.

"Yes, Mrs. O'Riley, speak up. What is your question?"

The crowd stirred itself even louder now. Curtis and his mother were pushed and shoved to the front of the room. They moved out from inside the crowd, facing the lord mayor, board, and important officials of Fatima Mansions.

"Mrs. O'Riley, I presume."

"Yes," she said nervously.

"Do you have a question or not? This entire meeting has reached unpretentious proportions. What is it that you could want?"

She was quiet. Curtis stared at the ground. The crowd started to shout about what was to come next.

"Excuse me, Sir O'Malley?" a voice cried from above the loud rumble. "Excuse me!"

Dirk stood on top of a chair, whistling a loud

shrilling sound with fingers in his mouth. The crowd quieted, turning their attention to where Dirk was standing. "Dirk Shannigan."

"Yes, yes, I know. From the church, correct?" O'Malley cited.

"Yes. Most of you know me, or have seen me around Fatima," he said, turning his attention back to John O'Malley. "Sir, I think I may have caused the attendance in your monthly meeting to rise tonight."

"Oh, really. How, might you say?"

"Well, it's just that I invited Curtis's mother, to come down tonight and share about something that I think is much more important to this township than a community phone box on a certain corner, or the blueprint for the new community center, or a license to open a new pub. The agenda item I have brought down with me to this meeting is a changed life."

A few fans of Dirk's message so far applauded his opening remarks. A few old-timers looked confused, but most of the individuals there knew exactly who Dirk was talking about. They wanted to know the truth.

"Most of you are aware that our community is a broken-down drug haven for addicts." A few of those standing close to Dirk shook their heads. "And it hasn't always been that way."

"I'll say!" a woman standing close to the door called out. The crowd seemed to agree.

"But I believe something has changed in our community because someone has changed. Most of you know who Mrs. O'Riley is, right?"

Curtis looked as white as a sheet. He knew what was coming.

"And most of you know her son, Curtis."

"I'd like to give that boy a good battering," a woman screamed.

"He's ruined my boy's life," cried another.

"Arrest him," yelled an angry father. Most of the crowd seemed to agree. Dirk tried to settle the fickle, angry crowd.

"Now, I know you've seen him on our streets selling drugs to our kids, but I'm telling you, you're not going to believe this, but Curtis O'Riley has changed."

A core of those in the room got really charged.

"I don't know if he'll talk about it, but you need to know it's true."

Curtis focused his eyes on a piece of trash on the ground. He didn't seem prepared for the attention he was receiving. His mother put her arm around him.

"Tell us, Curtis," O'Malley stepped forward to say, "tell us if this is true."

The room was finally quiet. The rumblings, the stirring, even the whispering had stopped.

"Well?"

Curtis raised his head and looked into John O'Malley's green eyes. "Yes," he said almost silently.

"What did you say?" John said back, even gruffer now.

"Yes."

John O'Malley's chin looked as if it was going to touch the ground.

The Irish crowd hushed even more. The quiet seemed to scare a few. Never had they seen a group of Irishmen so sober.

"Dirk, if I may ask, is this some sort of joke?" O'Malley questioned. And he wasn't the only one. Most of those in the room hated, even feared the boy's name. He had wreaked havoc on Fatima Mansions ever since he had been a small boy, ever since his father had left. *How, many asked silently, could a change like this be real?*

"What kind of change are we talking about here, Curtis? You tell us. This community deserves to know."

Dirk had pushed his way through the tangled web of bodies. He reached Curtis, placed both hands on his shoulders, and looked him in the eye. "Curtis, you must tell them. Tell them what your mother has seen. Tell them what I have seen. Tell them how real this all is. I believe in you, and so will they. Look at them," Dirk said intensely, turning himself and Curtis to face the crowd. Curtis glanced out at the crowd then back at a sweet bar wrapper on the ground. "They need to know. Just like you needed to know."

The arm Curtis had used so often was still slightly bruised from the needles that had punctured their way through in the past. His thin frame and unkept wavy hair still gave him the appearance of a heroin addict. But there was something different in his eyes. It was evident he was not the same person.

"Uh," he started, "I, I haven't used anything in three weeks. I haven't used any drugs in three weeks."

The crowd wasn't quiet any longer. Words of unbelief were being expressed. Whispers of truth were being challenged. Many just didn't think it could be true.

"Tell them how, Curtis. How could you stop this?"

Curtis looked up now. His eyes were filling with water. "I found Jesus. Jesus Christ."

That was all he needed to say. Several women from the back of the room started to cry. A number of men started to pray. Everyone seemed to be in a state of shock. If Jesus could change Curtis, He could change anyone. Curtis fell on his knees and began to weep. The room stood still. Irishmen are not known to cry often, if ever. Curtis's cries could be heard over the crowded room, up the stairs, and onto the street.

Curtis wept openly for the lives he had led astray and for the parents who hated his heart. And with a heart of gratitude for the Spirit of God, who could change them all.

CHAPTER 27

THE SPIRIT OF HARLEM, NEW YORK, had changed. The evidence was everywhere. Lenny Johnson's work was cut out for him. A hunger for God had broken out inside some of New York City's toughest schools. Lenny flipped the on button on the coffeemaker. The hot, steaming mixture started to drip into the glass carafe. He was nervous. Several principals from around the city were meeting him in his office this morning to discuss the spiritual "awakenings" that were happening on their campuses. Men and women from all different cultural and religious backgrounds were looking for an answer to the phenomena at hand. Lenny smiled to himself, pouring the first cup of coffee into his usual mug. He didn't have all the answers; all he knew was that prayer had been answered. He sat down at his desk and opened his Bible. He had been reading about the church in Acts. It was the only thing that seemed to give him solace. Lenny suddenly was identifying with the day-to-day spirit that could be seen everywhere he turned. He couldn't stop the move of God, even if he tried. The church of God was breaking out. His eyes spilled across the second chapter, starting with verse 17 . . .

> *It shall come to pass in the last days, says God,*
> *That I will pour out of My Spirit on all flesh;*
> *Your sons and your daughters shall prophesy,*
> *Your young men shall see visions,*
> *Your old men shall dream dreams.*
> *And on My menservants and on My maidservants*
> *I will pour out My spirit in those days;*
> *And they shall prophecy.*
> *I will show wonders in heaven above*
> *And signs in the earth beneath:*
> *Blood and fire and vapor of smoke.*
> *The sun shall be turned into darkness,*
> *And the moon into blood,*
> *Before the coming of the great and awesome day of*
>   *the LORD.*
> *And it shall come to pass*
> *That whoever calls on the name of the LORD*
> *Shall be saved.*

Lenny couldn't help but wonder if these were "the last days." God's Spirit seemed to be pouring out all over the city, the state, even the country for that matter. Harlem hadn't been the only community touched. Suddenly, what began as a perverse tragedy in a small Arizona suburb had become the fuse to an explosion of God's hand all around the world. Lenny's students were prophesying over their needy city, a group of principals from around Harlem were meeting to dream about what to do next, and miraculous signs from the poor to the rich were taking place. Just last night three gang members confessed to the murder of a fellow member and turned themselves in because Jesus Christ had told them to.

Lenny shook his head and took another sip of coffee. God had called him and his wife there. Now there was no doubt. What if he would have left, given up, and just quit? "Well," he said to himself, "I wouldn't be meeting these turkeys today." He opened up the box of donuts he had purchased at the grocery store and picked out his favorite.

"Mr. Johnson," his secretary buzzed in, "I have a Mr. Wentworth from New Jersey Heights Junior High here to see you."

"Send my man in," he said with a laugh. "Send him on in." This was going to be fun, he reasoned. The funniest thing he had ever done.

CHAPTER 28

"I THINK THEY ARE READY for you now," Mr. Connely addressed Marjorie, who had dozed off on a chair in the district's main office.

"What?" she said in a sleepy tone.

"They've made a decision."

Marjorie sat up, glancing down at her watch. She was awake enough to do the math in her head and realized she had been snoozing for more than three hours. She covered her mouth and yawned. "Long meeting."

"In more ways than one," he said sternly. "I think everyone is ready to put this behind them."

Marjorie stood up, pulled back her hair, licked her lips, and tried to rub out the puffy dark rings she knew were under her eyes. Her feet felt like cement blocks—one step, then another. Marjorie kept yawning, hoping to fully wake up before she got to the boardroom. Connely tapped on the door.

"Everyone ready?" he said.

The door slid open. Tired eyes met Marjorie's. She stepped inside and sat where she had before. Connely shut the door with a slam. Everyone jumped, including Connely himself.

"Sorry," he mumbled.

"Well," Mr. Cromer began, "it seems as though this

decision took us longer than we expected. We got to talking about everything and almost felt time slipping by. None of us realized that it had been over three hours. I apologize for the inconvenience."

Marjorie crossed her legs, sitting up straight. "No need; it gave me some time to catch up on my sleep."

"Yes, I suppose losing sleep during a time like this would be normal. It must be terribly stressful."

"You're right. Not to mention that tomorrow morning I'll get up and keep a school running. All this attention has drained me of everything I have."

Cromer cleared his throat. "Has it now?"

"Yes."

There was an awkward silence.

Marjorie looked around the room at the faces. She felt for them. This was no easy decision to make for anyone, even your enemies. It was obvious Cromer was stalling, hoping somebody else would lay out the news to her. "Listen," she spoke up, "let's just get right to the point. I'm guessing nobody wants to share the good news, so what we have is bad. Can somebody explain to me what you've decided?"

Connely started to talk, but Cromer interrupted him. "Marjorie, I know this must be a taxing time for you. And I wish we could work out an agreement, but it seems we cannot."

"Mr. Cromer," she cut in, "please stop trying to make this so easy for yourself to say. Please stop worrying about how I'm doing and just tell me what you decided."

The board wiggled around in their seats.

"As a group, we have decided that it would be in the school's best interest if . . . if—"

Connely broke into Cromer's stuttering. "They want you to step down."

Marjorie's eyebrows wrinkled up. "What?"

Connely took a sip of water. "They want you to resign. The only way to stop this behavior on campus is to pull out the root. And we see the root at Washington as being, well, you."

Marjorie had expected the worst, but that didn't make it any easier to hear it from Connely's lips.

"And, being the school district's legal representative, I need to help protect it from any kind of lawsuit. We believe the most proactive thing we can do is try to help you relocate out of state and reestablish what we believe is the most important aspect of Washington— education, not spiritual renewal. After all, we are talking about a public institution here."

Marjorie couldn't even hear his words anymore. All she could see was his lips moving. She crumpled her left hand into a fist. She knew her rights. She understood the system. And there was no way to win the game today. "Bull—," she whispered, then stopped. *No*, she thought, *this isn't worth it. It's not worth losing my temper in front of them. That would give them too much pleasure. Then they really would win.* She looked Connely in the eye. "Well, since you have suddenly become the school's legal counsel and already forgotten about its former principal, then I need to get myself some legal counsel."

"I can help you with that," he said back.

She laughed. "Are you kidding? No, I don't need your suggestions. I'll find my own help. Just be prepared, because if you were hoping your decision would keep you out of court, you're wrong. You just got your ticket to ensure you'll be there."

"Now, now," Cromer chimed in.

Marjorie turned to face him. "Please don't patronize me. I'm not fighting for myself or my reputation; you will ruin that anyway. What I'm fighting for is every student in my school. They deserve the right to experience God's renewal if they choose to. And you or I won't stop that. You watch, God is bigger than any of us."

"Please, Ms. Harrison, let's not get ugly—"

"Ugly? No need to worry. All I'm after is the truth."

"And we are, too. If the court needs to decide, then we will let them."

"Courts? Forget courts; I will push this one for the sake of every student in this country."

Connely moved closer to her. "What court are you talking about?"

"The Supreme Court, Richard. If you want a fight, then I'll give you one. Besides, I've got the almighty God behind me." She stood up, pushing in her chair. "Oh, and don't take the nameplate off the door until this is all said and done. I'm not finished being principal yet."

The door didn't slam this time, but shut with the normal sound that signaled someone was leaving.

Marjorie clicked down the hallway. No tears this time, just fire. There was fire in her eyes. Not to redeem herself, but to bring freedom to her students. All she could think about was the students.

CHAPTER 29

SEVILLA WAS CONFUSED. She had never done any kind of trick in a hospital. *A hospital for the heart?* she thought to herself. *Maybe this guy is a heart doctor? Yes, that must be. That's why he will pay triple.*

Sevilla walked behind the man through the front doors of the building. Inside seemed to be an entirely different world. It looked like a warehouse. Instead of hospital beds and patient rooms, all she could see was a cement floor, a few lights and a group of people gathered in the center of the room.

"Welcome to a hospital for the heart," he said to her, encouraging her to follow him.

She reluctantly dragged her feet. Something inside told her this wasn't going to be about sex. She tapped the man on the shoulder.

"I'm ready to leave," she whispered.

"You can't; I still have twenty-five minutes."

"I don't care about the money, I just want to leave."

He paused, taking her hand in his. "Don't be afraid. Everything is going to be all right. Trust me. I have not brought you here to hurt you, but to help. You'll see." He nudged her on. Sevilla followed as slowly as she could. She wanted to take up as much of the twenty-five minutes as possible.

As they walked closer to the group that was centrally located, Sevilla could hear a song being played by a man with a guitar in the middle of the circle. Those who surrounded him weren't what she expected. Many of them seemed to look similar in age to her, a few younger and a few even older. Eyes were closed, hands were lifted high, and the group seemed focused on one thing. "What are they doing?" she whispered again.

"Worship," he whispered back.

Worship? Sevilla wanted to run and hide and just get out.

The girl standing next to her looked familiar. Sevilla looked closer. She had seen her on the streets trying to raise some cash to live, just as she was. A muscular young man stood across from her. She had seen him before, also. In fact, he had taken some business away from her several months back. He was hitting up the same men she had been. After an argument with her boss, she hadn't seen him back. There were others. Several she had seen selling themselves just like she had. But the look on their faces. Something was different. No longer did they resemble the look of living lost, but now had a look of peace unknown to her. The girl standing next to her smiled. Sevilla smiled back.

"Hey," she said in a lower tone, "where am I?"

"Magdalene."

"What?" Sevilla said with confusion.

"Magdalene. It's a Bible study for anybody who used to sell themselves on the streets of Bangkok."

"What is happening here?"

"Didn't anybody tell you? This is for anybody who's tired of searching for love on the streets. It was started by that girl over there." A pointed finger led to a young woman with blonde flowing hair, tanned skin, and a black dress. "That's Karissa. She's from America. Came over here about six months ago because God told her He was going to help her get girls off the streets. I'm glad she came; otherwise I'd still be out there."

"Who's that?" Sevilla said, pointing to the man next to her who was now singing along with the rest of the small crowd.

"Oh, that's Jaython. He works with Karissa. I thought he bought me for sex, but then he brought me to Camilla. You've got to hear her testimony. It changed me."

Part of Sevilla wanted to run, part of her wanted to stay. If these people that she recognized could change, then why couldn't she? But what would she do with her life? What would she do about her boss? Even with doubts considered, something felt so right.

The guitar stopped playing. The small ensemble sat down quietly. Sevilla followed whatever the group seemed comfortable doing. She crossed her legs and clutched her purse tightly.

"My name is Karissa, Karissa Dalton. Most of you know me because of the stories I have told about my brush with death. God saved me from being murdered in a shooting disaster in my hometown of Chandler, Arizona, over in America. I used to be like a lot of you.

The only difference is that I didn't give my body away for money. I gave it away for love."

Sevilla was starting to feel uncomfortable. Karissa was talking to her directly, and she knew it. She wondered if this entire thing had been set up to target her. Maybe they had watched her for weeks selling herself on the street. Maybe this was some sick game of control her boss was playing on her. Or maybe this could be totally real.

"It's no secret what most all of us are doing, trying to find love in a way that hurts our perspective of love more than it helps it. I never understood love. My dad made me do things with him for years. Things that I thought defined love. Now I know they did not. You need to know what you do out on those streets isn't the kind of love that I know God has for you. You're just too scared to believe."

Sevilla was scared. Scared that this could be the truth. She glanced at her watch. Her hour was up. Jaython came up behind her, whispering in her ear. "Hey, your hour is up. Do you want me to take you back?"

Sevilla was trying to listen to Karissa. "Back?" she said softly. "No, no. Not yet."

Karissa looked into her eyes, penetrating the mask she had on when she had come in. "After I graduated from my high school, I decided that only I could change my life. It's funny, even after being in the classroom in the middle of the worst school shooting in American history, it still didn't change me. But coming here did. I wanted to get away from my life in Chandler. So I came here, hoping to find myself. A few friends of mine convinced me to come on a missions trip with them. And when I saw some of you on the streets, I saw myself. I came back six months ago to give my life to telling as many of you as I could the truth. And the truth is that you are looking for something. You wouldn't be doing what you're doing if you weren't. God wants you to know that you don't have to look anymore. He's found you. He has found Himself in you."

Sevilla couldn't stand it anymore. She wanted to leave. This was too real. Never had she heard words like this. Her heart felt like it was on fire. She felt a hand on her shoulder. It was Jaython.

Karissa continued. "If this sounds real to you, would you be willing to stand with me? I know it might feel weird, but nothing will ever change what it was like to see a few of my friends die for their faith. And I wasn't even a believer then. I know it sounds like a lot to ask, but will you?"

Sevilla's stomach was in knots. She had been with hundreds of men, engaged in things even she wouldn't talk about, but this commitment made her more nervous than anything she had ever experienced before. Her sweaty hands unclenched her bag. She nervously dug through it for the picture of her mother. She held it up with shaking hands. "Mama, what should I do?"

She knew her mother would want her to stand. But did Sevilla want to stand? That was the question. She glanced at her watch again. She was losing precious time to make the cash that would bring her through another day. What it wouldn't bring was freedom.

Sevilla closed her eyes. In the darkness of her mind she saw a little girl running through the streets of the village. Her feet weren't bound by anything. They ran freely across the hot soil. She opened her eyes, staring at her feet. They weren't the same little feet she saw with her eyes closed. They represented somebody older, bigger, and more complicated.

She stood on those feet quietly. She noticed another girl standing with her. A hand was on her shoulder again. This time, though, it wasn't Jaython's; she could smell Karissa's sweet-smelling perfume.

CHAPTER 30

THIS WASN'T SOMETHING JOHN HENSON had been ready for. His house was packed, not to mention the fact that it smelled like a liquor cabinet. Although the buzz had long since worn off, the smell of Lucky's Dance Club was heavy on the clothing of those who had been there. Darlene put on another pot. She was almost out of coffee. This was the fourth pot she had made.

Ryan sat with John in the living room. Eyes were tired, bodies were weak, the events of the previous evening, although exciting, had been long. Even so, the room of onlookers listened. None of them had ever experienced what they would never forget. The question continually asked was, "What do we do now?"

"What you experienced last night wasn't just a one-time event. I can't explain it, but I also don't want it to go away. It mustn't go away."

The room agreed. John took out his Bible and tried to lead the group through some passages that would introduce them to who Jesus Christ really was and who He is today.

Ryan said, "I've got to tell you guys, I tried to pretend it all wasn't real. That God was one big jerk. You know, I convinced myself it was His fault, what happened to Liz, so I had every right to hate Him. And I think about all the time I put into fighting Him. Man, I've totally missed the last year of my life."

Jackie sat by his side, listening intently. She knew this was real, but the reality of the entire change in her life was just breaking through. "Where do we go now, honestly?"

"Well, we can't give up. People are going to call us crazy. They will say what happened last night was a lie. We must believe in the truth. For that is what set us free."

The bartender and owner of the club, who had been laid out for three hours on the smelly floor behind the bar, stood up. His massive frame intimidated most in the room. "John, I've got a question. What do I do about my bar? Do I open it tonight as usual?"

Some of the other employees from the club nodded their heads. John wouldn't give him a pat answer. "Well, Lance, what do you think you should do?"

He cursed again, rubbing his face. "Aw, I don't know."

"Then what do you feel?" John said, lifting his cup to Darlene, who filled it with more coffee.

Lance thought for a moment, then responded from his heart. "I think we need to have some kind of meeting there tonight. If God chose to land there, then maybe He wants to stay. I don't know. Let's get a band, and I think that Ryan should tell his story again. There are a lot more people that need to hear this. If I just shut things down they never will."

"But isn't that what a church is for?" someone questioned.

The room was quiet. John looked around the room, then spoke with confidence.

"Traditionally, yes. But let's take a look at where Jesus was. He spent time with the prostitutes, with the drunks, and with the thieves. I mean, He died on the cross next to one. Maybe that is exactly why He moved there, because that is where He wants to be. He is tired of staying inside the buildings we build. He wants to be where the hurting people are."

"Well, look at us. I think a few of us fit that description," a tough-looking woman dressed in black leather remarked. "Look at us. We aren't exactly churchgoin' material."

"Right on!"

"So why not make the club our church. Set up business as usual—no, even better. Let's do it better. Bring them in and let them experience what we have."

The room started to rumble. The same enthusiasm that was with these Aussies just hours before was starting to burn again. Ryan turned to Jackie. She was starting to tear up again.

"Sorry," she said, wiping away a tear. "My mascara—it keeps running, you know? It's just that I've never experienced anything like this. After my pop died, I just let every thought go about ever having a father. Now I have more than I can ask for."

Ryan thought about his father for a moment. Mark wasn't perfect, but it was his constant encouragement and concern that had helped Ryan hold on to any hope at all. Watching his father deal with the death of Liz had been overwhelming. So overwhelming that he ran to Sydney, hoping to make it go away. He looked around the room; there was no denying what he was in the middle of. There was nowhere else to run. He wanted to experience the same sense of God's power that his friends were experiencing back in Chandler. He hoped God was breaking out the same way there as He was here.

"Man, this is awesome. God is awesome."

Jackie smiled. "He is."

The morning sun broke out across the bay, splashing itself across the top of the Sydney Opera House. It was far from just another day. God was moving. The church was breaking out. Out of the buildings and spilling into the bars, clubs, and places where God's awakened hearts could be found.

CHAPTER 31

THE CITY OF DUBLIN WAS TALKING and Fatima Mansions was the subject. Something completely unexplainable was happening there. Local Irish news was covering it, the newspapers were printing it, and Irish tabloids couldn't get enough of it. God was moving in one of the toughest neighborhoods Dublin had to offer. Drug dealers were surrendering their drugs and themselves to local authorities. Addicts were throwing away their needles. Heroin sales were on the decline. Musicians came there to write songs about it. Artists were drawing and painting pictures because of it. Ireland's premier pop/rock band stopped recording in downtown Dublin's Warehouse Music district to ride through Fatima Mansions in a limousine to catch a glimpse of it. Meetings were being held. Cathedrals that had a few candles burning in them were now full of hearts that were on fire to experience this God who was changing even the seediest of characters in that part of town. Catholics and Protestants were embracing peace that could only come from the unity Christ could bring. Word on the street was that this type of spiritual renaissance hadn't been a part of Irish culture since the days of Saint Patrick. Hailed for driving out all the poisonous snakes of Ireland, Patrick's heart for his country was now resting on another young man who was chasing away the vipers of sin, Curtis O'Riley.

Curtis grabbed his new Bible and book bag and headed to the DART station. Since he didn't have a car, the train would normally take him anywhere he wanted to go. Today was no exception. He was traveling into the heart of Dublin to Croke Park. Famous for its football games and championships through the seasons, tonight's game had far more to do with life than a simple winning score. The DART was packed wall-to-wall with people. Curtis squeezed in, grabbing onto a metal pole.

"Are you heading to the stadium tonight?" a nearby Irish woman with a blue scarf over her head asked the friend she was riding with.

"Wouldn't miss it for the world. I've been hearing a lot of things about Fatima, and I want to know what this—what do they call it?"

"Awakening?"

"Yes, what this 'awakening' is all about."

Curtis pulled his hat down tightly on top of his head, covering his forehead and nearly over his eyes.

"Do you think we could be seeing what they once saw in the days of Saint Patrick?"

"Dear God, I hope so. Look at where we have gone. There's murder in the news almost every night. And the drugs—this younger generation is into the drugs. I don't think we even know how to stop them. Maybe this entire thing can."

The women paused, noticing that Curtis was listening. He slid his forehead between a few bodies in front of him.

"Do you think this young man they keep talking about could be sent from God?"

Curtis strained through the noise of the tracks to hear the answer.

"He's got to be. Only God could care about Ireland to send us what He did with Patrick."

"God bless him, wherever he is."

"Yes, God bless him."

The train came to an abrupt stop. Curtis slid forward, his book bag piercing his side. The doors of the train opened, pouring out the people. Curtis stepped off the train while watching the women who had been talking about him walk away.

Thank You, God, for blessing me. I don't deserve this, You know. I'm just an addict with a reason to live now, he prayed silently. He could see the football stadium in the distance behind the station. His heart started to race. God was going to use him, "just an addict." He reflected on the hundreds of people walking by him. "God wants to use each one of you," he whispered. "Just like me."

The lights inside the stadium burned brightly, spilling light into the darkness of Dublin's downtown. Every chair had a body sitting in it, not to mention those standing in the aisles. The city counted it as the second largest crowd to fill the stadium next to the 1995 World Cup match when Ireland faced England.

Ireland didn't come out victorious that night, but tonight was another story. A spirit of victory was looming on the horizon for a country that had been punctured with the wounds of a struggling economy and a fiery battle within its own culture due to conflicting religious beliefs. Curtis's mother had spent the day praying for peace. If there was anything the Irish needed it was peace. Not just within the culture, but in each Irishman himself. After this night, no longer would they feel like the little island in the European union, but soon they would break out, leading God's fight to bring that part of the world to its knees.

Dirk had been working with several churches to provide leadership for the event. They had hoped to fill the bottom floor of the stadium but never dreamed of filling it. A few pastors prayed, and a local worship team led a few songs with an audience six hundred times what they were used to.

Curtis held on to his Bible tightly. Sharing his testimony in Fatima had been easy compared to this. His mother had promised she would be in the front row, and if he needed to focus on somebody, she would be there.

A local pastor introduced him. A few hundred from Fatima clapped, cheering wildly as Curtis took the stage they had built. Otherwise, the crowd was quiet, waiting to hear his words fall on their ears.

"Hello," he said, clearing his throat nervously into the microphone. "Hello, my fellow countrymen."

The crowd echoed back a staggered greeting.

"I am here to tell you about something that happened in my life."

A rock the size of Curtis's fist flew onto the stage, landing with a thud next to his right foot. It startled him. He stopped talking into the microphone, trying to see into the crowd through the bright lights. No trace.

"Who do you think you are?" a voice heckled from the highest balcony.

"Shut up. Let the boy talk," said another.

"It's all a lie, I tell you!" someone screamed. Then more voices cried out from the crowd stating personal opinions and cheering points of view.

Curtis looked down at his mother. He could see the silhouette of her head. He tried to picture the encouraging look he knew she would have on her face. The night was turning into a disaster. The quiet young former addict knew something had to be done. *But through me?* he wondered. *Would they really listen to me?*

An unexplainable power like he had never felt before came over him. It shot through his head and down to his feet. No longer did he feel like a weak, wretched soul saved by grace, but in that moment he knew his life had purpose. He knew Saint Patrick must have felt the same thing. "Speak," he whispered to himself, "you must speak."

"My fellow countrymen! Listen to me! LISTEN!" he repeated into the microphone. The crowd immediately ceased from its arguing.

"You will listen to me tonight. For my life carries a message to each one of you. Throw rocks at me if you want, roar and shout if you want, but your words and stones won't stop what God is doing in our city. He IS breaking Dublin out of where it has been for hundreds of years. He is breaking us out!"

"Speak to us, Curtis O'Riley," a young man cried from the lower balcony. "Speak to us!"

And He was. God had taken the most foul, heroin-filled, HIV-positive addict from an empty cathedral and put him inside a packed stadium to speak to his country. Dirk had dreamed of filling the cathedral, but God dreamed something bigger. The Spirit of God hovered over the stadium like a blimp over the Super Bowl. Dublin would never be the same. Ireland's spiritual sleep had been awakened. God was preparing this small island to change the European world.

CHAPTER 32

SEVILLA CLUTCHED HER PURSE TIGHTLY as she had done during the first ride out of Bangkok with Jaython. This time, the tight grip came as they headed in.

"How long has it been since you've seen your mother?" he asked, trying to make the ride a little more comfortable.

"I left a year ago," she said politely.

"Does she know where you've been?"

"Some friends of hers back in the village I grew up in told her that they had seen me."

"In what capacity?"

Sevilla paused. "As a whore."

Both lost any words to try to change the reality of what had been. Jaython broke the silence. "Do you think she will still allow you to live at home?"

Sevilla held on to her mother's picture. "I don't know. Custom is that I should be disowned. I've disgraced my family." Sevilla shifted in the front seat. Those words made going home more uncomfortable than she wanted to admit. "But I've changed, you know."

"I know. Don't forget that."

"I won't. If everything works out I plan to be at Magdalene every week. I would miss it, not going. And Karissa—I would miss her, too."

"When you live with someone for a few months you learn to love them in a special way."

"Yes, you do. I love her. She found me. Believed in me. I can't thank her enough."

Jaython turned down the street Sevilla had written down as home. "I think going home and facing your mother is all the thanks she needs."

"I'm so nervous," she spilled out. The homes they drove past were simple shacks painted white to keep cool in the blazing sun. They weren't mansions, but for Sevilla, it was home.

"Which one is yours?"

"It's down here. Last one on the right. Beats the shack we used to live in out in the country. I wonder if my mom is even there. She likes to visit with the neighbors—," Sevilla said, then swallowed hard. Her mother was kneeling down in front of a small garden in front of a wooden porch.

Jaython parked the car across the street from Sevilla's home. They sat inside the car for a moment before Jaython opened his door. "You can do it," he said with assurance.

Sevilla tucked the picture into her pocket and got out. The door slam didn't seem to affect her mother's deep concentration while planting a group of wildflowers. Sevilla stepped slowly across the gravel. "Mama?" she said under her breath, then repeated it louder. " Mama?"

Sevilla's mother turned her head toward the gravel road. She dropped the planter, staring, then screaming.

"Sevilla! My little girl, Sevilla!" Her hands pushed her up off the sandy floor, and her feet moved as fast as they could until she was embracing her daughter with everything she had. "Oh, Sevilla, you came home. I knew you would come home!"

Jaython watched from a distance for a moment or two, then climbed back in the driver's seat of his tiny car. "Welcome home," he said to himself, watching Sevilla get swallowed through the front door of her home, her mother leading the way. He drove from the southeast shack district back into the downtown area. He sensed that the mission had been complete. Another life breaking out from a pattern of destruction to a life of hope. Sevilla now had hope. *That's what this is all about,* he thought to himself. *Another one has broken out.*

He put his turn signal on and turned left down the crowded Bangkok street. The red-light district was just ahead. He drove his car into the shady area, staring at the girls who lined the streets. The car pulled up next to the cement curb and drove up on top of it. He reached over and rolled down the window. A beautiful young girl caught his eye, her long black hair blowing in the wind. He lifted a wad of money, showing it to her. She stepped closer to the car. "Hey, can I buy you for an hour? Just give me an hour." In Bangkok, God was breaking out. One heart at a time.

CHAPTER 33

THE CAMERA FOCUSED IN on Maria Severson. She was primping her hair and checking her eyeliner with a compact mirror in her hand.

"Maria," said the News 4 cameraman, "can you move over a little to the left? I'm trying to get the back of the Washington Monument in the shot."

"Sure," she said, stepping aside a few inches. Washington, D.C.'s most famous tower was now in view.

"Great—it looks great. Yes, that is a great shot."

"Two minutes until we are linked with Chandler," a second crewmember reminded the team. "Stand by."

Maria licked her lips. Field reports made her nervous since the shooting at Lincoln. Her field report there had been a disaster, and left a scar on her face she couldn't forget. At least this was thousands of miles away from the memory of the shooting spree, although it was still making headlines today.

"And we're on in thirty."

Maria lifted the microphone and smiled.

"And in fifteen."

She could see the reflection in the camera lens of another reporter doing a report a few yards behind her. She thought she recognized the voice and tried to catch a quick look.

"And in ten, nine, eight, seven, six, five, four, three . . ." Two and one were counted down with the cameraman's middle and index fingers. He pointed to her, signaling they were on. The red light on the camera started to blink.

"Hello, John. This is Maria Severson, reporting to you live from the nation's capital, Washington, D.C. It is here where a very important decision will be played out today. The Supreme Court will be deciding if what many have called 'spiritual awakenings' are going to be allowed on the public school campuses across this nation. The Supreme Court justices seem to be split on the decision, John. A number of the judges are citing the fact that schools, townships, and cities have improved greatly due to the outbursts. Crime has been on the decline in several of these cities, as well as general behavior, and ultimately what this case seems to be stemmed from, violent behavior."

Maria was trying to do two things, report and listen. Just a few feet away the other reporter's voice was feeding a nearby microphone . . .

"The entire case started a few months ago when one of these 'awakenings' was reported on a junior high campus in Roanoke, Virginia. Participating in the spiritual event was the school's own principal, Marjorie Harrison. A few weeks after the event, Marjorie lost her job due to her involvement in keeping the spiritual renaissance on the campus. So began a case against the school district for the students' rights not only at Washington Junior High, but for students around the state, regarding a student's right to bring 'God' onto the campuses of America. A debate over the separation of church and state has not taken place in our nation like this since prayer was taken out of the public schools of America in 1963. Today, the line once again will be drawn in the political sand. The argument has dropped on the steps of the Supreme Court after the state of Virginia passed on the decision. This moved it to the higher court due to the sensitive issue of the suit. The justices are once again in the news following last year's painful decision in the presidential election.

"If this bill is passed today, it will open the door to allow these spiritual awakenings to take place whenever and wherever they begin. No matter what decision is made, the evidence is clear. Something is shaking up our nation, causing it to 'awaken' to the thought of having God lead this country once again. This has been Janet Warren, reporting to you live from Washington, D.C. . . ."

"This has been," Maria said, stopping midsentence. *Janet Warren? I don't know a Janet Warren,* she thought, *but I do know a Janet Theisen.* The cameraman waved at her, trying to get her out of the trance. "Oh, Maria Severson reporting." The blinking red light stopped. Maria turned her head, tossing her shoulder-length hair back onto her left shoulder. Nothing there. The voice, the crew—gone. "Say, have you guys ever heard of Janet Warren out of L.A.?" she asked, pulling her earpiece out.

"Who cares? God, what happened to you, Maria?"

he said, ignoring her question. "You almost ruined your piece."

Maria wasn't listening. "Do you remember what Janet Theisen's maiden name was?"

The two-man crew started to wind up the wires. "Now there's a name I haven't heard of in a while. How about you, Mike?"

"Nope," he replied back to his friend.

Maria wound up her mic cord. She hoped to hear the voice again.

Mark, Bernice, and Seth stood outside the courtroom. Seth sipped some coffee from a Styrofoam cup. "What do you think they are asking him?" he said.

Mark rested his head on the marble wall. "Well, Taylor has been at the helm of this thing from the beginning. From what we can gather, Chandler was the first place these awakenings hit. The problem with Chandler is that guys like Jake Forrester couldn't get anywhere with their anger because the city wasn't going to fight something that seemed to be healing the wounds. Too much publicity. So I think they are going to question how it began and how it spread."

"Right, like they are going to figure it out," Seth shot back. I would give anything to see these justices trying to figure out how God moves. Do you think Forrester's testimony will do damage to the case?"

"It depends on how big his mouth is," remarked Bernice. The guys laughed. "No, I mean it. If he wants to damage the case he will. Unfortunately, he will speak on behalf of the parents of this nation. Ugh," she sighed, "I wish I could get in there!"

Marjorie sat inside the courtroom, breathing quietly. She wanted to hear every word Taylor answered when questioned. He was doing an awesome job, she reasoned. Her stomach growled, reminding her she was next. Her mind drifted past Taylor's words. She couldn't believe where she was sitting. It had been such a long road getting here. This case had not only brought her to testify in the nation's capital, but had put her entire life in jeopardy. It was on a daily basis that she would ask herself if serving God with her life, her heart, and now her job was worth it. And it was almost hourly that she would remind herself how worth it everything was. Even if that meant she had to sell her new Volkswagen. This was something worth sacrificing everything for. Marjorie knew it went far beyond who she was. This was about the Kingdom.

Connely sat across from her. He was looking smug, feeling as though letting Marjorie go a few months back was the best decision they could ever have made. He didn't care about the students; he didn't care about the desperate need for God they had. All he was concerned about was winning. If the Supreme Court ruled in favor of allowing these "awakenings" to happen on campuses across this nation, he would have to live with a great deal of humiliation. The opposite vote would make his district, state, and this entire case politically correct. After all, he figured, it's all in how you look to the public, not what is actually true. He saw the facts. In each one of these cities, acts of God had taken place; there had been defiant changes in the lives of the junior and senior high school students living there. The newspapers didn't want to report it, tabloids wouldn't touch it, and powerful people tried to hide it because they lost the power they selfishly needed when God was in charge instead of them.

"So, what you are saying, Taylor," one of the judges asked stoically, "is it that you do not know how any of this started? All you can remember is bowing your head to pray, and when you lifted it—bang—something had changed?"

"Yes," Taylor said with confidence, "but what you don't understand is that I started praying for that a year earlier."

"Let me get this straight. The result of what happened at Lincoln was the culmination of praying for this day after day for over a year. So what you saw happen on that day was a result of not just one prayer, but the effective prayer of many others gone before?"

"You said it," Taylor replied, almost laughing.

The judge paged through his notes and sighed. "All right. I guess that's all I have. Anyone else?"

The courtroom was silent for a moment. The only female justice on the court raised her pen. "I do, if I may?"

"Go ahead."

She took off her reading glasses and set them next to her water glass. "I must commend you, Mr. Shepperd, for your valiant desire to see your school and community changed after the tragedy we are all aware of that took place in Chandler. But today, your school, gun control, education about violence, many other concerns are not what is at hand—"

"Ma'am, if I may?" Taylor interrupted the Supreme Court justice.

Connely sat up. Marjorie leaned forward and smiled. That's why she loved working with students; sometimes they just didn't know better.

"It's just that," Taylor continued, "those things are being decided on today. Don't you guys get it? All that stuff is the result of taking God out of our schools a long time ago, and now we have a chance to see Him come back and change the students I go to school with every day. If you make the right decision today, you won't have to vote on things like education about violence, gun control for minors, and other things, because they won't be a problem."

The court was silent again. "May I finish?" the justice said in a tone that let Taylor know he had overstepped his boundary as a witness. "What is at stake here is a law that gives the right to protect every student in this country. If we allow your God to move freely on our campuses, we must allow any God. Complete religious insanity."

"But there is only one God," he replied into the microphone.

She sighed, putting her glasses back on. "It's not

that easy, young man. It's just not that easy. This is complicated."

Taylor cleared his throat and spoke up again. "I thought it was, too. That's why I waited for so long after the shooting to do anything about it. And then one day God just shows up. Uncomplicated, clear, and simple. I think we make things a lot harder than they really are."

The justice was getting angry now. She shifted from one side to the other, waiting for Taylor to finish. "My final question is this: What has been the effect on your campus from this event?"

"Well, where do I start? Because we have allowed God to move on our campus—"

"Which I might remind you," she interrupted him firmly, "is against the law until we pass it."

Taylor tried to ignore her intimidating techniques. "Um, well, God is doing stuff on our campus every day. We have seen any kind of violent behavior and talk become obsolete. And, Seth and I have started a program for students who are made fun of a lot. You know, down-and-outs. We try to get other students in-volved in their lives to build friendships with them so they aren't so angry with their peers or the school. And, Liz's parents, the Claraboughs, are teaching about how to deal with anger in a few classes and are just being a mom and dad to kids that might not have one or the other."

"So, what then are the benefits of this?" she clamored on.

Taylor paused. "For the first time, in a lot of my

friends' lives, they are excited to come to school. They have found a purpose for being there, not to mention a reason to live. Our campus is a safe place to learn again. Safe not just from guns, but from hate altogether. You wouldn't believe it. And it all goes back to God. He's done it. None of us ever could."

The justice wasn't going to let him go any further. "That's all I have. No more questions."

"You may step down, young man," the head justice said to Taylor.

Maria gave him the thumbs-up sign as he stepped down from the witness platform. He sat down next to her.

"Great job," she whispered.

"Thanks," he said, taking her hand and squeezing it. "God is in control."

The red light signaled Maria was on again. Today was the big day. The court had been adjourned for several days as they discussed the fate of the "awakenings" in public school institutions around the nation. The judicial system had been under complete scrutiny by the press. Journalists, newspaper reporters, student reporters, major networks, cable networks, and Internet news sources were everywhere. Maria enjoyed seeing all her news journalist mentors and had even had lunch two booths away from the *Today Show* morning cast one afternoon. It reminded her of the buzz that surrounded Lincoln. Because of the accident that happened while she was reporting, she wasn't as much a part of the hype as she wanted to be. Her vengeance had come on this trip. This was a news anchor's dream.

John, her co-anchor in Phoenix, had been scheduled to cover the landmark decision, but declined when his son came down with the flu. He kept in touch with her from the office. Besides the live broadcasts, there wasn't much work in between her live appearances on Channel 4. So she got to see as much of D.C. as she could. But that would all end today after the Supreme Court made its decision. Appeals would take months, even years, not to mention a ton of red tape and legal action. If the ACLU had any say at all in the matter, God, prayer, and anything that had a spiritual context to it would never be allowed in a public institution.

"We've been through this before. You guys ready?" Maria's cameraman responded. Maria and a News 4 intern nodded their heads. "And here we go. Ten, nine, eight, seven, six, five, four, three . . ."

"This is Maria Severson, reporting live again from Washington, D.C. Hello, John."

After a brief pause, she heard John's familiar voice come through her earpiece. "Hello, Maria, greetings from Phoenix."

"John," she said, smiling, flirting with the camera, "I have to ask, is it sunny there?"

He laughed, then replied, "Need you ask? Maria, 330 days of sunshine a year. You're missing all of them."

"Well, John, as you can see, it has just stopped raining here for a brief moment. In fact, it wouldn't surprise me if it started to pour on us before the end of the broadcast."

"Tell us, Maria, what is happening regarding the decision?"

"Well, John, we are all waiting for the judges to deliberate and let the public know their decision. A few inside sources have told us this was not an easy decision for the Court. I don't think the decision would be a difficult one if there wasn't so much evidence supporting the changes that have taken place in communities and schools where these 'awakenings' have fallen."

"Maria, do you have any guess which way the Court will vote?"

"John, I don't. The judges, even the country seems divided on the issue. Groups like the ACLU are working hard to convince the public this decision is a legal matter, not about the change a spiritual experience can bring. Other religious organizations are staying involved in the evidence that is seen on such campuses as Lincoln High School in Chandler, Arizona, Roanoke, Virginia, and many others."

"Maria, I am sure you are aware of news of these 'awakenings' happening outside the country—around the world. Do you think seeing the global effect in these other countries will slant what the Court decides?"

"John," she said, pulling out an umbrella, seamless in her transition to keep the report moving, "I'm not sure. Take a look at the country of Ireland. The testimony of the young man we've heard about, Curtis O'Riley, has changed the spiritual tenor of that particular nation. Many are wondering if there is a Curtis O'Riley somewhere in America who can bring all this unusual activity to a point of action. Many Americans seem very reluctant to allow any kind of spiritual conditioning to go beyond the four walls of churches. That is why this decision is so important. Many believe if the Court votes to ban these occurrences, any hope for a spiritual renaissance in our nation will be lost."

Maria grasped her earpiece. A voice from inside the court building was speaking to her.

"John, just a moment," she said, focusing on the new information she was receiving.

"We are talking with Maria Severson in Washington, D.C., where the Supreme Court will make a landmark decision—"

"John," she came back seriously, "I have just received word that the court has resumed. A decision will be read—"

"We interrupt your already scheduled programming . . ."

"We're off," the cameraman said out loud.

"Shoot, I didn't even get to finish," Maria said angrily. "Network?"

"Yep. Network. They are early. We need to get set up after their coverage is over. The judges will be leaving through the side entrance. We need to be there. Let's load up."

The three of them started to wind up the cords and put the cameras into cases. Maria heard the voice again.

"This has been Janet Warren reporting. We now go

live to Tom Brokaw in New York for the network coverage of the decision."

Maria stepped toward a woman with short blonde hair and wearing a black power suit. Maria did not recognize her from the back. But maybe from the front—"Janet?" she said, tapping the woman on her padded shoulder.

"Yes?" the unrecognizable voice replied.

Maria stared intently under her umbrella. "Janet. Janet Theisen?" The short blonde hair was confusing her. The facial features seemed the same. "Is that you?"

Janet was quiet and didn't reply right away. She looked away, catching the attention of a news crewmember putting a camera away in a van. "Sid, I'll be right back. All right?"

"Make it quick. We've got to get over to the side entrance before the networks go on standby."

"I will; this will just take a minute," she replied, stepping away from the area she had been reporting in. Maria followed her without a word being said. The two women stopped, standing with black umbrellas in a grassy area located in D.C.'s central park area.

"Janet, is that you?" Maria said again.

Janet took out a pair of Gucci sunglasses and put them on despite the cloudy weather. "Yes, Maria, it is."

Maria stood shocked. This wasn't something she expected on her trip. She stumbled to find some words. "It's just that—I didn't—what are you doing here?"

Janet seemed cold toward her. "The same thing you are. Reporting."

"I knew you moved out to L.A., but I had no idea you stayed with television."

"Well, I'm not an anchor. Just a reporter. I changed my name, went back to school for a semester to get some space and basically start a new life. They hired me based on my experience before Phoenix."

Maria looked confused. "So, they don't know."

"Know what?"

"Who you are?"

"They know me by who I am at this point in my life, Janet Warren. My maiden name. Reporter for Channel 6 in Los Angeles. Not an anchoring position, but at least it's a job."

"But your face, your name, it was all over the news for months."

"That's why I went back to school. It's amazing what a face-lift, a new hair color and style can do for you."

"But, are you happy?"

"I'm as happy as I can be on a day-to-day basis."

The women were quiet. A downpour of rain could be heard spattering across the cement next to where they were standing. Splashes of water covered their expensive shoes.

"How are you dealing with everything?" Maria questioned.

"Is this on or off the record? I don't do interviews."

"Off."

Janet sighed and took a cigarette out of her inside pocket. She lit it, blowing out a puff. "Honestly? Better. I almost went off the deep end about a year ago.

Dealing with the press, the pain, the hell. But I'm better."

"I'm happy for you."

"Well, I appreciate that, but I'm just surviving day by day. What brings you here?"

Both women chuckled. "I guess I know why you are here. Exclusive report, right? I'm sure you have done a fabulous job replacing me."

Maria cleared her throat. "You're a hard person to replace. You did an excellent job. The best in the business. Not every person gets asked to possibly go network."

Janet took another puff. "Well, don't pat my back that much. It cost me everything. My career in Phoenix, my, my . . ." She paused. "My son." She sucked on the cigarette, taking a deep breath to ease the tension she felt. "It's funny, I hate smoking. I always told John never to pick up the habit. And here I did."

"Well," Maria tried to console, "we all have to do something to deal with life."

"Yes, you're right. You know, I am here reporting on these awakenings, and I had the chance to do a story on one that was happening in a small Hispanic church on L.A.'s east side. And when I was there, I really felt something. The same thing I felt at Liz Clarabough's funeral. I know these 'awakenings' are the real deal. I think I'm going to go back when I return to L.A. I need Him back in my life, Maria."

"Who?" Maria asked.

"God."

A streak of lightning flashed and a crash of thunder flew through the air, causing both women to jump back a few inches.

"Wow," Maria said, "I think you may be right."

Janet focused on something over Maria's left shoulder. "Gotta go. Van's packed. I'm sure you're heading to the same place I am."

"Side entrance," they said together.

Janet pulled off her sunglasses.

"Do you think we could stay in touch?" Maria asked.

Janet paused, thinking deeply. "I . . . I guess. Maybe via E-mail."

"I promise I won't tell your secret."

"Thanks, at least not right now. I know I'll face it at some point."

"Don't we all."

"Well, I should go. Your scar healed nicely."

"Not as nice as your face looks. Did they change your nose?"

"Just a little," Janet said, smiling. "Keep in touch."

Maria watched Janet walk away in the pouring rain. She hoped she would look back to give her a comforting wave, or a friendly smile at least. But Janet climbed in the unmarked black van and sped away. Maria wondered how long it would be before the secret got out. For now, she wouldn't tell a soul. Nobody needed to know Janet was the mother of John Theisen, America's most well-known school killer.

CHAPTER 34

THE COURT WAS SILENT AS THE JUDGES took their places. This kind of recess and return wasn't new for them. In fact, it was routine. They hadn't seen the press like this—buzzing about like bees around a nest—since their presidential decision months ago. They looked like statues, smiles gone, expressions faded, and eyes bloodshot.

Marjorie got to be in the courtroom when the decision was read, along with Connely, because Washington Junior High was at the center of the decision. She stood when the justices entered. Her stomach growled due to the nerves that were stirring around inside. Reports on each of their decisions were placed on a table in front of them, as well as a synopsis describing the decision. The senior judge stayed standing to read the decision.

"You may be seated," he said firmly, backing away from his microphone. He conferred with a fellow judge, then spoke into the microphone so everyone could hear.

Newspaper reporters were waiting outside anxiously, television journalists waited with cameras poised and ready, radio stations waited for a document to come through from the Associated Press, even the president received a phone call stating he would be the first to find out the answer.

"The Supreme Court of the United States of America has reached a final decision regarding the State of Virginia's deliberation on whether to allow or ban a spiritual awakening on a campus, whether brought on by a student or through an act of God. Based on the evidence, facts, and testimonies, we have reached a decision. The Supreme Court has voted . . ."

Marjorie made two fists. Connely clutched his briefcase. Taylor chewed on his gum as hard as he could. Outside, Mark, Bernice, and Seth waited impatiently, walking and talking in the lobby area of the courthouse.

" . . . that it is unconstitutional and against the laws of the nation that separate church and state to allow these occurrences on the public school campuses of this country."

The courtroom erupted in shouts and screams. The justice hammered his gavel on the table. Its loud bang echoed through the halls and into the lobby.

"Furthermore, if any of these occurrences take place, school administration has the right to stop them immediately."

"The Supreme Court has just banned the awakenings. They will not allow the 'breakouts,' a man screamed into the lobby, causing a trail of individuals to flood out the doors.

"No!" Seth said, pounding the thick marble column he had been leaning on.

"God help us," Bernice whispered. "God help us."

Outside the Court, the streets were a mess. reporters were shouting, cameras were rolling, and the verdict was shaking the country.

A late-evening newspaper landed outside Cameron Hutchinson's front door. The headline read:

SUPREME COURT MAKES CONTROVERSIAL DECISION: NO MORE SPIRITUAL BREAKOUTS

CHAPTER 35

THE NEWS HAD HIT THE SMALL Midwestern town of Beloit, Wisconsin, as it had anywhere else. Dixie Creme Donuts had already sold out of its morning edition of the *Beloit Daily News*. Not to mention glazed donuts. The small donut dive was packed. The topic seemed to be at the center of every conversation.

But for the students of Turner High School, things seemed very much the same. The parking lot was full of cars loading up, teachers were bustling through the halls, and the boys' basketball team had taken over the gym for an early practice due to the game planned that evening.

Richard Meyers, FCA president, junior class officer, and local football star was waiting in the library in Study Room 3. "Another week of no one showing up," he said to himself, disappointed. That didn't matter; all he knew to do anyway was pray. He started with as much passion for the students of his school as he could muster. It wasn't long before three more students entered the room and started praying with him. Shortly before classes started, a few more arrived.

Mrs. Grigglesbee, Turner's librarian, wandered into her domain for another day of managing books. "At least they don't talk back," she reasoned. She noticed the group of students praying in Study Room 3 as they normally did every Thursday morning. She started placing the daily newspapers from around the state in the newspaper carousel they had recently purchased. The headlines echoed not just the state of Wisconsin, but the state of the union.

COURT BANS BREAKOUT AWAKENING MEETINGS

RELIGIOUS ACTS STOPPED

BAN ON SPIRITUAL ACTS SEPARATES CHURCH AND STATE EVEN MORE

ACLU ECSTATIC ABOUT DECISION

A SAD DAY FOR EVANGELICAL BELIEVERS ACROSS THE COUNTRY

Mrs. Grigglesbee got so engrossed in reading the articles she barely noticed the hour that had snuck by. A few students hustled in and out, but not even one of them needed to check out a book. Instead, they were checking out something else. She noticed a few students standing outside a study door. She immediately went over to see what the problem was, like a good librarian would.

"Can I help you students?" she said in soft but firm voice.

None of them spoke.

"What's going on here? I asked you a question."

Finally, one them uttered a few words. "We're just wondering what is going on in there."

She noticed a few students on the floor. Richard Meyers, the group leader, was wiping away a face full of tears. Something was going on inside beyond her control, the school's control, even the government's control.

She opened the door. It squeaked as it opened. Only Richard made eye contact with her. "What's going on in here?" she asked him nervously.

It took a few moments for Richard to gain his composure, then he spoke through the cries of his friends. "I don't know, Mrs. G., I just came in to lead the Bible study this morning. No one showed up, so I started to pray like I've done a million times before. And then, God, He just moved. God is moving, Mrs. G., He's moving."

The headlines for Beloit's evening paper had nothing to do with the decision in Washington, D.C. anymore; this time they resembled something closer to home.

AWAKENING BREAKOUT AT TURNER HIGH SCHOOL

ABOUT THE AUTHOR

MARK A. REMPEL (www.markrempel.com) is the author of Thomas Nelson's Extreme Fiction series, including the titles *Point Blank, Breakout,* and *Real.* He is also the author of the upcoming novel *The Waiting,* a modern-day parable about the story of the prodigal son. Mark has been writing, creating, and ministering for more than fourteen years. He recalls making up crazy stories as a kid and then acting them out in front of his family. As he has grown, that desire to touch and see people changed through creative communication has inspired him to dream the dream of creatively capturing the world for Christ.

In an effort to reach people, Mark has been speaking to audiences around the country. After working with hundreds of students at Cross Current Outreach on a weekly basis, Mark has dedicated his life to reaching people through the art of telling parables. He is the author of more than fifteen plays including *The Extra Mile* and *Legacy,* which have been filmed as live stage productions. He has written for *Wireless Age* and *Teen* magazines, Charisma Life, Group Publishing, and has also scripted the recent Bob Carlisle Father's Day Special. He has written several screenplays and wrote and directed the independent film *The Iris.* Mark also took a creative edge in writing and developing the script and story for Treetop Studios/Brentwood Records' three-dimensional animated series entitled *Tails from the Ark*.

As an author and speaker to teens and adults, Mark shares frequently with young adults around the United States at conferences, camps, and in junior and senior high schools. His transparent heart, humor, and honest message give him incredible favor with teenagers. He is known by many for his vulnerable and genuine spirit.

Mark and his wife, Brenda, live in Phoenix, Arizona, with their three children—Zion, Azsia, and Ezekiel.

Speaking engagement bookings are available in association with Brent Gibbs and the Literary Division of Mitchell Artist Management, 209 10th Ave. S., Suite 214, Nashville, TN 37203 (info@mitchellartist.com).

ACKNOWLEDGMENTS

I MUST SINCERELY THANK MY WIFE, Brenda, for allowing me to stay up late, travel long distances, and allowing me to passionately use my gifts for the cause of Christ. I truly honor you.

My three wonderful children who inspire me everyday—Zion, Azsia, and Ezekiel! Thanks for letting Daddy do what he does!

Mom and Dad—when you adopted me you didn't know what you were in for! The vision to tell these parables comes from your ability to allow me to be exactly who God has created me to be.

Thanks to all my Irish and Australian friends who helped me get the words right. God is breaking out across this planet using individuals like you guys!

The teams at Xt4J and Thomas Nelson—you have taken a chance to allow reality in young adult fiction . . . thanks!

Brent and the team at Mitchell—you guys rock!

Finally, to the close-knit group of individuals who stayed up way late to help create and edit this story . . . this was a team effort. Your sleepless nights are helping change a generation. Thanks for playing your part.

Breakout was published in association with Brent Gibbs and the Literary Division of Mitchell Artist Management, 209 10th Ave. S., Suite 214, Nashville, TN 37203 (info@mitchellartist.com).

SNEAK PEEK

Check out this chapter from book three in the Extreme Fiction series,
REAL

CAMERON HUTCHINSON LIFTED THE GUN, resting the end of it on the left temple of his forehead.

Just kill yourself, a voice shot through his brain. *Nobody cares, right?*

No, I do, another voice argued. *I do. I don't want to do this. I don't want to do this.*

A bead of sweat rolled down between the cold metal and the skin on his scalp. He picked up the picture of Chloe, staring at her delicate face. For being three months pregnant, she sure didn't show it.

"I love you," he whispered.

Pull it, you failure! another voice blasted. *Pull it!*

He rested his head on the end of the bed, the gun still pointing at his temple. *I can't do this.*

His mind had been reasoning for over an hour now. One minute the small handgun he had dug out from his father's closet was against his head, the next minute it wasn't. A phone ringing startled him, causing him to flinch. He didn't answer it. He fell down onto the floor and buried his face in the carpet. He started to sob uncontrollably. After a few minutes, he stopped crying and tried to relax. Cam's eyes were heavy. As he felt himself falling asleep, his mind rested on the awful situation he had gotten himself into . . .

"Hello. Is Chloe there?"

"Just a moment," said the voice on the other end of the line. "Chloe, phone! Can somebody go up and get her?"

Cameron glanced at his watch. The sixty seconds he had to wait were excruciating. He heard the phone being jostled around then finally somebody picked it up.

"Hello?" Chloe said quietly.

"Chloe. Thank God. You all right?"

She didn't have any words. The silence said enough.

"Chloe, you there?"

"Yes." She paused. "It was awful, Cam."

"Are you hurt?"

"A little."

More pausing.

"So you did it, right?"

"What do you think?" Chloe responded in anger. "Yes, I did it."

Cameron breathed a sigh of relief. "I knew you would. I knew it. I just knew it."

Silence.

"Did they know if it was a boy or a girl?"

"NO! They didn't know. Just a minute."

Cameron heard a door shut, followed by Chloe's trembling voice again.

"I didn't want to know, all right? Why would you? Cam, it's over. I don't want to talk about it."

Cam shot back another question. "Did anybody see you?"

"No, nobody saw me." She paused. "Except for . . ."

"Except for who? Who?" Cameron gripped the phone cord in his hand, leaning against his bedroom wall.

"This girl who was picketing outside. Before I went in, she stopped me and she remembered praying with me at the awakening meeting that happened at the high school a few months ago. She told me she didn't want me to go in. Cam, she literally begged me. I thought she would never let go of my jacket."

Cameron was quiet. All of his worlds were crashing together. He knew exactly who that girl was, and she would know exactly who he was. "She didn't get your name, right?"

"No. I'm not that dumb. I tried to play off that I didn't know her and that I was never at the meeting. But we both know she got our names that night. Remember, she filled them out on a card? Why did this happen, Cam, why?" Chloe started to cry. "What have we done? What have we done?"

Cameron rested the gun back on his head. What had he done? How could such a nice Christian kid make so many bad mistakes in such a short span of time? He drew back the trigger. His heart was beating as fast as it could. Cameron thought if a bullet didn't do him in, his heart would.

"Oh God," he prayed out loud, "is any of this real?"

Check Out These Other Groovy Products from Extreme for Jesus™

BIBLES

The Extreme Teen Bible (NKJV)—HC	$24.99	0-7852-0081-9
The Extreme Teen Bible (NKJV)—PB	$19.99	0-7852-0082-7
The Extreme Teen Bible (NKJV)—Black	$39.99	0-7852-5555-9
The Extreme Teen Bible (NKJV)—Purple	$39.99	0-7852-5525-7
The Extreme Teen Bible (NKJV)—Orange	$39.99	0-7852-5678-4
The Gospel of John	$1.50	0-7852-5537-0
Extreme Word Bible—PB	$19.99	0-7852-5732-2
Extreme Word Bible—Black	$39.99	0-7852-5735-7
Extreme Word Bible—Chromium HC	$29.99	0-7852-5733-0
Extreme Word Bible—Blue Snake HC	$29.99	0-7852-5796-9
Extreme Word Bible—USA	$29.99	0-7180-0153-2
The Extreme Teen Bible (NCV)—PB	$19.99	0-7852-5834-5
The Extreme Teen Bible (NCV)—HC	$24.99	0-7852-5835-3
The Extreme Teen Bible (NCV)—Retread	$39.99	0-7180-0063-3
The Extreme Teen Bible (NCV)—Reigncoat	$39.99	0-7180-0062-5

BOOKS

30 Days With Jesus	$7.99	0-7852-6626-5
Breakout	$6.99	0-7852-6547-3

Burn	$9.99	0-7852-6746-8
Daily Groove	$9.99	0-7180-0086-2
The Dictionary	$19.99	0-7852-4611-8
Extreme A-Z	$19.99	0-7852-4580-4
Extreme Answers to Extreme Questions	$12.99	0-7852-4594-4
Extreme Encounters	$9.99	0-7852-5657-1
Extreme Faith	$10.99	0-7852-6757-3
Extreme Find it Fast	$2.99	0-7852-4766-1
Extreme Journey	$14.99	0-7852-4595-2
Extreme for Jesus Promise Book	$13.99	0-8499-5606-4
Genuine	$13.99	0-8499-9545-0
God's Promises Rock	$3.99	0-8499-9507-8
Fuel	$12.99	0-7852-6748-4
Point Blank	$6.99	0-7852-6546-5
Real	$6.99	0-7852-6548-1
Sisterhood	$12.99	0-7180-0085-4
Step Off	$19.99	0-7852-4604-5
Unfinished Work	$16.99	0-7852-6630-5
Wait for Me	$13.99	0-7852-7127-9
Walkdawalk	$10.99	0-7852-6747-6
Why So Many Gods?	$16.99	0-7852-4763-7
Xt4J Journal, Plastic Cover	$9.99	0-8499-5710-9
Xt4J Journal, Spiral-bound HC	$9.99	0-8499-9508-6

AUDIO ADRENALINE

Put four crazy friends together, throw in some music and blend on the highest speed and you get Audio Adrenaline. These guys are best known for radio hits like "Big House" and "Mighty Good Leader" and they keep on cranking 'em out on their latest CD, *LIFT*. We'd like to offer you a deal to pick up a copy of the CD using the attached coupon. If you already have it in your collection, feel free to give the coupon to a friend who is missing out on the action.

For the latest

AUDIO ADRENALINE

info, check out

www.audioa.com

to see pictures,

hear music,

buy merch

and get

tour updates.

Save $2 NOW on LIFT

EXPIRES August 31, 2003

AUDIO ADRENALINE
LIFT

CUSTOMER: Save $2 with this coupon. ONLY valid off the suggested retail price of $17.98. Coupon valid only at participating Christian Retail Stores. Limit one coupon per purchase of specified product(s). You may pay sales tax. Not valid with any other offer. **RETAILER:** Redeem as one (1) 'Frequent Buyer' coupon provided this coupon is redeemed by a customer purchasing this product. Any other use constitutes misuse. Must be redeemed within 90 days of expiration date. NO CASH VALUE. Chordant Distribution Group, PO Box 5084, Brentwood, TN 37024-5084

www.audioa.com
www.forefrontrecords.com

5 24382 99282 6

Dedicated to Black people, whose creativity, resilience, brilliance, power and grace continue to soar despite living in a country where their sense of worthiness is under constant attack.

Do not be conformed to this world; but be transformed by the renewing of your mind so that you may discern what is the will of God; what is good and acceptable and perfect.

Romans 12:2

Copyright 2017 Hollinger Publications, Inc. All rights reserved.

No part of this book may be reproduced or transmitted in any form by any means without permission in writing from the author except in the case of brief quotations cited with proper attribution to the author. For further permission, contact the author directly through Worthythebook.com.

Library of Congress Cataloging Publication Data
Hollinger, Michelle

>Worthy: Simple Steps to Strengthen Your Sense of Worthiness and Change Your Life

ISBN 13:978-1985856462

Contents

INTRODUCTION	5
My Worthiness Story	10
Born Worthy	15
Pseudo Worthiness	16
Worthiness and Our Social Media Obsession	18
Worthiness and Validation	22
Worthiness and The Oprah Effect	24
Wounded Worthiness	26
Signs of wounded worthiness	28
Worthiness and #Metoo	37
Worthiness and the glass ceiling	41
Worthiness and the African American community	44
Worthiness and Colin Kaepernick	51
Worthiness and Sisterhood	54
Worthiness and Forgiveness	56
Revive Your Worthiness	59
4 Principles for Reviving Worthiness	61
Worthiness, Denials & Affirmations	63
Affirm Your Worthiness	67
The Self-Validation Vision Board	70
Get Off Social Media	74
Write a Letter to Your Younger Self	77
#IAMWORTHY Gratitude Journal	80
The Worthiness Prayer	84
The Weight of Worthiness	86
See What Happens	91
Epilogue	93

INTRODUCTION

Worthy. What a loaded word. Many assume it should be relegated to self-help books for people who are depressed or suffering from low self-esteem.

The truth is, far more people are dealing with worthiness issues than you might believe. Even people who appear to have it all together experience worthiness issues.

That's because of its subtlety. Like carbon monoxide, <u>wounded worthiness</u> is odorless but potentially lethal. We don't realize how it is impacting us until its lowkey pattern of mediocrity shows up one time too many and we finally decide to figure out what's really going on.

+ Illusion of Unworthiness

Something happens, and we have an insight or an epiphany that tells us something deeper is happening to cause this specific issue to continuously show up in our lives again and again. Someone says something to us that we've heard before but THIS time, it resonates within us and we know unequivocally there's more to our story.

There are so many common scenarios that people settle for because they do not feel worthy enough to experience something better. And in the age of social media, our sense of worthiness has been exploited; got us believing our obsessive participation with Facebook, Instagram and Twitter is making us feel better.

It's loaded when we use it to assess whether someone else deserves whatever it is we're judging them about, but it's even more weighted and life-defining when we use it to judge ourselves.

And we're judging ourselves unworthy far more often than we realize.

Worthiness is powerful yet elusive; it shapes us and what shows up in our lives. It feels so harmless because we could be living a satisfactory life that feels normal; but a sense of unworthiness lurks just beneath the surface blocking us in ways we cannot see with the naked eye.

A very talented artist friend of mine, for example, was doing her thing; using her talent and putting her work out there. When she had the opportunity to enter a prestigious art show, her wounded worthiness reared its head. Other artists with comparable art had priced their work at far higher prices – and their art was selling and selling briskly.

She, on the other hand, had placed extremely paltry rates on her work; prices that really were not in alignment with the sheer beauty and brilliance of her work. She initially blamed other factors for her decision to price her work so low; but when she got real with herself, she was willing to admit that ~~wounded worthiness~~ *t* was the culprit behind her choices. And even though her prices were significantly lower than other artists - she ended up selling very few of her pieces.

+ Illusion of Unworthiness

Illusion of Unworthiness

Here's why: there's an energy surrounding ~~wounded worthiness~~ that acts as a repellent. When YOU don't believe you're worthy of a price that aligns with the quality of your work, people can sense it and although they may not be able to articulate why, they are not drawn to it.

Our childhood holds many clues regarding our sense of worthiness. Whether we had experiences that convinced us that we were worthy or unworthy, both impact how we view ourselves and what we manifest in our lives. Our sense of worthiness lingers just beneath the surface and affects our quality of life.

Here's why the topic of worthiness is so important. Worthiness has an indirect impact on the legacy we leave because it has a direct impact on our potential. Legacy and potential are intertwined. To live and die without actualizing your potential results in one type of legacy. A legacy of regret. A legacy of "if onlys," and "coulda, woulda, shouldas."

What legacy are you interested in leaving? What do you want said about you in your eulogy? Your relationship with your worthiness holds the answers to both questions.

We're not talking big, grand levels of accomplishment that result in fortune and fame. Everyone was not born to be famous, but everyone is designed to create, live and leave a legacy that informs people that they were here.

If ~~wounded worthiness~~ *illusion of unworthiness* informs our legacy, what we leave behind isn't entirely true. It's incomplete. It's only a portion of what we were capable of leaving.

Everyone is born with a unique purpose, however. And if you're walking around with **+** ~~wounded worthiness~~; the likelihood that you're living your unique purpose is very small.

+ Illusion of Unworthiness

My Worthiness Story

National treasure and spiritual teacher extraordinaire, Iyanla Vanzant, frequently says you must do your work if you want to heal and create a life that works for you.

I've done my work. I've forgiven people who harmed me. Forgiven men – some relatives, some not – for sexually violating me. Forgiven my father for not raising me. Forgiven my ex-husband for his role in our toxic marriage. Forgiven myself for my role in it, too. Forgiven myself for hanging on to resentment, grudges and anger.

Beyond forgiving, I did the work to rise from victimhood. I've immersed myself into spiritual development that transformed my way of seeing things. I've worked hard to renew my mind, change my thoughts, live from gratitude.

Even with all the work, something continued to linger just beneath the surface, shaping how I saw myself and my life and consequently, what showed up in it. It clouded my results and served as a very effective obstacle to me manifesting more.

It's true we teach what we most need to learn. As the publisher of a women's magazine, I encourage women to live their best lives. To feel the fear and do it anyway, to step outside of comfort zones and to discover their life purpose. The intention of the publication resonates deeply with women who want more from life.

Yet, even as I would hear myself speaking truth about how our thoughts create our reality; about how important it is to spend time in the silence; the power of gratitude and forgiveness; about how to silence our inner critic by listening to her and challenging what she says, there was an intangible essence limiting the magnificence of my life because deep down inside, I did not feel worthy.

The residual effects of childhood abuse, growing up without my daddy and being in an unhealthy 26-year marriage took a larger toll than I'd realized. The cumulative effect of these events did emotional damage that shaped my perception of myself in ways that were difficult to comprehend with the naked eye.

Worthiness is slick like that.

Acknowledging that we have worthiness issues takes courage. I came face to face with my own recently (not the first time) when Ann Charleus, my business consultant, challenged my unacceptably low prices for high quality products and services.

Because I've done a tremendous amount of spiritual development over the years, when I'm faced with an issue, owning it and growing through it takes far less time than it used to.

So, when Ann asked me, "What's up with the low prices," I instinctively knew, almost immediately what the deal was. I knew the low prices were a symptom of something deeper. Something that had to do with how I see myself. My sense of worthiness.

I also knew I needed to mull it over to really get to the root and heal it once and for all. As the publisher of a women's magazine that encourages women to live full out; to take risks, face fear, step out of comfort zones. How could I NOT address my worthiness issues? I thought I had faced them, but apparently, I hadn't.

Getting to the bottom of this issue was so important, I shut things down for a few days and spent a lot of time in the silence asking tough questions and fully expecting – and receiving – sacred answers. It's how I figure things out.

Silent introspection led me to worthiness issues I thought I'd already resolved. There they were, staring me in my face, daring me to deal with them or continue shortchanging myself – and not just by charging cheap rates.

This book is my response to my brilliant business consultant who respects me enough to challenge my limited view of myself and my prices. It's for everyone brave enough to acknowledge that they, too, are dealing with worthiness issues and are ready to face them, to see what's there.

There are a handful of powerful activities to get you going on this sacred worthiness journey. As is the case with any sincere effort to heal, if more is required, your gut instinct will guide you to what you need to continue growing - the right book, the perfect sermon, the ideal therapist – whatever you need to get a grasp on your worthiness and restore it to its full, life-changing status.

Becoming aware of the state of my worthiness and how it was curtailing my ability to manifest has set me free. I'm still working on standing fully in my truth; however, I have come a very long way.

Writing this book was therapeutic for me. As its vessel, I have been blessed in ways I did not anticipate. My prayer is that it blesses you even more abundantly.

Born Worthy

Despite what you may have heard to the contrary, you were born worthy. Everyone is.

Religious beliefs about original sin are up for debate because that notion simply doesn't match up with the idea that we're all made in the image and likeness of the Higher Power responsible for our creation.

Besides, "sin" means "to miss the mark," so that's a difficult accusation to lay on a newborn baby. (That declaration alone might be enough for some of you to toss this book. I hope you won't. I encourage you to continue reading – with an open mind and an open heart.)

The truth is, within you is a sacred space where your worthiness exists as one of the spiritual qualities (love, faith and innate wisdom are some of the others) you come automatically equipped with.

What happened afterwards largely determines the status of your worthiness today.

Pseudo Worthiness

As a society, our sense of worthiness is seriously damaged. It's the reason that social media exploded in popularity and is showing no sign of letting up.

We're desperately searching for something to soothe our ~~wounded worthiness~~; which feels flawed and scarred instead of pulsating with life-affirming vitality that guides us to lives that fulfill us spiritually, emotionally, mentally and financially.

Illusion of Unworthiness

One significant factor skewing our sense of unworthiness is seeing example after example of people becoming famous for questionable reasons. And because they have all the trappings of success, we assume they're worthy of it and we're not.

We experience the "woe is me" angst that comes from living a life where ends don't meet, the job is a pain and our relationships are inharmonious and draining. Wrapped in our woe is a strong belief that everyone else gets all the lucky breaks.

Our sense of unworthiness takes even more of a beating because it feels like we're really trying to get ahead. Problem is, we're trying to use an externally focused approach to something that only permanently responds to an inside-out method.

Even the folk with all the trappings of success are still dealing with worthiness issues because things are incapable of filling the void. Amidst all the busy external stimuli, the assault on their sense of worthiness continues.

<u>Our sense of worthiness</u> has shriveled and shrunk and needs a major reminder that not only does it exist, but that <u>its growth requires something only we can give it: attention, intention, cultivation and preservation</u>. We're trying to soothe our worthiness, but we're looking for the balm in the wrong places.

Worthiness and Social Media

Facebook founder, Mark Zuckerberg, brilliantly predicted that social media would benefit from normative social influence, a type of collective social sway that leads to conformity. Social psychologists define it as "the influence of other people that leads us to conform to be liked and accepted by them."

Who knew we'd become so obsessed with something that literally involves being "liked?" Who knew what a hit it would be to our worthiness? Apparently, Facebook's founding president, Sean Parker, knows how damaging it is because neither he nor his children use social media.

Social media engagement is an example of a normative social influence that is so widely accepted and deeply entrenched that we look at anyone who is not on Facebook, Instagram, Twitter, etc. as though they have three green heads and a purple horn protruding from their nose.

Zuckerberg and his co-creators understood psychology and used it to hook people on their product. Sean Parker, former Facebook president admitted that when they were working to get the social media company off the ground in 2004, he and others sat around figuring out: "How do we consume as much of your time and conscious attention as possible?"

Their solution?

"...We need to sort of give you a little dopamine hit every once in a while, because someone liked or commented on a photo or a post or whatever. And that's going to get you to contribute more content, and that's going to get you ... more likes and comments."

Their strategy worked. We're taking selfie after selfie in search of validation from external sources - friends and strangers on Facebook, Instagram and other mediums. Think about it: we take a picture of ourselves, share it with a group of people (some of whom are complete strangers) and then check to see what those people think about the picture we took of ourselves.

If that behavior existed back in the day, it would be akin to taking a polaroid photo and then standing on a corner, showing it to family, friends and strangers and asking them what they think.

Excessive social media engagement in general and the obsessive use of selfies specifically is viewed as normal because of such widespread acceptance.

But just because something is accepted in mass does not mean it's healthy. Even the folk who created it are feeling tremendous guilt about how successfully they were able to exploit our need for validation. Parker, Facebook's founding president, criticized the way the company "exploit[s] a vulnerability in human psychology" by creating a "social-validation feedback loop."

For people walking around with ~~wounded worthiness~~ **+Illusion of Unworthiness**, this social validation feedback places a band-aid on the wound, making it feel and appear to be healed when it's not.

We're all guilty. To some degree or another, most people have participated in this national selfie obsession that is now a normal part of our lives. It seems like such a fun, innocuous and cool way to connect with friends and family. So, what's the harm?

Is it really unhealthy?

Yes, if what's floating behind the selfie is sadness, disappointment, frustration with your life; with who you are and what you're doing professionally and personally.

Posting selfies and live videos result in a temporary high that comes along with the 'likes' and positive comments; but it really does nothing to soothe the deep emotional and spiritual void we're seeking to fill. It's external validation and using it to feel good about yourself is like applying a bandage to an infected cut without disinfecting it, then seriously expecting it to thoroughly heal.

Worthiness and Validation

Our sense of worthiness and our need for validation are intertwined. The social media obsession did not create our deep need for validation; it only revealed it. We've been expecting validation since the day we were born.

As infants, being fed to satisfy our hunger validated us. Also, we felt validated when our dirty diaper was changed; when a parent or caretaker held us when we craved human contact, and when our requests to "look at me" were met with loving, attentive eyes.

If, as we ventured into toddlerhood and beyond, our needs were ignored, and/or we got cues that we were not enough from the people in our lives, our validation took a hit. The more hits, the more damage to our sense of worthiness. Years of hits without corrective messages lead to a deep craving for something to fill the resulting void.

Apparently enough of us are experiencing this craving to make social media a multi-billion-dollar industry.

But are we really willing to continue going through the motions; accepting short term gratification that exacerbates the wounds to our worthiness?

Or are we ready to step into our truth so fully and completely that the validation we innately crave rises to embrace itself? Are we courageous enough to poke around the wounded worthiness to find an opening that takes us to a better life?

Worthiness and The Oprah Effect

I feel it necessary to discuss Oprah Winfrey when examining the word 'worthy' because of the impact she has had on our collective psyche, specifically as it relates to an awareness of our innate worthiness and our need for validation.

Although in its early years her show's format was similar to the others, Oprah Winfrey quickly realized the opportunity she had to positively impact society. Oprah shifted her show's structure from destructive topics that pitted people against each other to spiritual topics that offered us wisdom, information and inspiration to live our best lives.

The phenomenal 25-year run of the Oprah Winfrey Show, the highest rated ever, is evidence that she effectively tapped into and soothed our collective need for something more. The end of Oprah's talk show in 2011 left a huge societal void that is, to some degree, being filled artificially via social media.

She's offering similar content on her network; but because her audience is more varied, and her bottom line demanded it, OWN's programming is designed to resonate with people at different levels of consciousness; and some of it is solely for entertainment purposes.

Rich, substantive shows like Super Soul Sunday, Queen Sugar, Black Love, Iyanla Fix My Life, Master Class and others align with the values of the Oprah Winfrey Show and provide viewers with the spiritual nudge that her talk show did.

Unfortunately, but understandably, Oprah's impact has been diluted because it is spread across various types of programming instead of being singularly concentrated via one phenomenal show.

But we're still hungering for Oprah's consciousness, as evidenced by the massive response to her at the 2018 Golden Globes Awards show during her acceptance speech for the Cecile B. DeMille award.

We're still hungering for a reminder of our innate worthiness and our need for validation.

Illusion of Unworthiness
~~Wounded Worthiness~~

Many of us had experiences that wounded our sense of worthiness. Childhood abuse of any kind, abandonment, rejection, rigid expectations from parents and other authority figures as well as societal norms that minimize the value of certain groups (African Americans, women, immigrants, gays, etc.), impact on our beliefs about the SELF that affected our perception of our worthiness.

Living from ~~wounded worthiness~~ *Illusion of Unworthiness* impacts the quality of your life because it colors your view of who you really are and what you're really capable of.

Thing is, if you're unaware that your worthiness is wounded, you can spend your entire life living beneath your true potential; falsely believing you were doing the best you could. ~~Wounded worthiness~~ → *Illusion of Unworthiness* distorts your view of what's possible and of what you're divinely designed to accomplish.

I read an article a few years ago where a middle-aged woman was saddened by her 80-year old mother's statement that she (the 80-year old mother) was just getting her stuff together. How sad for this woman to have reached this beautiful stage of her life without realizing her true worth.

Thankfully, she unwittingly reminded everyone who read the article that life is short and rapidly moving forward whether we're getting our stuff together or not. I'd be willing to bet that she was dealing with worthiness issues and had no idea how awesome she really was.

The beautiful thing about becoming aware that your worthiness is wounded is this simple truth – <u>all wounds heal</u>.

Signs you're dealing with wounded worthiness

You're involved in an abusive relationship.

Being in an abusive relationship is one sure sign that your sense of worthiness is damaged. Allowing another person to abuse you in any way means at some subconscious level, you feel you deserve the abuse or that you can't do any better. It is probably stemming from an unhealed childhood experience involving abuse. Enlisting the help of a skilled therapist might be necessary to help you navigate your release from victimhood.

You dim your light to "keep the peace" with a mate, family and/or friends.

You have what it takes to significantly improve your quality of life and you know what you should do to make it happen; however, whenever you begin to take the necessary steps, you stop. The reason? Someone close to you says or does something to indicate their displeasure in your attempt to improve yourself. A part of you knows you deserve to continue moving forward; but another part of you is concerned about losing the approval of people close to you, or worse, losing the person altogether. Ultimately, if the people close to you are not supportive of your growth and development, perhaps they do not belong in your life. Tough call but Marianne Williamson said it best in her phenomenal book (which I highly recommend as a worthiness restoration tool), A Return to Love: "There is nothing enlightened about shrinking so that someone else won't feel insecure."

You hate your job.

You spend an enormous portion of your life working. Second to the amount of time you spend at home is the amount of time you spend at work. Why would you accept devoting such an enormous portion of your life doing something you hate? The reason is your underlying sense of worthiness has convinced you it's OK because it pays the bills. You've accepted that other people can find and live their calling, but not you. But what if finding and living your calling - that thing that has YOUR name on it - is what you're supposed to be doing? When you revive your sense of worthiness, don't be surprised if it brings a strong desire to either bloom where you're planted by finding reasons to love your job; or diligently discovering your unique calling and doing whatever it takes to make it happen.

You have never asked for a raise or promotion.

The qualifier here is that you feel you deserve to be paid more or elevated to a higher position. If under those circumstances, you have never asked for a raise or promotion, it is very likely due to your poor sense of worthiness. You've had the internal conversation with yourself several times and end up talking yourself out of asking because of how you assume your employer will respond. Your assumption is based, not on how your employer values you, but in how you value yourself. And how you value yourself stems from your sense of worthiness. Asking for what you deserve is an action a strong sense of worthiness makes possible.

Your self-talk is always critical.

We all talk to ourselves, all the time. We're talking to ourselves even when we don't even realize it. If we have not taken control of our thoughts, chances are the conversations we're having with ourselves are negative. Instead of congratulating ourselves when we've done well, we spend more time criticizing ourselves when we've messed up. Instead of expecting good, we expect the worst. We actively live up to the saying "we're our own worst critic," because our sense of worthiness dictates that our thoughts and words about ourselves match its low energy.

You are haunted by regret.

We've all used poor judgment and made mistakes. We have all done something we wished we hadn't; or not done something we wished we did. It's a part of the human dynamic. If you're still beating yourself up by playing a 'coulda, woulda, shoulda' game, however, it's a reflection of your sense of worthiness. A strong sense of worthiness makes self-forgiveness possible and self-forgiveness provides space for new ideas, new goals and new opportunities to manifest.

You engage in passive-aggressive behavior.

Someone asks you to do something that you don't want to do. Instead of politely refusing, you say 'yes' and then grumble your way through it. A co-worker invites you to attend an event that you're not interested in. Instead of thanking them for the invitation then politely declining, you show up and your attitude is toxic because you didn't want to be there in the first place. Someone says something you don't like. Instead of expressing your displeasure to them, you gossip about them behind their back. All are examples of passive-aggressive behavior that stem from a poor sense of worthiness. You're reluctant to disagree with someone because you're afraid of disappointing them. You're assuming by declining their invitation, you will hurt their feelings. You fear losing something from them so you mask your authenticity by saying 'yes' when you want to say 'no.'

You do not speak up at work or in personal relationships or you apologize when you do.

You have an idea about how to cut costs at work; improve productivity or enhance morale, but instead of sharing during the staff meeting, you remain silent. Or you apologize before sharing your thoughts by saying "sorry, but…" You're unhappy about the choice of restaurant your mate chose, but you go anyway, silently kicking yourself for not suggesting someplace else. Your mother-in-law routinely says something blatantly disrespectful to you, but you say nothing to address it. A poor sense of worthiness makes these scenarios possible. A strengthened sense of worthiness makes it possible for you to be fully present, allows you to connect with your authenticity and honor your voice by using it to respectfully advocate for yourself.

You attend a church out of habit, convenience or tradition; not because it feeds your soul and helps you to live a better life.

This is a biggie that many people participate in for their entire life. The specific church, type of church or denomination you're currently attending might have been chosen years ago when you were younger and had different spiritual needs; but even though you've outgrown it, you continue attending for reasons that do nothing for your soul's growth and development. It might be the church you attended with your family when you were a child and you continue going even though the message no longer suits you. Even though the discomfort, guilt or unidentifiable nagging feeling is really your soul urging you to find something that helps you to live a better life, you remain because you're afraid to "rock the boat," potentially upsetting family, friends, fellow parishioners, your pastor, etc. You may even have religious fears about what might happen to you when you die if you make a change that is more in alignment with your spiritual needs. A strong sense of worthiness boosts your confidence and acquaints you with parts of yourself that reveal what you really need to step into your truth. It also allows you to make difficult decisions that others might not understand.

Worthiness and #Metoo

The topic of worthiness is all over the "Me Too," campaign, which was launched more than a decade ago by Tarana Burke, a Black activist who wanted the grassroots movement to provide "empowerment through empathy" to survivors of sexual abuse, assault, exploitation and harassment in communities that typically don't have access to rape crisis centers or counselors.

In 2017, following the despicable allegations of sexual assault and harassment by a powerful and controlling man, Harvey Weinstein, actor Alyssa Milano suggested in a tweet that survivors use the hashtag #MeToo to bring attention to the prevalence of sexual assault and sexual harassment. Unfortunately, several other men have since been accused of sexual assault, harassment or other related misbehavior.

There are millions of women and girls (men and boys, too) walking around with wounded worthiness; many quietly. Their silent suffering is exasperated by society's tendency to do what designer Donna Karan did – blame the victim and make women who have been sexually assaulted responsible for their attackers' criminal behavior by suggesting that women's attire or behavior somehow encouraged men to rape them.

I know firsthand that sexual assault and harassment do a number on a woman's sense of worthiness. Because I was violated by men who were members of my family (a brother, an uncle and a cousin by marriage) as well as harassed and sexually mistreated by men who were strangers, it was easy for me to walk in lockstep with the "blame the victim" mentality rampant in society. With so many different abusers, surely, I HAD to be doing something other than existing to bring on their unwanted vile behavior.

To say my sense of worthiness was wounded is a colossal understatement. It was battered and bruised; coming dangerously close to what felt like annihilation. Thankfully, a part of my healing included the awareness that my abusers were damaged men. "Hurt people, hurt people." More importantly, I forgave myself for believing that I had ANYTHING to do with my assaults.

A tidal wave of collective worthiness is empowering women to come forward with sexual abuse and sexual harassment reports. No longer willing to remain silent and embracing the strength in numbers, women are increasingly speaking out about past violations and demanding that men be held accountable for their misdeeds.

Escaping from under the immobilizing cloud of victimhood did wonders for the way I feel about myself. I empathize with the millions of women who have been sexually assaulted and/or sexually harassed. I stand with you as you recover the truth about your worth and encourage you to seek professional assistance with the process if you're not able to navigate it on your own.

Although your body was violated, who you are deep within could never be touched. It is as strong as it's always been but needs your permission to thrive. You are not alone.
#MeToo
#Timesup

Worthiness and the glass ceiling

When we attack traditional glass ceilings, the use of policies and procedures to level playing fields for women can be used. A collective energy from the affected group can be galvanized to plow through; yet, even those traditional glass ceilings are difficult to penetrate when the collective is comprised of millions of rigidly constructed personal glass ceilings.

A patriarchal society needs women to agree to play small for it to thrive. Fifty three percent of white women voting for a self-avowed sexual predator to lead the country is an example.

Another is inequitable compensation between genders; a vicious cycle. A patriarchal society created pay disparities, which are perpetuated, in part, by women afraid to demand their worth; also fueled by a patriarchal society.

Women who are afraid to demand their worth are dealing with personal glass ceilings that are only shattered when they step fully into the truth of their being; sparked by the reviving of one's sense of worthiness. Traditional glass ceilings may be built by a patriarchal society, but they are partially supported by personal glass ceilings.

Public policy can reduce their occurrence; however, no amount of policy can shatter traditional glass ceilings. They will only dissolve when personal glass ceilings dissolve. And personal glass ceilings dissolve when women do the work necessary to heal, revive their sense of worthiness and then boldly fill the resulting space with verbal and behavioral affirmations of their worth.

We have examples of women living from their true worth.

Harriett Tubman's decision to escape slavery and then make multiple returns to help others do the same was fueled by an awareness of her true worth.

Jessie Daniel Ames worked from her worth. In the 1930s, she and members of the Association of Southern Women for the Prevention of Lynching (ASWPL) courageously demanded white men cease the horrendous practice of lynching blacks.

Bree Newsome's courageous climb up that pole in South Carolina to snatch down the Confederate flag was fueled by an unabashed knowing of her true worth.

Congresswoman Maxine Waters' refusal to be talked over by Treasury Secretary Steve Mnuchin by repeatedly stating, "Reclaiming My Time," had an awareness of her self-worth stamped all over it.

Worthiness and the African American community

This country's systemic assault on worthiness is a stranglehold preventing millions of Blacks from realizing their true potential. Beginning with the viciously intentional destruction of enslaved Blacks' sense of worthiness, America has made it its business to convince Black people that they are not worthy.

Keeping slaves illiterate by refusing to allow them to read was but one of many strategies for distancing them from any awareness of their true worth.

Using religion's depiction of God as vengeful and the use of scripture to justify complete obedience to masters was another way to annihilate Blacks' sense of worthiness.

Publicly killing or maiming outspoken slaves was not just punishment for their audacious attempts to stand in their truth; it was also meant to keep other slaves in line.

Instances of this country's efforts to control Blacks' sense of worthiness are everywhere; from Rosewood to Emmitt Till; from the assassinations of Medgar Evers and Martin Luther King, Jr. to its centuries' long, unpunished annihilation of Black men and women that continues today.

George Zimmerman deemed Trayvon Martin unworthy of existing; unworthy of walking through Zimmerman's neighborhood minding his own business, so despite being told not to approach him; he did and shot him to death.

The country's interest in minimizing Blacks' sense of worthiness is evident in the labels used to describe Blacks and their communities. No other group in this country is labeled as consistently as the African American community. "At-risk," "disadvantaged," "underprivileged" – have all become synonymous with being Black.

When you tell a person who they are long enough, if they don't know any better, they begin to believe you and not only accept the labels, but also use them to describe themselves.

Self-fulfilling prophecy says what people believe to be true becomes their reality. And just like the parable of the jumping flea that was encased in a jar with a lid that continued to jump only as high as the lid, even when the lid was removed; many African Americans abide by self-imposed limitations, some of which are perpetuated by systemic limitations via the public assistance system, public housing, etc. A poor sense of worthiness is the foundation for this mass control of people.

An insidious consequence of Blacks' racially wounded sense of worthiness is a healthy repulsion for racism intertwined with an underlying desire to belong to the society controlled by racists. A great example of this duality is manifested during awards season.

On the one hand, Blacks complain that racism rules the exclusion of Blacks from certain awards categories and that Blacks should not look to be validated by this mainstream recognition.

On the other hand, when Blacks win awards from organizations like the Grammys, the Academy Awards, Miss America, etc., the excitement is palpable.

Here's my theory: It's normal to crave acceptance from your country; the place you call home. It's also normal to be skeptical that Blacks will not be recognized for their talent and skills based on the country's history of racism; not just in the entertainment industry, but in virtually every facet of life.

Educationally, young Black children are funneled into learning disabled programs at higher proportions than their white counterparts, suspended at much higher rates and poised to populate the nation's prison industry via disparate sentencing guidelines and systemic racism at every stage of the criminal justice process. Little Black kindergartners are suspended at higher rates than their white counterparts. Kindergarten!

Many innately brilliant Black students are more likely to be tested for emotionally handicapped designations than they are to be tested for gifted programs because they fall into the ubiquitous "at risk" inner-city school category.

And since designations based on predetermined categories are attached to schools' ability to secure certain funding; these revenue-generating labels are assigned to students whether accurate or not.

Many Black students' sense of worthiness is under assault from kindergarten to twelfth-grade. The part of them that knows better duels with the labels placed on them by educational authority figures. They know who and what they are, and their actions are often attempts to express this truth; but little Black children expressing themselves is frequently labeled as misbehavior.

Religion has also played a role in some African-Americans' sense of worthiness. In poorer communities, there are several churches on every block; and these are churches with traditional religious doctrines of heaven and hell, born sinners and the serious notion that event saints are not worthy of God's goodness.

Many of these churches have outreach programs that provide social services; however, most are designed to help people make ends meet, not rise above them. And traditional church messages can do a number on a person's sense of worthiness by teaching duality. That is, by preaching to congregants Sunday after Sunday that the power to change their lives rests not with them, but with a capricious god in the sky who has already demonstrated for hundreds of years that their plight is not a priority.

New Thought, a powerful spiritual movement that holds that humans are divine and create their reality via their thoughts is one of the most user-friendly and powerful philosophies in existence. Unity, over 120 years old, is one of the more popular New Thought movements.

Unfortunately, New Thought churches are not popular in the Black community. This, despite one of the most prolific, the Universal Foundation for Better Living (UFBL), being founded by the late Rev. Dr. Johnnie Colemon, a powerful African-American woman who was the first African-American to live at Unity Village, and one of the first African-Americans to be ordained a Unity minister.

The absence of UFBL churches in the communities that need them most is complex. The typical UFBL sermons are rich, transformative messages but without the pomp and circumstances, whooping and hollering expected from many Black church experiences. They are big on self-love, self-empowerment and self-responsibility; and void of the traditional religious messages of sin, punishment, judgment and heaven and hell as post-living destinations determined by whether you have accepted Jesus as your personal Lord and Savior.

So, because their message of empowerment is packaged differently, and the content takes a very practical, "you have the power within you to change your life" approach, it might not be received by congregations accustomed to more rousing services.

(For the record, Rev. Derrick Wells, senior pastor of Christ Universal Temple for Better Living in Chicago does an excellent job of delivering the powerful UFBL message in a robust and spirited manner. The man can preach!)

Another factor is the deeply entrenched acceptance of traditional Christine doctrines that unwittingly wound practitioners' sense of worthiness with the belief that all have fallen short of the glory of God.

Many people are so immersed and allegiant to their religious beliefs that questioning how those beliefs impact their lives is unacceptable; and exploring whether a different philosophy or religious approach might be more beneficial is, unfortunately, frowned upon.

Worthiness and Colin Kaepernick

Former NFL quarterback Colin Kaepernick is an example of this country attempting to remind a Black man of America's power to determine his worth. Kaepernick has protested the widespread unjustified killings of Blacks by the police; the majority of which, even when captured on video, result in the police either not being charged or if they are charged, being acquitted.

Since Kaepernick began his silent protest by kneeling during the playing of the national anthem, he has lost his job, been the recipient of death threats and blacklisted in the NFL.

Even the president of the United States weighed in on the issue by encouraging NFL owners to fire players who kneeled during the anthem; going as far as calling players daring to protest, "sons of bitches."

Kaepernick's strong sense of self-worth and his belief in the worth of Black lives led to his protests. Many whites, our president and NFL owners included, are dumbfounded that this Black man has the gall to stand up for himself and other Blacks by taking a public stand. They have inaccurately made his protests about the American flag, however, Kaepernick made it clear from day one that his protest was against this country's deadly treatment of Blacks.

It takes a Black man with a strong sense of self-worth to take a risky stand for what's right. His sense of worth is apparently an affront to many in this country who want Black NFL players to "stay in their place," by refraining from using their platform for the higher good of marginalized people.

Many other Black NFL players appear to be operating from wounded worthiness as they remain staunchly obedient to their bosses' demands. Even those who agree that it is wrong for Blacks to be killed by police without cause are afraid to take a public, sustained stand because they are afraid to face the consequences that might arise.

Athletes like Colin Kaepernick see the bigger picture and understand that his sense of worthiness demands certain actions. He understands that his worth extends beyond the football field.

Kaepernick followed in the worthy footsteps of athletes like Muhammad Ali, whose strong sense of worthiness had the world agreeing that he was, indeed, the greatest.

Worthiness and Sisterhood

Worthiness and sisterhood are naturally intertwined. Women have the power to impact each other's sense of worthiness by either wounding it or blessing it. And our desire to do either is informed by our own sense of worthiness.

Women with a strong sense of worthiness have compassion for their sisters with wounded worthiness. They are aware that they are more than their sister's keeper, they are their sister.

Women with a strong sense of worthiness have a consciousness that allows them to bless other women with ease; and their tribe is typically comprised of others also living from a strong sense of worthiness.

Conversely, while it takes wounded worthiness to wound worthiness, it's still a sad experience to see a woman saying or doing something to inflict harm on another woman. The intention is probably not to damage her worthiness, but it is a consequence when women are unaware of their authentic power.

One of the beautiful results of healing our sense of worthiness is the impact of our recovery on the women and girls in our lives. When we're living from a strong sense of worthiness, our ability to have compassion for others with wounded worthiness goes to a higher level. And when we're mothers, aunts, grandmothers or in any role where we influence young women and girls, we learn to proactively protect and cultivate their worthiness.

In addition to developing genuine concern for women and girls living from wounded worthiness, we begin to attract other women living from a strong sense of worthiness into our space. Our tribe begins to shift, and we eventually find ourselves surrounded by women who are a reflection of who we are and how we're showing up in the world.

Vibing with a tribe of authentic women is a powerful blessing. The energy flowing in and through this group is life changing because there's an expectation for growth and constant progress.

Worthiness and Forgiveness

Taking steps to revive your worthiness requires courage and power. Acknowledging that it's wounded will undoubtedly lead you to revisit past experiences that resulted in its woundedness.

You can't revive your worthiness if you're not willing to forgive the person/people who had a hand in wounding it.

This step is so crucial that if you find it difficult to forgive, please seek the help of a highly skilled professional whose job it is to help you understand why forgiveness is a part of healing and necessary for a strong sense of worthiness.

Trying to revive it without forgiving someone responsible for its wounds can become emotionally draining. That's because a powerful but elusive obstacle that shows up as (expressed or unexpressed) anger, resentment, grudges and/or pain keeps you stuck.

You might be seething, expecting the person responsible for your wounded worthiness to say or do something to make things better. It might make perfect sense to you that the person who harmed you should play a role in your healing.

The responsibility for what they did rests with them. However, your forgiveness has nothing to do with them and everything to do with you experiencing the peace that comes from letting go of what you cannot change.

Forgiving is not saying that what happened was OK. Forgiving is about you no longer being held hostage to it.

It's not minimizing your pain; it's giving you permission to feel something different. It's making a choice to experience more joy in your present, which is difficult if you're still chained to the past.

When you've not forgiven, you're essentially making someone else responsible for your happiness. What if they're unwilling, unable or unaware that you're expecting something from them? What if they don't care? What if they're no longer here? What if?

Leaving your peace in someone else's hands leaves you powerless. And the energy that you use to keep your past alive could be put to better use – like reviving your worthiness and living the life you deserve.

Revive Your Worthiness

Reviving our worthiness is one of the most important things we could ever do. Especially since without it, creating the life we were born to live is difficult, if not impossible. When we go about our lives focused on working, acquiring things and participating in relationships from a poor sense of worthiness, what shows up in our lives reflects it.

If we're dealing with worthiness issues, it's no wonder we're working at jobs we hate, seeking to define our worth by our possessions and settling for unhealthy relationships and/or marriages.

Living from a strong sense of worthiness - from the inside-out - positions us to attract into our lives people, experiences and material possessions that reflect our true value. A strong sense of worthiness allows us to enjoy said material possessions without being so attached that we don't know who we are without them.

A strong sense of worthiness serves as a very accurate life purpose compass. Strengthening your sense of worthiness begins to attract to you everything you need to discover your life purpose and live it. It's not a quick process, but so worthwhile.

Attempting to create a great life without healing wounded worthiness is counterproductive and ultimately results in feeling inadequate; in part, because the acquisition of the things that are supposed to bring fulfillment doesn't. Things can't fulfill.

Even though our worthiness has always existed, it can become so wounded that it feels nonexistent. The good news about worthiness is its resilience. Despite being smothered for years, wounded by life's experiences; it can be dusted off and invigorated.

Fortunately, wounded worthiness sits in wait, poised to respond when our attention shifts to it with attention, intention, cultivation and preservation. You don't acquire worthiness, you revive it.

Four Principles for Reviving Worthiness

ATTENTION

The first step to reviving wounded worthiness is shifting your attention to it. Think about your worthiness. Embrace it and believe it exists to serve your highest good.

INTENTION

The intention behind any idea or action is what fuels it; gives it power and affects whether and how it manifests. In the case of your worthiness, expect it to work on your behalf. Expect it to reveal wonderful parts of yourself you have not yet discovered.

CULTIVATION

A vibrant, healthy sense of worthiness takes work to revive and work to develop. The more you cultivate a strong sense of worthiness, the more you dissolve the energy from the life experiences that wounded it. In this cleared space, your worthiness can stand strong and tall as the foundation for creating the life you want.

PRESERVATION

Once your worthiness is revived, your work is not done. It takes work to preserve your sense of worthiness. One of the most powerful things you can do in your life is to find those things that nurture your worthiness. They're different for everyone. What does it for me, might not resonate with you – and vice versa. When you discover ways to nurture your worthiness, make a commitment to do them consistently.

Tapping into and cultivating your sense of worthiness is not a one-shot deal and it doesn't happen overnight; but it is so worth (pun intended) the effort.

Worthiness and Denials and Affirmations

A very powerful New Thought spiritual practice deals with using your thoughts to create your life. It is also a powerful way to revive your worthiness. The use of denials and affirmations can help change the way your think about your worthiness.

Denials are statements of release. You're not denying facts or feelings or emotions; you're denying that those facts, feelings, or emotions have power over you.

Using denials does not mean you are "in denial" that challenging events happen; you use denial statements to remind yourself that no matter what is going on, you are always free to choose your response to that experience.

An affirmation is a statement of truth. It's a statement of what you want to have – stated in the present tense. It is a powerful tool for retraining your way of thinking.

An effective denial in the worthiness building process is "That experience has no power over me and does not determine my worth."

Follow it up with an affirmation like "I am worthy of the best life has to offer!"

Because most of us are accustomed to a great deal of negative mental "programming" in our day to day existence, we unwittingly solidify a sense of unworthiness with our thoughts.

Using denials can loosen up rigid negative thinking and affirmations can help you think more in alignment with what you want to experience in your life.

The use of denials to change error thinking and a belief in scarcity, limitation, illness and unworthiness is extremely powerful; however, the empty space resulting from the removal of these error thoughts must be filled with thoughts that enrich you, that affirm life, goodness and worthiness.

If not, other variations of error thoughts could replace the old versions, leaving you poised to have "new" experiences that are really rehashed old stuff.

The Universe abhors a vacuum and fills newly emptied spaces according to your consciousness. That explains why a woman might leave an abusive relationship but end up in another. There's something within that knows she deserves more or she wouldn't have left; however, there is work to do to cultivate that part of her.

If she hasn't followed her denial of the first abusive relationship with affirmations of her worth; with truth statements about what she deserves; if she hasn't done the work to heal the brokenness that resulted in the first relationship AND filled her consciousness with higher level thoughts about herself, chances are extremely high she will attract another abusive relationship into her space.

An example of a denial and affirmation for this scenario are:

Denial: This relationship is no longer acceptable and has no power over me.

Affirmation:
I deserve a healthy, loving relationship.

That formula holds true in other life scenarios, as well. You leave a job where you feel unappreciated, undervalued, underpaid and end up in another where you're voicing the same complaints because, while you removed yourself from the limited experience (denial); you did nothing to heal, nothing to change the consciousness that landed you at the first job.

Using denials helps you recognize that the situation has no power over you. Affirmations help you make a purposeful declaration of your wonderfulness; a deliberate celebration of your worth.

Affirm your Worthiness

If you're not familiar with using affirmations, this next activity is one that will definitely require an open mind. It's an extremely powerful process that takes affirmations to a higher level as it requires you to state your desires in the present tense – as though they are already happening.

The I AM statement used with affirmations has its source in the bible and it is historically known as the verbal key to manifesting whatever the words that follow it describe. (It's one reason I don't agree with having recovering addicts to state their name followed by, "I am an addict." I understand the belief that recovery is a life-long process, however, words are powerful, especially following I AM; and for that reason, I believe I AM Recovered would be a more powerful statement for recovering addicts to use. (IJS)

Stating affirmations might make you feel like you're engaging in wishful thinking by stating your desires before they manifest, but it's a powerful process that yields positive results when used consistently for the long-term.

Using them might also feel counterproductive because, when used effectively, affirmations dredge up old thoughts and/or beliefs that block their manifestation. It feels like you've taken two steps forward and one giant step backwards when you engage the affirmation process; but it signifies progress.

Here's why:

In order for underlying obstacles to your progress to be healed, you must, 1) be aware that they're there and 2) they must rise to the surface to be addressed. It might seem like just as you begin to inject positivity into your life, all hell breaks loose; but to give up then is to guarantee that nothing changes.

If "negative" things begin to happen, it's a sign that your affirmations are working. Keep affirming them - especially if/when things appear to be going wrong.

Additionally, as the gunk comes up for healing, do not ignore it. Deal with it; with the help of a professional, if necessary. Once it's healed, it won't continue to resurface and what you're affirming has a clearer space in which to manifest.

So, when and how do you use affirmations to revive wounded worthiness? First take inventory of what's not working in your life. If you feel stuck in a dead-end job, 'I work at a great, fulfilling job' is powerful. If you're charging too little for your products and/or services, try, 'I receive high income for high quality products/services.' If you're in an unhealthy relationship, how about, 'I AM involved in a harmonious, healthy relationship.

The idea is to begin to speak into existence what you want to experience by acknowledging what's not working and then creating a statement that affirms what you want.

The Self-Validation Vision Board

Take an amazing selfie.

What you do with it next might be difficult, but it's powerful. Do not, I repeat, do not post it on social media. At all. I know the urge to share it with others in anticipation of all the likes, loves and comments about how great you look are so very tempting. But on the worthiness building journey, the external validation that comes from social media is counterproductive.

Self-validation is far more important, so instead of sharing your awesome selfie with others, you're going to keep it all for yourself and use it as a beautiful reminder of who you are, to strengthen great qualities you're already using and to cultivate other wonderful qualities you want to begin to express.

Here's what you do with your selfie:

Look at it. Really look at it and notice what you love about the person in it. Start with your appearance. What's your favorite part of your face? What do you like most about this selfie? Look into your eyes.

Now, write a mini-bio. Where were you born, when? Where did you attend elementary school, middle/junior high, high school? Did you attend college? Vocational school? If so, where?

Make a list of your strengths.

Recall an accomplishment that you felt great about. Re-live it. What was it? When did it happen? How did you feel? Which qualities were necessary to make it happen.

Write them down.

Next, print your selfie and place it in the center of a poster board. Now go back to the strengths and qualities you identified about yourself. Either type them up and print them out individually; or find large versions of the words in magazines or newspapers and cut them out.

The qualities you already use, place them closely around your selfie and glue them to the poster board. Now around those words, glue the qualities that you want to begin expressing.

The final step of creating your Self-Validation Vision Board™ is to cut out images, photos, etc. that represent the most important goals you have for yourself. If it's traveling, cut out an image of a plane, train or whichever mode of transportation you plan to use to get there. Cut out an image of the destination you plan to visit.

Starting a small business? Cut out an image that represents the type of business you'll be starting. What is the name of your business? Type out the name, print it and glue it to your board. Add other images that represent your dreams and goals to the outer areas of your poster board.

The idea for this powerful visual image is to reinforce awesome qualities you already use and set an intention to cultivate the additional qualities you want to express. Ultimately, the purpose of your vision board is to elevate your sense of worthiness by combining a visual image of your amazing qualities with the power of visualization to manifest your dreams and goals. The foundation for living the life you want to live is a strong sense of worthiness.

Looking at your Self-Validation Vision Board™ regularly is powerful, so carve out a few minutes when you first wake up and just before you go to sleep to spend quality time quietly, alone, with it.

Get Off Social Media

OK, calm down. Don't get off permanently. But do get off for ONE FULL DAY – each week. On this weekly social media-free day, the idea is to be FULLY PRESENT and to do things that deepen your connection with yourself.

If you're at work, notice when you're tempted to engage social media for personal reasons. (If it's a part of your job, that's allowed.)

When you eat, really focus on your meal. Take your time and enjoy every bite.

If you're with others, pay attention to them and what they're saying. Participate in the conversation. Resist the urge to pick up your phone to check in on social media.

If you take photos, instead of posting them for public consumption, how about printing them and placing them in a photo album or a frame? Buy a special "Thinking of You' greeting card and mail someone a copy of the photo.

Wherever you are, be fully present. If you're participating in something that you would normally share on social media, share it with yourself by thinking about how the event blessed you and anyone else involved. Talk to the people involved about the experience. Share what your favorite aspect was. Ask them to share theirs.

Try to remember how you used to spend the time you now spend on social media. Think of a few of the activities and during your weekly social media sabbatical, indulge in them.

Prior to Facebook, Instagram and Twitter, did you used to enjoy reading a book? Did you spend more time listening to music? When is the last time you got up and danced all by yourself? Discover or rediscover simple joys - like completing a crossword puzzle or taking a nap.

When you get the urge to engage social media, stop, take a deep breath, think about what you're doing at the moment and ask yourself what you really need. If necessary, remind yourself that you can rejoin social media tomorrow - but honor yourself with this day by devoting it to yourself.

Taking occasional breaks from social media is very healthy. People who do so recognize the need for a more balanced approach to social media engagement and wisely decide to shift their focus from the external to being more present in their actual life.

Write a Letter to Your Younger Self

You've probably seen in magazines or on certain TV shows encouragement to write a letter to your younger self. The typical invitation to write this retrospective letter is to offer advice about how you could have done things differently or been a better person.

Sitting from this vantage point, Monday morning quarterbacking our past allows us to see what we could've done differently; how we could have been more - if only we knew then, what we know now.

But that's impossible.

It's a deficit-focused approach that implies that you could have done things differently when you couldn't. It's an unfair approach because at this vantage point, years later, you have amassed more wisdom, courage and insight, so of course your assessment of past misdeeds is different.

The letter I'm asking you to write isn't that type of letter because - what's the point? You cannot change one thing about your past or your younger self and offering advice to her does nothing to help you improve the quality of this current phase of your journey.

The letter I'm encouraging you to write is strength-based and its intention is for you to draw power from your past to use NOW. To that end, the letter that you write to your younger self is a letter of gratitude.

Make it a special, sacred occasion. Find a quiet space and carve out some solo time. Get some nice stationary and a favorite pen. Light a candle. Be fully present.

Think about what your younger self achieved and thank her for it. Think about what she endured and thank her for it. Think about what she survived and thank her for it. Think about her talents, gifts and skills and thank her for them. Think about how her navigation of her life's circumstances made it possible for you to be here, now, and thank her for it. Think of all the wonderful qualities your younger self possessed but, perhaps, went unnoticed and thank her for them.

There is no page limit to this love letter. And you don't have to finish it in one sitting. Add to it over the next few days, weeks, months. Shoot, continue to add to it for as long as you like. And while you're at it, consider how the qualities you're thanking your younger self for are still present within you – NOW.

How can you put them to use?

#IAMWORTHY Gratitude Journal

Gratitude journals are extremely powerful ways to shift your focus and change your life. Gratitude is a huge part of the Law of Attraction; which is all about using your thoughts and words to attract what you want into your life. It is based on the premise that what you focus on most expands.

The Law of Attraction is all about drawing goodness into your life by focusing on it and expecting it to manifest, but the law works both ways. When you focus on what's going wrong in your life or you constantly complain about what you don't have – you draw to you those kinds of experiences; negative situations and circumstances of lack.

An #IAMWORTHY gratitude journal takes a fascinating spin on the Law of Attraction by placing the focus on you and the wonderful things you do. It is for your eyes only – not to be shared with anyone.

When you notice the wonderful things about you and celebrate them by putting them in writing, you become even more mindful of how awesome you are – a powerful way to heal wounded worthiness, while also attracting more goodness into your life.

An #IAMWORTHY gratitude journal makes you your biggest cheerleader because ultimately, what you think about yourself and your experiences matters most. You validate yourself and heal your sense of worthiness.

Below is a list of ideas to get you started. Trust me, once you do, you will discover other awesome things to journal about yourself!

Here's how it works: purchase a beautiful journal and each day, write at least three things about yourself that you are pleased with, proud of, thrilled about, etc.

Sample journal entries:
- Someone cut you off in traffic and instead of giving them the finger, you wished them well.
- You finished a work assignment ahead of schedule
- You worked out
- You relaxed

- You redecorated
- You took a special trip
- You took a risk
- You practiced a random act of kindness (and told no one)
- You placed a difficult phone call
- You had an important conversation
- You went out and had fun
- You stuck to your diet
- You enrolled in the class
- You attended a seminar
- You said positive things to yourself
- You congratulated yourself for a job well done
- You sent yourself flowers
- You took a relaxing bubble bath
- You politely declined an invitation
- You said 'no' without apologizing
- You skipped social media
- You were fully present with someone
- You took yourself on a special outing

Include experiences in your journal that celebrate who you are. Tell no one about your journal and make it for your eyes only. On those challenging days where writing positive things about yourself might be a struggle, look through some of your previous entries to remind yourself of your goodness.

In your effort to revive your worthiness, the words you speak about yourself go a long way. Writing them down solidifies them in your consciousness.

(You can purchase an #IAMWORTHY Gratitude Journal at https://worthythebook.life)

The Worthiness Prayer

I am worthy.
Just because I am.

No one else defines my worth.
No circumstance limits my worthiness.
I reclaim the power of my worthiness through forgiveness.

I am worthy.
Just because I am.

I am worthy of the very best life has to offer.
I am worthy of love, health, prosperity, peace and joy.

I unleash the energy of my worthiness
and it shapes my journey.

I am worthy.
Just because I am.

I am worthy of harmonious relationships, and because they reflect the relationship I have with myself; I honor me with love, compassion and respect.

I am worthy.
Just because I am.

Every day I embrace my worth.
I intentionally celebrate my worthiness.
I cherish my worth with thoughts, words and actions.

I am worthy.
I use my voice.

I am worthy.
My opinion matters.

I am worthy.
I do not play small.

I am worthy.
Settling is not an option.

I am worthy.
I face my fear.

I am worthy.
Just because I am.

The weight of wounded worthiness

I had no idea how my life would change by delving into my worthiness, learning to revive it and incorporating worthiness preservation practices into my life.

I had no idea that I would postpone publishing my magazine until I felt more authentic about what I was saying to women on its pages, taking a great publication to even higher heights. I had no idea that I would manifest more money or that I'd make one of the biggest decisions of my life – to become intentional about transforming my body.

But that's what happens when you revive your worthiness. The life you want to live comes into focus because you're no longer mired down by the weight of wounded worthiness. You gain a much clearer perspective on what you want.

One of the most significant benefits to emerge from my revived worthiness has been the loss of about 15 pounds. That might sound insignificant, but it represents a monumental achievement for me.

I have carried around at least 100 extra pounds for more than 20 years. I discovered a long time ago that the weight, for me, represented protection. Protection from men looking at me in ways that made me feel publicly naked; like I was a sitting duck for assault. As a sexual abuse survivor, extra weight accumulated subconsciously to protect me until I felt safe.

Revived worthiness leads to an awareness of divine safety and a refusal to spend another minute hiding behind weight.

Revived worthiness reminds you that the future you envision is actually happening now, in this moment, with every choice. It reminds you that freedom from self-imposed limitations is self-directed.

Revived worthiness sparks the energy and courage necessary to shed the physical shell guised as protection. It creates sacred space for the real you to emerge; standing tall with dignity and spiritual grace.

Since I began writing Worthy, I have changed my eating habits and made exercising consistently a mandate instead of an option; but the real work is happening inside of me. Once I began the work to revive my sense of worthiness, self-love that flows from knowing my worth illuminated my life, how I was living, how I was hiding. It flipped excuses on their head and forced me to decide, once and for all, whether I continue crawling when I can walk; walking instead of running; settling, not soaring.

My weight represented fear. When fear dissolves, so does the weight. Reviving worthiness involves reinterpreting the messages of the subconscious, which is fed by the conscious mind. Reviving worthiness empowers the conscious mind to enlighten instead of enslave.

Revived worthiness informs you that you have choices.

When you're living with revived worthiness – you want the best for yourself. You are no longer willing to settle for a plus sized existence when you can live in the body you feel most free. Your fighting weight. That weight you look and, most importantly, feel your best.

Revived worthiness convinces you to take a 'by any means necessary' approach to being your best self – mind, body and soul.

It's not an easy road to travel but when you know you're a worthy traveler, you pack what you need by way of perseverance, self-discipline, self-control, self-trust and you decide, once and for all, to do what you need to do – one day at a time – to be who you really are.

Here's what I decided to do. I tossed diets. I trashed trying to stick to some specific way of eating because whenever I try that approach, it leads to a feeling of deprivation. When I feel deprived, I think about everything I can't have and eventually eat too much of it.

I thought about what works for me and put together guidelines to keep me focused. I then decided to immerse myself deeply into this new way of BEING.

I started moving my body consistently several days each week. Some days it is stretching. Other days I swim. Depending on what I feel like doing, I might ride a bike or work my way through a 30-minute weights/cardio circuit. I could also be found doing aerobics or Pilates at home with an online show or at the gym with a room full of sweaty souls. Bikram yoga and belly dancing, I found, are good ways to rejuvenate my body between more strenuous work-outs.

An important aspect of honoring me means on some days I do absolutely nada. Just rest. Chill out in a hot bubble bath with a glass of wine and my music. I treat myself to manis, pedis, massages, facials – all in the name of honoring my very worthy body.

I'm no longer fixated on a specific weight. I'll know how much I should weigh when I arrive at it and it feels right for me. For the first time in a very, very long time, however, I know that I'll get there because I'm worthy.

See What Happens…

Embarking on this worthiness reviving journey takes courage. It takes courage because you really do not know what will awaken within you and into which direction you will be pushed.

For me, it meant meeting parts of myself I had yet to discover. It meant becoming a better businesswoman. Working from a strong sense of worthiness plays a tremendous role in how I see my work and what I'm bringing to the world.

There was value surrounding it, but my wounded worthiness distorted my view of it. It's like I was walking around wearing dirty glasses which made it hard for me to see clearly.

Revived worthiness gives you a clear view of your life, all your assets, flaws, strengths and areas in need of improvement. It shines a light on those areas where you've settled; including things like carrying extra weight.

Revived worthiness wakes you up to what you deserve and by cultivating your worthiness; the path to achieving what you deserve is revealed.

Revived worthiness resulted in my commitment to lose weight and reclaim my body; as well as a more successful business. Reviving my sense of worthiness illumined my inner power and the ability to embrace what I deserve.

As you contemplate the way your worthiness shows up in your life, I encourage you to try the activities with a "let's see what happens," mentality.

Some will resonate while others might not. Use what works for you. If an activity sparks an idea for something different – go for it. When your worthiness is thriving, it goes to work for you in ways you might never have considered.

Above all else, enjoy the journey.

Epilogue

Boosting your sense of worthiness leads to a better life. Period. It's an inside-out approach that results in positive results. While it's a serious endeavor, it can also be fun. Cut yourself some slack as you revive your worthiness. Especially as you release old behaviors that resulted from your poor sense of worthiness.

When we know better, we do better. And when our worthiness gets revived, we make different choices.

Participating in the activities will surely direct you towards rediscovering your stronger, more vibrant sense of worthiness. I have one more recommendation. A book. There are numerous books that help navigate the worthiness journey, however; this book absolutely transformed my life.

'You Can Heal Your Life,' by Louise L. Hay was published over 30 years ago and still packs a powerful punch in the worthiness arena. The book's goal is not specifically to boost worthiness but because of its comprehensive, sacred approach to loving the self, a revived sense of worthiness is a beautiful by-product.

Hay passed away on August 30, 2017, leaving a rich legacy of self-love, vibrant worthiness and her masterpiece of a book. I strongly recommend it.

These simple steps to revive your worthiness will probably lead you to other activities because of the uniqueness of your individual journey. You will discover other fascinating ideas. I'd love to hear what else you come up with as we all navigate this worthiness journey.

Please tell me about them by writing to me at michelle@thesisterhoodmagazine.com.

You could win a #IAMWORTHY gift pack that includes an '#IAMWORTHY Gratitude Journal, #IAMWORTHY T-shirt, #IAMWORTHY mug and a free subscription to The Sisterhood magazine.

Made in the USA
Columbia, SC
01 November 2018

HOW I GOT BETTER FROM A
TRAUMATIC BRAIN INJURY

For anyone who ever had a TBI, past or present

MADELEINE WELTON

FriesenPress

One Printers Way
Altona, MB R0G 0B0
Canada

www.friesenpress.com

Copyright © 2023 by Madeleine Welton
First Edition — 2023

Please do not substitute this information for medical advice.

All rights reserved.

No part of this publication may be reproduced in any form, or by any means, electronic or mechanical, including photocopying, recording, or any information browsing, storage, or retrieval system, without permission in writing from FriesenPress.

ISBN
978-1-03-913938-1 (Hardcover)
978-1-03-913937-4 (Paperback)
978-1-03-913939-8 (eBook)

1. BIOGRAPHY & AUTOBIOGRAPHY, MEDICAL

Distributed to the trade by The Ingram Book Company

This book is dedicated to Dan
for your unwavering commitment to our marriage,
that enabled me to recover…
and to our sons, Jack and James,
who supported me throughout the process
of becoming whole again.

HOW I GOT BETTER FROM A TRAUMATIC BRAIN INJURY

TABLE OF CONTENTS

Part I: Introduction — 1
  My Story: What Happened — 9
  My Injury Meant . . . — 21
  Transfer to the Riverdale Rehabilitation Hospital — 33
  Physical Therapy was not like Physical Education — 43
  The "Squeaky Wheel" Gets a New Walker — 51
  Christmas and Our Treasure — 59
  Emotional Lability — 67

Part II: Living with A Brain Injury — **71**
  How To Live With A Brain Injury — 73
  Short Term Memory Problems — 81
  Criticism — 89
  Three Tbi Issues Leading To Chaos — 93
  Neuroplasticity — 97
  If It Isn't My Coordination, Then What Is Wrong? — 101
  Chronic Neck Pain (Whiplash) — 107
  Brain Injury Associations — 111
  Social Interactions — 119
  IT Problems — 123
  Sexuality — 125
  Acquired Attention Deficit Disorder — 131

Part III: The Insurance Game — **133**
  What I Did When Payments Stopped — 143
  The Invisible Injury — 149

Part IV: SPECT Scans — **155**

    What is SPECT? — 155

    SPECT Scan Procedure — 161

    Interpreting My SPECT Scans — 169

    How to Get a SPECT Scan in Ontario — 173

    Costs of SPECT (in Ontario) — 175

Part V: Other Factors That Helped Me — **177**

    Exercise & Fitness — 177

    Supplementation — 183

    Yoga — 187

    Nordic Walking — 189

    Golf — 191

    Right Brain/Left Brain — 197

    Music Therapy — 203

    Spirituality and Healing — 205

    The Prayer Wheel — 207

Part VI: Life After SPECT — **209**

    Pace Yourself Forever — 209

    Epilogue — 211

    The Future of Brain Injury Recovery — 215

    References — 219

PART I: INTRODUCTION

I WROTE THIS book because I want to share hope with others who have sustained a severe brain injury. My recovery has been complex and multi-faceted. This is my story about how I found a helpful treatment for my injured brain. It should not be mistaken for medical advice, but as something for you to further explore.

I sustained my traumatic brain injury in October of 1993. After awakening from a twenty-six-day coma, my immediate concern was what do I do to get better? Like the analogy of falling off a horse and getting right back up to ride again, I wanted to know how I could get back up. I asked everyone I encountered in the hospitals and all my therapists, but no one could provide me with an answer. I made it my mission to recover from a Traumatic Brain Injury (TBI) and after almost two decades, I finally succeeded in finding an answer. I believe that I was fortunate enough to have met the right people at the right time in my life. I was very persistent about trying new options to heal from a TBI. Now, I feel both privileged and obligated to share this knowledge with other brain injured individuals.

A few of the common characteristics of traumatic brain injury (TBI) are provided. I also sprinkled the book with a few survivor tips to assist you in your recovery. I did not have a guide. I share with you a few of my own difficulties to let you know that some of these behaviours happen to many of us, and we still survive. It would be easy to dwell in the past, thinking of what might have been. Instead, this is a new beginning where you may even enjoy many of your favourite things all over again while discovering new experiences.

I always hoped that I would find a way to achieve the best recovery possible. My rational was that: *If human beings can build such a complex world, then we, as a species, should have the capability of fixing ourselves.* I had this idea that the knowledge I needed was out there, somewhere, waiting for me to find it.

At the time of my injury there was no manual on brain injury recovery. Today, there is still no "one-stop shopping" for brain injury recovery in Canada, but we are getting closer. There are brain injury clinics that treat many of the various problems acquired from the injury. Unfortunately, there is still no single organization in Canada who can make you whole again.

Throughout my journey, I tried many different therapies. Some, such as massage and chiropractic, were for physical symptoms I experienced. Other treatments, such as triathlon training and hyperbaric oxygen therapy, attempt to oxygenate parts of the damaged brain. I was willing to try any treatment to the extent it would not cause me harm, making me physically worse than my starting point. I believe that it was my personal investment in the research that enabled me to search for possible solutions. It was my life, and my family's life and I wanted it back.

Eventually, I met a Canadian psychiatrist who knew of a treatment. He wanted to make this procedure available to all Canadians with brain injuries. However, problems were encountered everywhere he turned. How could he deliver this procedure across the country? How would he publicize its availability? How could this be done if there were not enough psychiatrists trained in this procedure? Currently, psychiatrists trained in this method can use the results obtained from SPECT scanning to identify the problematic areas of your damaged brain. They look for hot spots, which are parts of your brain that are overworking. They also look at cold spots which are parts of your brain that are underworked and sometimes dormant. Their goal is to balance your brain, so no one part of your brain is exacting a greater influence on the rest of your brain. The properly formatted SPECT scan is read by specially trained psychiatrists who then suggest treatments. I am hopeful that this procedure becomes a recognized treatment (through referral to specialists) for patients with traumatic brain injuries (TBIs).

When I had a head injury, I decided to make recovery my life's work. But I was forced to put that work on hold. I was living with numerous effects of traumatic brain injury, especially constant fatigue. At a certain point, the health care supports were removed by the insurance company, and despite the fatigue, I resumed the activities of daily living. I had to temporarily ignore my personal search for a cure. My daily life included caring for myself and our two young sons, taking care of a home, a garden, and trying to support my husband My husband's work necessitated frequent moves, which included preparing the house for real estate showings and setting up a new house (new banks, new grocery stores, often new schools for the boys). Every little thing I had to do required enormous effort. I was exhausted planning the steps required to get ready for each day.

I now see that the disillusionment I felt during the first decade after my brain injury was unwarranted. At that time medical health professionals did not have the ability to "fix" me. What they saw back then were only the parts of the brain that were non-functioning. They were doing the best they could and assumed that once severely brain injured you would always remain that way, to a certain degree.

Over my first decade of recovery, many people suggested that I write a book about my traumatic brain injury. I balked at this idea because I knew that I had not really become much better. I felt like I was seeing the world through a filter which turned off my access to communication and knowledge. I also thought there was absolutely nothing new that I could add to the knowledge that was already available. It would take a miracle to get me to write a book about brain injury.

Fast forward eighteen years and I found my miracle. I met John Rossiter Thornton, M.D. F.R.C.P.C. Dr. Thornton uses SPECT scans and their interpretation to improve the oxygenation of my brain. I met Dr. Thornton at a workshop for traumatic brain injury and Hyperbaric Oxygen Therapy (HBOT), organized by Dr. Angela Colantonio, University of Toronto. Dr. Colantonio was the research director of the Canadian organization called Brain Injury Canada (formerly named the Brain Injury Association of Canada).

After the workshop everyone networked. Dr. Thornton approached each of the TBI survivors and asked if we had heard of SPECT. He tried to engage us and gave business cards to each of us. Dr. Thornton invited us to contact his office to learn more about what he could offer us.

Over the next week I thought about following up with Dr. Thornton. It had been well over ten years since my accident, and I was frustrated that my brain was still not better. The re-training of my brain through different therapies did not make it work faster or more nimbly. Was this Dr. Thornton offering something too good to be true? I made my decision to follow-up based on three facts:

1. Dr. Colantonio, a professor of Occupational Therapy at the University of Toronto, had invited him as a guest speaker at the workshop which suggested that she supported his ideas.

2. A literature search revealed that Dr. Thornton had an established and esteemed reputation in brain research.

3. Dr. Thornton was offering a scientific, evidence-based opportunity that might improve my condition.

I decided to phone Dr. Thornton. There was a lot resting on this call: this treatment might be my Holy Grail, my last hope. I was going to try something that had the potential to improve my brain function. I needed to know if the treatment was safe. I contacted Dr. Thornton who agreed to accept me as a patient, and we decided to proceed.

This book <u>How to Get Better from A Brain Injury</u> is about what came next. It is about the current use of SPECT scanning and its specific use in traumatic brain injury recovery. SPECT is an imaging strategy that measures blood flow in your brain and provides pictures of the same to your psychiatrist. It shows where the oxygenated blood flows well or does not flow at all. How it works will be discussed in this book.

I want to emphasize that there is no time limit to the success of trying this treatment. Individuals who have had brain injuries, either recently or a long, long time ago, are all able to obtain successful results. Everyone follows the same protocol to reveal the physical workings of their brain through photographic mapping of blood flow. It is one hundred percent non-invasive. Then, depending on what is discovered, there will be different treatments recommended in the form of medication(s) and psychotherapy. Imaging with SPECT (single-photon emission computed tomography) scanning is used during treatment to track the changes and improvements in the brain.

MY STORY: WHAT HAPPENED

ON OCTOBER 7, 1993, I was going to the Fitness Club early enough to attend babysitting services for my two boys, both under two years of age. We were temporarily living in a condominium building as we were "between houses", and it required a bit more time, effort, and organization for me to get going. We exited the condo with a large stroller and the days' paraphernalia and paraded through the building to the underground parking lot. After loading the car, I secured both boys' car seats in the back seat. This simple act was the key to their survival.

Off we drove. It was a clear day, and the visibility was good as I drove eastbound along the North Service Road in Mississauga toward the Fitness Club. Shortly after the morning rush hour a small black car travelling westbound on the QEW exited the highway where there was no exit. He moved all the way across the highway from the inside lane and crashed through the chain link fence which separated the highway from the service road. His little black car caught some air as he hit the fence and he landed on the body of my car before rolling off.

Kaboom!

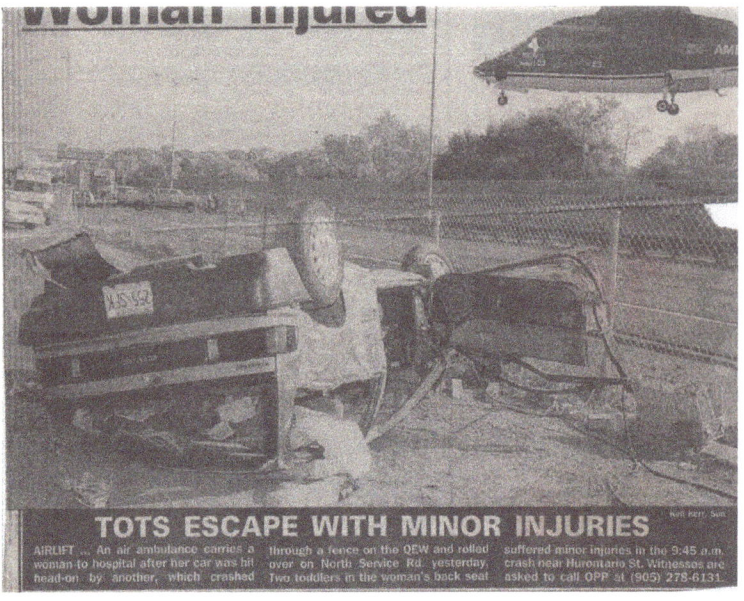

This is a photo of the car with the helicopter in the background. I saw nothing. I heard nothing. This story I share with you was pieced together from my copy of the police report, newspaper clippings and the reports of my family members. Many lives were abruptly changed forever in that moment: my life, our two little boys' lives, my husband's life, our extended families' lives, and the life of the young man who hit me. My sons would grow up with a severely brain-injured mother in charge of their development. Absolutely terrifying, to say the least.

The young man who hit me was charged with careless driving. This charge relied on other drivers having noticed poor or reckless driving behaviour prior to his launch off the highway, but no other driver recognized any irregular driving behaviour <u>immediately</u> prior to his launch, so the charge was dismissed. The driver was cut very badly by the glass from his windshield and taken to a local hospital. At the scene of the crash, he apparently appeared to be in much worse shape than me because of all the blood and broken glass. Fortunately, he was let go from the hospital the next day after the hospital had patched him up.

The story that came out of the investigation was that the driver's big toe had been run over by a forklift at work. He had gone home first and was now on his way to see his doctor. There was no drug or alcohol test administered at the scene and there was no pain assessment done. The retired judge who presided over our mediation questioned what may have caused his car to swerve across the highway so out of control. We will never know.

I was covered by the initial no-fault insurance which I quickly topped out. Prior to no-fault I could have sued for ten times as much money as I eventually received.

The next photo is of me in my car surrounded by firefighters. I carry a special place in my heart for firefighters. The most severe impact was made to the front passenger seat which was empty. Both my babies were in the backseat, buckled into their car seats, and they were fine.

My head hit the side window and I was unconscious in a nanosecond. Air bags did not become mandatory in Canada until 1998. My accident was in 1993. You can see my face (in the photo of the crashed car surrounded by fire men) by looking directly at the steering wheel and allowing your eyes to drift slightly up and to the right-hand side. I am under the roof of the car in the middle of the photo. The neurosurgeon at Sunnybrook Hospital said the strength of the steel in my car may have saved my life.

The Peel Region Fire Department used the "Jaws of Life" to extract me from the vehicle and I was airlifted to Sunnybrook Hospital in Toronto. The boys were extremely fortunate in that an off-duty policewoman had been driving on the highway behind the other car. A trained first responder, she exited the highway and turned onto the service road to where the crash was located. I was told that she took care of the boys at the scene. When I finally telephoned her to thank her for her kindness, I was told that she had left the force. The boys were taken by ambulance to the local hospital which was five minutes away. They were checked out and found to be in good health.

Regrettably, I had been negligent in changing my address on my driver's license within the required time, as I was waiting to change the address on my identification until we moved into our new home (three months later). At the time such a change required visiting a government licensing office, a twenty-minute drive, waiting several hours and with two babies. Of course, the police went to our old house to tell my husband about the crash. Thankfully, the new owners were able to find the address of his workplace and they directed the police to his office. What a horrible day for Dan. He heard that his wife was in a coma and that his two babies were at the local hospital waiting to be picked up, all the result of a fluke accident.

For the remainder of the month, Dan commuted from our home and his work in South Mississauga to Sunnybrook Hospital (now called Sunnybrook Health Sciences Centre) in North Toronto. Initially, Dan's parents, their friend Betty, and his sister all pitched in to help look after the boys, but this would not be a long-term solution. Dan still had to go to work, and he needed to finish building our new house. Also, I suspect that once out of the coma, I begged him to spend more time with me in the hospital.

At the time of my accident. my parents were on a ski vacation in Europe. Fortunately, a partner at Dad's law firm used the travel itinerary he left behind to track them down with the news. They flew home as soon as possible. I understand the serious distress they must have been experiencing. My parents and Dan all listened to the doctors' predictions regarding my prognosis which are just forecasts of expectations based on statistics.

My super-organized type A personality mother quickly devised a plan for Dan and our baby boys to move into my parents' house in mid-Toronto. Back then it was only a fifteen-minute drive to Sunnybrook hospital. I had become the centre "attraction" in the family, not something that I have ever desired. Dan and our sons stayed there for the remainder of the month. My family's relatives were scattered throughout Canada. They responded rapidly to the news of my mom's babysitting enterprise with co-ordinated visits to help her with the boys. Meanwhile, Dan commuted to work each day, spent time with our boys, and visited me several times each week. I imagine those were very busy days for everyone but me. I was having the best rest that I had had in years.

At the scene of the accident, I was unconscious and had suffered a traumatic brain injury. The degree of one's unconsciousness is measured on the Glasgow Coma Scale (GCS). The GCS was designed in 1974 to determine the degree of head injury or consciousness using a standardized assessment. It is a numeric system with "1" being the lowest and poorest measure available on three different items: eye opening, motor response, and verbal response. The scale ranges from 3 to 15, with 3 indicating the deepest level of unconsciousness. At the site of the accident, my reading was a 3. Later at the hospital, I had readings that ranged from 3 – 6.

Total sums of these readings ranging from 3 - 8 are classified as severe. A score between 9 – 12 is classified as moderate and a sum equal to or greater than 13 is classified as minor. It is important to note that "minor" does not mean that a person with a minor brain injury may not also have very serious difficulties.

Shortly after my arrival at Sunnybrook Hospital a CAT scan was performed. The neurosurgeon inserted a Richmond bolt into my head. I looked like Frankenstein. No one has a photograph of me from this time as it was before cell phones. Thank goodness!

As a precaution, I was placed on 300 mg of Dilantin per night to prevent seizures. I remained on this drug for over a year but, fortunately, I never experienced any seizures.

At Sunnybrook Hospital, I was put into the intensive care unit (ICU) for ventilation and monitoring. I was extubated on the eighth post-operative day which is when they considered me to be "medically stable" but still comatose. The hospital put me in a wardroom with three other people. This was a short stay as I was quickly moved to a single room. Apparently, I made too much noise and the other patients complained saying that I "talked too much." I could understand this if it were the case, but it was reported that I was constantly "moaning." Others may have heard moaning, but I know that I was trying to communicate to the outside world that I was still somewhere inside my body. "Please help me get out of here!" But no one in the hospital was conversant with TBI moans.

When I was finally awake, I existed in a small space with all my needs being met. I knew nothing. My world was clean, white, and peaceful. It felt like I was in a storybook where I could view everything objectively. I was pleased to realize that I thought about what I was going to say before I said it. I had no idea this was because all my communication skills were badly damaged. I had to retrieve the words, stored somewhere in my head, before speaking. I was also pleased to remember that I needed to arrange these words in the correct order before I said them. Of course, I had no idea that my spoken word sounded nothing like I imagined. I realized that I had a nasal twang, but it was not until other people told me that I sounded drunk that I knew there was more to it than just a twang.

My first attempt at this information sourcing occurred when I asked the nurse where I was, followed by the question of why was I here? She turned the questioning back to me and asked me what I thought had happened. Then she let me ramble on about my own made-up situation of nearly drowning. I suspected that was inaccurate because she then suggested I ask my mother about my accident. Surprisingly, I *did* remember, probably because something cued me to ask the question.

One day when Dan visited me, he took me in a Geri-chair to the end of the hall. We stopped by the window at the end of the hospital's hallway. When Dan was me around, I felt a happiness and warmth throughout my body as I realized that with him by my side, nothing could stop me. I could see the empty hospital corridor stretching out in front of us, beckoning me to run. In my most earnest and pleading voice, I asked Dan to help me escape! Suddenly Dan had the same look on his face that frequently appeared on my mother's face. Poor Dan, he looked helpless and lost, as he scrambled to explain why my idea of escaping was not feasible. It wasn't that we couldn't achieve it, it was that he did not want to, he said.

Dan said: "Mad, remember you had an accident? You need to stay here a little bit longer".

Me: "C'mon Dan, you can talk to the people, they will listen to you." I thought that Dan would side with me no matter what. I was impatient and unaware of any plan designed to get me better. Apparently, I was being given time to heal sufficiently before progressing to the next level of recovery. Dan and I stayed at the end of the hallway for a long rest. He knew that some extra time would prevent me from remembering my idea of eloping from the hospital.

To this day, whenever there is an issue that I am not able to fix on my own, I will say, "But Dan, you can talk to the people—they will listen to you."

The amount of paper that was generated by the medical and legal teams related to the crash and my hospitalizations easily filled a banker's box. I kept the box for years after my court case because its contents comforted me by explaining the trauma I experienced. Of course, I never did need anything in the box, but it gave me a sense of security to have it. The box was my teddy bear.

MY INJURY MEANT . . .

I WOULD HAVE to learn to walk, talk, read, write, and swallow again. Everything I had taken for granted each day of my life was now a major task to be mastered. Most people have little knowledge or experience of what a brain injury really is or what the expectations are of surviving one. This truth is magnified because every single brain injury is unique. As we gradually became educated in the world of brain injury, we expanded our vocabulary too. I will provide some definitions to ensure every reader has a basic knowledge with the language of brain injury.

Dr. Donna Ouchterlony was my medical doctor at the Rehabilitation Hospital. She provided us with an analogy for a traumatic brain injury (TBI) that was easy for Dan to understand. Her suggestion was to imagine that your skull is a football and it's filled with Jell-O. When the football is thrown, what happens to the Jell-O inside? That football can do many things at many different speeds. Likewise, it may be caught, dropped, tackled, rotated, or crushed by a player, so there are many different outcomes for the Jell-O inside the football, just as there are many outcomes for the sloshing around of your brain inside your skull, especially in a motor vehicle accident.

There are two types of brain injury: open and closed brain injuries.

Open brain injuries are visible, and they include any holes in your skull, for example, from a gunshot wound.

Closed brain injuries occur when your brain gets sloshed around inside your skull. These may be from vehicle collisions, falls, or beatings. I had a closed head injury.

We discovered that medical professionals see three specific aspects within your brain, the physical, cognitive, and emotional components.

A "**contrecoup**" occurs when the brain rebounds off the inside of the skull (maybe several times), causing further damage. For example, if the left-hand side of your head hits the side window in a car (as mine did), there can be additional damage to the right side of the brain as your brain sloshes back and forth within the enclosed skull.

"**Edema**" is the swelling within your head from increased blood flow to the injured areas. If it pools, it can form a hematoma or blood clot which increases pressure on the brain tissue within the skull. Neurosurgeons will insert a shunt in the skull to relieve the pressure that is building and pressing against the tissue of the brain, potentially causing further injury.

The following statistics are copied from the website of "Brain Injury Canada" with permission given years ago.

> **By 2031, traumatic brain injury (TBI) is expected to be among the most common neurological conditions affecting Canadians, along with Alzheimer's disease and other dementias, and epilepsy.**
>
> **Traumatic brain injury (TBI) is a leading cause of disability globally. In Canada, 2% of the population lives with a TBI, and there are 18,000 hospitalizations for TBI each year. One-third of individuals with a TBI are women, and TBI is particularly common early in the reproductive years (15-24 years), with intimate partner violence and accidents being major causes. Women with TBI are more**

likely than men to experience mental health problems post-injury.

Please note: The following series of stats has been extrapolated from United States data to the population of Canada.

TBI occurs at an annual rate of 500 out of 100,000 individuals. That is approximately 165,000 in Canada per year. This equals 456 people every day, or one person injured every 3 minutes in Canada.

TBI occurs at a rate of 100 times that of spinal cord injury.

When injury due to stroke or other non-traumatic causes is included, close to 4% of the population lives with a brain injury. That equates to over 1.5 million Canadians living with acquired brain injury.

It may seem odd, but I was overwhelmed by my own bravado. I believed that I could take on this challenge to recover. In hindsight, that was a highly unrealistic expectation. My brain was truthfully not functioning well at all. I had no scientific training or scientific contacts in my life. Why on earth was I so sure of myself? Outside my own family life, I had never been that confident about anything before.

Were there health care professionals who had failed to communicate the information about treatment for brain injuries to me? I only knew that I wanted this more than anything else in the world. This was the one life I had been given and I was going to get better. I had Dan, and we had Jack and James, our baby boys. I could not give them up to wallow in my own daily failures and self-pity. Yet, in suggesting that I was going to accomplish this I was described as "impulsive, "disillusioned" "unrealistic" and "lacking insight" by nurses, family members and therapists—quite correctly, on the face of it. But who else had anywhere near as great the motivation as I had?

A key to my bravado can be found in Dan's response to a friend of ours who recently asked him, "What was Madeleine like before the accident?" Dan's responded by saying, "Mad was…always very determined." Thankfully that did not change as a result of my brain injury, or I certainly would not be here today writing this book for you.

My editor and my psychiatrist suggested that I include milestones of my progress in this book. My response has been to try and incorporate a few of these milestones as readers may find them useful. I suggest that such milestones were probably more exciting for my loved ones than for me, as they represented progress to them, while to me it felt like "watching grass grow".

At Sunnybrook hospital, I spent days and days lounging in a Geri-chair or lying in bed. The time passed quickly—or was it slowly? "**Geri-chair**" is the short form for geriatric chair, which is a specific chair for people who can no longer move independently. It is also use in seniors' facilities and rehabilitation centres. I do remember feeling that time moved slowly for a while but that was only because I had so few things occupying my brain. Also, I was never awake for very long. What I do know is that visitors visited, meals were delivered, and walks were taken in the hallway. This is a bit of a misnomer as I was not actually doing the walking. I was rolling along in a Geri-chair or a wheelchair while being pushed by someone else doing the walking for me.

I remember learning prior to my injury that, if a memory is related to a strong emotion, it is less likely to be forgotten. This happened to me repeatedly. I found that no matter how severely brain damaged I was, I still have memories from this time in my life.

There was the time when I ate my first solid food. Throughout my coma, I had been on a liquid diet via a naso-gastric tube. My Mom, my brother (who had flown in from Vancouver to visit me now that I was awake) and a nurse were all standing around my bed. The excitement and tension were palpable. This would be my second recovery milestone, allowing that waking up from the coma was my very first. My Mom and brother were more excited about me eating than I was.

There was a lot of verbal coaching taking place that went something like this: "Madeleine, you are going to eat your first solid food through your mouth. Let's get you sitting up straight so that it will be easier for you to swallow." Doesn't Jell-O slide down your throat? The bowl of Jell-O sparkled under the bright hospital lights. I can't remember thinking about Jell-O very much, but suddenly it took centre stage in my life. The hype and attention from everyone else present may also have helped to brighten its allure.

But problems quickly presented such as how to work the spoon? I found it very awkward and difficult to grip. My audience suggested I just use my hands which I thought was an excellent idea.

Enthusiastically, I dug my hands into the bowl and removed a large blob. I raised my hands to eye level so that I could see the blob on the spoon up close while continuing to move the Jell-O to my face. My brother Graham was laughing at me for some reason. Did he know that I lost the Jell-O? I had no idea where this spoonful of Jell-O went, but I did not taste anything in my mouth. Graham told me that the Jell-O was all over my forehead. Surprisingly, my mother was quiet. I believe she was traumatized once again by seeing the realities of this latest disability. Fortunately, I discovered that I was no longer sensitive in front of others about my inability to do things which would bode well for my recovery because I would try just about anything without being self-conscious or worried about failure.

Voila, my proprioceptive system is on public display. It did not work well. Then again nothing of my physical self worked well. My attempt at using my mind to control my body is an excellent illustration that "mind over matter" doesn't work when your brain is badly injured. I was lying in bed when I announced to my mother that I had to go to the washroom. She immediately said that she would call a nurse to help me. I brushed her off and announced that I could do it on my own. Of course, I could go to the washroom on my own. I had been doing it for most of my life. Why, oh why, did I always have to learn through trial and error? My mom was unable to convey to me why it was a bad idea for me to try and walk. I made up my mind that I was going to try right now and that was all there was to it.

Hospital staff had told me that I could not walk, yet I had not even tried to walk, so how did they know? Wouldn't it be better to find out first? How could I not remember something so obvious? Were they referring to the 'knowing how to walk', or the 'knowing that I had a brain injury and could not walk? Regardless of which, I still had to go to the washroom. As I lay there, I devised a plan. I was proud that I had been able to coordinate enough focus to devise a plan in the first place. This meant that I had overcome a symptom of brain injury and that was my distractibility. Yet, how distracted is a patient in a single hospital room? This is my brain injured self, being practical. I thought at the time that if I could overcome a symptom of brain injury such as distractibility, then what on earth could go wrong? I formulated the steps:

1. Swing my legs over the side of the bed.

2. Use my hands to steady myself on the edge of the bed.
3. Put my feet on the floor.
4. Proceed to stand up, while still holding on.

All went according to my plan until I swung one leg forward and away from the bed. I fell flat on my face. This was baffling to me as nothing physical was broken. Why didn't the messages I had sent from my brain to my legs not work? My mother called for a nurse to get me off the floor and I really hope I was laughing in my mortification. Who knew? Everyone who understood what a brain injury was did and that was not me at this point.

Many years after, I asked my mom how she handled the accident. With further prodding she decided to share her worst memory of my stay at Sunnybrook with me. Mom said she stepped off the elevator and there I was seated directly across from the elevators. My head was hanging down and I was slouched over in my Geri-chair with drool flowing out of my mouth. While my mom was expressing her terror at my life being reduced to this, I happily told her how significantly positive a moment this was for me. Here I had been left alone, out of the hospital bed, and outside of my hospital room, (even though I was still in full sight of the nursing station). It made a strong impression on my mother, and I wished that I could have shared what I saw was going on at the actual time this occurred to spare her from her sadness about my condition.

My final memory of Sunnybrook hospital was also the most motivating experience there. A nurse had once again parked me in my geri-chair beside a window. Right below the window I watched a young woman pushing herself with her walker. I did not know that it was a walker she was using as they were unfamiliar to me. Yet there she was, young like me and she was moving independently, unlike me. I felt an overpowering urge to achieve that same independence. Later, when the nurse came by to pick me up from my window spot, I remember stating, "I want to do what she's doing down there. I want to stand up like her and walk!"

TRANSFER TO THE RIVERDALE REHABILITATION HOSPITAL

(The Riverdale Hospital has been replaced by the Bridgepoint Rehabilitation Hospital)

I SWEAR THAT it was only the next day that they transferred me by ambulance to the now defunct and demolished Riverdale Hospital. However, my sense of time was so vague that for all I knew, the transfer could have been the next day or the next month. It makes me feel good to think it was the next day. I worshipped that memory for months because it provided me with a motivational goal. This would be my third achieved milestone. I was being transferred from a trauma unit to a hospital for rehabilitation and recovery. Yippee!

Beside the hospital was the Don Jail. I had never seen a jail before and now I had a view of it out my hospital window. Rehabilitation hospitals focus on rehabilitation through positive reinforcement of desired behaviours, compassion, and nurturing. It was a weird dichotomy, having these two institutions situated side by side.

At the time of my hospital transfer I don't think that I stopped talking. In my tiny world which was composed of peoples' explanations and living in Sunnybrook hospital, the thought of moving from a place where everyone knew me to one where no one knew me was very scary. I was consumed by the idea that at the Riverdale Hospital I would get lost. In retrospect, I do not know of anyone ever being "lost" in a hospital, so I wonder what psychological construct explains this? Fear?

Upon my transfer I was again placed in a wardroom. This was fine until a loud female was put in the bed across from me. She was noisy just like I had been at Sunnybrook Hospital. I asked a nurse how to get a private room and was told that I needed private insurance to get one. She suggested that my family would have likely organized that upon my arrival.

Finally, something clicked in my brain as I experienced my brain turning "on" like a light switch. We had discussed the topic very seriously when Dan had to decide if he would buy into the plan at his work. We thought it prudent since we enjoyed physical and somewhat dangerous sports, and we were planning to start a family at the time. How would I ask Dan about this? I sat in the hospital dining room and wrote out lines for him which said, "we have private insurance".

Following this conversation, I was moved into a semi-private room. Many of the nurses felt sorry for me because all my roommates were older women who had suffered from strokes. What the nurses did not realize was that I was in such bad shape I did not have the energy to engage with a roommate. If they did not speak any English that was even better. I did not even have a rental television because I slept most of the day.

When I was awake, I ate, performed self-care rituals such as getting dressed or undressed and I engaged with visitors. Otherwise, I slept. Eventually, I did finally have a young roommate who was a young mother of twin three year old girls. I felt so badly that I was not more energetic with trying to get to know her, but my communication skills were so impaired it was not possible for me to initiate a relationship with her.

Now that I was established at the Riverdale Rehabilitation Hospital, I recall the most common questions from my visitors were: "Do you remember anything from your coma? What was it like? Did you have dreams?" First off, I do not remember much from much of this time. There were flashes where I knew that I was trapped and unable to communicate with the world. Sometimes I sensed there were people were around me. It is highly likely that this was the time when I was moaning in my coma at Sunnybrook hospital, "Let me out, let me out." My sister Jennifer did one of the few things that is helpful for coma patients. She played music for me. I think we heard an awful lot of one musician (initials C.S.) because he was familiar, and "clean" enough for public consumption. A friend of mine used to read, out loud, newspapers and magazine articles that were only about politics. She would have read them anyway, so why not to me? For almost the past two decades, I have been involved with political campaigns, never having previously done so. Can one develop a new hobby while in a coma? Seems possible!

I loved being in the rehabilitation hospital. I could not understand why people speak negatively about being in hospital. This hospital was old which was why it was scheduled for demolition within the next decade. Yet, to me, it was like being at an adult camp. My room was cleaned, and I was served three prepared meals a day. I did not have to decide on a menu, buy the food, prepare the food, serve the meal, or clean up after. Why do people complain about hospital food? It was healthy. I did not have to count grams of protein and I did not have to prepare it. I felt that I was on vacation. This meant that all my energy could go towards healing, which is what makes rehabilitation hospitals work so effectively, in my opinion.

My hospital room at the rehabilitation hospital was as pleasant as Canadian hospital rooms get. I had a lot of cards and many plants and flowers in my room. It felt and smelled a lot like my childhood home. Mom had always been an avid indoor and outdoor gardener, and I was used to our house smelling like a greenhouse. My mom and my sister had put photographs of family and friends above my bed to personalize my space. It was a great comfort to me because whenever I returned to my hospital bed from therapy sessions or even a walk around the floor, I felt that same sense of "coming home" to my space that one feels when you open the front door of your own home. Comfort and security await, as you cross the threshold.

The importance of visitors and social interaction when in hospital is essential to one's recovery and cannot be overstated. I had read that social interactions play a positive role in healing but to empirically support this statement for the purpose of this book, I include the conclusions of a study done by M. Matteri in 2016, on <u>Research into Increased Social Interactions during Convalescence</u>. They found the effects of sensory stimulation led to significant increases in the level of cognitive function and basic cognitive skills. Having many visitors in hospital benefits one's recovery as opposed to the historical recommendations of not disturbing a patient who is convalescing.

This is a photo of me in my room at the Riverdale hospital.

The rehabilitation hospital was truly like summer camp for me. We had regularly scheduled activities throughout the day. My program included:

- physiotherapy (physical games)
- occupational therapy (OT) (mental games)
- speech therapy (very difficult for me)
- occupational therapy group sessions (miniature parties!)
- meals served three times a day.
- weekly visits by my M.D., Dr. Ouchterlony.

The variety of planned activities was designed to enlist the use of different parts of the brain. There was more testing by occupational therapists for my cognitive abilities (*testing* is just another word for a game). I love games and I remember my father teaching me to play cribbage when I was six years old. The Riverdale Hospital tested me extensively because they knew that eventually there would be a price tag on my accident and the resulting deficits with the insurance company. Testing also assisted by directing therapists in my rehab.

Most of my testing was for cognitive issues. The OT was very helpful and would explain throughout what she was testing for. I believe these explanations were provided because I always asked. I also always asked my therapists if they knew how I could improve from my brain injury. I don't recall anyone ever admitting that they could help me with that but maybe I am just not remembering their answers.

The occupational therapist worked to help determine what I could and could not do in therapy. She also visited me in my room shortly after I arrived to help organize me with all the new activities. I was given a paper calendar that looked identical to the ones we used in high school with times and boxes to fill in with "classes" or appointments. This schedule was taped above my bed on a bulletin board so that everyone—except me—could see what I was supposed to be doing. Initially I did not have anyone to move it to a place where I could see it, so I was oblivious to what was going on. Fortunately, my mom and other visitors seemed to know, and made me aware of my upcoming activities. Occasionally, and only at the beginning of my stay, did a therapist have to come to retrieve me for a therapy session that I had forgotten about.

I wanted to write the schedule out myself. My writing was worse than my pre-injury illegible handwriting. I saved an attempt of my handwriting from a page I tore out of the exercise book that my mom had left to communicate with hospital staff and visitors.

Occupational therapy group sessions were surprising and tricky. At the first session, there were seven brain-injured individuals all sitting around a square table. We were each handed a small piece of folded paper and told not to open them. On the outside of the paper was our name and on the inside was a number. The therapists explained the Glasgow Coma Scale (GCS) to us. They also explained how two people with the exact same GCS reading could have very little in common with each other's situation. We were then told to open our pieces of paper and say what our GCS reading was and how we felt about it. Being slightly competitive, I was pleased to have the lowest score in the room. I thought that I had won, as in coming first in a sprint race. How disturbing is that?

We took turns listening to each person give their answer and how they felt about it. That was the point of this exercise, **"listening"**. Characteristics of newly brain-injured people include extreme self-centredness, self-absorption, and the willingness to talk about themselves constantly. Interrupting others' conversations is quite typical, showing a lack of control and no sense of timing during a conversation, although my experience would allow that a common reason for doing so is to not forget what I was about to say. Of course, the information you were afraid to lose by not blurting it immediately is usually not important to others anyway.

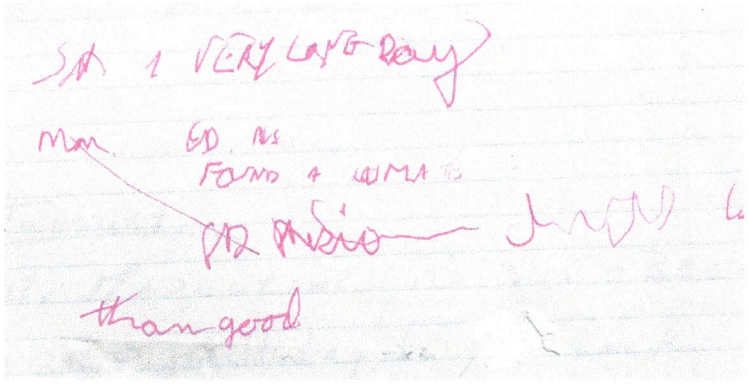

SURVIVOR TIPS

1. Have an exercise book and pen available at the bedside for staff to communicate with your family.

2. Make your space your own with anything you find comforting such as plants and photos. My young roommate had her own comforter for her bed. Going to her bed felt like arriving home to her.

3. Encourage visitors to visit you at the hospital.

PHYSICAL THERAPY WAS NOT LIKE PHYSICAL EDUCATION

AT RIVERDALE REHABILITATION Hospital, I started my new life in a wheelchair. That glimpse of the woman using a walker out the window at Sunnybrook was still just a future dream for me.

Initially, I found the physical therapy (PT) sessions quite annoying. Why on earth was I not being taught how to walk? And what about my bendy, swaying torso? Was mobility not the most important function for me to learn? The first few times I went down to PT, I was excited. I expected Physical Therapy be a close relation to Physical Education. I loved Physical Education classes at school, and I anticipated that PT would not differ by much.

I expected to be doing workouts focusing on the muscles required to help me walk. Perhaps some leg weights, and movement patterning? At the time, I anticipated working in tandem with the therapists to achieve my goals. I envisaged having a small discussion about goals, like plans with a personal trainer.

I knew that I was knowledgeable enough about my fitness to express what my body needed. I knew that core work was required to stabilize my mid-section.

This was not to be. The therapists had me perform much smaller activities. Eventually, I progressed to the point where they let me try to hold on to a bar and stand. Another move that I mastered was pushing a chair. I was aware of my decline from my former abilities, but I was still excited to be learning. Many baby steps were taken and whenever I was standing upright, I was guided by a physio. These physiotherapists obviously knew what they were doing, but it sure wasn't gym class. I never even broke a sweat. Since returning home from the rehabilitation hospital in 1994, I believe that I have spent more time at my physical therapy clinic than all other therapies combined. As I recovered more and more after being treated by Dr. Thornton, I was able to participate in more activities (tennis, biking, and activities which require two or more physical skills). I often discovered there was still a weak link in the performance of the activity, however. Then, I would injure myself. Best solution is to focus on all around fitness training and take it very slowly (not my nature), pacing yourself.

Thankfully, I did not become depressed even though my world was surrounding me with negative feedback regarding what I could NOT do. At this point in time, I had no short-term memory which fortunately acted like a built-in safety mechanism that made the situation tolerable.

There was testing for speech issues such as my inability to find words. I wish they could have helped me sound better but that was not to be. I asked repeatedly to get rid of the nasal whine that many TBI individuals have, but the speech pathologist said that I was fine. I did discover, over the years, that other brain-injured people also have a distinguishing whine to their voice so that we are able to identify each other without being told. It is almost like a secret club! Industry professionals, such a speech therapists and nurses can also identify brain injured individuals easily.

I have tried over the years to make my speech smoother and crisper. I found a good speech therapy program which I had problems fitting in to my schedule. One of their recommendations was to see an "Ear, Nose, and Throat" (ENT) specialist who I finally saw about three months later. As a side benefit in trying to heal other issues, I found hyperbaric oxygen therapy to have positively improved the slur in my speech.

There were also weekly doctor visits scheduled. I think I slept through many of them, although I remember being awake for a visit from a room full of residents. That was the most exciting it ever got.

My morning routine in the rehabilitation hospital remained the same. There was my main morning nurse who took great care of me. On other days, I was still well taken care of. I would be awakened each day and breakfast would be delivered. The nurses would then take me down the hall to the co-ed single bathroom. There were no private washrooms in this old hospital. Some days, I was treated to a shower making use of a shower chair that rolled right into the shower space.

At first the nurses would help me to get dressed or at least retrieve the clothes from the closet which I could not reach on my own. I remember that I used to be interested in clothes and fashion, yet it made me cringe to look at the cupboard. Why did these nurses have to ask me what I wanted to wear? Absolutely nothing from in there!

Apparently, I had lost so much weight in my coma that nothing I owned fit properly. To meet my wardrobe needs in the hospital, my mother once again came to the rescue. While she was passionate in her hatred of clothes shopping, due to the gravity of the situation (I literally had nothing to wear but a hospital gown) she now had a mission. Mom bought me at least four mix-and-match cotton lounge outfits with little colour-coded markers to indicate which top and bottom should be worn together. While I was somewhat disgusted if not mortified by the concept of this, I did appreciate this selection had bright, flattering colours. This would help ensure that I was not lost or misplaced in the new hospital.

Another small milestone occurred when the nurses on my floor were extremely busy. I recognised this as a significant event because it changed my role from that of being a dependant lump to having some control over my own destiny. This may have been scheduled into my rehabilitation protocol by the occupational therapist. On this wonderful day, there was not a spare nurse to take me there.

Yes, I certainly would try. This may have been a scheduled small milestone, but to me, this was huge! It signaled my first taste of independence. My biggest difficulty was trying to remember what to do and when to do it. The progression of steps was still an abstract concept as my brain did not understand "cause and effect". Once again, I relied on a list of steps.

1. Wheel myself down the hallway.
2. Press the elevator button.
3. Wait patiently for the elevator to arrive.
4. Wheel myself onto the elevator.
5. Exit on the opposite side of the elevator which ensured that I did not need to turn around in a wheelchair.
6. Press the correct button to go down to the correct floor (pressing the button was the most difficult part of this experience).
7. When I did forget to press it, nothing happened. I would sit there in the elevator forever, with a brain that did not know that anything was wrong.
8. Eventually, as the time passed, I became aware that I was stopped. Hmmm, what did I forget? I think I have been sitting on this elevator for quite a while…
9. Eventually, other people came along and wanted to get on the elevator.

10. They asked me what floor I would like to go to. The "cueing" of needing to press a button was enough for me to realize that an action was required.
11. Finally, I exited the elevator and headed for my therapy.

What did happen after a few weeks was the ability for me to get on the elevator and to realize when I had forgotten to do one of the steps, so some learning did occur.

I was still in a wheelchair, but I was now able to manage my own mobility within the hospital. I started to pull myself on the handrails that run along the walls of the hospital corridors. I could literally fly down the hallways. These railings on the walls are there to assist people to walk down the hallway but for me, they served as boomerangs in my wheelchair. Everyone seemed to be telling me to slow down but they didn't realize that I was invincible. Again, I could not see the effect I could have if I crashed or ran into someone. However, I did eventually learn to slow down to what I considered to be a controlled speed.

Fortunately, the physical therapists finally started to teach me how to walk. I figured all I needed was "practice", but it was slow going. The physical therapists were probably looking for things larger than fitness, whereas all I wanted to do was exercise. After I returned to the hospital after Christmas break, I remember finishing my dinner and looking out the door. I saw a man walking by my open door on his walker. Either he stopped to say "hi" or I initiated the conversation and asked him what he was doing?

He invited me to join him the following evening on his walk, and naturally I said "yes'. I did ask him if we were even allowed to do such an independent activity since I was still feeling rule bound to the hospital administration's policies. He reassured me that it was okay, and off we went.

Every night after dinner, we would practise our walking by circling the hallway a few times. It reminded me of my high school's indoor track practice. Eventually, I was left to do laps on my own. I guess he escaped!

After four months in the two hospitals, I finally left the rehabilitation hospital using only a walker.

THE "SQUEAKY WHEEL" GETS A NEW WALKER

ONE EVENING, A nurse standing behind the nursing station, asked me to stop walking and told me to go back to my room. I was mortified that someone was scolding me. What had I done? When I timidly ventured to ask her "why", she said my walker was making too much noise with its squeaking and creaking. She used that no-nonsense tone of voice, peculiar to nurses and teachers.

The next morning my physiotherapist started our session with her customary, "Hi, what's new?" Finally, I had information to give her. I eagerly reported that on the previous night the nursing staff had complained about my "squeaky" walker. My therapist asked why I was even using my walker at night. I proudly explained to her that I walked laps each evening with a fellow patient both for fitness, and to improve my walking ability. I truly felt like I was disclosing my secret training regimen and hoped that I had impressed her.

Later that day when I returned to my room, there was a surprise waiting for me - a brand new walker! The moral of the story: "The squeaky walker . . . gets a new walker!"

I was still a long, long way from walking independently, or even on my own with a walker outside. It was a warm winter day and my mother felt that I should be taken outside for a walk in the fresh air. Well, they could not spare a nurse so my tiny, petite, fierce mother declared, "I will take her outside myself." Even having lost a great deal of weight from being in a coma, I was still heavier than she was.

I resisted the whole idea of going outdoors thinking that I was in no condition to face the world. Would people stare at me, make negative comments, shun my existence? Somehow, I convinced myself to venture out. We would be on hospital grounds which are designed for sick patients in the hospital like me. Yes, it was glorious to be outside. This is a photo of me going outside for the first time. Location: Riverdale Hospital in 1993.

There is no shame in re-learning something, even if you are bad at it. Keep going, no matter how foolish you may feel, you will improve. The harder you try the better you will become, and frequency is the key to success. This was my life and the greater my effort, the greater the benefits. It is the perfect time to be selfish, which brain injury individuals are predisposed to being anyway.

The best visits I remember having at Riverdale hospital were when people brought their little kids with them. Babies were the best because they could just crawl around on my bed with me. I remember Dan's two-year-old nephew crawling all over my bed and it just triggered great happiness within me. I could not wait to get home and hug my boys. I believe that floodgate of positive emotions I experienced encouraged the staff to let Dan bring my babies into the hospital.

The following is a letter in my notebook to my family from a social worker on the unit, explaining that bringing my children to visit me would be a huge benefit for me.

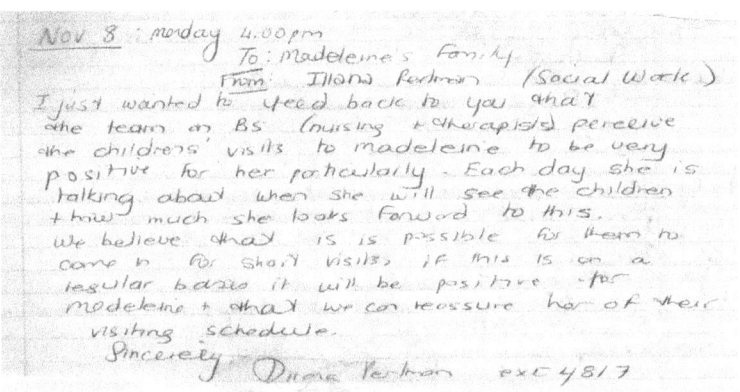

The next time a social worker visited me it also had a significant effect on my life. This young social worker innocently asked me who I resembled more, my mother or my father. I suppose that I surprised her by breaking down in tears and telling her that I was adopted. It had never bothered me to be adopted. In fact, my parents instilled in their three adopted children what they saw as the increased value of being adopted. My parents were required to meet many conditions and fulfill numerous regulations to be worthy of parenting us.

For a second time my brain clicked "on". It occurred to me as I lay in the hospital bed, post-coma, with a TBI that "here is a social worker who has access to social registrars and government type information". I could see it in her eyes that she wanted to be helpful, so I blurted out the question to ask if she knew how to find my birth parents. She offered to start the process for me. I received something in the mail in a few months which would explain the process allowing me to decide and what steps to take, if any. Now, one can just register with a DNA matching site and hope that a parent has also had their DNA done.

I had always wanted to know where I fit into the world. My Mom was a good organizer which complimented her control streak. I was organized, but my personality was quite the opposite. I could not see myself following in her footsteps. Mom was involved in many different organizations, setting up committees, handling her own financial portfolio (she had been a stockbroker before she married), and from my perspective, she led a complicated social life that would exhaust the average person. Yet our house was always well maintained. How did she do it all?

Approximately a year after my discharge from the rehab centre, I received a letter from the Children's Aid Society. This letter contained non-identifying information and a form to complete to match with a request from the other side. The rules were very strict, and the information was sealed. I completed the request form and sent it off, not to be thought of again. A full decade later, the Children's Aid Society contacted me by mail. I finally met my birth mother with my brother, as she lived in Vancouver. I learned how I came to be. My birth mother never told my birth father of her pregnancy. She was very conscientious and thoughtful about my prenatal health. She even changed jobs to work as a nanny to make it easier to carry her pregnancy. The most unusual coincidence was discovering that when she married a few years later, she lived only five minutes from my parents' home in Toronto, so our paths would have crossed many times at the local grocery store, community centre and other local venues.

The question by the social worker was initially meant to discover more about my personality, which had changed significantly. Apparently, 70% of brain injured individuals have personality changes. My good fortune was a glorious transformation, turning my introverted self into more of an extrovert. I also suspect that disinhibition from the injury played a role too. I no longer had any fear of misbehaving or making any type of mistake (this was not necessarily a good thing). My Mom had always been overpoweringly strict. She was quite surprised by my freedom to speak and commented frequently about the changes in me.

It is common for individuals emerging from a coma after a TBI to be different from what they were before the injury. Is this because so many parts of your brain are shut down while other parts are compensating by over firing? I will leave that conundrum to medical professionals to determine.

SURVIVOR TIPS

Something I learned through this experience was the need to let others know what was going on with me. I had been brought up to not discuss most personal things or emotions with others. Communicating about my squeaky walker led to a wonderful outcome and the positivity of this experience encouraged me to speak up more and more. Of course, I suspect many people wished I had never found my voice! But remember that it is your life, and the consequences of your behaviour will belong to you alone. Please remember not to abuse your voice too frequently or it will lose its strength. Think of the "boy who cried wolf".

CHRISTMAS AND OUR TREASURE

AS A PATIENT of the rehabilitation hospital, I was thrilled to discover they sent you home for Christmas! We were avid downhill skiers and we had always enjoyed winter and snow. In fact, our romance started through the University Ski Team. It was not until my second or third year that I realized how awesome Dan was for me. I knew that I needed someone who was stronger willed than I was. I also appreciated how kind and straight he was, and untainted by external influences. He checked almost all the items on my checklist as the "perfect guy for me". His one flaw in my books was his diet. He was a meat and potatoes type of guy and that has not changed in thirty years. Instead of taking dance lessons prior to our wedding, I went to cooking school to learn more about cooking meat for Dan. The biggest beneficiary of these classes was my brother, who got to eat whatever I brought home from that week's lesson.

Back to wintering up north. Who would take care of our children while Dan skied? Thankfully, mom's abilities to problem-solve shone brightly once again. She found us a nanny/housekeeper, through a friend of hers who lived near the ski area. This woman, named "Treasure", encouraged me to conjure up numerous origins for her name. It turns out that she was originally from Niagara Falls, Ontario. This sounds corny but I have to say it, Treasure literally became *our treasure*. She took care of all of us. She ensured that Dan and the boys were happily fed. She organized me and whatever household tasks I might be able to accomplish, and I was able to nap while she was there. In the afternoons, the boys and I usually did art and crafts activities together. Again, the boys excelled way past my mediocrity.

That first Christmas after my accident, we had a full house. Treasure came after Christmas day, but I had lots of help. There were the four of us, my parents, and my brother who flew in from Vancouver. Dan's parents were a five-minute drive away. It was a wonderful and very special Christmas.

We started a routine that continued until I was let out of the hospital for good. I have to say that Dan was a good planner. Late every Friday afternoon, Dan would pick me up at the front door of the rehabilitation hospital in the middle of Toronto with the boys in the car. We would then drive up north to a chalet. By the second winter, the boys would be greeted by Treasure with plates of homemade cookies. To prevent any dissonance between them, Treasure strategically made a different flavour for each boy. The second winter, both Jack and I took ski lessons and we continued to have Treasure work for us. She became a part of our family for almost a decade.

I think that skiing can be a great family sport. If you live in Canada, we have the winter season which always involves snow. Now, there were a few sporty activities that I would choose to pull all of us together, but Dan was only interested in downhill skiing. Fine by me! My parents took up downhill skiing when their children showed an interest in finding the hills. While cross country skiing, my brother, Graham, and I walked up and skied down a hill repeatedly. Mom was not much of a skier, although her effort and attitude were admirable. Sometimes, she would sit at the bottom of the hills for an entire day and wait for us. She was happy to have successfully exhausted her children.

I love being outdoors and knew that I was very fortunate to have learned to ski because I absolutely loved it. I wanted to pass that enthusiasm on to my children in the hopes that we would all share in the same activity on weekends and winter holidays. Dan had been an excellent skier growing up and had ski-raced at the International Ski Federation (FIS) level. I was fortunate to have learned to ski when I was young and fearless.

Now, at 30 years of age and having downhill skied for at least two thirds of my life, I had to learn to ski again from the very beginning. Dan arranged at the ski school for me to take private lessons from a proficient and kind older instructor who managed to keep me safe and eventually more competent at it. I can still remember him encouraging me to sing as I went down the hill so that I would stop over-thinking on my way down. I am happy to report that I am downhill skiing again, as well as travelling to the Rockies each winter to ski there with my family.

I recall the hospital staff repeatedly saying that my self-awareness and insight were concerns. Brain injured individuals do not know the limits of their abilities because everything is "new" again and you do not know what you are capable of. In my past life, I had utilized a "trial and error" approach to most everything in life. I was usually successful, and I had never even broken a bone prior to this motor vehicle accident (MVA). The two things broken in this MVA were my clavicle and my brain.

Can you imagine how dangerous this "modus operandi," was for me when I aspired to participate in the activities I used to do? I kept trying and trying to participate in inappropriate activities in my first five years post-injury, none of which I was capable of tackling. I fell off my road bike going around the block because I could not unclip my pedals quickly enough. I also tried the "Adult House League Ski Racing" which turned out to extremely unsafe for me. Thankfully I kept crashing near the beginning of the course before I picked up any speed.

Socially, Dan shielded me at the ski club by explaining to his friends about my condition before I spoke to them. I spoke with a slow and slurred pronunciation, often being mistaken for being drunk. Dan also involved us in extra activities such as Scottish dancing. The second year back, a friend of his was organizing a "Robbie Burns" dinner which is a celebration of the Scottish Poet Robbie Burns. It included a demonstration of Scottish dancing and Dan signed us up for the weekly Friday night practices. Surprisingly, Dan turned out to be a strong dancer. The other ladies appreciated his smoothness and co-ordination, as we twirled in and out with different partners. My feet did not work very well, but I somehow managed to stay upright.

I was just not aware of my physical limitations and was encouraged to believe they were all related to my head injury. Most were of course, however there was other "collateral damage" by way of what was initially diagnosed as a drop foot. Turns out this was a misdiagnosis, and the real problem was an ACL tear, which I eventually had repaired. I mention this because this contributed to my difficulty in being able to re-learn how to walk.

Still, nothing seemed to be working very well. I was a terrible skier. Our boys were learning to ski much better than I was which is a common refrain of many parents eventually, but not when they are under 5 years old! I kept plodding along and I trained at the fitness club with the goal of improving my performance on the hill. It did not happen. I just never got into the rhythm of dancing down the hill like I used to. However, after being treated by Dr. Thornton 18 years after my accident I found myself finally able to achieve some degree of skiing ability. Not perfect, but better than not at all.

EMOTIONAL LABILITY

I HEARD THE term, "emotionally labile" being used frequently in the hospital with reference to me. Remember, my brain is not fully operational, and I became indignant at the accusation. How could I be emotionally labile? Being "labile" meant that I had done something wrong. How could I be at fault for anything when I could hardly do anything? I looked up its definition and discovered there existed a second interpretation of the word which is more accurate for my situation: "a person or thing whose presence or behaviour is likely to cause embarrassment or put one at a disadvantage." Yes, I excelled at being emotionally labile! I have tried very hard to bury my cringeworthy brain-injured behavior deep in my subconscious. Unfortunately, this behaviour persisted for almost two decades before any treatment occurred.

My children grew up not knowing their mother to be anything other than brain injured. When the day came that Dr. Thornton treated my emotional lability, there was a big improvement in their own levels of anxiety and comfort. It was easier for everyone to relax without Madeleine having a meltdown. What I learned from Dr. Thornton is that behaviour-management techniques to treat my outbursts did not work very well with my kind of brain damage, which was primarily in the frontal lobes of my brain. My mouth would open almost as fast as my blood surged into my head. Once I reached a certain peak of emotions, reasoning conversations did not work with me. I needed the appropriate medication to bring me down from these intense emotional over-reactions. I now understand the terminology of being "hot-headed". That was me, in top gear.

A significant milestone for me occurred after my treatment with Dr. Thornton. We were all sitting in a fully loaded car in our driveway and Dan was going through his vacation checklist prior to driving our family to a ski hill for the week. Jack spoke up, adding to the list by asking "Does Mommy have her medication"? This was a victory, all thanks to SPECT, medication, and psychotherapy.

I suggest that the best way to get through to a person in an emotionally charged state is to agree with them. Dan was the one who introduced me to this technique. He aligns it to the marital tactic of saying "Yes, dear," rather than to argue about something trivial. This is a two-way street in which my reply should also be "Yes, dear" to avoid unnecessary escalations in emotions.

PART II: LIVING WITH A BRAIN INJURY

I HAVE INCLUDED the topics that are often issues amongst a large proportion of TBI's, however there is still a vast number of individual differences. Areas of concern may be with any of the five senses, or they may be cognitive, emotional, or physical. My challenges were in all three domains.

It is very difficult to live with an unbalanced brain since you do not realize what areas are dominating and which brain areas are not functioning.

Certain tasks were modelled in therapy sessions after I left the hospital. Tasks for meal planning and looking up recipes, writing a shopping list and buying the ingredients before trying to cook something are examples. A speech pathologist recommended I read out-loud to improve my diction, which was also helpful.

Dr. Thornton wrote a mini book for his patients on <u>How to Live with a Brain Injury</u>. The guidance provided is helpful before you undergo the SPECT Scan procedure and treatment. Unfortunately, I did not have this book for a very long time into my brain injury. I know I could have behaved better if I had known about his treatment and seen this book earlier.

His tiny book is credit card sized so one can copy it and carry it in a shirt pocket or wallet. I have copied and inserted it with permission.

Please see the following pages <u>How to Live with a Brain Injury.</u>

HOW TO LIVE WITH A BRAIN INJURY

Page 1:

Heal Your Brain, Heal Your Soul, Heal Your Life.

4 + 4 = Balance

John F. Rossiter-Thornton M.D.

Page 2:

Be yourself by using…

The Fourfold Path for Every Day

4 Steps to a Happier Life

MEDITATE

PRAY

EXERCISE & EAT RIGHT

DO WHAT MAKES YOUR HEART SING

These Four Steps Work When You Use Them

Spend a little time with each step Every Day

Page 3:

For Interacting with Others:

Follow The Four Agreements: A Practical Guide to Personal Freedom by don Miguel Ruiz

BE IMPECCABLE WITH YOUR WORD
DON'T TAKE ANYTHING PERSONALLY
DON'T MAKE ASSUMPTIONS
ALWAYS DO YOUR BEST

Challenging Interactions? Do an Agreement Scan on Everyone Involved.

Understanding the Issues Can Show a Way Forward

Page 4:
My book is intentionally short,
so that time saved can be used to
put the steps into practice, a little bit every day.

Further reading:
The 4 Agreements, by Don Miguel Ruiz

The Prayer Wheel Program,
J.F. Rossiter-Thornton M.D.

For more information: www.theprayerwheel.com

A Shirt Pocket Shrink Publication
Copywrite 2010 Rossiter-Thornton Enterprises Inc.

A common term I heard from many health care professionals was that of referring to me as a survivor. For many years, I refused to acknowledge or identify as a "survivor." I thought it was a bit corny giving myself this title and I was a little embarrassed, even ashamed, to have that label. In my mind, the term survivor was for individuals who had survived cancer. I had not recovered in the way a cancer patient has after enduring agonizing treatments. How could I truly be a survivor? Yes, I was alive, but I was not cured, as cancer patients frequently are. Once I was 100%, then I would call myself a survivor. Again, these are the thoughts emanating from an only partially functioning brain.

One of the first things I did when I got home from the hospital was to check myself out in the mirror. Would I be able to see my invisible injury? I was hoping that I'd look good from all that weight-loss, but I had done nothing to maintain my muscles, so I had zero shape. All I saw was the reflection of a sickly and -unhealthy looking woman. I did not want this to be permanent and I realized my external self-image was easier to repair than what was inside my head. This was valuable because people tend to treat others better if they convey a positive image of themselves. Things such as a good haircut, co-ordinated clothing, attention to accessories and make-up are all useful ways to accomplish this. Simplicity in addressing these areas is also very important. A quick routine with clothes that are mix and match will save you energy. You do not need to have expensive haircuts or clothes, rather focus on being clean and as well-groomed as possible (hair brushed, beard trimmed).

My next issue was to pinpoint exactly where on the continuum of abilities I had landed. I sat down and read my way through all the hospital and therapists' reports about me. How discouraging it all was. I felt even worse. There was a ton of paper used to document my deficits and disabilities.

That day was the first and only self-directed pep talk. I said: "Madeleine Janet Welton, is this all that you will amount to for the rest of your life?" "Are you going to crawl under a rock and hide forever?" I answered myself and lacking the verbal wordsmithing skills of my husband, I borrowed his phrase: "Yes it is time to take names and kick ass". Interestingly, I wrote down names and put them into one of two lists. The "good" list was for those who were kind or helpful to me (or family) during this time. There was also a "bad" list which were the names for those who never called or offered support and seemed almost afraid to engage with me. The only ass kicking I did was pushing myself in the gym.

All of this was made slightly more difficult because of my high anxiety levels. I had felt this overwhelming angst since I woke up in the hospital which eventually felt like my normal state. I was consumed by the following thoughts, which went through my head on a continuous recorded loop:

1. When I arrived home, I was worried about almost everything.
   - I was worried that people wouldn't accept me in my new brain-injured state.
   - I was worried that I could not realistically raise our two children, Jack and James.
   - I was worried that I was fat, not eating properly, not exercising enough, and not wearing the right clothes.
   - I was worried that I was a lot dumber than I had been before and maybe I was so stupid I just did not realize it.
   - I was worried that Dan, underneath ignoring me, really thought I was super disgusting and would leave me floundering on my own.

- I had worries that just did not stop, and they replayed on and on.

Eighteen years later, I finally admitted some of these worries to Dr. Thornton. He suggested that my high anxiety levels may have helped my recovery up until that point. Because I had never felt good enough in my earlier life, I had continued to try and become better. I even researched a few things on-line that purported to fix an injured brain but were dismissed by me as from snake-oil salesmen!

One big surprise was my ability to focus intensely on a topic. That is likely why I was able to pull together enough information (off the internet, from Pub med, and by emailing doctors about scientific treatments) to do my own lit review about brain injuries. This became my full-time job.

The first time I realized this intensity of focus was after a case manager had encouraged me to return to school for an interior design class. Here I was severely brain injured yet I managed to score an "A" in the class. I was able to focus with intensity on one assignment because I had no competition from other parts of my brain. Do not be stubborn. Have an open mind, take your time, and then make your decision about what you want focus on. It is YOUR life, and this is the only one you are going to get, for better or worse.

SHORT TERM MEMORY PROBLEMS

IN THE NEXT interior design class, I managed to forget my book bag one day. I took that as a sign for me to focus on life that was closer to home. What was the point of getting me ready to work if I could only manage one thing? In my early condition, (anything within the first five years post-injury) I did not expect to be productive in the work force. All my energies would have to be directed at a job, driving there, working, and driving home. I could not do it. I knew that I would be too tired to work out at the gym or play any role in our sons' lives.

As only a part of my brain was working back then, my cognitive abilities were severely compromised by the injured parts, and over-powered by the parts that were working at a furious pace. Such a combination caused significant personality changes. Fortunately, the short-term memory problems allowed me to forget what caused me grief as well as my own abominable behaviour. I wonder if such memory issues are built-in mechanisms for survival. When I expressed concern about forgetting to explain myself properly in conversation, Dan replied to me by saying, "Mad, don't worry about it, people know that you do not have an agenda. First, you would need to remember what your agenda was and secondly, you would tell everyone about it." While this comment could be interpreted negatively, I was greatly relieved that I was seen as guileless.

Word finding could have been a big issue (and was) but having spent years of my life reading books for pleasure, I could find synonyms quickly. I had learned a large enough vocabulary to express myself properly. If I was stuck, I would revert to a synonym. However, as the years have passed by, I have found myself less fluent with my words.

The saddest and cruelest example of my short-term memory deficit was its impact on others. During my stay at Sunnybrook hospital, my mother told me of a situation she felt that I should address with Dan. As he was leaving my hospital room, my mother was coming in. She asked me if I had seen Dan recently. I broke down in tears and said, that "he never comes." I carried on and wailed that he didn't "want anything to do with me, and that I was an inconvenience to him." Dan overheard yet was disciplined enough to attribute my words to my brain injury. I cannot bear to think of how much I must have hurt him over the years.

"Out of sight and out of my mind." It just did not register with me. I always figured that when my brain had healed enough to retain more memories, then it would. In the meantime, my little brain would work on repairing itself to the best of its abilities. But how effective could the healing be if those abilities were so compromised? I knew how to be healthy, as in eating properly, exercising, and taking supplements—but was that enough?

Health-care professionals tested me many times to make sure they had my short-term memory loss documented to a precise degree. Testing took place initially in hospital and then both sets of lawyers (the insurance company's legal team and my lawyers) sent me to be tested again. All this documentation of my abilities, or my lack thereof was for the lawsuits that were to follow.

I recall sitting at a testing table that belonged to a psychologist hired by my lawyers. The tester wanted to know why I had such a poor grasp of literature if I had graduated with a Bachelor of Arts Degree. I was completely stumped as I tried to recall the names of the books she referenced. This was one of the happiest "losses" which I experienced because I could read any book in the world as if it were my very first time. Pure joy.

In occupational therapy at the Riverdale Hospital, I was taught many strategies to cope with my memory. I still use many of these skills and have found that the more that I try to accomplish, the more I need them. One example is always leaving things in the same location. We have bowls of car keys near the front door and the garage door. This ensures that everyone leaves their keys in one of the bowls—otherwise, pandemonium ensues while we investigate coat pockets, purses and drawers. Obviously, this is not an issue for just those with brain injuries.

SURVIVOR TIPS FOR ORGANIZATION

1. Always leave such as coats, keys, and cellphones in one certain place.
2. Write reminders and lists. I had grown up with lists (Mom, school, activities…). The difficult part is remembering where I put the list!

3. Today one can put everything on a phone, which I am no longer likely to lose, thanks to my new more balanced brain.
4. Use a day planner or a cell phone calendar religiously.

After I returned home, I tried to make use of these "memory helpers" every day. They did not work when I was at the gym, nor later when I would be on the golf course. It is hilarious that I thought I could participate in golf when I literally could not remember if I had taken five shots on a hole or seven shots. When I played with Dan, I usually put in my maximum just to keep up. (Please be assured, the Pro shop told me to do that if I picked up my ball).

At this time, most MDs knew little about brain injury and the options available for their patients. The brain is so complicated that medical doctors must spend many extra years to become psychiatrists or neurologists specializing in brain injuries. I think that referring brain injured individuals to a psychiatrist should become the standard of care.

My former family doctor referred me to a psychiatrist once, a few years after I had returned home. This was after I experienced the nightmare of visiting the inside of a police station for the first time in my life. This was not because I was upset about something that happened to me, but rather I was infuriated regarding what someone had done to Dan. This situation wasted my energy for a very long time. The solution that was provided to me was easy to follow:

1. Avoid the people who incited me to anger
2. Continue with psychotherapy.

It appears that I have been involved intermittently with psychotherapy for most of my recovery. Still, I did not see a real difference in my psychotherapy sessions until I met Dr. Thornton. He combined what he saw on my SPECT scans with what he uncovered during my psychotherapy session to prescribe the appropriate medications. Simply defined, *Psychotherapy* is "talk therapy".

The biggest **oxymoron** in medicine that I noticed is this: most **people who experience traumatic brain injuries are unable to investigate and select their own options for recovery. Even if the information is out there, how do they connect with it?**

If we can enable individuals with TBIs to restore function to their brains, they will be able to navigate their own futures. A balanced brain will allow individuals to select possible treatments and therapies, however, it must be stressed that the symptoms need to also be linked to the appropriate therapies. How many people know what to do or where to go for specific therapies? That is why your family doctor (the quarterback of your health care needs) is so important.

CRITICISM

UNFORTUNATELY, CRITICISM PLAYED a large part in Dan's personal strategy with me. Current studies on behaviour modification conclusively agree in a greater success rate using positive reinforcement such as praising a desired behaviour versus negativity. I was criticized and corrected for much of what I said and did. The more Dan tried to help me in this way, the more I hated him. It may have worked when coaching little league football and teaching young boys new plays (as in, this is the correct action, and this is the wrong one). But I was often unable to do what he was trying to suggest to me because of my long list of disabilities. He had no idea the information he was sharing did not make it through my neural network properly. This resulted in my feeling like I had failed him yet again, and I resented him for it. Dan had nobody to show him how to maintain a marriage with a brain injured wife. The majority of marriages dissolve after a spouse has a brain injury.

While I was physically included in many activities, I often felt like a piece of furniture. I could never figure out what to say fast enough in a group situation and realized that some people understood and just let me be. But I wanted to contribute so badly… I was aware how diminished I was intellectually, physically, and emotionally. Deep down, I only wanted Dan to see me with the eyes he once had for me. We had complimented each other in many ways because each of our strengths would cover the others' weaknesses. But now, absolutely everything became Dan's responsibility. I had nothing to offer anymore.

As the years progressed, Dan started to speak over me to others, dismissing my attempts to contribute. I hated that I was such a foggy-brained simpleton. My brain was not working well enough to even attempt to contribute on an equal playing field. Or, if I did succeed in stopping the conversation to interject a few words, I would have forgotten what I was going to say.

This stopped the day we rode a ski lift with an uncle of Dan's. This gentleman interrupted Dan, in response to him cutting me off mid-sentence by asking if I could please repeat myself and mildly scolding Dan that I had been speaking first. I felt visible and was forever grateful to this kind man. Dan did not realize how hurtful his behaviour was for me or that he should care what I had to say.

Exasperated with my inability to live up to his standards and the continuous stream of criticisms, I said "enough." We did have a discussion wherein I explained that "If you cannot stop criticizing and constantly correcting me, I want out (even in my disabled state). I can no longer live like this". I briefly questioned if my existence was dependent upon his evaluation of me.

I still really wanted to be married to the Dan I had married. But not only had I changed, he changed too. Our relationship had deteriorated under the weight of my stagnated recovery and his high-stress business. The construction industry during the first twenty years of our marriage was difficult, (a.k.a. a buyer's market). He started building low rise townhomes shortly after we married and worked for a different builder (referred to by his father). After learning how to build one phase of townhomes, he continued to do the next two phases on his own. The trickiest part of building is finding financial support. We mortgaged everything we had for many years, and I contributed my own finances to the business. We saved all the profits of his projects to use for equity for the next phase of building. It was stressful always having to bargain shop for most of the year and then maybe have a month at the end of a project (every 2-4 years) to buy some needed things. I was spoiled rotten by my father who after several years of wondering why I never had any money, started gifting me a cheque at Christmas to cover my expenses such as the golf club membership dues.

I apologized frequently for not being the woman he had married. I was a mess. I was not as smart, athletic, or good looking as the woman he was used to. One of these attributes might be a considerable loss, but everything? The worst issue with the changes in me was that I yelled a lot, or argued with him just to avoid accepting that he thought I was wrong. It was exhausting and demoralizing being at home with this going on.

But I was determined that one day, Dan would see me for who I had become, and not who I had once been.

SURVIVOUR TIPS FROM BEHAVIOURAL THERAPY

- Positive reinforcement works much better than negative reinforcement.
- Positive reinforcement helps builds new neural pathways and helps the brain heal.

THREE TBI ISSUES LEADING TO CHAOS

(1) SENSE OF location or geography used to be second nature to me. I always ended up where I was supposed to be. I had a summer job once as a securities messenger which involved running around downtown Toronto delivering things. After my accident, I had difficulties finding my car in a parking lot. Strange as it may seem, I did not realize that this issue was specifically related to a part of my brain that was injured. I assumed that I was just slower and less able overall. Fortunately, it is once again automatic, but for almost twenty years, I had to devise methods to assist me in finding my car.

When I went to the fitness club, I always tried to park my car in the same row to avoid losing it. This strategy worked well if the parking lot was not super busy. I devised a methodical system in my head for parking on busier days. Short of having flashing lights and sirens installed, I tried to park in a spot within visibility of that first row, so that I would see it when I looked over in that direction. Bad things happened when I drove a different car and inevitably forgot that I had driven a different one.

(2) Distractibility is a basic characteristic of traumatic brain injury. It presents as acquired attention deficit disorder (AADD). Frontal lobe damage occurs commonly in TBIs so acquired AADD is also common. Learning how to focus and having the discipline not to let your mind wander is the key to addressing this problem, and it is easily treated with proper medication. Ritalin has been replaced by a newer medication (Vyvanse) that works in the body differently and without the jittery side effects.

(3) Disinhibition is another prevalent issue. The only solution for disinhibition is to train yourself not to react to things and then not to act on that reaction. Depending upon the situation, behaviours such as taking a deep breath or counting to ten before reacting can be a useful technique. However, with more volatile concerns, reactions are unlikely to be quashed without more serious interventions.

Positive role-modelling is more effective than negative comments and discipline. Behavioural corrections, no matter how kindly intended, did not stick in my brain. Remember, you are re-learning everything. Does something need to be pushed out of your brain to take in the new suggestions? Do you have time to evaluate what? Some survivors will have recall of their behaviour but maybe only in certain settings. Others will have blank canvases which need to be fully re-created with healthy age-appropriate behaviours.

Furthermore, different types of learners benefit from information being presented differently. Reading about behavioural suggestions may help visual learners and can be reinforced by repetition. Others are auditory learners, and account for about half of the population. Kinesthetic learners (or tactile learners) account for a much smaller proportion. If one is not an auditory learner, how can the person recall a correction on top of everything else? Disinhibition may be acquired from damage to numerous parts of the brain. It may present as a lack of judgement, lack of insight, and lack of foresight in committing anti-social behaviour. Again, based on the premise of this book, I advise seeing a psychiatrist for medical advice for these issues.

Once I was treated and my brain was tweaked as close to perfection as it was going to get, the many negative emotional characteristics which I displayed such as disinhibition, distractibility, anger, impulsiveness, hyper-sexuality, and lack of sensitivity to others just disappeared. Interestingly, I can pull out those scandalous behaviours when I want to, but now I have made a conscious decision not to do so. My brain has been balanced and I can finally go forward and learn more efficiently and more effectively, through repetition, and thanks to neuroplasticity.

NEUROPLASTICITY

MY ACCIDENT HAPPENED years before Norman Doidge discovered neuroplasticity which is the ability of the brain to reorganize itself (adapt and change) by forming new neural connections throughout life. If parts of the brain are damaged, the brain will compensate by reorganizing and forming new connections between intact neurons in different regions. However, for this to work, the neurons need to be stimulated through activity and new learning.

In layman's terms, neuroplasticity is using undamaged parts of the brain to do what the damaged parts of the brain used to do. While neuroplasticity may seem to be the great solution to brain injury, by itself neuroplasticity does not repair or open dormant parts of the brain or correct any of the damage that is present from a brain injury.

One thing that concerned me at the time was that I did not know how to direct any of this 'learning" into a new segment of my brain. I tried to ask people how to do this and was often met with blank stares. As it turned out, I did not need to know how to achieve this because our brains do it automatically. Any newly learned information either goes to a new or repaired part of the brain and this information is then stored there. We do not need to know where, only that it is there.

Three years ago, we built our "forever home". I was thrilled to be able to make selections that I wanted. I used the professional services of the friend who returned my book bag from that final decorating class. I was flummoxed as I could never find the words to describe what was flashing in front of my mind's eye. I would find myself talking and then inserting the phrase, "my left brain and my right brain are not communicating with each other right now. I know what I want, but I cannot seem to verbalize it." One day, I asked myself why this was happening and practiced trying to recall what I was thinking. I discovered that the items I was storing were visual images which I could retrieve but I still could not verbalize my vision. A solution or easy fix for this issue was to verbally describe things out loud as I visualized them. This improved recall of the images and allowed me to communicate what it was I was visualizing. The moral is this story would be that to retrieve certain information, you need to store it by using the same method you will be using to retrieve it.

Neuroplasticity can work far better if your brain is balanced through use of SPECT scanning, psychotherapy, and the proper medications as prescribed by your psychiatrist.

IF IT ISN'T MY COORDINATION, THEN WHAT IS WRONG?

WHEN OTHERS SAW me walk many assumed that I had a balance problem. However, in yoga classes, I was able to hold and maintain the poses if they were not standing poses, although I did start to master stationary standing poses too. Also, I could downhill ski (because my feet were stationary and encased in hard ski boots) and ride a bike. I tried to strengthen my ankles which never seemed to help. I realized that my issue was connected to some type of agility or mobility concern. I knew that but for most of my adult life, I did not know why I could not walk well. Where do you go for answers to solve this issue? Again, after all this time, I am wondering if this is a job for my new and amazing family doctor?

Year after year, I stressed over learning how to walk better. I could not figure out why my body was not cooperating. I did not know what a torn ACL entailed or what a dropped foot was. Why would I think to look that information up if it was not even on my radar? I guess I had expected a therapist or doctor to figure this out for me or direct me to the appropriate resource to figure it out. No one ever said anything about it, so I did not think it was a big deal. Until it was. It was obvious to me that I had something wrong, but I did not know how to get to the bottom of it.

All that I could contribute to this issue was practice. I practised walking methodically which is "heel-toe, heel-toe." I often spoke these words as I marched along. Why on earth was it so difficult to get this back? Both my boys learned to walk before they were a year old, and in a very short time were walking far better than I was. No matter how much walking I did, I never seemed to improve. I started with the laps in the rehab hospital and continued by walking around large blocks in our new neighbourhood, I walked pedestrian trails on the major traffic routes, I walked laps at the gym. If I was out of the city in northern Ontario, I would walk along the highway. I love forest walks and so does our dog, Duke. Over the years, I have read several times about "forest bathing," and that trees give off chemicals which reduce stress and improve one's mood. I asked for technique tips from physical therapists and personal trainers to know what to think of as I walked. It has been almost 30 years now and I still think of my movements when I walk. Duke and I "bathe", rather than "walk". Fortunately, Nordic Walking Poles are turning out to be a great success for my technique of "bathing" in the forest.

Initially, I had mild right-side paralysis which was an obvious cause for my walking disability. I was forced to be left-handed which meant holding the cane in my left hand, writing with my left hand, and even eating with the spoon or fork in my left hand. I was not very graceful or co-ordinated. Still, I thought to myself, there is a positive aspect in having to use my non-dominant side. Both sides of my brain needed to be activated and then used in my daily life. I interpreted it to mean that by working both sides of my brain, I would undoubtedly get better faster. I think that optimism helps, although the right side of my brain turned out to be the more impaired side.

Writing with my left hand was not pretty. This was solved with the evolution of personal computers which were beginning to go mainstream. I decided that it would be in my best interests to take all the free time I had (which was most of my day) and re-learn how to type. I bought a child's typing game and an adult learn-to-type program. The typing not only provided me with a legible way to communicate, to write grocery lists and to-do lists, but it also improved my fine motor skills, insofar as my handwriting also improved.

When I discovered that there was no standardization for treating a brain injury, I had to build my own team. Trying to integrate many different specialties was difficult enough, but I was also trying to determine what specialties I required. Don't forget, my quintessential definition of an Oxymoron: "trying to use your injured brain, to fix your brain." As a result, this "team-building event" took many years. I did waste time on tangential activities such as having a triathlon coach. What was I thinking? Yeah, yeah. I was going to get more oxygen into my brain. Again, not in itself a successful route in its application. But the underlying hypothesis was correct.

Serendipitously, the triathlon training led me to search out a highly regarded sports doctor recommended by the athletes I encountered at the health club. His quick analyses complemented my journey of increasing the amount of oxygen reaching my brain. Dr. Galea had just started treating soft tissue injuries with Hyperbaric Oxygen Therapy (HBOT). The use of this method was a far more advanced concept than my basic idea of increasing the duration and frequency of cardiovascular workouts. Without a soft tissue injury (my knee) interrupting my life, I may never have recovered the use of my brain. I became a devout proponent of HBOT which has many uses. Not all are covered by the government health care system in Ontario.

CHRONIC NECK PAIN (WHIPLASH)

CHRONIC NECK PAIN is common with individuals who experience motor vehicle accidents (MVAs). In my situation, it was far down the list of my concerns related to the brain injury, but consistent in its effect since I had never really thought about it. I just took care of it. I started by visiting chiropractors during the first five years to address this issue. I experienced relief from neck pain temporarily, but this never goes away permanently. The problem was created by the stretching of the neck muscles and surrounding ligaments as a result of the impact of the accident. There are several methods of temporary treatment for this condition.

1. Chiropractors:

    I first sought out chiropractors to alleviate this pain in my neck. One practitioner suggested the following exercises:
    - Rotating your neck in both directions.
    - Tilting your head side to side.

- Bending your neck toward your chest.
- Raise your shoulders up towards the ears.
- I still perform this routine if my neck is bothering me, and I have no further ideas about treatment for chronic whiplash.

2. Atlas Orthogonal Adjustment:

   After a few years of attending sessions with Dr. Thornton, he noticed me massaging my neck one day. He then referred me to a chiropractor named Dr. Baird, located in Stouffville, Ontario. Dr. Baird performs a procedure call the "Atlas Orthogonal Adjustment", which is a non-invasive procedure. The neck is lined up with the "Atlas machine", that has a small, soft protruding knob (the size of a pencil eraser) and pressure is gently applied. X-rays of my neck were required beforehand to determine the precise point of contact.

   Dr. Baird also uses Bio Flex Laser Therapy after performing his orthogonal adjustment. The intention of the laser is to instill permanence to the adjustment. The only drawback for me was the driving distance to his office. I had one of the most frightening experiences driving there one time, and it would have been my fault.

3. Osteopathic:

   I also had my neck pain manually treated by an osteopath. These professionals specialize in soft tissue injuries. He showed me how to alleviate the pain myself and where to massage the vertebrae of my neck.

4. Massage:

   I used massage to alleviate my neck pain during the first fifteen years of my recovery. Insurance covered a certain number of chiropractic sessions and a certain number of massage sessions. I tended to run out of chiropractic sessions but somehow always forgot to utilize massage therapy.

5. Acupuncture:

   I am seeing an acupuncturist/naturopath for my shoulder, face, and whatever else needs healing. I mentioned my neck problem to the acupuncturist, and it got treated right away. One acupuncture visit enables me to have all problem areas on my body treated for one fee.

BRAIN INJURY ASSOCIATIONS

FOR SEVERAL MONTHS after I returned home from the hospital, my mother urged me to contact my local brain injury association. She had found the Ontario Brain Injury Association extremely helpful for educating her about brain injury. Finally, I attended a Brain Injury Association meeting in the mid-1990's with Dan. At this meeting, there were professionals who dealt with brain injury as well as survivors, and a speaker. Before the speaker's presentation, there were refreshments, which provided an opportunity for attendees to mingle. I suppose that was meant to be helpful, but Dan and I pretty much kept to ourselves. The only thing we, as a group, had in common was our injury, which doesn't bode well for interactions. A main symptom of traumatic brain injury is an incredible degree of self-absorption. In reflecting on my own anti-social behaviour, I realized that other survivors did not really want to engage with me either. Check that experience off my list. I could now tell my mother that I had done it and had no intentions of attending another one.

Little did I know what my future would hold. In 2003, ten years after my injury, I joined the board of the Brain Injury Association Canada (BIAC), now Brain Injury Canada (BIC). It was all because of coffee! As I have mentioned several times over, fatigue had a large impact on my life. Caffeine was a great short-term fix to spark the neurons in my frontal lobes and to help battle the fatigue.

I frequently stopped at the same coffee shop because it was located centrally to most of my activities. Once a week, many other mothers whose children went to the same school as my sons gathered there. One of the ladies was concerned about being late to attend an Annual General Meeting located almost an hour out of town. I inquired of her what AGM she was attending and found out that she was the chair of the Ontario Brain Injury Association's (OBIA) fundraising committee. I am sure it was obvious to her that I was brain injured. I still blurted out, "I was brain-injured and said that I would like to help her if I could. I no longer had any connection to the world of brain injury, and this seemed like a good place to start my search for an answer to my question. Well, I was very useful as a face of brain injury for her fundraising activity.

This serendipitous encounter turned out to be the first step in my journey through my brain injury's "road to recovery". The former chair of fundraising for the Ontario Brain Injury Association was Bonnie Crombie. At the time of writing this, she is the current mayor of Mississauga, Ontario. Bonnie asked me to join the committee of an Ontario Brain Injury Association (OBIA) fundraiser. All I had to do was attend the planning sessions, (which always included dinner at her house) and to fill a small table for the event. The next event was much more work, as I was tasked with the Silent Auction. My visible disability enabled me to collect gifted items easily in exchange for a taxable exemption receipt for the donors.

Soon after this successful event, Bonnie phoned me to ask my permission before she shared my telephone number with another member from the OBIA fundraiser. Howard, a member of the OBIA board of directors, wanted to know if I would be interested in being part of the newly formed Brain Injury Association of Canada (BIAC). The initial organizational structure was to have a brain injured "survivor" from each province, as well as a non-injured representative.

Howard was the non-injured representative from Ontario and the chair of fundraising. He asked me to be the survivor representative in his fundraising endeavours. I agreed to go to Quebec and join the BIAC. I was nervous the first year when I had to speak in front of all the attendees at the brain injury conference and be nominated to the board of directors. This was less of a feat when I look back at the event. Yet, it was the first time I had ever put my name out there for any election. I joined the board of the BIAC in the second year of its inception. The idea behind its formation was to strengthen the awareness of brain injury with a cohesive voice across the country. These conferences were full of brain injured people from all over Canada. It brought us together because of only one thing, but it was a "thing" that made us unique and separate from the rest of society. It was not an interest that brought us together but our very essence of being. Because the conferences last a few days, we did have time to interact and share our experiences personally.

The fundraising platform we used at the beginning enabled BIAC and the local brain injury association to generate funds which were spilt 50/50. BIAC's fundraising committee was to provide a fundraising vehicle for local brain injury associations to avail of. The local associations were required to generate guests, prizes and perform all the functional tasks in running a fundraiser. Howard like to call them "Fun Raisers". The theme that year was the 'Hawaiian Oyster Odyssey".

One major roll I played at these Hawaiian Oyster Odyssey fundraisers was to speak at these events. Public speaking was something that had always terrified me, yet here I was able to speak because of two new factors. First, I was intimately familiar with my topic and secondly, I had no inhibitions. I could get up in front of people and talk forever. Another good outcome of frontal lobe damage.

What did I speak about? My good fortune here was to be provided with the theme of that year's event. Howard would suggest a topic aligned with that year's guest speaker, whom he recruited. I would allocate at least a week trying to write out a speech, edit it and re-write it several times. I do recall trying to leave the stage with an upbeat or funny remark. When I spoke, the room was so silent you could hear a pin drop. One year, my mother was the one to drop! She literally fainted after I had finished speaking.

This story of our travelling adventure to the annual BIAC Conference in Pierrefonds, Quebec, illustrates our lack of awareness. There were many people who helped behind the scenes, without our being aware of the need at the time. We would all meet at Union Station to buy our tickets for the train. Howard would bring several young female professionals to act as chaperones for the survivors. I do not think that any one of us believed they themselves needed chaperones. It is likely that we each assumed they were for other people in our party. These women would quietly and inconspicuously spread out amongst us. They lowered the dynamics of the group while keeping us company and providing any assistance required. One kind lady taught me how to play Sudoku.

As chair of the fundraising department, Howard flew all over the country to be present at these Hawaiian Oyster Odyssey events, until one day he could not attend an event in Prince Edward Island (P.E.I.). Using my airmiles, I happily flew down. I shared a room with the first president of the BIAC, Mireille, in a motel next door to the event. This event was a great deal of fun for me. They had games, prizes and a celebrity chef named Michael Smith shucking oysters. I was awe struck and ate as many oysters as I could. Was it possible to absorb some of his cooking talent through his presence? I then won a box of lobsters in the raffle, which were cooked when I picked them up the next day. I had a wonderful time and love P.E.I.

Eventually, the success of the initial fundraising efforts enabled the BIAC to host larger conferences in larger hotels. Now, they host at least one major conference a year. The conference schedule can be found at: braininjurycanada.ca (bic.com). The name was changed to Brain Injury Canada (BIC) to make it easier to say and easier to remember.

The Ontario Brain Injury Association, (OBIA), had developed a significant outreach in the province of Ontario. The OBIA had been in existence since 1986 and chose not to join BIAC. This may have been due to OBIA's already well-developed organizational structure. Each of the other provinces needed to design their own unique network, compatible with the health care model that existed within their province. In 2010, educator John Kumpf took over as executive director of OBIA and made extensive improvements to Ontario's brain injury network. He developed many educational courses for caregivers and health-care workers with brain injury. The first course is called "Brain Basics". Many of us at BIAC have taken this course.

The OBIA holds an annual conference in Niagara Falls. It brings together survivors, caregivers, and professionals in the brain injury industry. There are lectures on a variety of issues. It allows for education, social interaction, and storytelling. There are also booths of many sponsors who play valuable roles, such as the top brain injury association plaintiff lawyers, therapeutic businesses to treat brain injury concerns, and many assistive devices. There are also many booksellers there.

Unfortunately, I think the brain injury associations miss a lot of people. I remember that I felt too injured and unable to interact properly to even attend a function. If 160,000 people have brain injuries every year, is it just the luck of the draw who gets involved or has a serendipitous encounter? What happens to all the other individuals who are injured brains, living in isolation?

SOCIAL INTERACTIONS

INTERACTING WITH OTHERS and being in public places has its challenges. Your megaphone may be turned on or turned off. This could be due to the excitement from the stimuli you may experience. Or, if you are in a group situation, you may be trying to talk over others. Obviously, this is rude and inappropriate. It is still rude when your reason for trying to speak over someone else is because you know you will likely forget what you wanted to say. It is better just not to try. Your time will come.

Brain-injured people need to realize that their self-centred tendencies will affect their behaviour negatively. This is difficult to do in the moment. Often, I will realize what I have done after the fact, and lament to myself, "Oh, why did I not shut up?"

Maybe you could have one or two stories that you can use as examples. Get someone to help you select two stories and practice rehearsing them with you. I used to write ideas out. There is always a need for repetition. After SPECT treatment, you may still need to repeat something a few times. I still require some things to be repeated twice before they are embedded in my brain. Compare this with several years of repetition for an untreated brain.

I thought my simple life was exciting. I even bought a cell phone cover that said, "Life is a Party" if for no other reason than to make me laugh at myself.

At the other end of the continuum, you may be too quiet, even timid. While I am personally familiar with being both an introvert and an extrovert, I have only experienced brain injury through the eyes of the latter. If you have previously experienced life as an introvert, imagine the difficulties if you are brain injured.

1. See a psychiatrist. There is medication that can alleviate your anxiety. SPECT Scans are ideal tools for determining levels of anxiety and the degree to which it may be influencing your life.

2. Who do you socialize with? Your family. They will hopefully be able to provide you with unconditional love. If you follow the instructions for getting a SPECT scan, then your behaviour should be stable in just a few years. Mine took over twenty years since it takes about two years or more for the new learning to help.

The Law Family: James and Jack. Back Row: Dan, me, brother-in-law Bruce with baby Rosalynd, my sister Jennifer, Mom, Dad, brother Graham.

3. Special Interest Groups: sports, the arts, education, volunteering, faith-oriented programs, clubs or associations that are special to you. If you do not belong to anything at all, maybe this is a good time to think of what interests you such as participating in political campaigns or going back to school. Do whatever it is that makes you tick.

The photo below was of me in a playoff after sitting down to dinner at a charity golf event. They realized there was a tie and had us hit off golf mats to a target in the valley below. Let me just say, we won!

SURVIVOR TIPS

1. Try to make a habit of using well-rehearsed replies to others' questions.

    Q: "How are you?"

    A: "Fine, thank you. How are you?" Try not to go on for ten minutes about your brain injury.

    Q: "How are you coping with your brain injury?"

    A: "I am learning a lot about brain injury. I had no idea there was so much to learn".

IT PROBLEMS

LEARNING TO DEAL with impulsive behaviour was my Achilles heel. Whatever my impulse in responding to an unpleasant event, it was usually the wrong one. Once triggered, my survival mechanism kicks in, and ugliness follows.

    I have two horrible examples of events that occurred to me in the past year. The past year means that I had already been treated by Dr. Thornton and everything I could do was done. There was the situation where I forgot my evening medication the night before an airline flight. That will never happen again as I now carry reserves in my purse. My second unfortunate situation involved the sending of an impulsive and angry email. Even after being treated and being medicated, I found myself listening to my angry husband regarding a situation which kept evolving into more of a serious problem. In an impulsive and hot-headed moment, I found myself writing the most horrible email I could conjure up. Designed to be as nasty and spiteful as possible, I erased it from my computer immediately when I finished putting all thoughts down, but not before I had hit "send". Why I did not have a file for personal thoughts like a diary is beyond me. Of course, it did come back to bite me.

How to Handle E-mails with a TBI:

1. Never send new emails directly from your mail. Try to ensure that you compose emails in "word' first. This is very important for those times when emotions are running high. It formalizes the action of writing and hopefully prevents you from doing anything rash.
2. Avoid directly replying to emails.
3. File it away and do not send. Re-read it later and modify it. Being rude or abusive never gets the response you really want. Being kind and understanding is much more effective, and you are more likely to get a positive response to your complaint.
4. Once the angry email has been sent, it becomes permanent on the internet.

SEXUALITY

I WANTED TO add this topic to my book because it should not be avoided by the brain injured population. When only part of your brain is working, the heightened or diminished interest in sex may contribute negatively to your behaviours. Yes, one can sublimate this area of your life, but the two ways it manifests can cause major problems especially, if you are in a relationship. Talking about this topic makes many people uncomfortable. It made me uncomfortable, and while I knew something was very much "off" for me, who could I talk to? I have added the subject in the hope you may recognize aberrant symptoms around your sexuality that you can address with your health care provider. Again, sexuality is an issue for every single individual with a traumatic brain injury.

How on earth does someone with a severe brain injury talk about sex when so many people without brain injuries shun this topic? I realize that while there are many definitions and identifiers for people's sexuality, there are two major concerns that are mutually shared. The first problem is the most common issue, and that is having too little sexual stimulation. This may cause you to try and close off this portion of your life forever. How will that play out with your partner or spouse if they want to stay with you and support your recovery? Alternatively, you may become hypersexual, which can also cause problems, as with this heightened sense of arousal you may think everything in the world revolves around sex. Unfortunately, this was my issue. To all those I may have embarrassed, please accept my apologies.

An increased interest in sex is referred to as hypersexual and a decrease is referred to as hyposexual. Increased sexual desire occurs in some TBIs, but apparently a decreased sexual desire is more common. The best advice as a TBI survivor that I have to offer you is to identify if either of these scenarios affects you, and then talk to your health-care provider (your family doctor, nurse practitioner, or psychiatrist). There is a whole field of information designed to assist and guide you, although having your SPECT scans done and treatment prescribed could nullify this need.

Addressing this issue properly is much better than being constantly embarrassed by what you do. For me, I was hypersexual and, combined with my disinhibition and impulsiveness, I cringe at what behaviours may have occurred. Once my brain was treated by Dr. Thornton, there were no lingering issues whatsoever. In fact, he was surprised when I read a short presentation that I was to give as part of a seminar that he was presenting. I explained that after I had been treated, my hypersexuality had completely disappeared. We had never discussed this area of my life in psychotherapy.

At the time of my injury, Dan and I had been married only a short time, although we had known each other for over five years. My self-image suffered from the brain injury which included feeling physically unattractive, and sexually unappealing to my husband. I could not determine if I was any good at sex which is probably an unnecessary worry for most heterosexual women. Sometimes, my "slightly" competitive nature emerges in very unpredictable scenarios. Simply put, I always wanted to be above par at everything I did. I did not have to be the best, but I needed to be better than average. So, I took a reading detour and read a handful of self-help books.

Of course, this was quite unnecessary, but the practice was fun.

I may have said things and behaved inappropriately to those outside of the brain injury bubble. The problem for me was not knowing the correct response in a timely manner. If this seems ridiculous, let me be the first to say, "it was". The distinction between what was allowed, what was partially accepted, and what behaviours were not allowed under any circumstances was no longer clearly defined for me. Growing up, my mother, through her own behaviour and explanations about social etiquette, (basically that there was very little leeway regarding what was permissible) guided me. She was able to convey the rules of etiquette and behaviour to a degree that I feared interacting with most of society. Now, my brain had been wiped clean of all her teachings. I initially thought I needed to re-learn them, but it was a blessing in many ways that I did not. The added stress of all those rules is exhausting and demoralizing. Yet, because I had forgotten a lot of behavioural mores and norms, it could be very awkward for those around me. Now, who was there to teach me?

I was fortunate through my memberships at several sports clubs to have exposure to many awesome women. Over the many years, following their leads, or simply imitating them helped me behave correctly. Once we were on a group vacation and a friend of ours from the ski club pointed out a very hurtful a comment I had made to Dan. I really needed that wake-up call to recognize that my behaviour was inappropriate and mean. We shared many dinners with other couples who Dan played sports with. This allowed me to practice proper etiquette, although the introduction of alcohol was debilitating. All I can say about alcohol is don't touch the stuff. Its impact is magnified two to three times in strength depending on your brain injury, hydration level, food consumption and other external factors. Think of it as poison running through your body. Alcohol was involved in almost every behavioural mishap in my post injury life, but now that you can be treated earlier in your recovery, you will not need substances to quiet your mind. Yoga and meditation are good alternatives, as are forest walks.

Dan never, ever complained about lacking a normal life. Looking back, I realize he was consumed with work and caring for the boys and me. He was trying to run his business alone to maintain zero overhead. I was concerned however, that because of the extent of my brain injury, he would not find me good enough to keep me around. My daily outbursts would have made other men run far away. At the time of my accident, many friends of my in-laws suggested divorce to Dan because we had only been married a short time. I know they were looking out for him, but Dan and I had known each other for almost a decade by the time of the accident and I knew two key things about Dan.

1. He was in love with me.
2. Dan was a man of his word. In everything Dan does, he is strong and true. He took his wedding vows literally and believed the words in sickness and in health to have meaning.

ACQUIRED ATTENTION DEFICIT DISORDER

THE TRUTH SHALL set you free. It didn't. During the first several years of my recovery, I could not lie. It is a symptom of acquired attention deficit disorder (AADD). My brain was so impaired that I did not know when I should avoid telling the truth as I knew it, all because others might be embarrassed, vindictive, or hurt. I was unable to see the consequences for me and for everyone else.

Here I was, a grown and married woman, but I still talked to my parents constantly to ask their advice. My father would tell me to be truthful. Unfortunately, this caused me a lot of grief and alienation. This "telling it like is," was already part of who I was prior to my injury, however I knew when to hold off discussing delicate topics. Not anymore, my new brain had no filter and everything I knew that related to a question would spill out. By not having a filter, I said and did some unspeakable things.

Situations abounded where it was obvious that I was struggling just to engage properly in conversation. My walking and talking problems were obvious to everyone, but no one expected me to have "truth serum" seeping from my pores. Fortunately, it was easy to discredit or dismiss me because people could easily say, "she had a brain injury".

You may have the expectation of trust, but I learned the hard way. Be careful who you trust. Outside of your tight circle, most people will have no idea what is going on with you.

SURVIVOR TIP

Shut out all the negative people in your life, that is anyone who upsets you or makes you feel inadequate. They will steal bits and pieces of your positive energy, energy that is needed by you to heal and to live a good life.

PART III:
THE INSURANCE GAME

THIS TOPIC IS very important! To navigate through this world requires patience, which most of us TBI's do not have in abundance. Brain-injured individuals must choose between the accessibility/necessity of services, and the cost of these much-needed services if you pay privately. The good news is that with the knowledge you will obtain here, you may not have to have lengthy and acrimonious relationships with insurance companies and lawyers.

I was golfing recently north of the city and was joined by a young, retired speech language pathologist who had loved her vocation. Being much younger than me, I questioned why she retired so young. Apparently, this lady had worked primarily with brain-injured individuals. She said that she finally had to quit working because of the inner turmoil and anger it was causing her. While she loved her day-to-day job with her clients, she hated that the insurance companies would cut off her clients long before they had achieved the potential ability they were capable of.

Once you leave the safe and nurturing environment of the hospital, you may be very fortunate and find yourself surrounded by the same types of people. They will be in outpatient programs and private therapy companies. But when the money runs dry and the insurance coverage is cancelled, you will be thrust head-first into the mean and ugly world of the need for money to continue your recovery. The money train just stops. Without insurance coverage you are left without any guide to show you how to progress on your own.

This is also the time when you hope your lawsuit gets settled quickly. But it won't. It should if SPECT neuroimaging is used but, in my time, the insurance companies try to bleed you dry first. Lawsuits will exist between you, the victim and the insurance company representing the other party. Also, you may have a lawsuit against your own insurance company to acquire all the funding that your coverage entitled you to.

This private world of health care operates on profits. Insurance companies are large players in both the health care industry and in the business world.

Their revenue comes from premiums and investment income. For those with traumatic brain injuries, the claims department is where all activity occurs. They will also have their own legal departments or law firms familiar with their organization. There are two major objectives that explain the existence of insurance companies.

1. These insurance companies pay their medical expert witnesses a lot more than the province pays their medical experts to testify and say what the insurance company wants them to say. The Ontario Health Insurance Plan (OHIP) rates are standard and not variable. OHIP cannot purchase the best expert testimony.

2. Insurance companies are in business to make money. Even knowing there is fraud when one has a catastrophic injury such as a TBI, it is incomprehensible how they can assume you are committing fraud. I was not capable of living alone, let alone developing a "plot" for my financial gain.

3. Insurance companies were a thorn in my side for the many years it took for my case to be settled. I would like to refer to a book called *So,*

You Think You're Covered! The Insurance Industry Rip-Off. It was written by Jokelee Vanderkop in 2013. This is the printed word of truth that describes the process and treatment you may expect when you file a claim. You are the client who paid the insurance premiums year after year. If insurance companies are granted the opportunity to sell their product as a mandatory requirement for driving a car, why are they allowed to profit from this delivery of contracted services? It is the investment division that should be profitable not the claims department. Introducing no-fault insurance, as Ontario has done, ensures that the insurance companies are paying out a great deal less money. In a perfect world, the excess money could be funnelled into service distribution for accident victims rather than shareholders' pockets.

To my consternation in catastrophic injury cases, one's own insurance company is not a free-flowing source of funds for the injured party. Once one's basic needs are met, anything more requires the injured person to request and demonstrate why something is needed. Who are they to judge if you're walking, speaking, or behaving adequately? Well, those medical experts they hire will tell you that you are as good as you can ever expect to get. The industry only gave me two to three years of recovery funds and then wrote me off. I was an expensive client, but I was not much better. In fact, I think it would be less expensive for insurance companies to provide their clients with SPECT and the associated treatments. In this scenario, the insurance companies would pay out a lifetime of pharmaceutical costs which is less than the sum of current expenses. Such expenses would include hospital costs, additional therapies and various supports, personal caregiving, child-care, plus a lump sum. This would be the best solution for both traumatically brain injured individuals and for the insurance companies.

Our insurance company did provide childcare for up to forty hours a week. In fact, they did cover a lot of things as I had an active life before my injury. Their coverage of childcare and my care allowed my husband to continue to work, but only that. There is no wiggle room for chores, meals, even a workout, let alone a life. That is not even accounting for the decades of untreated brain injury symptoms that I struggled with. My emotional roller coaster was also my family's roller coaster.

Favourably as it turned out, there was a conflict-of-interest lawyer present at my father's law firm. My Dad's law firm represented both the rehabilitation hospital and my own insurance company. As a result, they had to find a different lawyer to represent me when communicating with my own insurance company. The firm's plaintiff litigation expert, who was representing me in the tort case was asked if he could recommend someone. My tort lawyer referred me to the then-president of the Plaintiff Lawyers' Association. One neurologist who was testing my ability levels asked me who my lawyer was. When I explained that I had two and mentioned their names he chuckled and said that I was most definitely over-represented.

At the outset, my insurance company wanted to take control of my situation. A woman phoned me shortly after I returned home to set up a time for her first visit. I was brain injured. She was manipulative. She introduced herself by saying that she was my case manager. I know my doctor had recommended post-hospital care so I expected that this was who she was. The worst part of this misguided experience was my belief that she was working on my behalf.

Why did this woman intervene so quickly? She immediately enrolled me in the provincially funded local hospital out-patient program. This allowed her to save the insurance company a lot of money and made me occupy a space that could have gone to someone who was injured without private insurance. It was not in my best interests, nor was it in the public's best interests for me to attend this program.

Now I had two mysteries to solve:

a. How to Get Better from a Brain Injury.
b. What evil activities take place at insurance companies?

The outpatient hospital program was a huge disappointment to me after the rehabilitation hospital. The program goals were very different. The hospital's outpatient program was a community-oriented program to integrate you back into the community. There was zero likelihood that it could make me better. I fired my care manager after completing the first month as an outpatient. This was my first step in building my own team—a power team to get me where I wanted to be. This woman had the nerve to ask Dan if he thought that I knew what I was doing. Dan, bless his heart, told her that I knew exactly what I was doing.

I knew without a doubt that she was not looking out for my best interests.

The increased commotion and new stimuli in my world led me to forget where my rehabilitation doctor had referred me. I was surprised that my mom did not have notes telling us what to do, but she still solved the situation for me. My mother and I contacted my doctor at the rehabilitation hospital who was wonderful and sent me in the right direction.

Insurance companies want quick settlements for less than the value of your injury. Often the insurance company will offer you a quick settlement to get your claim off their books. If you are short of money (likely because you can't work) these insurance companies may seem to be offering you a lifeline. But they are trying to take advantage of your misfortune by paying you far less than you may be entitled to.

Hiring a good lawyer is very important. As many television ads for plaintiff lawyers state, "You don't pay until you are paid." The fact that these firms can afford to advertise on television (which is very expensive), would imply that they win law cases. The larger law firms are also visible sponsors at brain injury association conferences and events. I believe—and I am not advocating for anyone in particular—that some legal firms will even assist your ability to survive financially by adding any borrowed amount to your legal fees after your court case.

Even though my father was a successful lawyer, he knew nothing about my situation's insurance claims. He asked his top injury lawyer to lead me through these uncharted waters. My tort lawyer was at the top of this plaintiff game, yet he was respectful and attentive to my frequent concerns. What I considered to be enormous problems were just blips in the legal procedure. There is a procedure for filing claims and lawsuits. There is also a procedure for settling lawsuits. Currently, we fall under the second application of "No Fault" Insurance.

I was medically mandated by my primary-care physician at the Riverdale Hospital to have "taxicab rides" available for all the places I would formerly have driven. For me, that included taking the boys to nursery school and picking them up, grocery shopping, and a ride to the gym while the boys were at nursery school. These taxicab rides should have been available until I had my driver's license restored. I lived in the suburb of Mississauga in <u>1990's</u>, and it was quite a stretch for me to walk to a bus stop with two young children, to take the bus, transfer buses, and return the way I had come. This was impossible. I could not even imagine carrying groceries or anything else on me. I still faced many difficulties. I could still barely walk.

WHAT I DID WHEN PAYMENTS STOPPED

AT FIRST, THE cab company had been very accommodating. I had been given a regular driver named Bubba who seemed to understand enough about my situation to tolerate my incessant chatter. Eventually the cab company stopped accepting my requests for a drive unless I paid them directly because my insurance company was not reimbursing them. This was confusing to me because I thought insurance companies were supposed to pay the bills. It was an eye-opener to discover that just paying premiums to an insurance company does not mean they will take care of you.

I clearly remember one day when I walked out of the church doors after picking up the boys at the nursery school there. There were two men photographing me as though it was a promotional photo shoot. Why would the church or the nursery school be randomly taking photos for publicity? I had no idea they were insurance adjusters. It was only me they were photographing as I held my child's hand and led him from the church doors to the waiting cab. I must have had a premonition of something to come that morning because I insisted for the first time that our support worker/nanny join me in the cab ride to pick up the boys from nursery school. This gave extra emotional support to help me get from the doors of the church to the doors of my car while we each held onto one of the boys.

I mentioned this scene in conversation at the fitness club the next day and was told it was not normal. Someone, possibly a fireman, gave me crash course on insurance adjusters. As a result of this, I lodged a complaint with the insurance company by stealing a page from mother's playbook. She had always insisted that if you have a problem with a corporation you should telephone the president of the company directly. So, I did.

The first time that I telephoned the president of my own insurance company was after my taxi rides were denied coverage. I was only able to leave a voice message. Unfortunately for him (or his voice machine) it was like opening Pandora's box as he heard from me more than once. I could go on forever and there was no one to interrupt me or suggest that I stop calling.

After I encountered these conflicts with my insurance company, I became full of indignation. Questions abounded, such as: "Where did all these mean people come from?" and "What did I do wrong?". I was extremely fortunate to have people behind the scenes who could feed and clothe me. It made it easy for me to dig my feet in and take a stance against the insurance company. They were not going to get away with anything on my watch. I even hoped that after winning my own battle I could figure out how to prevent this from hurting everyone else with a TBI. Well, that never happened although now I can at least share this solution of how to regain function.

The investment department of an insurance company should be capable of making enough money for the insurance company to support their claims department while providing its shareholders with a decent profit. I was fortunate that I had financial support behind me. Although it was a financially tight existence I could hold out long enough to see this through. The anger and rage in me created by the insurance companies with their games gave me cause to chase recovery even harder.

I remember helping my husband on one of his building sites where the colour selections had to be redone, as some items had been discontinued in the time it took for him to get permits. The project had been delayed many times by the municipal planning department with the local councillor causing interference. Dan had run out of cash and my services were free. One of his purchasers worked for an insurance company dealing specifically with brain injuries. Gradually, I shared my own situation with her, not ever thinking this would come back to bite me. But in her attempts to acquire "more house for less money," she wrote my husband a letter accusing him of various irregularities and included an entire paragraph bashing me. She was using her insider knowledge of brain injuries, attempting to incite my anger into something that she could be compensated for. Fortunately, I had already been treated by Dr. Thornton and was able to brush off her attempts to discredit me quite easily.

The reason I bring this up is to illustrate how immoral these players can be. This woman had been trying to reassure me that the insurance companies had changed since my own experience, when, in fact, she was using her insider knowledge of brain injury for her own personal and financial gain.

SURVIVOR TIPS

Find yourself a personal injury lawyer.

There are legal guidelines in place to provide services to you. Insurance companies must follow these rules, but unfortunately, it often requires a good lawyer to ensure that they do.

THE INVISIBLE INJURY

COMMUNICATION IS SO important, yet brain injury disrupts everything about it. Visually, I appeared drunk with my uneven gait and my very slurred speech. If I saw a policeman or woman ahead of me in the distance, I made sure that I displayed my pronounced limp as a visual explanation for my walk and to prevent a possible encounter that would require me to speak. If I spoke, there was always a lengthy and frustrating explanation as to why I sounded drunk and walked like I was drunk. Not just one symptom, but two! This frustrated and annoyed me more than anything else. I couldn't just get on with life with this negative feedback. This personal horror show of mine suggests just a little of what racial profiling must feel like.

Over the eighteen years it took before I had my SPECT scan treatment, I would estimate that I was questioned by "concerned citizens" or refused service at least once a week. It was not always servers who would refuse to serve me, but those in totally unrelated industries. Maybe they thought I was too drunk to make the correct decision or that I was trying to use stolen funds to pay for something. I have no idea why that is the "go to" assumption, but I have no sympathy for their ignorance.

Those establishments never got my business again. An example of such a misunderstanding occurred in a major supermarket chain store. It was a huge store and people would lurk in the aisles and beg for money. I decided that because I had the time and I had become used to people helping me, that I should speak up to help others. So, I waited for a long time at customer service to speak with a manager, and we then went back to the aisle. But there was no one there. Meanwhile, the manager had seen me both walk and talk. I went home without any self-awareness of the mess that I had caused. I was still in my dirty gardening clothes and had displayed my vulnerabilities at the store.

Less than an hour after talking to this manager, my doorbell rang. The policeman standing at my front door started by saying how he hoped it was not me. He had been my master's swim team coach and knew exactly what was wrong with me. Again, serendipity intervened. Or maybe God was looking out for me? Anyway, I felt safe in the knowledge that this policeman would be able to communicate with the supermarket manager as to my invisible disability. The silver lining of this event was to see this supermarket fail.

What a dilemma. I was wasting my limited energy by repeatedly trying to explain my invisible injury, time that could have been better spent repeating information to aid in my recovery. Why couldn't I just have worn a sign on my forehead? "No, I am not drunk, I have a traumatic brain injury." Would I feel like an idiot wearing such a sign? Yes, I would. Having lived with an invisible injury which I am sure honed my sales skills, I would now select "feeling like an idiot."

Again, it bears repeating that I was very aware of my personal presentation. I always tried to try to have my clothing and make-up look finished. I knew that first impressions make a big difference in how well you are treated, and I most certainly needed all the help I could get. This was an area I had conquered, having been self-taught about clothing and styling techniques. My biggest frustration was my hair, so I wore it up a lot. I suggest to others to find an easily manageable hair style and keep it cut regularly. For women, simplify your beauty routine if it works.

I still remember my mother entering my hospital room one day and announcing that I should always be wearing lipstick. A friend of mine was present at that time, and we laughed about the wearing of lipstick for a long time. Clothing can also be easy but expensive, so long as everything you buy co-ordinates. Second hand stores can be awesome treasure troves for "new" clothes.

After I had been treated by Dr. Thornton I experienced a nightmare situation—quite recently. I was returning home from Vancouver where I had gone to visit a friend. The night before I flew back, I forgot to take my medication. This resulted in my trying to convince the flight attendants that I should be allowed to fly, that I did not mean to slam the overhead bin shut, and that I was not a danger to the flight. I may have sounded drunk. I walked unsteadily. My eyes were red because I'd had a bad sleep from having forgotten my medication. What a mess. Unfortunately, I am still too embarrassed to fly that with that airline again.

SURVIVOR TIPS

- I now carry extra medication in my purse for any emergency.

- I also did not know at the time that I could take my "nighttime" medication as soon as I remembered it. This would not harm me. For five years, I had been waiting until the next dosage time, experiencing all the symptoms of withdrawal for up to twenty-four hours. That was always a horror.
- Being clean and well-groomed helps first impressions by showing that you care about yourself, and how others perceive you.

PART IV:
SPECT SCANS

WHAT IS SPECT?

THE CURRENT USE of SPECT technology allows for every person who has acquired a brain injury, at any time in their life, to regain use of their brain. SPECT scans identify which area of your brain are receiving oxygen and which are not. Treatment to balance the brain ensures that specific issues can be eliminated, and other abilities may be recovered. There is no time limit for the effectiveness of its use. It works two years, eighteen years or thirty plus years after your brain injury. SPECT scans and three-dimensional interpretation of them will work on all the variations of brain injuries, independent of the time elapsed.

SPECT scans make use of a radioactive tracer to show where the blood is flowing in your brain. The heavier the flow of oxygenated blood, the lighter and brighter the coloured tracer. The final format that these SPECT technicians use to read the scan is composed of different shades of colours. The most active areas are brightly lit and show where the blood flow is heaviest. There may be areas that are solid dark holes which represent parts of the brain where there is little or no oxygen. The brightly lit areas are working well although some may be overworking. The darker coloured areas or solid black spots are where little, or no blood is flowing. There is no oxygen reaching these areas of the brain which means they are not working at all.

The difference is the use of the word efficiency:

Efficient is using a functioning and balanced brain to learn both old and new information.

versus

Inefficient trying to instill knowledge or skills with a broken brain.

Not everything can be improved immediately with the use of SPECT scans and their three-dimensional interpretation, even when followed by the appropriate treatment plan. Some issues can be improved just by taking the appropriate medication, such as your emotional control. Other things must be re-learned all over again through repetition, followed by more repetition. Once your brain is balanced you can re-learn things efficiently, whereas prior to SPECT, you are trying to instill information utilizing a broken brain. And yes, there are even a few things that I deemed too ambitious and unnecessary to re-learn.

Dr. Thornton follows the teachings of Dr. Daniel Amen, of the United States. Dr. Amen is a well-respected pioneer in brain SPECT imaging. He currently has several clinics located throughout the United States. These clinics are available to anyone with the money to attend and it is a lot of money. It has been a long road to where Canadians can be treated with this method. I will explain how the cost of SPECT scans in Ontario is not as prohibitive as it is in the United States of America. This information can be found in the chapter titled "The Cost of a SPECT Scan".

Roadblocks arose in the delivery of this technique for Dr. Thornton and every time he was stalled I unconsciously withdrew my writing commitment. Several difficulties became apparent in the delivery of this procedure. The most valuable concern was obtaining suitable images for non-nuclear medicine doctors to read. Canadian radiologists were not available to read and prepare his SPECT scans in "non-nuclear medicine" interpretations. These scans are taken and produced within hospitals for the purpose of treating patients, but not by psychiatrists There are fewer than ten doctors in Canada who can provide this therapy. So, the next process would be for Dr. Thornton to design a system that could treat a larger number of people. This technicality and many other medical issues have been addressed and there is now the beginning of a system in place.

Much of a hospital's research is enabled by monetary grants and there was no funding for this niche area of brain injury care. It is quite appalling to have to refer to brain injury as "niche" when it is so widespread (two percent of the Canadian population have experienced brain injury, or approximately 1.5 million Canadians.).

Within the context of my brain injured self, I dove headfirst into trying to find a way to make me better. I believe that Dr. Thornton also dove headfirst into finding a solution for Canadian brain injury survivors. Fortunately, he demonstrated persistence and created a procedure so that we now have a solution that could be available to all Ontarians. Dr. Thornton has sourced appropriate hospitals that provide the SPECT scans and now sends the SPECT scans to radiologists in the US. The American radiologists convert the scans into a readable format for Canadian psychiatrists to interpret. The only requirement is to have a family doctor or psychiatrist to organize this protocol with Dr. Thornton. You will also need regular follow-up with your treatment plan.

My first attempt to share my information with others was a dead end. I presented my story to TBI survivors and others who were attending a brain injury conference in Gatineau, Quebec. I knew that I had a problem guiding others to treatment resources, but Dr. Thornton continued to encourage me to prepare and to present. I felt awkward talking about a treatment to a room full of people, but not being able to tell them where to find it. Ontario did not yet have a centralized source for this information. That meant that my success was only half-realized. I was pleased to have succeeded in generating interest and desire, but I had failed in providing direction. I had asked Dr. Thornton for an answer in anticipation of such requests, but he was experiencing his own problems.

My previous family doctor would not take over the filling of prescriptions for my brain injury treatment, claiming to be unfamiliar with the treatment and the psychiatrist. To renew my prescription from Dr. Thornton, I had to ask him to write a new prescription for me at my monthly visits. What would happen when I stopped seeing him?

Dr. Thornton encouraged me to find a better option, so I asked Dr. Tony Galea, my sports medicine doctor. The Galea clinic had a pharmacy within their building which made it easy for Dr. Galea to fulfill such requests. Many of the recommended treatments for traumatic brain injury are off-label medications. When something is referred to as off-label, it is the use of medications for unapproved indications. Providing off-label medication for brain injuries is likely done because there is no available drug that is approved specifically for the injured brain. To achieve that status is time consuming. I felt secure using my psychiatrist's recommendation for his referral of off-label medications. I now have a new family doctor who has assumed this role.

SPECT SCAN PROCEDURE

WHEN YOU REPORT to the nuclear medicine department of the hospital:

1. You will be required to change into a hospital gown and complete a questionnaire.
2. You will drink a radioactive tracer, or have it injected. You will wait twenty to forty-five minutes for the tracer to flow to your brain.
3. You will then be taken to the SPECT scan machine which is physically like an MRI machine. You will lie down on a narrow bed which then pulls you into the machine.
4. At all times, you will have a technician monitoring you. While you are in the machine, images will be taken from a variety of angles. You are not supposed to move at all! I was nervous about twitching. The technicians may play music for you to help pass the time or to help you relax.
5. Photographs of your brain are taken from many different angles.

6. These photographs must be prepared to be read by radiologists and converted into a readable format by non-nuclear technicians. They are then interpreted in 3D by the psychiatrist who ordered the scans from the radiology department.

Treatment depends on what the images show in combination with the person's symptoms. To determine the effectiveness of these treatments it is necessary to have regular psychotherapy sessions with your psychiatrist.

TOP-DOWN VIEW: A HEALTHY BRAIN VERSUS MY INJURED SKULL

I compare a normal healthy brain (on the left) to my injured brain (on the right).

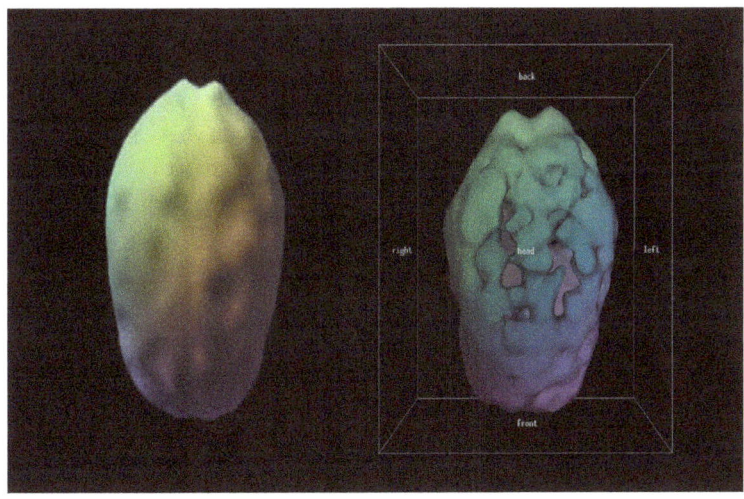

TOP-DOWN PHOTO

The *before* picture of my brain is on the left. The photo on the right is my brain *after* being treated by Dr. Thornton.

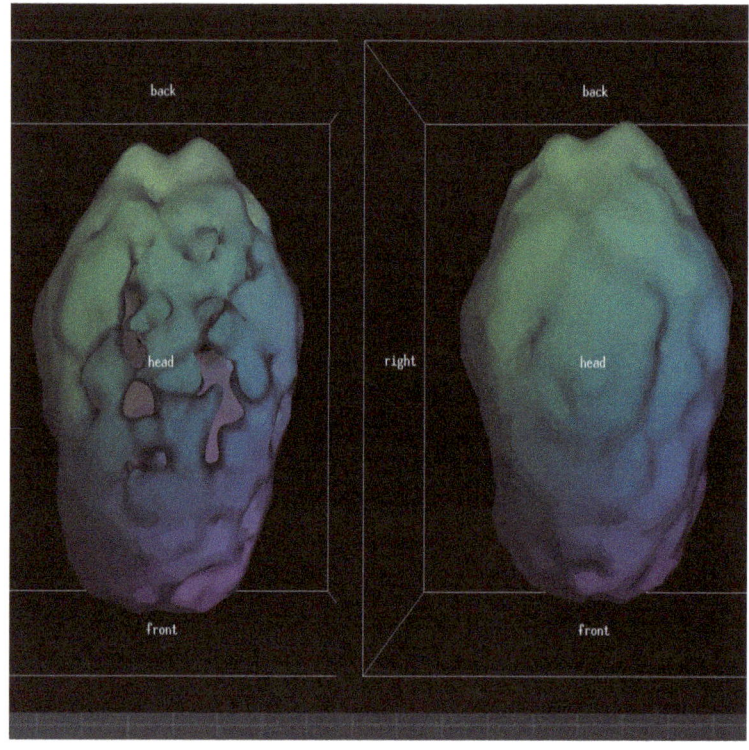

BOTTOM-UP PHOTO

Again, the photo of my brain on the left is full of holes. The photo on the right is my brain after being treated.

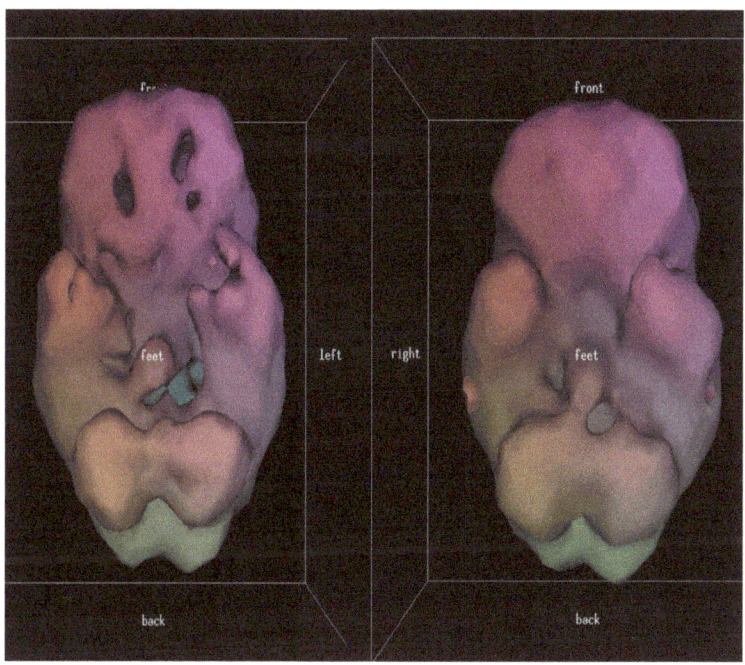

TEMPORAL LOBES

The temporal lobes control many functions of the body. They may work in combination with other parts of the brain to deliver these abilities. The temporal lobes are responsible for behaviour, judgement, emotions, speech, hearing, vision, and memory.

Wow, that seems like everything! The area of this region on my SPECT scan was completely blank. It was just a black hole.

I realized that:
- I was not a bad person.
- I was not crazy.
- I was not drunk.
- I just had no oxygen reaching my temporal lobes.

MY FIRST SPECT SCAN

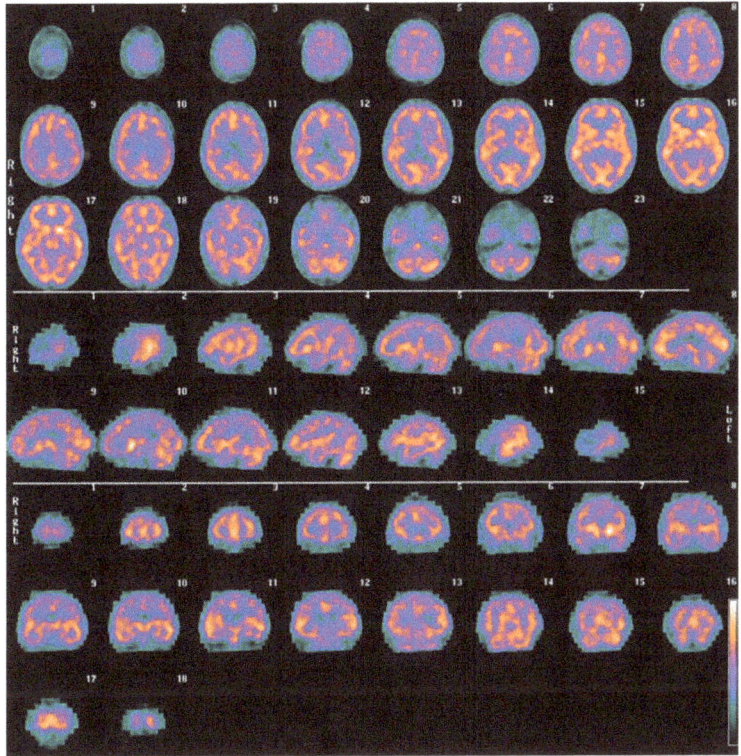

There was a lack of illumination in both the frontal and temporal lobes of my brain. The discovery of my temporal lobes as almost dormant sent me home with an urgency to look up their function on the internet.

MY SECOND SPECT SCAN

My second SPECT scan is of my brain being illuminated. The areas are lighter and brighter. The increase represents greater blood flow (which is carrying oxygen) reaching more parts of my brain.

The treatment plan, as prescribed in the form of medication, caused this improvement.

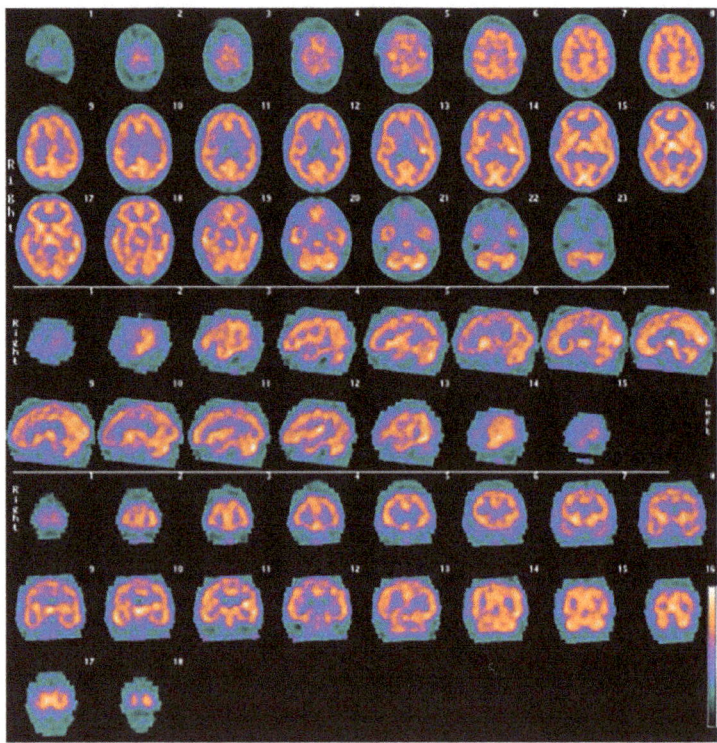

INTERPRETING MY SPECT SCANS

ONE OF THE areas that the therapist tested and re-tested in hospital was visual memory. I do find that it's much easier to recall something that was visually presented to me than something I've heard. Yet, as I mentioned earlier, it was impossible for me to verbalize what I recalled. I found that after my brain injury, I could address part of my short-term memory loss by being able to see things. If I read something several times (at least twice), I was more likely to remember it. I am still that way.

The internet was a wonderful thing in many ways for my brain injured self. All it required of me was to enter "maps of the human brain" and many choices appeared before me. Caution should be employed though, as a lot of things one looks up on the internet charge money and are looking to sell you things, such as books. You do not need to spend money. Scroll past the ads, and you will find what you need. If not, read the small print next to a site's URL and they will identify themselves in small print as an ad or not.

For my injury, the most impaired areas were my frontal lobes and my temporal lobes. The temporal lobe deficit did lead me to some regrettably inappropriate conduct. I did try to blast another person with my torrential anger and he found a solution to get rid of me. I felt quite rightly at the time of this behaviour, that the guy who drove his car onto mine should know what he had done to my life. One day his sister answered his phone and told me how upset he was to have caused this accident. By her being there and taking my call, I felt that my message must have succeeded in conveying the seriousness of my anger. I apologized. This was the first of many people to whom I feel apologetic, but please consider this to be for anyone who feels they deserve one. I am trying to learn not to recall past emotions especially the severely negative ones. According to a recent podcast I listened to on regret, it was suggested that there is "value in regret", and that is to guide you in future behaviour.

Dr. Thornton's SPECT scan with three-dimensional interpretation is what saved me, and my family from me. After starting the medically supervised and prescribed drug therapy, I no longer let my frustration or selfish pursuits lead to heated outbursts. There have been instances where Dan has riled me up and caused me to misbehave but that usually only happens within the confines of our house. My family has never met Dr. Thornton, yet they all know who he is and sing his praises. If I made no other improvements, at least "my people", are all happy to have me emotionally stable in much better control.

HOW TO GET A SPECT SCAN IN ONTARIO

DR. THORNTON WILL provide psychiatric interpretation of your SPECT scan. He will work with your family doctor or psychiatrist to help interpret and implement the findings of the SPECT scan. To obtain a SPECT scan for treatment of your brain injury, ask your family doctor to refer you to Dr. John Thornton of Toronto. His contact numbers are on-line, or can be found through Canadian Psychiatrist channels. Dr. Thornton has retired from his office counselling sessions so your family doctor or psychiatrist will need to connect you with other mental health professionals in your local area.

The easiest way to connect with Dr. Thornton is for you or your family doctor to leave a voice message on Dr. Thornton's answering system. With permission given by Dr. Thornton, his telephone/fax number is: 416-926-8944. Dr. Thornton will recommend to your doctor the locations of the appropriate nuclear medicine facilities based on where you live in Ontario.

1. You will undergo the first SPECT scan which has been described for you in this book.
2. A procedure is now in place for the images to be returned to Dr. Thornton in a readable format for him to interpret and analyse.
3. You will need to have a psychiatrist or family doctor monitor the therapies as recommended by Dr. Thornton. Both the medication itself, and the dosage of the medication may need to be adjusted.
4. After you have stabilized, a second SPECT scan should be done.
5. This will show if the medication is correct and if it has improved your brain function ……………… or if medication adjustments are needed by a qualified psychiatrist.

COSTS OF SPECT (IN ONTARIO)

1. **The following issues are covered by OHIP:**
   - The appointment to obtain a family doctor's referral for a SPECT scan.
   - The SPECT scan itself.
   - Psychiatric counselling or psychotherapy (talk therapy) to help determine which medications and dosages are suitable.
2. **There are two major components that require you to pay out-of-pocket. (Payments that need to be made by the Patient).**
   1. The interpretation of the SPECT scan by a qualified technician. This may cost several hundred dollars.
   2. Medication costs, which will be for a lifetime of treatment. You may have coverage from private insurance, your lawsuit, or a workplace health plan. If you are not covered, there are generic drugs which are less expensive.

- SPECT is far less expensive than a PET or MRI procedure.
- SPECT may be available in other provinces under reciprocity agreements.

PART V:
OTHER FACTORS THAT HELPED ME:
EXERCISE & FITNESS

I FIRST WENT back to the gym after only a few months after returning home. Exercise seemed the logical next step to assist me with my recovery. Boy oh boy, did I ever have a problem. I found it difficult to do much of anything and I found it difficult to decide what to do. I tried lifting a few small dumb bells, but I was directionless and kept switching my movements. I tried to sit on the stationary bike but was easily distracted and could not work it properly. Being a good swimmer, I decided that I should go for a swim. I knew this would provide a full body work out. The club had a large pool which was most often empty and was unguarded, except for family swims and children's lessons. I slid into the water and proceeded to do several laps until I became bored (as opposed to physically tired). When I relayed this activity to my physical therapist who visited me at my home, she bombarded me with questions. Upon realizing that I had been alone in the pool for the entire time that I was swimming, she requested I not swim until she had organized something for me.

The following week, my physical therapist assigned me an extraordinary physical therapy assistant to me. Cassandra patiently taught my body how to function, starting with holding onto my feet as I rode the stationary bike. Without her, I would not have made any significant physical progress. She was my lifeline to the world that I used to know very well. My confidence increased and the workout itself made me feel 100 percent better. An artist might be more comfortable in a studio, a musician in front of a musical instrument, but I was most comfortable with exercise equipment.

I could have worked-out in a different environment such as my home but being in a fitness club with a personal physical therapy assistant prevented me from getting distracted. The members at this fitness club were gentle and kind toward me. I guess having an accident no more than four hundred metres from the club encouraged an awareness of my situation. I really felt that I was part of the community there. There was little judgement. Those people who knew my story would share it with those who did not.

After my Insurance Company stopped paying for my therapies, I discovered personal trainers. Of course, the head trainer had to gently show me some new exercises before I realized this was an option. Again, my lack of self-awareness allowed me to think that I was just bored from working out. I needed someone to organize my workouts for me, expand my exercise repertoire, and keep me engaged. By making an appointment for training, the money was spent whether you showed up or not (within reason). My first thought was to improve my walking. My physiotherapy assistant had focused on re-building my strength. Once I hired a trainer, I continued down this path. Then, one day I received the local brain injury association's newsletter publicizing their own five-kilometer run. Now I wanted to learn how to run. I hired a wonderful trainer who happened to be a distance runner herself. For three months, I ran at least three times a week in preparation for it. The run was for the local brain injury association and was organized by the non-brain injured personnel who worked for the association for with brain injured people.

I thought it would be no problem as I had trained specifically for this distance and my running gait was a great deal smoother than my walking ability. Yet, I was exhausted before I reached the finish line. I did not stop and walk; I persevered and finished the run.

Ironically, the organizers (who were not brain injured themselves, but oversaw brain injured individuals) of this event had not factored in that Canada had switched to the metric system. They were holding a five-kilometer race on a five-mile course! Five miles works out to just over eight kilometers. Yes, I was "pretty pleased" with myself!

I knew that aerobic exercise is good for your brain. The fitness club was trying to organize some triathlon programs, specifically a swimming program in the pool. I decided this might work for me, as I could benefit the most by having three aerobic activities in one sport. I even went so far as to hire a top triathlon trainer to design a workout program for me. By the way, this was completely unnecessary, and I realize that I wasted money and time. Rarely could I keep up to the programming.

Even so, my training allowed me to complete three triathlons one summer. Swimming was my best part because I had done a lot of competitive swimming in my youth. The biking was fine due to my acquisition of an ultralight bike. However, the running was my weakness because of my partially torn ACL and unknown issues with my left leg and foot. I could not recruit all the leg muscles necessary to run properly, although I did realize my running was superior to my walking. In my one and only Olympic-distance triathlon, my muscles were so tired that I literally dragged my left foot across the finish line. While I was maximizing my aerobic fitness, fitness itself will not fix your brain. At a certain level of fitness, you do generate more energy within yourself. But not enough to enable me to fins sufficient time to train for these triathlon races.

I would only recommend this activity to other brain-injured individuals who may have engaged in this activity before their injury. Triathlon training, followed by a race, is a big-time commitment. I used to take my sons running and biking with me on the weekends. It became part of their fitness routine as well, and I even went so far as to enroll them in "Teens of Steel". The name "Teens of Steel" was a big help in their motivation since chronologically they were not yet teenagers.

SUPPLEMENTATION

I HAVE ALWAYS supplemented my diet with vitamins and minerals. As a teenager, I started making myself protein shakes to support my vegetarian diet. I also took a variety of over-the-counter vitamins. For guidance, I read magazines, books, and newspapers to help inform my nutritional intake. There was an unfortunate smelly period in my youth when I ate garlic pills and slathered Vitamin A oil on my face.

Vitamins and supplements can be an important facet of healing and maintaining brain health. In his holistic approach, Dr. Thornton recommends the following to all his patients:

1. Vitamin D
2. Omega 3's
3. Magnesium Glycinate

After using several systems such as pill cases to help remember to take them, I have finally moved entirely to liquid supplements as they are absorbed into your body more quickly. I keep the bottles in the fridge and have them prior to my morning coffee. It is all about routine. My prescription medication is in the bathroom and I take my medications after I brush my teeth in the morning and evening. Again, this is my routine.

There are benefits to utilizing as many apparatuses and accessibility aids as available. Not only will they provide the benefits for which they are designed, but many more side benefits will appear (more doors being held for you, groceries carried to your car, and so forth).

Accessibility Aids will:
- Reduce fatigue.
- Keep you focused on the task at hand.
- Notify others in your line of vision that you need to expend part of your energy on tasks that they do not. Wearing any type of leg brace when hiking or even on walks will alert other people to your extra efforts and I found most people lean toward helpfulness and will give you the right of way.

SURVIVOR TIPS

- Forgive yourself for your mistakes. Learn from them and move on.
- Live in the present and enjoy the journey.
- Try things that interest you and don't give up at the first, second or third setback.

YOGA

I WAS NERVOUS to attend my first yoga class but it was wonderful. Yoga is allowing your mind and body to connect through breath. That means anyone and everyone can do it. The class that I started with encouraged participants to be compassionate towards themselves and others. We were encouraged to go at our own pace and it was expressed that Yoga is never competitive.

The importance of yoga as a mind/body-strengthening exercise for brain injuries has garnered a lot more interest in recent years. Yoga starts with breathing. So even if you can only sit in a chair, you can do chair yoga and practise your breath awareness. This can often lead directly into meditation which Dr. Thornton suggests should be practiced every single day.

One year, I brought my yoga instructor to one of our conferences in Pierrefonds, Quebec. We sat on the grass of a Monastery, with the river flowing beside us. Anne joined us from Mississauga, Ontario and led us in a very relaxing and holistic form of yoga that made people smile when they finished. We were ahead of the curve as yoga has become a very popular breakout topic at most brain injury conferences.

Yoga classes that are called "therapeutic" or "gentle" are ideal and a good place to start. Look for classes that incorporate different abilities by offering several levels of difficulty.

NORDIC WALKING

THIS YEAR, I bought dedicated "Nordic walking" poles. Their use increases cardiovascular fitness and makes use of the core and upper body at the same time. It is gentle on the body while also allowing for social interaction. I recall being invited to join a group of women many, many years ago at the health club. Back then, I wanted to maximize my workout in the time limit that was available to me. I wanted to exhaust my body and walking certainly would not do it. I tend to be my own worst enemy when I am offered something new. There have been many things that I did not try or go to see which I regret. I felt that I could participate in this when I was older and had more free time. This woman realized that it could improve my walking, but still I resisted. I was not quite sure what to make of them—were Nordic poles "uncool", or were they "just for old people"? It turns out that I was my own worst enemy.

Recently, when Covid-19 shut everything down, I explored options such as Nordic walking. Many

physiotherapists have Nordic walking poles and recommend their use to improve one's technique and posture. Articles tout the many benefits of this activity including:
- The use of some upper-body muscles and your core.
- Developing a rhythm and a faster pace.
- Not only has Nordic walking added to my array of cardio activities, but it makes walking our dog, Duke, much more exciting. They are my new toy and are assisting me in the re-patterning of my walking gait. With my Nordic walking poles and a large dog on a leash, I visually take up a lot of space. People give way to me on sidewalks which is super.

SURVIVOR TIP

If you do invest in poles, order tip covers for walking on concrete. The poles spikes in winter are very effective for stopping slips and falls on ice.

GOLF

GOLF WAS INCREDIBLY difficult to learn well enough to play even nine holes. I had never been a regular golfer, but I knew how to swing a club and how to use a putter. These were tasks that my father encouraged me to do in my youth, and even gave me lessons. As adults, I was able to join a beautiful golf club, on an annual basis, in the country. My father had an equity membership there. His one membership allowed for all his family members (children, their spouses or partners, and his grandchildren) to join each year for the price of the annual dues. Back in the early years the price for our sons as juniors to join was very minimal, but the hours they could play were tightly restricted. The Club really wanted to encourage the next generation of golfers. We would drive up north on Friday nights and stop at the Mad River Golf Club. Initially, Dan would play nine holes, while the boys and I might hit a few balls on the range and occasionally would take a lesson. Motivating our young boys involved a lot of grilled cheese sandwiches and chocolate milk dinners.

This itinerary evolved over the years until we were all able to play nine holes together. When James turned thirteen, he shot a hole-in-one!

Dismally, I found that I was still unable to improve enough through weekend practice to play a respectable round of golf. This encouraged me to try and find somewhere to practice my golf in the city, so I tried local public golf ranges until an aunt of mine passed away and left a substantial amount of her estate to many of her nephews and nieces. I thought of what she would have liked me to do with it. After ensuring the family cottage would survive, I realized that joining a golf club would satisfy her value of women's independence. Or did it just fit my purpose?

I told Dan that maybe this might be a good opportunity for me to learn to play golf. Dan suggested that I investigate the golf club down the street from us. It was five minutes by car and fifteen minutes by bicycle. The best part of riding my bike was the ride home which was a gentle downhill glide. This golf club had spectacular gardens supported at the time by a large greenhouse to entice me, plus a small indoor pool, exercise rooms and a manicured golf course. I met with the membership Director and after chatting outdoors on the patio where I could see the gardens, I was invited to join. I said "yes" on the spot. Two weeks later, Dan asked me how my interview at the golf club went. I said, "Oh, didn't I tell you? I joined it." Yes, all my therapists would have explained my behaviour as impulsive. But I had my own funds, and I knew that with all the sequelae from my brain injury, this sport might take a lot longer than usual to learn.

Over the years, I have taken more golf lessons than my level of play ever demonstrated. Finally, I noticed that over the past two years (before Covid), I saw an improvement. My success was from taking a course on the mental game of golf. Of course, I took this course after I had been treated by Dr. Thornton. Most amateur golfers are not able to experience mental golf coaching. It was the best thing I ever did for my golf and helped with everyday mental behaviour. There are as many mental golf coaches as there are swing coaches and putting gurus. The most important strategy that I learned in this course also helped me cope with everyday life post-TBI.

- A "negative response" to something that is ingrained in our psyche is three times as strong as a "positive response".

Example:

Golf: You might say to yourself, "Darn, what a bad shot". To reach neutral, you need to congratulate yourself three times for similar shots. I find it extremely embarrassing to perform self-praise.

Life: "Darn, I burned dinner again". Yes, I needed to stay in the kitchen and be aware that I was cooking something. This should always be the case but my TBI symptoms of impatience and distractibility would lead me astray.

Golf is very social and maybe good as a healing activity. Referring again to research showing that increased social interactions play a positive role in healing, I believe that in many ways, golf has been important to my process. The membership at these clubs have been very forgiving. Apparently, some of the women knew about my situation and shared their knowledge with others who might have thought I was peculiar or possibly drunk all the time!

Then Covid struck. I kept hurting myself at activities I was physically unprepared for, as all the health clubs had been closed. For two years, I was unable to golf. I spent two years waiting for the elective surgery backlog to clear so I could join my surgeon's list and be scheduled for my ACL repair. During this time, I took a lot of long walks, and hikes, accompanied by Duke.

SURVIVOR TIPS

Three positive comments are equal to the strength of one negative comment. Focus on the former, and let the rest go.

Regarding cooking, do not leave anything on the stove if you leave the room.

Try to use oven timers whenever possible. I set my oven timer even when I must heat something on the stove for a set time.

RIGHT BRAIN/LEFT BRAIN

AGAIN, CAN A TBI individual have success in healing their own brain? Well, embarrassing as it seems now, I do recall thinking early in my recovery that I had uncovered yet another stroke of brilliance using my injured brain. Having studied psychology as an undergraduate, I anticipated finding some guidance for healing my brain in my textbooks. When I read the chapters of how different hemispheres of my brain are responsible for performing different tasks, I thought that I was on to something. Yes, the hospital had tested both side of my brain but how were these results being utilized in my everyday life? It really did not matter. The first activities I explored for each hemisphere were so much fun that I never explored any further. Everything I did, I did because I liked it!

Left Brain: I enjoy reading and I was thrilled to discover that I had forgotten everything that I had read. What else was I capable of doing? There was a caveat to this. If I had taken notes or written something down then it was still in my brain, stored in my long-term memory. But who writes notes when pleasure reading? I used the library a lot prior to them uploading books on-line. I still take our books from the library but now they are e-books.

I took up bridge, thinking that would stimulate my left brain. After I attended some church group sessions, my mother-in-law gave me a gift certificate at Christmas for the local bridge club lesson program. I loved it! Unfortunately, bridge requires a partner, and I did not have one. I experienced having a regular partner recently, and I am thinking that having random partners is easier. There is also a lot of free on-line bridge today.

Currently, I am trying to study new languages to generate new neurons by playing on-line language games. The difficulty is to stick with one language. I want to master my French because I live in Canada, but because my brother lives in Mexico, I have tried to learn a bit of Spanish. Then, if we vacation somewhere else, I think it is only polite to know the basics of language in that country. I am not a natural at languages by any means, so I think it is the fun playing the language App that I have been using.

Right Brain: For my right brain, I was initially at a complete loss. I liked art and I enjoyed listening to most types of music. It was easy for me to remember that I was terrible at performing in both these arenas. I am estimating the time here, but it may have only been about eight-, or nine-years post injury, when a lady at the fitness club had a block of ten tickets to a concert in Toronto and she asked if I would like to join them. The concert was a Canadian musician playing in Toronto at Massey Hall. I was unsure if I would even know any of his music. Since I had forgotten all the novels I had read, and all the movies I had seen, what would be different with music? To my surprise and delight, I *did* recognize the music. Music soothes the brain. You hear it, you feel it, you move your body to it, and on an emotional level, you rejoice in it.

I was so excited when this rock star came on stage, and I proceeded to watch him intently. I could not sit still. I suspect that by dancing in my seat, I was annoying those seated around me. Noticing that many other people had run up on stage and were dancing, I asked those seated beside me if they thought it would be OK for me to run up to the stage. I did. I loved it.

After the show, I learned that most of these people were members of his fan club. They also were able to purchase better seats at a pre-sale or in a reserved block. I had many years of excellent concert viewing through this route. Unfortunately, the sophistication of scalpers has made such access difficult.

I was surprised at the undivided attention I was receiving from this rock star. He kept staring at me. Over the next several years, I attended more of his concerts and spent time in his chat room. I particularly enjoyed being in his chat room because no one could see or hear me. There was a moderator in his chat room so that threads of conversation never got out of hand. The people who populated this man's world were mostly good, kind people. Still, I would question myself as to why he continued to recognize me at future concerts. My brain could just not retrieve the necessary information to place him in my life. Eventually something must have "cued" me during a chat room conversation. The lights seemed to be slowly turning on, one bulb at a time, until I could put all these fragments of information together. Apparently, I had met him a few decades before when he was still relatively unknown. He was curious and concerned with the difference he saw in me and wondered what on earth had happened to me.

Music Appreciation has now become my right-brained activity. For a short window of my life, I even knew how to get good concert tickets. I also went to see many other bands when they played throughout the G.T.A. On occasion, I even travelled to see this musician elsewhere. It was surprising to realize that I could still be o.k. out in the world in my restricted and limited capacity. Being new to asking for help from anyone, I discovered the joy of being less independent. You still need to be vigilant and careful if you look like an easy target. So, travel light and be organized.

Music was therapeutic because it led me to a place that was all mine. It provides many physiological benefits but the basic psychology of it worked for me too. People are not interacting or talking with each other. There may be hundreds, or thousands of people and they are enjoying the music individually. No one else could feel the music or even interpret the same feelings to it that I did.

Music is powerful. In fact, after a concert, I would feel a natural high. This is because listening to music modulates serotonin and dopamine levels in your brain.

MUSIC THERAPY

MUSIC PLAYS AN important role in our lives, our well-being, and our healing. I looked on the internet for examples of music in therapy and why it works so effectively. I found plenty of support for music improving mental health and well-being, from reducing the amounts of pain medication to stimulating brain activity. Music therapy has been used in rehabilitation settings to stimulate brain functions involved in movement, cognition, speed, emotional regulation, and sensory perception (Bredt, Magee, Wheeler & McGilloway, 2010).

Neurologic Music Therapy is based on neuroscience (Smith, 2018). Neurologic music therapy uses the variation within the brain both with and without music and manipulates this to evoke brain changes that affect the patient. I have no idea how this works, but it has been proven effective.

Researchers have found that listening to music and playing music increases the body's production of the *antibody immunoglobulin A and natural killer cells*—the cells that attack invading viruses and boost the immune system's effectiveness. Music has also been found to reduce the level of the stress hormone cortisol.

Orff-Schulwerk is a music therapy approach developed by Gertrude Orff (Smith, 2018). When she realized that medicine alone was not sufficient for children with developmental delays and disabilities, Orff formed this model "Schulwerk, or "schoolwork" in German). It uses music to help children improve their learning ability. This method also highlights the importance of humanistic psychology and uses music to improve the interaction between the child and other people.

I made up my own form of music therapy. This involved listening to live music or recorded music which I sang along to when driving. I also learned music-assisted relaxation techniques, such as progressive muscle relaxation and deep breathing.

SPIRITUALITY AND HEALING

I WAS BROUGHT up in the United Church of Canada. We belonged to a beautiful church in the centre of Toronto called Timothy Eaton Memorial Church. As children, my siblings and I grew up attending Sunday school and confirmation classes and then attending church services. My parents always ensured we went to the 9:30 a.m. service, which as teenagers, was a nightmare. Then in my late teens, in search of guidance, I would attend the Sunday evening service, which was much more conducive to my sleep habits.

When I married Dan, our lifestyle did not leave any room for Sunday church services. I still believe in the spirit of Christianity and feel comforted holding onto this belief. I do not believe one has to believe the actual biblical stories themselves but to believe in their teachings, as a guide to live one's life. Could I ask God to help me find a way to get better? I prayed and I asked him to show me "how to get better". If prayer is "intention setting", this intention was achieved. If prayer is talking to God, then God answered me.

At first when Dr. Thornton introduced me to the idea of his "Prayer Wheel", I thought, "Uh-oh, what did I get involved with", "Is this going to be a cult"? Fortunately, I learned that the lines are blurred more than I ever would have thought, between religion and psychology.

THE PRAYER WHEEL

by John F. Rossiter Thornton, MD

Why Pray?

Prayer has been shown to benefit health and is a self-help technique and spiritual practice that costs nothing, requires no special equipment, can be used anywhere, and for any situation. Dr. Thornton created this wheel which he calls "the ancient technology of intention-setting."

The Prayer Wheel is a circle of eight categories that interconnect to form a circle:

1. Count Your Blessings, to harness depressive thoughts and anxiety.
2. Sing of Love, healing
3. Request Protection and Guidance
4. Forgive Yourself and Others, - heals as it clears your mind of anger and negative feelings.
5. Ask for Yourself and Others – this is intention setting or goal setting.
6. Fill Me with Love and Inspire Me, healing.
7. LISTEN with Pen in Hand

8. Your Will is My Will

In this five-by-nine-centimetre pocketbook, there are tips to help you follow each step. He also offers special uses of the Prayer Wheel.

www.theprayerwheel.com

PART VI: LIFE AFTER SPECT

PACE YOURSELF FOREVER

POST-TREATMENT, MY HARDEST battle is to pace myself. Some days I wake up feeling energized but if I try to do everything on my to-do list, I end up exhausted. With exhaustion comes a decrease in my abilities to function. My speech may start to slur, I lose some stability and my ability to problem solve goes out the window. I used to feel that I must get things done or I will forget to finish them. Why? I now know that writing a To-Do list is a much better option.

Be aware that it is critical to maintain your muscle strength. Human beings lose 10 percent of our strength each decade after age 50. Less strength means less energy and everything you do takes more out of you. Injuries are more likely as a result. With that in mind, I have tried to figure out what works best for me with reduced energy reserves from a treated (but not invincible) TBI and aging.

We need to maintain our strength-training a few times per week through body weight activities and gym work. I tried to cut back on some of my strength-training from my regular schedule because I find it hard to self-motivate, but I found that if I do not maintain my fitness level my body tires more easily and physical abilities start to fall apart (my limp increases and my balance decreases). It is a fine line between doing too little and overdoing it.

Fortunately, I discovered functional training circuit training. Functional training refers to exercise that looks like movements you make in your daily life. It helps with athletic performance, injury prevention, and other everyday fitness tasks. There are seven functional movements: pull, push, squat, lunge, hinge, rotations, and gait. Performing these movements will stimulate all the major muscle groups in your body.

SUMMARY

Sufficient rest with the right balance of exercise and nutrition will provide you with a healthy baseline. This will allow you to engage in whatever makes your heart sing.

EPILOGUE

IT CAN BE frightening waking up and wondering who you are. Where do you belong in this world? Who are your people? Questions are everywhere. As I gradually woke up, I needed to be prompted to recall most things, including having two baby boys. Time and sleep are your best answers at the beginning of your recovery (for me that lasted several years). Once you are medically stable you can decide if you want to engage in what SPECT scanning entails.

A great deal of my adult life has been lived under the cloud of a traumatic brain injury. I had to relearn many things since being treated by Dr. Thornton and I hope that I have lots of time to learn more. I am a happy person, with a beautiful husband, two great sons, and our fabulous rescue dog, Duke.

Now that our sons are both finally on their own, Dan and I are forging an easy and comfortable life together. I am so thankful he asked me to marry him all those years ago. Without his support, my life and my search for treatment would not have succeeded.

Even though we had difficult situations and he had to endure my behavioural and emotional roller-coaster, the gratitude I have after coming out on this end of it all is titanic. We share a resilience. Through all that we have experienced together, whether raising our sons, my adventure with brain injury or his struggles with his business and his family, we survived together. To refer to a previous goal of mine, Dan now "sees me". In fact, I think that Dan might know me better than I know myself now. I have come to really appreciate his humour and anticipate a splendid humour-filled future with him.

I believe that we need holistic traumatic brain injury centres. Maybe this could be within a specialized rehab hospital with follow-up guidance and out-patient programs set up upon discharge. A central point of contact which all doctors could access and support their patients with relevant TBI information is needed. What other illness or injury requires someone to use their damaged faculties to solve their own crises? This needs to be done by bringing all the hospitals who treat traumatic brain injury, and all the specialties that work with traumatic brain injuries, together under one roof. Another possibility would be to have questionnaires given to patients to cover all possible areas traumatic brain injury might affect. The person could complete these at home prior to a doctor's visit. How does a brain injured individual remember all their deficits with a short-term memory problem? Even if a doctor has a checklist, a thorough visit could take hours. Designing a questionnaire for patients to complete (either on their own, or with caregiver assistance) could flag certain issues that will trigger advice and/or referrals by the Family Doctor.

While I do not have the level of physical function I would like, I love being physically active because that is what makes my heart sing! I am finding there is still a lot more fun to be had by approaching sports from a different ability.

Mentally, I came out of this situation with more confidence in myself than I have ever had. Gosh, is it ever fun to not be worried about every little detail! I maintain my on-line bridge and I am attempting to increase my fluency in a second language. Sadly, we experienced many covid openings, closures, and re-openings of sports activities. I physically injured myself badly on two occasions due to my excess enthusiasm for doing what I had been deprived of doing all season. I did not listen to my own caution of "pace yourself" forever.

Being eternally enthusiastic has opened doors to new experiences. Not golfing has encouraged me to travel the Bruce Trail with our dog, Duke and my Nordic walking poles. Not being able to regain my downhill ski proficiency led me to learning how to Telemark ski. Editing and re-editing this book may lead me to prepare for another brain injury conference. Life can be more exciting when you try new things.

One thing that I have noticed in re-reading sections of this book as I edited it for the hundredth time is how positive I am. Once you ask to yourself, what have I got to lose? the answer is "nothing at all". I had nothing to lose by trying to tweak my brain. I was at my lowest point, and every time that I tried something new, it helped. Just the act of trying was better than doing nothing. A busy mind is much happier than a lazy mind. Everything you do may not be successful, but who knows? You still might like it!

THE FUTURE OF BRAIN INJURY RECOVERY

BACK AT THE beginning of this book, I said that there was no central information desk for brain injury in Canada.

1. There is now a knowledge desk at Brain Injury Canada (BIC). The new website is worth your time to explore. You can find their website at: https://braininjurycanada.ca/.w
2. There is also a fantastic library and educational resources at: http://Ontariobraininjuryassociation.ca, (OBIA.ca).

Fortunately, the knowledge surrounding brain injury has changed a lot in the past twenty-five years. Today, two major players have accelerated the progress of brain injury research:

1. The many professional athletes who have sustained brain damage, both present and past.

2. Military personnel in the United States and Canada with TBIs from IEDs. Many who also suffer from post-traumatic stress disorder (PTSD) can also utilize the functional neuroimaging of SPECT for treatment.

The Canadian and U.S. military are both involved in brain research and are leaders in TBI treatment. In the U.S., the military has an integrated treatment system, unlike the public health-care systems of both our countries. The medical world looks to be trying to conquer one of their last frontiers, the brain. Is the reason because of the brain's vast complexity?

In reviewing what has been going on with brain injury research over the past twenty-five years, I was pleased to see the multi-disciplinary approach more recently being utilized by the American Air Force. Unfortunately, there is a big problem with their program and that is that you can only access it if you are a member of the Air Force.

Dr. Thornton has published three papers on the topic of SPECT Scans and their current use in the American Journal of Psychiatry. He has ensured that there are guidelines within the Nuclear Medicine Departments to be followed for people with Traumatic Brain Injury.

Dr. Thornton has also presented his work at many seminars for family doctors and medical specialists.

Looking forward into our future, there are several industries who can benefit from the use of SPECT. The first is my personal antagonist: the insurance industry. The second industry that would benefit from the use of 3-D SPECT analysis is the pharmaceutical industry. Treatment is a lifetime of medication. It is a chronic condition, like diabetics requiring insulin forever.

With the knowledge in this book and knowledge provided to me by Dr. Thornton, brain injury recovery can be significantly improved. In fact, to my mind, it will be a speedy recovery compared to the time it took for those of us who came before this knowledge. I sincerely hope that this knowledge becomes available to those in need and that it is used across Ontario. As the Canadian rock star, Bryan Adams sings in his album, On A Day Like Today, "But ya never know what might be comin' round your way". For those with traumatic brain injuries, it has come around for you.

REFERENCES

1. *Brain Injury Canada/Lésions Cérébrales Canada BrainInjuryCanada.com*
2. *Canadian Association of Nuclear Medicine/ Association de Médecine Nucléaire (CANM/ACMN)* CanadianAssociationofNuclearMedicine.com
3. *"Frontiers in Psychology" July10/2015, on-line magazine.* *https://archive.news.iupui.edu/releases/2016/02/02 adaptedyoga-brain-injury.shtml*
4. *"On A Day Like Today", Bryan Adams 1998*
5. *Ontario Brain Injury Association (OBIA.ca)*
6. <u>So, You Think You're Covered! The Insurance Industry Rip-off</u>: *Surviving the Fight for Long-term Disability Benefits* Jokelee Vanderkop. *2013*
7. <u>The Prayer Wheel</u> *Dr. John Rossiter-Thornton*
8. <u>This Is Your Brain on Music</u>, *Dr. J. Levitin, Plume/Penguin 2007).*

Printed in the USA
CPSIA information can be obtained
at www.ICGtesting.com
JSHW070156071223
53164JS00010B/77

God gave Pat a special dose of "inner strengthening with power by His Spirit" to be able to put her faith to work in a powerful way. Her journal reveals a woman that was living somewhere between earth and heaven in an illness that was preparing her for heaven while bringing a touch of heaven to all that received the emails that became the content of this book. Read with the expectation of learning the reality of a faith-walk that will be an encouragement when you need that extra dose of faith.

Rev. Dr. Glenn Havumaki
Director of Christian Ministries of Elim Park.org
Author-<i>Trashed or Treasured</i>

Her writing is engaging making me feel as I was on the journey with her. I appreciate the fact that she stated things (her condition) as they were. Pat faced the realities of a myriad of emotions. Her strength of character shines through her journaling. I now know how to be strong and courageous during my own trial.

Betty LoPrinzi

I had the blessing of knowing and treating Pat in our practice for over 30 years before she received her diagnosis of cancer. Pat maintained the same positive funny and caring spirit during her battle as she did before her surgery. "Walk With Me" is an excellent example of how detailed attention to the narrative of medical procedures, interwoven with personal and spiritual narrative can be a tremendous comfort to anyone who has been touched or affected by the diagnosis and treatment of cancer. It is a gift to know Pat through her 'story'.

Jeffrey J. Bisson, D.M.D.
Cheshire Dental Associates- CT

Wow, even though I never had the blessing of knowing Pat, personally, I feel like I have had a glimpse into her character through her journey of faith. Her love for Jesus is so clear and precious and the trust she put in God is inspiring to me. Her approach in faith to the circumstances she faced in the months before she was released and freed from the cancer gives me great encouragement. Pat's story would be of great help to many people facing similar situations.

Anne Wood

Walk WITH Me

Patricia Jahrstorfer

Illustrated by Judi F. Niemann

Copyright © 2013 by Patricia Jahrstorfer

Walk With Me
by Patricia Jahrstorfer

Cover painting and interior illustrations by Judi F. Niemann

Printed in the United States of America

ISBN 9781626975057

All rights reserved solely by the author. The author guarantees all contents are original and do not infringe upon the legal rights of any other person or work. No part of this book may be reproduced in any form without the permission of the author. The views expressed in this book are not necessarily those of the publisher.

Unless otherwise indicated, Bible quotations are taken from New Living Translation (NLT). Copyright © 1996, 2004, 2007 by Tyndale House Foundation. Used by permission. All rights reserved. New International Version (NIV). Copyright © 1973, 1978, 1984, 2011 by Biblica, Inc.™. Used by permission. All rights reserved. New American Standard Bible (NASB). Copyright © 1960, 1962, 1963, 1968, 1971, 1972, 1973, 1975, 1977, 1995 by The Lockman Foundation. Used by permission. All rights reserved. Amplified Bible (AMP). Copyright © 1954, 1958, 1962, 1964, 1965, 1987 by The Lockman Foundation. Used by permission. All rights reserved.

www.xulonpress.com

Blog link: www.we2jars.wordpress.com
Email: throughitallwithpat@gmail.com

> The illustrations accompanying Pat's text were added by her husband and family after her passing. They seemed an appropriate way to enlarge upon Pat's words. Some of the illustrations are family photos. Others, both photos and artwork, are from various public domain sources. In some instances artist Judi Niemann of North Carolina used her artistic skill at our request, to produce both original drawings and sensitive renderings of images from other artists and photographers. We extend our deep thanks to Judi for her service.
>
> Despite our extensive search to properly credit the original sources of images used here, we were unable to do so for several of them. We trust that this public declaration of our good intentions will suffice and we would welcome hearing from you, our readers, if you are able to provide their sources. We want to honor Pat in every way through this book, including due respect for copyright of nonpublic material, both quoted text and artistic rendering of illustrations.
>
> -The Jahrstorfer Family

PREFACE

*T*he most important reason for putting this journal into print is to Glorify my wonderful God and Savior, Jesus Christ. Without HIM I do not know that I would be writing or, indeed, if I would be here to write. HE has been my constant companion and strength during this trial, and HE has kept me in a place that is indeed "looking down from the heavenlies." My journey has been a grand "bubble experience", as I have sensed HIS protective, loving hand in mine throughout many difficult times.

I also want especially to pay tribute to and thank each and every one of you for being constant in prayer, faithful in service, and most tender in your love and compassion for me. Your cards, calls, meals, e-mails, transportation, and presence in my life during this time have been the undergirding of my uplifted and positive faith. I am amazed at the love you have for me, and my value and humility before God has soared as never before.

There has been a special one whom I cannot neglect to mention. My husband Carl has been there truly through thick and thin. He's been there to sort out the timing of medications, the insurance issues, the home care responsibilities, and has been there when I was too weak to stand, too unconscious to know who was with me. He

dressed my wounds, held my hand, read to me, prayed with and for me, and believed even through his own tears that God would heal me.

These pages are a compilation of 5-6 months of e-mails that I felt impressed to write while I was undergoing chemotherapy and surgery for ovarian cancer. At this point I am free of all cancer and have been given a clean bill of health. We serve a wonderful Savior.

Many thanks to my family and friends who showed me their love which encouraged me to keep writing and going forward.

Pat

Editor's Note: The preface was written March 15, 2012. The words, thoughts, lyrics, and Bible quotations in her journal are all expressed, written, and recalled at the moment of inspiration by the author. Because she read and used several different Bible translations during her lifetime, Pat's spontaneous recollection of scripture makes for an interesting read.

HOLDING ON

AUGUST 5, 2011

Thanks everyone for being so flexible. Last night (Wednesday, 8/4 /11), I just did not feel well enough to have you all over and be a participant. When we say we will pray for God's will we usually want our will with HIS blessing, especially when it involves pain. Yet our God is the one who is big enough to take us through as HE has shown in the testimonies that have been shared so far. HE is awesome and always worthy of all our praise.

The physical truth that showed up in the tests (8/2/2011) was that I have a 6-7" growth in my abdominal area. The analysis of its nature has not, and will not, be revealed until it is removed. Pray that we are following God's leading as to hospital and doctor. Of course, if God would go the quick miraculous painless way, that would be most welcome.

We know you will be part of our sustaining network in prayer, and we are grateful.

Thanks especially to Ellen for volunteering to take me and help out. God provided, but your offer touched my heart and made me cry. I guess I have been doing some of that today and God says it's O.K. As I bring my fears and human responses to HIM, HE shows me how much I will keep you all informed as more information becomes

August 5, 2011 (continued)

available. Carl has been a wonderful help, and when I had to go back to radiology for two additional tests beyond the three this morning, he was with me. I was thankful I could say "I need some emotional support right now" and not try to be the stoic woman I was taught to be".

So we wait upon the LORD while we **hold on tight** and we are glad that you are there **holding onto HIM** with us.

Bless and Miss you all,

Pat

P.S. It is now early Friday morning (8/6), Pat had a very difficult night. The doctor is prescribing high pain meds (she is not on them yet) and making arrangements for admission to hospital. Pat wants this to be over quickly. Pray for her relief and my thinking clearly. We will be in touch.

Carl

THE NEWS THAT CHANGED EVERYTHING

AUGUST 11, 2011

Editors note: *The following e-mail was written very early Thursday morning (8/11) by Carl at home while Pat was in hospital after several days of severe night time pain. She was kept over night for observation.*

Hello Family and Friends,

Some of you know the details of Pat's three month long backache issues, but here is an update. Yesterday, Wednesday morning, I took Pat to HH Emergency Room after a week of suspicious abdominal pain coming only at night time. After many tests from different medical areas they couldn't find anything wrong so a CT scan was scheduled. She was finally admitted at 8 PM. The scan was done at 11:30 PM. Since it was an all women's floor, I had to leave the hospital at that time. Her surgeon, Dr B., is scheduled to do rounds this morning at 7 AM when we will hear the results of all the tests. I'm hoping for quick surgery, even tomorrow, Friday, to remove this seven inch tumor.

Pat is grateful for all of you keeping her in prayer. Continue to pray. Yesterday, she was feeling better, being in the hospital, even if it was a long wait (10 hrs) in ER. She is upbeat and positive (as always) and anticipates with excitement about losing 10 lbs and a few inches around her waist. I will keep you informed.

August 11, 2011 (continued)

My cell phone signal is weak in the hospital but I will still try to communicate that way as I will attempt to sleep in the visitor's lounge on her floor.

Carl

Later Same Day (Late afternoon)

Well, God is amazing...When He tells us that patience is the fruit of the Spirit, we really don't know what that means until we have to wait some more. Bottom line is: I am too healthy to need emergency surgery, plus my doctor will be on vacation next week, and I have two major tests I need to schedule before she does the surgery. So, although the tumor is taking up most of my abdominal cavity, and I will need a total hysterectomy, it will not be at least until the 24th of August. So I am home again.

God is good. I am calm and confident. I am in pain but will be taking my pain killers around the clock until the surgery. Pray that my confidence in all God's good plans remains strong. Thank you all so very much.

Love you all,

Pat

THE UNKNOWN

AUGUST 13, 2011

Editor's Note: *This entry was sent to the doctor's office.*

Pat had an uncomfortable night (Friday), more with hip and back pain than abdominal pain. Dr. B. gave her the okay to go for chiropractic adjustment which Pat did yesterday morning (10:30 AM). She felt alright after the adjustment, but, once again, trying to sleep caused her pain. She is still on Aleve®, alternating between one and two pills 3X a day. She used a heating pad on her belly, hips, and upper thigh where she complained of most pain, saying she felt a pulling in her lower left pelvic area and down her thigh. I suspect this all could be post-trauma from her morning adjustment. Could that be the cause?

I don't know if she will be able to deal with 12 additional days like this with these kinds of nights. While she has a high tolerance for pain, it is frustrating and exhausting her. On the positive side, she has very minimal pain during the day. She is taking two pills at night. What other suggestions (she has tried pillows, raising her head, sleeping on side) can you offer her to get the rest she needs? One other observation: her abdominal cavity appears to be expanding since 8/6 when it was 43 inches. While in the hospital there was no measurement taken that we are aware of.

August 13, 2011 (continued)

Thank you for taking the time to answer all my questions: One more-- can these tumors grow more rapidly after ultrasounds?

Carl

P.S. I've done a bit of editing of Carl's notes. Thank you for your willingness to help us walk through this. I am confident that "this, too, shall pass", yet it is so very hard for Carl to see me in pain, and he wants to do all he can to help me. You may not get this note until Monday, but it was important that Carl document what has been happening so that you are updated on my condition as you requested.

Thanks again. Perhaps we will talk soon.

Pat

LATER SAME DAY

Dear Family and Friends,

I now have a date for surgery: August 24th at 9AM. I am stable with bearable pain levels. I will be going for more outpatient tests.

Continue to pray for me to KNOW that HE is higher and deeper and wider and has good plans and is watching over me and that, bottom line, HE is much bigger than it all and has wonderful purposes for these trials. As we are HIS beloved children, even as we are inscribed on the palm of HIS hand and HE watches over us like a mamma lion her cubs, so there is peace and patience for the journey. Thanks for letting me preach to myself.

Love you all,

Pat

EXTRAORDINARILY HEALTHY

AUGUST 14, 2011

As to the whole truth, my tumor is about seven inches and is causing swelling that is pushing my stomach up. It also is creating havoc with my back and even down my legs at times. I will be having a radical hysterectomy, and everything will be gone related to child bearing, even my cervix. So this week I am slated for a breast biopsy, and next week a day before surgery, I will be having a colonoscopy. My pain level is tolerable, but I think I may have made a mistake going to see Dr. G. yesterday, because last night pain kept me from sleeping, and the lying-down position is not conducive to the tumor's rest. YET, I know that my Redeemer liveth, that HE is the one who leads, that I am in HIS care and there is no better place...and I can inhale HIM and go through all that is before me. I am not afraid but do want this to be over.

The doctor says the recovery time will be 3-5 days in the hospital and 6-8 weeks at home. God can do miracles and I am extraordinarily healthy. That is why I am home... because I am so healthy. My blood pressure is 116/61 and the doctor was amazed...so amazed that she sent me home, because she did not see me as an emergency and will be on vacation all this coming week.

Love you much,

Pat

Increased Pain

August 20, 2011

Hello Family and Friends,

It appears Pat's pain is increasing (it has never left since 8/4). She has been on acetaminophen 625mg extended release tablets for the last seven days after Aleve wasn't keeping her pain free. She is taking meds every 6-8 hours now to stay ahead of pain. Pray that on Monday morning she can be released from some additional pre-op tests that she is expected to take on Tuesday prior to her surgery on Wednesday. It seems so far away.

Carl (for Pat)

Almost Funny

August 23, 2011

I'm sorry I cannot say much since we are on our way to J.C. in W. H. for the colonoscopy. The pain last night was excruciating and now (believe it or not) I am wearing *Depends* ®because it seems the flow did not want to stop. Also just trusting God. It seems like as we are speaking I am feeling more comfortable about "leakage". If this weren't so painful, it might even be funny.

Yesterday God sent a wonderful friend from church to minister to me, and HE has sent so many at just the right time. Kristin is expecting a hurricane and Laurie Ann is inundated with work and her children leaving. We'll talk again...gotta go...no, not that way!

Love you and always pray for you, too...know that you truly understand me.

Pat

THE JOURNEY BEGINS

AUGUST 23, 2011

Hello Family,

It certainly has been a long 36 hours. And even a longer 22 days, and then even a longer five months, the time Mom (Pat) first remembers starting to feel low back pain.

I believe all but a few of you know of today's long outing with the clean colonoscopy report and then the aspiration (end of procedure) that kept her in West Hartford Medical Center for longer than expected. The 103 temp and inability to control the pain (that she has had for 22 days) didn't make any of us happy, including the medical staff. Because of her very high dosages of Tylenol® (over 4500 mg average the last 10 days) and her very bad reactions to narcotics, especially codeine and morphine, they weren't sure what to give her.

The plan was to send her home today by 3pm and have her return tomorrow morning at 9am for surgery to remove the 7-inch tumor plus all her female reproductive organs. We are grateful for all prayers and that her colon is clean.

However, because of her temperature and inability of the medical team to control her pain, Pat was transported to HH at 5 PM and admitted immediately to North

August 23, 2011 (continued)

8th, a "women's only" floor. This answered my prayer as she really needed more attention than what this little old caregiver was providing with OTC meds. She was given one gram Dilaudid®, which took the edge off her pain (finally some relief). However, because of original doctor's orders, she has to remain on a liquid diet till surgery tomorrow morning. Talk about a tired puppy! I'm thankful for my clinical (limited as it is) understanding because of my experience working at Elim Park, so I became Pat's advocate. I've come to the conclusion that <u>every</u> patient needs a personal advocate in a hospital. Staffing works very hard, but they are all caring for more people than they can possibly cover in a 12-hr shift. I kept details of all of her meds, symptoms, pain experiences (especially the night challenges) of this past week. Of course, there was little or no sleep for Pat. These records are valuable in providing info for the doctors to address her pain. There seems to be a propensity for duplicating tests. Pat is now on a drip of Dilaudid-- groggy, tired and hungry, but with less pain. Since there are no men allowed on this floor, I had to leave at 10 PM.

Let's pray that her temp (103.8) breaks and the small matter of aspirated bile in her upper left lung clears up by 9 AM tomorrow so surgery can proceed. I will make contact with some of you again via cell phone, others by e-mail, most likely tomorrow evening.

Pat has felt the love of all our brothers and sisters in Christ and has remained calm and peaceful during this medical issue. It is truly awesome to witness. I'm so blessed. This has been the biggest health test in our lives, but our God says He *will never leave us nor forsake us* and that Jesus our Savior will be there in the boat with us during the storms of life as we place our trust in Him. That is the faith we live by, and we certainly have seen it in action.

Keep on praying.
Carl

Sketch of card given by Pat to Carl.
Original photo by Kim Anderson.

DAY AFTER SURGERY

AUGUST 25, 2011

Hello Everyone,

I am sending this e-mail to give you an update from Carl and Pat.

The doctor has removed the tumor and was surprised to find it cancerous. She did not get all of it and has recommended chemotherapy (starting in a couple weeks) for five months. The doctor is fairly confident that this will put it into remission after the five-month treatment.

Pray for a miracle and for wisdom for Pat and Carl that they know the right option for chemo. (There apparently are four different options.) Pray for them as they move forward following God's will. HE IS SOVEREIGN!

Love to all from Pat and Carl. She hopes to be home by Monday. Please call before visiting (probably not before she is home from the hospital).

Thank you all for your continuous prayer and support.

In His service,

Ellen P

RECOVERY

August 27, 2011

Our daughter, Laurie Ann, who is up from Virginia, stayed with Pat last night. I went home after four nights in the hospital. Pat is still in pain postoperatively due to major surgery (5 hrs). Doctors can't seem to control her pain. Pat is weak. Last night she was given two pints of blood to help with anemia. She has walked a few times which is a good thing.

Thank you for all your prayers and support. Right now, no visitors. Pray for her peace to continue, that meds can control pain, and that her caregivers (including me) stay calm.

Carl

WHO WILL HOLD TOMORROW

AUGUST 29, 2011

To all my business partners and associates:

As most of you know, my wife Pat had been complaining of low back pain for the last six months. She tried PT, water exercises at Elim Park, and chiropractic adjustments. All the disciplines said, "I can help", but nothing improved her situation.

On August 2, she went for her annual physical. Her primary care physician (PCP) identified that her uterus was the size of a four-month pregnancy. On August 4, internal ultrasound confirmed a seven-inch tumor on her ovary which her PCP said "must come out quickly". Three weeks followed of increasing pain, a scheduled surgeon's visit, one emergency hospital visit, and doctor conversations. All her markers (no history of cancer in family, a clean colon, mammogram, pap and blood work, and the CA125 tests) were not conclusive in showing the presence of a malignancy. A full hysterectomy was scheduled for August 24.

Pat's cancer is called carcinosarcoma and is rare, microscopic, and aggressive. Pat is now in HH (5th day) and still recovering from 5-hour intensive major surgery.

Our faith is strong because we don't know **What** trials we face tomorrow, BUT we know **Who** holds tomorrow. Her

peace is secure in knowing our Lord and Savior, Jesus Christ, will hold her hand through this storm.

Scripture tells us . . . He (the Father) *sends rain on the just and the unjust alike.* (Matt. 5:45) The rain falls on the good and bad. **How we respond to our circumstances determines our purpose, our growth, and our destiny.** As you are led, pray for her health to improve and for the next step, one day at a time. Pray for the changes in our lifestyle, and pray for me to *be strong and courageous.* (Joshua 1:9)

Because of our business and club connections, my activities, contracts, appointments, and meetings will be diminished or cancelled until Pat's condition improves. If you need to know more, you can e-mail me. She requests no visitors at this time.

Thank you for your friendship, legal and/or professional advice.

Carl

FIRST WORDS

AUGUST 30, 2011

Hi Everyone,

Laurie Ann is typing for me and I am so thankful that I could communicate with you <u>personally</u>! God is good. HE has brought me home again, given me a family that loves and wants too much to serve me, and given me a sustaining sense of HIS presence and love.

At this point my pain is under control and I had a great nap today. God has given me HIS peace. I pray I remain sensitive to HIS wisdom. I know HE is with me. Your gifts of service, food, prayer and love are lifting me at this time. I am leaning on HIM for the quiet healing only HE can provide.

I look forward to seeing you when I am ready. Laurie Ann will be here until Kristin comes on Friday, and Kristin will be here till next Tuesday.

Miss you all.

Love,
Pat

MOVING FORWARD

SEPTEMBER 2, 2011

Thank you all for your love, prayers, food, cards, flowers, kind words, calls etc.....I so deeply appreciate all your investment in me during this time. Let me say that God has provided bountifully for me, both through many caring hands and HIS continuously healing touch.

Let me also say thank you for allowing me this quiet time with God and my family to look at HIM and see where I am and where HE is taking me. I am very positive about LIFE as this morning I remember the verse in Deut. 30:19 saying that God has *placed before us the choice of life or death* and that we are to *choose LIFE*. I know that this path may have challenges, but I am taking one day at a time trusting HIM for tomorrow.

I know how much you all want to see me and hug me, and I value that part of your love. When Kristin goes home next week I may want to begin visiting with you, but please know that the quiet I am experiencing is a wonderful balm for me. I will try to listen to my body and God and would appreciate your work in my healing as well. The work I am asking you to do is the work of grieving and shock and the need for

September 2, 2011 (continued)

information. My healing needs the GOOD WORD HE offers. I do not in any way want to rehearse the pain of the past. I am in a new place and want to go forward. Please allow me to do so. Your tears would only reinforce the phase I have come through. Thank you for allowing me to communicate in this way, and please forgive me if I seem harsh or unappreciative of all you have given.

Bless you all. May HIS love envelop you with HIS truth.

Pat

Thankful Praise

September 4, 2011

Hi Beloveds!

This is the day that the LORD has made. I will rejoice and be glad in it!! Today I was able to worship with some music that spoke to my heart. Yet I have been wrestling with the idea of seeing you all. And I still sense it is not the right time. I have not even seen those of you who come to bring meals. The risk of infection is something I must consider at this stage of my healing. This Thursday I will be getting my surgical staples removed, and I believe I need to wait until at least next week before making a decision about visitors.

Please know that you are all very precious to me. I have sensed your prayers that have kept my spirits high. As you pray remember my family members who are caring for me, especially Carl who is not familiar with this kind of health situation and is surrendering again and again to God's sovereignty and will.

In all, I remain blessed and so aware of my Loving Lord.

Thanks again for your love and prayer.

Pat

DECISIONS

SEPTEMBER 8, 2011

Well, here goes . . . .After praying on the way to the doctor's office and sensing I needed to be open to whatever treatment would be best for me--not what I wanted--it was easier to make a choice. I was at peace and courageous, even a bit funny with the doctor, and had an opportunity to share my Jesus vision (refer to journal entry September 30th) with one of the patients I met in the office.

My treatment will begin with a CT scan on this Saturday and then four days of consultation and treatment (Sept. 19-22). I will be in the treatment center for three days and each day I will be able to come home after treatment. I chose a treatment that historically works best with the type of cancer that was diagnosed.

Please continue to pray that I remain strong and courageous and make more of HIS Word a part of the deepest part of my being.

Thanks for your love and prayers. I stand amazed at all those who pray for me throughout our great country.

Love you all,
Pat

First Week of Chemo

September 19, 2011

Today we got lots and lots of info. Too many facts. We are looking to Jesus but are fatigued. This is the time to pray for strength and faith to continue to rise up.

Our schedule for the next few days has been set, and the number of pills and the times I take them is very detailed and often. I will be on an IV for Tuesday, Wednesday, and Thursday, and on Friday I will have an injection to avert some of the side effects. Enough of the details.

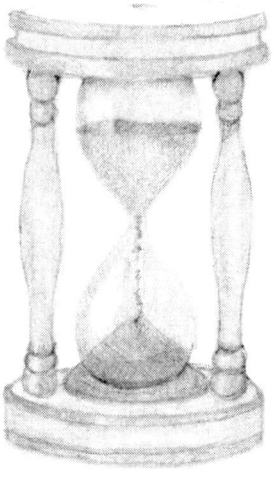

Carl and I realized that during this period of time, especially through Sunday, we may need more help than we anticipated. I guess we were planning on an easy way through. And although God is still in the miracle-working business, when we heard what will be involved, we did feel overwhelmed. We have to keep reminding ourselves that the way we FEEL has little to do with the love and presence of our God who is WITH us. Pray for us to know what and when and how we need help. At times it is difficult to sort through all we will have to do. So we are setting our faces like flints

September 19, 2011 (continued)

and taking one step at a time.

Thank you for praying and sharing the truth God has given you for us. We so desperately need HIM and now we KNOW it. This morning as we read Ecclesiastes we read the verse that says, "*A time to kill and a time to heal...*" (Ecc. 3:3). The time to kill is here in that the cancer must be killed and then the time to heal will come.

Thank you again. Carl will probably call on those of you who have offered to help when we know what that looks like.

Pat

CYCLE I

SEPTEMBER 20, 2011

Well, the Lord and I made it and, HALLELUJAH, WITHOUT SIDE EFFECTS!!! So please keep praying that God will create a wall against the side effects. They say they can occur at any time. Every time a new drug or treatment balancer was given, I was read the litany about what could happen and how I would feel. I realized the danger in administering the chemo, when each time the nurse changed the IV drug she put on <u>two</u> pairs of gloves and a plastic gown and face mask. She said that the drugs could cause cancer in a healthy person.

So I am home and tired, but you all want to hear the GOOD WORD, and this indeed is a good one, as I know you have been praying for NO side effects. Keep it up.

Today I woke up with an old Hebrew song... "dreidel, dreidel, dreidel, I made you out of clay"... I wondered what that had to do with anything. As I pondered, I thought about the word "dreidel" repeated 3 times. The stage the cancer was given was III C. Three, I

September 20, 2011 (continued)

pondered, what does God say about three? Then I thought of the conquering power available to us in the Trinity. Also a three-strand cord is not easily broken. And some others. But the overwhelming sense was that God has a much greater counterattack for anything the devil throws at us. The devotion we read today was about Hezekiah's battle with Sennecherib, and I was taken by the fact that the wars on earth and the wars we fight for healing are similar. We must be ruthless and be ready to go through the most difficult course of treatment, and then we will see as we did today that our Mighty God took all the side effects away.

Fear of the unknown tried to creep in before we went this morning and last night, but I just kept putting one step in front of the other, AND GOD IS FAITHFUL and blesses us in ways we can't imagine and are even afraid to believe.

Thanks for lifting us up in prayer. We know it is your intercession for us that helps us go through to the next step. Tomorrow and Thursday will be half days. I should be home for much needed rest by 2 PM.

Bless you all. May you ask for and God give you all the help you need to follow HIM so HE can grow you into HIS marvelous Holy image.

Pat

IN A BUBBLE

SEPTEMBER 21, 2011

Well, I made it through Day 2 and now only have two days to go. Tomorrow I get the last chemo dose and then on Friday get a white blood cell stimulator (Neulasta®) that will begin rebuilding the ones that were destroyed by the chemo. I have been advised that I will be resting on Saturday and Sunday and should keep outside contact to a minimum.

My spirits are high and I feel like I am in a bubble of God's protection and love. As to prayer needs: pray for this attitude to continue; pray that the chemo will be effective; pray for Carl as he gives more to me than ever; and pray that God will continue to use us as vessels as we talk of HIM whenever HE gives us opportunity--and there have been many. Today I sang a Jesus song with my nurse, and even though she didn't know all the words, she began singing with me and having a really good time.

Bless you all for remembering us. As you sow, so also shall you reap.

We Love you all!
Pat--and Carl, too!

Faith

September 22, 2011

Hello Friends and Family,

It is finished! It was another long day and as predicted, Pat is exhausted, so Carl here.

We left home this morning at 9:15 and returned at 4:15 PM. In chemo, timing is everything, and all the drugs given (including the 15 to 18 other recipients today) follow a protocol and precise sequence of events. So Pat's timing was a little later than we had planned. While she has had none or very little reaction to the drugs (God answered your prayers), her strength is at a very low level. This was told to us ahead of time to prepare for, so tomorrow and Saturday will be key days to pray for some of her strength to return along with increasing her white blood cells to ward off infection. Visitation is nadia, negative, nyet, no. Thank you for understanding.

Cycle I is complete. We now prepare for Cycle II in 18 days starting on 10/11 with two blood workups between now and then. Ok, that is the technical side of the treatment, now for what God is doing in all of this. God is sustaining Pat with His victorious right hand, holding her hand through this journey as she has shared with you about the dream and picture she has of Jesus leading her. With her spiritual strength firmly secured in knowing Christ as her Savior, her physical strength and then

her emotions come under control. So while Pat's pain has been severe at times during the last seven weeks, she has never blamed nor questioned anyone or anything in facing this battle. Like Job, she *"praises our God in the bad times as well as in the easy good times."* Blessed be the name of the LORD.

Your words of encouragement, scriptures, cards, e-mails, and songs of endearment continue to uplift Pat, so much so that she has shared her faith with several nurses, patients and volunteers. All are amazed at her acceptance of cancer so early on in the diagnosis yet with the mental strength of a "survivor", like being at peace in the bubble of her living, yet dealing with the reality of her condition. When the crises of life are right in front of you, your faith grows. Pat and I have reviewed our devotions and faith walk of the last six months and are in awe of what God has been doing to prepare us for such a time as this.

Carl and Pat

Came through the Night

September 24, 2011

Well, the night (9/23) and early morning is over, and it was a hard one. Was not sure what to take care of or how . . . did not want to use too many drugs and wanted to be sensitive to my digestive system.

Yesterday, Friday, the nurse said that the Neulasta shot I received would work to call all available white blood cells from my bone marrow to fight the potential enemies of my body and boost my immune system. She said I could possibly feel the pain in my bones and could also have a headache.

Enough of that . . . Carl said it was time for the sword and read to me from the Word this morning. I held onto all he read, my head is getting better, and I was able to eat some toast and peanut butter. The side effect that has been a challenge is the digestive process. Without being too graphic, I'll just say that after chemo there is a tendency to be too much in one direction or the other. Please pray for normal function. Please also pray for my blood test results next Friday. The last CA125 test gave me a score of 126 and 0-35 is normal. Pray for the lowering of this indicator.

I am so blessed with the care and love and gifts and prayers and the WORD and want to say thanks again to

all of you. The nurses at the treatment center keep remarking about my attitude and what a good patient I am as I allow them to . . . well, you know. I usually respond with "Jesus helps me" or "It goes faster without complaining or focusing on the pain".

I miss you all and would love to visit, but my immune system needs to be built up, and I am very tired. God has given me grace for writing, and I am so glad, because without contact with you I know my spirits would lag.

Thanks again for praying.

You are sustaining me in hope as you continue to look to our Father on my behalf. May HE grant all you need for this day.

Pat

BIRTH PANGS

SEPTEMBER 25, 2011

Dear Beloveds,

Just thinking about waiting for the time of birth and the birth pangs that assault us. Last night was very much like that, and I even wrote to our 18-year-old grandson at VMI that this was a form of my military training. It could also have been called the "agony and the agony", since yesterday at 1pm I experienced extreme intestinal distress with cold sweats and almost intolerable pain. After special meds and 12 hours my body decided to release its "cargo". (Forgive me for being either too personal or too graphic.) I thought of Psalm 23 and the phrase that says "*Even though I walk through the valley of the shadow of death, I will fear no evil; for THOU art with me*". Truly, I was almost choosing to be raptured and could not conceive of enduring any more pain. Carl was with me with cold, wet, washcloths and compassionate tears for my pain and GOD DID DELIVER!

During the night I was so tormented that I could think of little to console me. Carl read the 91st Psalm that our 12-year-old grandson gave me. Carl has been reading the Word to me often. (How blessed we are to have a grandson who sends me Scripture.)

One way the Lord speaks to me is in song, and last night's

song picked up on the 5th verse in Psalm 91...regarding the *terror by night*....I remembered this song from my teenage years... maybe you'll remember:

> *In the still of the night*
> *That's when I held you,*
> *Held you tight.*
> *For I love, love you so,*
> *I promise I'll never let you go!*
> *In the still of the night.*

This morning I am up a bit and writing waiting for my next nap. And in the middle of writing this update Patrick (our 18-year-old grandson) Skyped me. What a blessing to see him in his uniform and hear his heart for me. I guess that's it for now...I feel like singing "I will rejoice in YOU and be glad, I will extol YOUR love more than wine. Draw me after YOU and let us run together. I will rejoice in YOU and be glad."

I love you all,

Pat

THROUGH IT ALL

SEPTEMBER 27, 2011

"Tonight, tonight won't be just any night. Tonight there'll be no morning star"... or however it goes. I was definitely wondering about stars last night as they had seemed to disappear. The side effect relating to the pain that comes from the white cell producing drug was at times severe and lasted sporadically between 5 PM and 3 AM. Now I am stable, but the Doctor wants me on another narcotic (a low impact one that is a little stronger than the Motrin® I have been taking.) So, before I take it, I thought I would write, because it does cause drowsiness, and without much sleep, that may be likely.

Now, on to the good stuff. God speaks in the midst of the whirlwind (as He did to Job). Initially Job's response was: "Though He slay me, yet will I praise or trust Him." The disciples responded to Jesus by saying, "To whom else shall we go?" Paul talked about how long he lay in the "deep" and about his 39 lashes administered more than once. Paul did not say there was no pain associated with these trials. So, should I think I can and will be pain free? Do I want deliverance?. YES, and NO...if this is the way <u>through</u> that He has provided for me.

Someone recently shared that they felt God had prepared us for this all our lives. Isaiah talks of going **through** the water and not drowning and **through** fire

without being burned (Isaiah 43:2-3). I can clearly remember hearing God speak to me a long time ago as we were in a boat on Candlewood Lake. A storm came up and I asked HIM to move it. I sensed HE said, "I will not move it, but I will take you **through."** When we got home that day we saw  pock marks all over our aluminum siding evidencing a terrible storm. We were safe.

Then the thought came about Stephen and Paul and the pain or lack of it in the New Testament. Paul had all those terrible experiences, and Stephen looked into heaven to see Jesus standing at the right side of the Father. So...who gets the pain??? Does it make us any less valuable to God when HE allows us to suffer? Are we less chosen?

"A Mighty Fortress Is Our God"....came to mind and the verse that says that this earth is filled with devils who want to undo us but that Christ is the sovereign ruler, and one little word from HIS ALMIGHTY MOUTH will fell the enemy.

September 27, 2011 (continued)

He knows how much and how long, and sometimes I ask if it's done yet and sense again that in submitting to HIS plan there is safety and peace. There is a song that asks "How long till I awake in your likeness?" I need to remember not to continue to say I'm sorry for the plan HE has, because HIS use of these trials is always an exponential blessing. Jesus Himself said, "Shall I not drink of this cup? Surely it is what I was born for."

I pray you are all blessed. Love you all. Now I will eat lunch and take my drug.

Pat

TURNING A CORNER

SEPTEMBER 29, 2011

Well, it is midnight again...so, as some thoughts came to mind, I thought I'd share rather than sleep...Oh, well... AND THIS TOO SHALL PASS.

As my journey continues, I think of where I am today, and it seems like I've turned a corner. No intense pain, not even at nighttime; digestive system seems to be working; I have been awake during the day for most of it; and I did not take any pain meds at all today. Perhaps "drug brain" has left and that is why I am feeling a bit more alive. Of course, I still have healing pain and some fatigue, but it is much less than ever.

So, spiritually, where am I? Today two of my dear friends came to bring prayer and worship music, and they brought me rest and peace and a sense that God was so present and so confirming that EVERYTHING was in HIS ALL POWERFUL HANDS.

A song came to my mind as we were praying:

> *I cast all my cares upon YOU*
> *I lay all of my burdens*
> *Down at YOUR feet*
> *And any time I don't know*
> *What to do*
> *I will cast all my cares upon YOU.*

September 29, 2011 (continued)

So it seems that our sweet Jesus has taken me from the Scriptures that speak of HIS MIGHTY HAND to HIS tender, ever-present mercy and compassionate grace. I just sense HIM bringing a calm that is without any ripples, totally transparent, and powerfully encompassing to my heart. And I just am letting HIM hold me and sing to me (Zeph. 3:17) and be everything I need right now. What a blessed, holy place.

And, practically, you all are the extension of that peace and love and certainly HIS provision. May HE, by HIS most tender love and mercy, touch the very depths of your heart, and may you find total and complete rest in HIM.

Bless you all.
Pat

THE BEGINNING

SEPTEMBER 30, 2011

Hello Brothers and Sisters,

As I was pondering during the wee hours (notice I said pondering, not up writing, which is good, got at least 7 hours sleep last night), the beginning revelation regarding this journey came to mind. Perhaps you all have heard the story, but to set the record straight, and because I love to tell the story, I thought I'd document it.

It probably was Sunday, August 7th, that as I awoke I saw myself as a 4-year-old girl learning to ride a tricycle. I had a sweater on just like my Mom used to make me and pigtails that she would often put on top of my head. As I looked at the little girl, I saw Jesus beside me, and HE was holding my hand. The amazing thing about the picture, and even more than that, the experience, was that Jesus was smiling and waving HIS other hand as if to say, "No big deal; I've got this. It will be nothing for me, and I am with you." Then it seemed a song began to play in my mind:

> *Many things about tomorrow*
> *I don't seem to understand,*
> *But I know who holds tomorrow,*
> *and I know who holds my hand.*

September 30, 2011 (continued)

I wasn't sure about the music so I Googled it. It was amazing again what I found, for the song was on YouTube, and the pictures of the song were of Jesus holding little children's hands.

Then a thought came to mind...where have I seen that picture of me as a 4-year-old before...Laurie Ann made me a photo album for my 60th birthday, and I thought that's where the picture would be. Sure enough, there it was with the pigtails and sweater my mom had made.

The entrance of HIS WORD gives life and that's what happened that morning, and I still not only sense HE is holding my hand but also **KNOW** HE is when I do not sense anything but pain. BUT THE GOOD NEWS IS THAT THE PAIN IS AT A MINIMUM, and I am getting healthier and ready for my next round of treatments to begin on October 10th.

God bless and keep you,
Pat

Merciful Hand

September 30, 2011

Here is my second entry for today. As I was waking this morning I began to feel what some of you may feel as you think and pray for me. I was emotionally overcome as I thought of my sister and brother-in-law picking me up from my treatment. I could see in their eyes how they felt when they saw what the treatment took from me and how helpless and yet compassionate they felt. AND THEN...I had a wonderful sense of intimacy, of love, of the common ground we all walk on, on this earth. I also had a deep sense of God's empowering that held me up even enough to make light of my pain and discomfort and to be able to humbly and graciously say a sincere THANK YOU.

I can remember when I first came home from the hospital and the realization of not only what I had been through hit me, but also what lay ahead. The number of a Psalm came to mind, and I hadn't known it in the past with any real familiarity. It talked about being ripped apart and attacked and tormented. I looked at myself

and my surgical incision and said, "Look what they have done to me." Then as I came back to God as David so often did after his complaints...I remembered Isaiah 54:17... "*No weapon formed against me will prosper.*" Oh, yes, a weapon was formed against me, but it will NOT prosper.

Can we sometimes see those things as a result of an impure and unholy rebellion of God's people here on earth...yes, yet bottom line for me is the merciful hand of God in it all for HIS children and, as they say colloquially, "I is one!" And again it is the **through,** not the miraculous and sudden disappearance of all symptoms and disease, that HE's called me to. So for today I again rejoice, 'cause HE told us to in everything, and also I hold on in hope and faith, because HE showed me not only that HE IS WITH ME, but also that HE WILL NEVER LEAVE ME NOR FORSAKE ME. And that goes for all of you, too, if indeed you are choosing day by day to trust only HIM.

Love you all,

Pat

TO RECAP A BIT: A LETTER OF ADVOCACY

SEPTEMBER 30, 2011

Tomorrow is October 1. This journey began approximately in April, 2011, or maybe earlier. It seems like a long time, and in many ways it seems like the only life I've known for a while. And while we had traveled from March through June of this year, I just never felt right. Perhaps this letter is an encouragement to have yourself checked out. Let me share some of my early symptoms and be an advocate for early detection. To a degree my knowledge is limited but what I know personally I will share.

My identification of the ovarian tumor came on August 2nd when, during an exam, my primary physician determined that my uterus was the size of a 4-month pregnancy. Before this exam I was trying to treat the back pain I had with Motrin or Tylenol and was seeking out the help of physical therapists and a chiropractor.

When I showed them where the pain was they said it could definitely be an S.I. joint problem (sacroiliac). As we drew close to the end of my treatments that were interrupted by the real diagnosis on August 2nd, I even told a P.T. and the chiropractor that my pain prevented me from doing crouching front exercises because the abdominal pain was so bad. The ovaries, as a surprise to me, are located low and in the front of the abdominal cavity. This movement really stressed the tumor that was growing there.

Those who tried to care for me before the 2nd of August were not ovarian cancer savvy and did not recognize the pain that occurs in those areas when this type of tumor is present. We also live in a medical community which is so specialized that areas outside of their own are rarely addressed. Where is Marcus Welby, M.D.???

So, I mention all this to say that if you feel pain in your S.I. joint and it seems consistent and nagging...or if you have low abdominal pain that restricts certain forward bending or crouching movements....check it out. How? First by an internal exam and later an internal ultrasound. Believe me, it **IS** worth it. <u>**You** are worth it.</u>

The reason this type of cancer is called "the silent killer" is the fact that these types of symptoms are usually ignored. Ignorance is not bliss. For your sake and for the sake of all those who love you...check it out.

Now for the real commentary. I am still at peace, even though "mistakes" have been made. This is the world we live in, and although modern science has its benefits, it still does not know all, nor should it. Why did it all turn out as it did? Was God just letting all this happen in blissful unconcern for me, HIS child?

As Paul the Apostle would say, "NO, MAY IT NEVER BE!" Truly, I believe that my whole life is under HIS loving watchful hand and, as HE showed me early on, <u>HE would always be with me and never let go of my hand.</u>

SEPTEMBER 30, 2011 (CONTINUED)

Does HE see as we do?? NO...how else can HE be God if HE is not above and beyond us in all HIS thoughts and ways, and yet HE chose to make HIMSELF a vulnerable human like us so we could know HE has experienced life on earth fully and is aware of all our needs and indeed, all our suffering.

So dearest friends and family, do not ignore the subtle and persistent naggings in your body or the persistent love and presence of our God. They are the delivery system HE has graciously given us for our care and protection. Know HE loves you in a way you may not understand until you are "in deep waters" and can't swim without HIM holding you up. When this time comes in your life and you are able to rest in HIM, all the rest doesn't matter and does not even have to make sense. He is the great leveler of reason and the foundation of all real truth. And this TRUTH has no restrictors; it is unbound and more powerful than any human or earthly force, and when we believe, we have the power to live victoriously in the face of what the world calls calamity. That is how **AWESOME** our God is!

Thanks for "listening". I pray you have been cautioned and blessed and can rest in HIS peace because HE is always the eternal "bottom line". Love you, especially because HE loved you first and yearns for you to know more of HIM.

Pat

RAINY DAY

OCTOBER 1, 2011 (5:45 AM)

Just stuck my head out the back slider. It is damp and may rain all day today, BUT it is amazing how the day, the weather, struck me....it is almost like it is surreal. I can smell the moisture in the air and it refreshes and enlivens me. I can see very faint pink in the sky (maybe more grey) and I am filled with wonder. Wonder at the vastness of God and HIS infiniteness. Wow! I never thought looking out the back door on a mostly rainy day could affect me as it does. God must be speaking...because I don't think this is the way we humans see things. Bless HIM always for raising our sights always and in all ways to HIMSELF.

Pat

SELFISH OR SELFLESS?

OCTOBER 2, 2011

Now I've come from encouragement to . . . meddling??

Well, here goes. Woke up at 1:30 AM; was pondering on a nasty idea I am sure did not come from God. Bottom line was, why are we selfish or, better still, why are we unhappy? The idea that came to mind related to where I am today. If I choose to look within, I can be consumed by the thought of a wasting, consuming disease. And the parallel is that we can all do the same, but for everyone else it is called "navel gazing". So for me, I do not have a choice except to look up and out, up from myself and out to God who is above and beyond me...God who gives me hope to carry on and lights up my days and nights (sounds like a song again). So what does this downward, inward gazing accomplish? Well, you know, discouragement, disillusionment, despair, etc. When we choose instead to look to HIM we have LIFE and

all of its wonderful manifestations. And we have life like Jesus described to Martha and Mary...<u>resurrection life</u>... so that in this life or the next there is a fullness which is so above our comprehension that we are in a state where we see things from above and not below and where we ARE more than conquerors and where all those Scriptures we have read and studied are REAL.

So...I am thankful that I am captured by this wonderful God I serve in a place where HE is my choice (HE told me to choose LIFE) and where I can live every day of my life with a view from HIS perspective. This causes me NOT to look within at the decaying body but up at HIM for life and health and hope. What a blessing to KNOW that HE is the only place of hope. Oh yes, there are treatments and I will be here on earth as long as HE ordains. BUT while I am here it will be up and out and above and beyond that which is earthly and dying within me. I do remember the word from Ecclesiastes, Chapter 3, "*a time to kill and a time to heal*" and have believed that this was a time to kill the cancer cells so that it would be a time to heal me. So Praise God! HE has me. HE has my thoughts, my upward vision, and HE has me speaking what <u>HE</u> is doing and saying through me to you.

Is your perspective about yourself? Does it fulfill you or make you unhappy? Is it selfish or selfless? James says that when we ask God for something we ask with wrong motives in that we ask only to satisfy our own, *self-centered, self-focused,* pleasure. (James 4:3) (Words in italics here are my amplification for clarification only.)

OCTOBER 2, 2011 (CONTINUED)

He says in another place as he described wisdom that "*wherever there is selfish ambition there is disorder and every kind of evil.*" (James 3:16)

Please do not be offended and believe that I am now a totally sinless and holy person that has left humanity behind. I am still subject to this flesh I live in....BUT...I can see more clearly now the rain is gone (oops, another song again). My present situation has caused me to be locked into a wonderful place of upward vision, and it is a place that is so filled with life and hope and care for all of you that it is more life than I have ever experienced before. When Jesus' disciples said, "*To whom shall we go...You have the words of eternal life,*" (John 6:68), I believe they were aware that there was nowhere else they could see life as it really is except through Jesus' eyes. HE has begun to open my eyes to how HE sees it, and to whom else shall I go, since HE is the "*author and finisher of my faith*". (Heb.12:2)

So when you get to those places where you begin to look inside your flesh for answers and pleasure and power to conquer, try instead to look to Jesus. HE is the ONLY one who can lift you up beyond yourself to a place of eternal perspective while we are still here on earth.

Bless this sharing to HIS glory, and to your precious hearts,
Pat

GOD'S CALL FOR ME

OCTOBER 4, 2011

Here I am again. Missed two days, so you thought I was finished with my daily dissertations on the journey. Well, not quite yet. I am feeling much better. A drugless life is a real life. So this is what I have been pondering on...God's call for me. Right now (believe it or not) it is in part to write these daily messages. So how does it all happen? Usually I awaken with a thought about something that has occurred to me as I am processing what is happening and how God fits into it all. The strange thing about it is the pattern, or lack thereof. Pattern: The usual one is I awake at various night hours with a thought that comes to me, and then I just come to the computer and write. I am not really sure how I get here, but once I do it seems that I have much to say, and it isn't a striving of any kind; it is what is within me that just seems to pour out.

So back to God's call: It seems minimal and grandiose to see this "blog" as HIS call for me, yet whether it helps

October 4, 2011 (continued)

me see more clearly or is really something HE wants others to see, I will leave up to your judgment.

The pattern is the interesting thing...do I get these thoughts in the daytime? So far, NO. It seems all I have written has been during the nighttime hours. So why do I have to give up sleep? Well, it is good to write now. I enjoy the quiet, and it seems I can think clearly. The distractions of the day are gone, and as I awaken from sleep, I am refreshed and energized enough to be able to do this.

I might just be like another Michelangelo, who I understand slept a few hours and worked a few. Whatever the case, I am not tired during the day anymore than usual. I now take an hour or so nap in the late afternoon and otherwise seem almost normal. Oh yes, there is still some healing that has to come, but I feel rather stable at this time.

Yesterday a friend of mine from our small group at church was here to help me clean, or shall I say, she cleaned our house for us. As we chatted we both came away with a new sense of God's sovereignty and overriding control and yearning to bless HIS children. We talked about HIS nature and that HE does not cruelly withhold wisdom or guidance from us. (James, Chapter 1). HE also sets us on a path that we are not necessarily involved in choosing. Then HE uses that path

for HIS glory, to bring us intimately closer together. HE allows us to sense that others are really carrying our load (as the body of Christ should). As a result, we are all lifted and encouraged by the trial.

When HE says "the trial of our faith is more precious than gold", we really do know that is true, because there is nothing greater than the manifestation of HIS love which is given to us personally and through the love of our brothers and sisters. It is like seeing everything through rose-colored glasses or from a hot-air balloon on an early fall morning when everything is still and perfect.

So again I say, HIS WILL BE DONE, HIS KINGDOM COME, because it is the best and most perfect plan. Although it seems rather peculiar to us at times, it is far above what we could ask or think, and the pleasure and exhilaration of it all is better than any trip one could take. Also, it is totally drugless, and we don't have to go anywhere other than HIS will to obtain it. HE IS AND ALWAYS HAS BEEN AMAZING BEYOND OUR COMPREHENSION....AFTER ALL, HE IS GOD!

Bless you as you continue to seek to follow HIM.

Pat

A "Hairy" Day

October 5, 2011

"But blessed is the one who trusts in the Lord, whose confidence is in him. They will be like a tree planted by the water that sends out its roots by the stream. It does not fear when heat comes; its leaves are always green. It has no worries in a year of drought and never fails to bear fruit." (Jer. 17:7-8)

Well, last night (in the wee hours of Tuesday am) as I was sleeping, I felt very uncomfortable in the back of my head as if I had a tight pony tail and after the rubber band was taken out my head hurt. Well, I don't know if this is related, but as I took my shower this Tuesday morning my hair began to fall out. SOOOOO…..was it a little shocking? YES, too shocking, and NO….I was told this would happen. As it says in the verse above, "does not fear when heat comes" (or hair falls out), "has confidence in HIM."

Oh, yes, a woman's crown is her hair, but who we are goes beyond how we look. Is that hard to grasp? Yes, and no, because what GOD says about us is what we really are. The leaves of the trees are always green, and (again relating to the Scripture) this one "has no worries and bears fruit" even when there seems to be no source of nourishing water. SOOOOO…..I am awaiting my beautician who will be coming to our home this afternoon. I am so blessed to have so many caring for me. The

support system God has given me keeps me and holds me and blesses me when I could crumble, but HE is so magnificent that "this, too, SHALL pass".

"*When I walk through deep waters He will be with me and I will not drown.*" The one who trusts in the Lord (has his confidence in HIM) is truly like the flourishing tree regardless of how one looks or how one may feel. HE in me IS the one who WILL NOT...and that is all that really matters. HE is also the courage to walk **through**. I will write more later.

TUESDAY AFTERNOON

My beautician has come and gone and I continue to ponder. Selfishness was the topic of a previous e-mail (journal entry). Selflessness is the path **through**, because it is based on an upward and outward perspective. If I again choose selfless, other directedness, I will be looking more to HIM than inside of me. If I look to myself, I will be choosing to be filled with how everything looks and feels and of course what others think of me. I will be concerned more with their opinion of me than my healing, and I will be caught up in the grieving they may be experiencing. Should they grieve???

Of course, we all do when we lose something that has *always* been with us. But, will I be caught up in their emotion so that I lose my strength?...NO, not as long as my eyes remain on the One who keeps me.

October 5, 2011 (continued)

Practically speaking...it is "only" hair. It grows back...I won't have to wash it, style it, think about it, or move it out of the way. It is, in a way, a relief. Do I still need courage?...constantly... but that is who the God who will never leave me nor forsake me, IS.

Carl often comes home from work and says that his talks with his supervisor revolve around .... So What??? (alluding to the goal of any business endeavor). Again I ask, what is the goal of all this??? In my case it is what God wants from this...healing and growth (or maybe death so I can be conformed to HIS image) and an upward and positive faith-filled perspective which HE places within my reach. This can happen only **IF** I will choose to walk **through** it all with my Jesus holding my hand.

On Sundays at church we often sing this chorus to a song:

> *Oh no, You never let go*
> *Through the calm and through the storm*
> *Oh no, You never let go*
> *In every high and every low*
> *Oh no, You never let go*
> *Lord, You never let go of me!*

Today I am holding on a little tighter, and HE is big enough to make what I am experiencing an inconvenience instead of a terrible trauma.

Bless you all till next time,

Pat

A Good Day

October 6, 2011

Hi Everyone,

It's been a GOOD, GOOD DAY! I am celebrating feeling the best since my surgery...almost "normal". I have energy and a deep sense of truly enjoying life. I walked to the mailbox with my new "hairstyle", and everyone I saw today thought I looked great. The wind was blowing, the sun was shining, and as they would say in Jewish, "What's not to like."

Laurie Ann, Don, Allie and Dani will be traveling up from Virginia Beach to visit this weekend before my next round of chemo and I feel the best ever. It will be soooo good to see them. Much was accomplished today and God gave me grace to ask for help with driving tomorrow and asking someone to come to an appointment with me. The response I am getting from those I ask for help is often, "Thank you for asking me." God sure is going before me... and I am overwhelmed (sometimes with tears). What an awesome God we serve!!

Thank you all!!!

Pat

NOT EASTER SUNDAY

OCTOBER 9, 2011

No, it is not Easter Sunday, but it is <u>Resurrection Day</u>. Every day we awake and have breath and have all the gifts GOD has so graciously given to us is a resurrection day....especially those times when we see HIM answer prayer. All those times we obey the little nudges (even though we are often humbled by what HE asks us to do) and then we see HIM answer, and the answer is so much bigger and greater than the moment of humble obedience...It is RESURRECTION DAY.

HE is with us, HE speaks, we obey and HE answers...what else is greater than these moments except that they may occur more and more often......,**AND that is HIS glorious will**.... that these times may be the normal testimony of our lives.

We are enjoying this weekend with our daughter, her husband, and granddaughters, and even though our oldest grandson is not with us, we had an opportunity to Skype with him. GOD IS SO AMAZINGLY BEAUTIFUL...HE meets us where we are and fills our cup with HIMSELF, SO WE BOW AND WORSHIP, AND HE <u>**IS**</u>**!**

Love you all and pray that this day is one where HE is above and beyond all that this world could ever offer.

Pat

Joyful Anticipation

October 11, 2011

Morning

Thanks again for being there. This morning I begin Cycle II. It sounds a little like I am getting into a boxing ring with the bell about to sound for the round to begin, and I am jumping around to make myself agile and ready for the fight. I know I have been trained for this, because my faith and life experiences have made me ready. I feel encouraged by the good report I had yesterday at the doctor's pre-op visit, and as I write I am reminded that you are all praying and loving me from afar.

I began thinking about my CA125 (cancer indicator) test (results of which I will get today or tomorrow), and in my heart I began to celebrate. I don't know the results yet but am anticipating the number going down toward the normal range (0-35). The last time the test was given my score was 126. So the celebration had lots of HALLELUJAHS, and my spirits were really high, and I was ready to walk the path to the end of this long treatment time (approx. 5-6 months).

As I had this celebrating spirit in my heart, I heard whispers of..."It may not happen...,"etc. And in the midst of all the doubts and negative accusations that were thrown at me I remember: *"Faith is the essence of things unseen"* (Heb. 11:1), Paul battling as if he were a

boxer fighting so that he *would* conquer, and "be strong and courageous". So here's to the future and the "*future and hope HE has planned for me*" (Jer. 29:11)--which is always GOOD. Faith is a wonderful gift because it gives us a *present* hope.

Bless you all!
Pat

AFTERNOON

Thank you all for praying specifically for my CA125 test. As I shared this morning before results, a safe normal score is between (0-35)......TODAY THE MIRACULOUS SCORE WAS *21!*

We were up at 5 AM and came home at 6:45 PM. It was a long day and I am fading quickly. And yet God IS FAITHFUL!!!!

We had a wonderful party at the center today. My friend from the last chemo, a Christian, was there, and

October 11, 2011 (continued)

my Christian nurse took care of me, and a long-time Christian friend came to be with me. There were some glitches, and ones that could steal our joy, but God sustained us and gave us a great spirit of celebration.

Pat

Evening

I have to take new meds before bedtime, and I just can't wait to do so. Then I can go to sleep… don't think I will be awake in the night too much. Tomorrow we will leave a bit later, between 9-10 AM, and I am sooooo glad about that.

God always finishes what HE starts, and this morning I had a keen sense of celebration, you joined in, and HE brought it all to pass.

HALLELUJAH!! Thank you for showing that you are the true body of Christ.

Pat

PLOOPED BALLOON

OCTOBER 12, 2011

MORNING

Well, today I feel a lot like a plooped balloon. BUT there was good news yesterday, and my score was a winning one.

As for the boxing image. I was pondering a bit more on it this morning (because my instructions during chemo week are to walk, rest, and don't do much more), and an extension of that image came to mind. In the boxing ring I do not get to fight back with my boxing gloves, and I have to take all the punches that are pummeling me.....YET, because of my spiritual attitude of praise, surrender, and focus on GOD, HE fights for me and I win!! Carl says it's like the letters O.C.---HE is Over Coming, Ovarian Cancer!!

Be blessed, encouraged, and empowered today by all HE has for you!

Love,
Pat

October 12, 2011 (continued)

Afternoon

To add to my morning insight regarding the boxing image and the sense that I had no strength left....Here's what my morning devotion was entitled...."Drained of All Strength". The scripture reference was Isaiah 40:25-30, and today I was encouraged to do as it said, "*Wait upon the LORD.*" HE helped me get through the day (although my time at the treatment center was only four hours), and I was able to sit up and be energized enough to have supper with my sister-in-law who came from Glastonbury to take me home and bring me supper.

GOD IS TOO GOOD! And I am going to bed...Thanks again for your prayers and hands extended.

Pat

Trust and Obey

October 14, 2011

Often I will wake up with songs on my heart. This morning's was "Trust and obey, for there is no other way to be happy in Jesus, but to trust and obey....". I can clearly remember being in the Billy Graham choir back in the 1980's when his crusade came to Hartford. And this morning I am reminded about the message of the song that was meaningful to me in the 80's and so much more today.

THERE IS NO OTHER WAY TO BE HAPPY IN JESUS BUT TO TRUST AND OBEY. I can envision three pictures of what that looks like. One is my story of Jesus holding my hand as a little girl (as I will always be to HIM). Then there is the picture that comes to mind when we read the poem entitled "Footprints", and then the latest picture a friend gave me of a little lamb snuggling under Jesus' neck being hugged, in a very comforting and cozy position. Forgot one; there are four. There was the picture a friend gave me of Jesus in the hospital operating room with HIS hands around the doctors as they are performing surgery.

So many reminders, so much assurance and comfort. HE is always with us and will show us HIMSELF in so many different ways. In which way will you see HIM today...in a song, a picture, a memory, or in a way you've never seen HIM before? But however you see HIM, HE will be

October 14, 2011 (continued)

newer, deeper, more real, and because of this new view, you will be able to truly "Trust and Obey" in a brand new way, and you'll be happier in Jesus because you'll trust and obey.

Very practically for me today, trust and obey means going to my next chemo session with a smile and a confident assurance that with HIM I can do everything HE asks me to do. Now who else would we obey than one we totally trust whom we know loves us in this precious and deeply loving way??? Test your "trust meter" today and BE VERY, VERY HAPPY.

Love you all because HE first loved us.

Pat

Sketch of the picture referenced by Pat; artist unknown.

Little Rest

October 15, 2011

Hello Everyone, Carl here.

Yesterday, Friday, was to be a Day of Rest for Pat, but it turned out to be the beginning of a very tiring, exhausting 36 hrs after-chemo downer. Pat rested most of the morning, then in the afternoon I took her to the Gray Center for her shot of Neulasta. The next three days are ones in which Pat is at her weakest.

She came home last night tired, slept with a slight headache, and today till now (3 pm) Pat has been in bed. She might get up for five minutes but plops right down again. This cycle seems to be a little more severe than her first go around with Neulasta. But, believe it or not, medics say this is a normal reaction.

Thank you all for your continued prayer, meals, phone calls, letters, and encouraging words and even rides to Hartford. They are a real blessing to us while walking through this trial. It is in the testing that we find our faith and see how God is refining and defining that faith. Join with us in the hope that Pat gets stronger during the remainder of this day and that we see the bright hope of tomorrow (Sunday) along with the Son.

Keep on praying, keep on believing.
Carl

Statement of Faith

October 16, 2011

Hi Everyone,

Thank you all for understanding that at this point in my treatment, it seems easier to type than speak, yet I know there will be more energetic days. Today I felt so weak that holding my head up was a challenge. Now at 1:30 AM I seem to be getting a little strength back. "This too shall pass" has become a new statement of faith for me, as I can often do little but totally lean on God's power to bring me through.

I do pray you are experiencing a little more of HIS love for you each day.

Love,

Pat

A Thankful Heart

October 16, 2011

Hello Dear Friends,

This morning (6 AM...better than 1 AM) I woke up with a thankful heart that I can communicate my heart to you. I am sending this e-mail to a few of you who have been there to visit, give and help out in various ways. THANK YOU!!!

This morning as I pondered (and I do feel better today), my heart yearns for as normal a life as possible during the next five months. While I must be cautious and not exhaust myself, I do not need to be cloistered in my home. Yesterday I sat out on the deck for 20 minutes and felt like I was in another world. It was so refreshing and reminded me of my recent time, at the end of my last cycle, where I had almost normal energy and went to the apple orchards with my daughter's family. (Of course I did not eat any apples from the trees and did not pick any or forget to wash my hands.)

Right now I am thinking about how much, who, when and in what ways to stay as "alive" as possible. Being home is necessary in my peak weakness times and when I am in pain but does not work for the other times when I want to be out in the fresh air and try to do the things that are necessary for our household. We have a bit of an added element too these days in that Carl takes the car

October 16, 2011 (continued)

each day. I have not begun to drive and I guess I will have to make a decision about when I want to do that. I guess most of all having people back in my life is important.

I mention all the above to say that if you would like to do so, please give me a call, and we can go out together, visit, or just walk around a bit here.

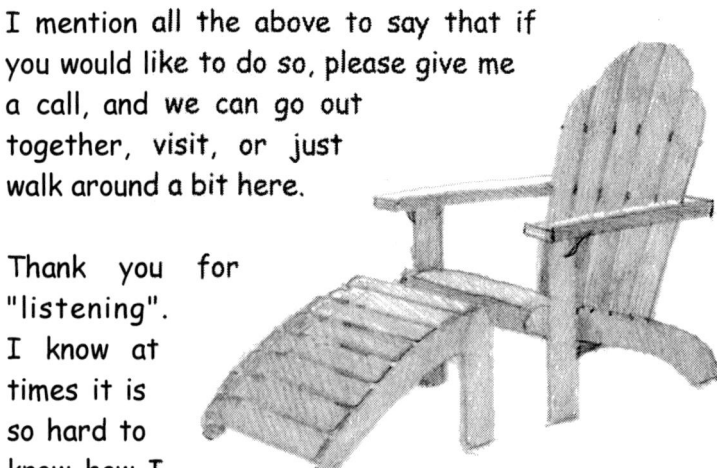

Thank you for "listening". I know at times it is so hard to know how I feel and what I need and we all want the healing to be unencumbered. GOD IS MY REFUGE and yet you are HIS arms.

Love you all,

Pat

WEEK OF "WEAKS"

OCTOBER 18, 2011

Today is the end of the week that was... Chemo last week and then debilitating weakness and terrible cold sweats....(maybe this is what coming off a drug addiction is like)...and then the Neulasta shot and the narcotic to ease the pain of white blood cells being pulled out aggressively at one time causing a stiffening of the body for a short period of time. (***Editor's Note:*** *Similar to one having a seizure*).

Sometimes I just do not want to do this anymore. This is not an appropriate attitude since there are four more 21-day cycles that await me. And now I am considering a permanent port in my chest where blood and chemo can be more readily given to me.

Yes, I know :
  "Young *men grow weary, but they that wait upon the Lord shall renew their strength."*
  (Isaiah 40:31)

And I know that sometimes we get weary and need to take a grip with tired hands and stand firmly on shaky legs, and
  "*Mark out a straight path for our feet so that even if we are weak and lame, we will not stumble and fall but will become strong."* (Heb. 12:11-13).

October 18, 2011 (continued)

So as the Word says and not like I FEEL, there will be better days and there will be triumph and I will live in the land of the LIVING. But for now there is the WORD of God and HIS promises and HIS love and of course yours as well.

Today I had some disappointment, some pain, much fatigue, little rest and a husband who loves me and listens and hugs me, sisters and brothers who want to help and reach out and see me, and of course a faithful God who will NEVER leave me nor forsake me and longs to sing over me and allow me to snuggle right under HIS chin when I have days like this. THERE WILL BE BETTER DAYS! BECAUSE WE HAVE A BETTER GOD!

May HIS grace fill all the places in your life that FEEL empty today.

Pat

No Drug Reaction

October 19, 2011

Thank you for believing with me that I would NOT have a reaction to my Neulasta shot that would require the narcotics that cause even other side effects. Yesterday was a relatively pain-free day. I did NOT get the usual pain associated with the drug. Your intercession made on my behalf reached the throne of grace and the answer was "I am here to help you."

As for the next prayer requests...Would you pray my blood test results would not only show a low CA number (the last great one was 21) but also make me eligible for a port so that chemo and receiving blood would be less painful and so much easier. Also, would you pray that my anemic condition would not worsen and that I would be strong enough not to have to take any transfusions of blood. Yet...HIS will be done. HE knows what is best and how HE wants me to remain strong during this time.

THIS IS THE DAY THAT THE LORD HAS MADE. I WILL REJOICE AND BE GLAD IN IT!!!

Love you all,

Pat

Letter To A Friend

OCTOBER 20, 2011

Hi Everyone,
Just wanted to send off what I wrote to someone today that you may be able to apply to your own lives. If so, <u>great</u>; if not, give it away.

Love you all,
Pat

October 20, 2011

My Dearest Friend,

Also there was another thought that came to mind... from Psalm 103. It says, "and heals all your diseases." I remember a Pastor sharing about disease as dis-ease. So as I thought about it what came to mind is that, as we are in a total place of ease in HIM, there is NO disease, only HIM and us. Just like my picture of Jesus nuzzling the little lamb, and even holding us as a weaned child, so are you and I, as we rest, rely, wait, trust and worship HIM.

Yes, there is NO disease. There is only peace in HIM, and because of that HE is in total control, and there is only blessed, hopeful, anticipated good expectation of what HE has for us.

WOW!! HE IS MUCH BIGGER AND MORE TENDER THAN EVER!

Love you too much!
Pat

SONGS

October 24, 2011

Good Morning!

"How are you this morning... feeling fine and dandy?" This line comes from a song in the play *Porgy and Bess*. Today I do feel better and have felt much better these past 5-6 days and so have not written, because I was enjoying the help from friends who took me to the places I needed to go and even brought me to some fun places. (Of course we made sure we stayed away from the crowds.)

"Holy, holy, holy, Lord God Almighty, who was, and is, and is to come...with all creation I sing praise to the KING of KINGS; You are my everything and I will adore YOU!" This was one of the songs that has been playing over and over in my mind, and am I thankful that God reminds me of who HE is and what HE has in HIS hand through the words of these songs.

Yesterday our Pastor and his wife came to share communion with us, and we had a wonderful time of worship, sharing and sitting in HIS presence. The body

October 24, 2011 (continued)

of Christ has changed location and number but is as close or closer than ever. God is better than so Good.

This week Tuesday I will be going for a consultation regarding the placement of a 'port' and will be getting one implanted on Thursday in my upper chest if I pass all my blood tests. Pray that God will make a way, because this will make my chemo treatments easier to administer.

Our daughter Kristin and her family will be here on Thursday, and we are thrilled to be able to see them again. It is rare that they come up to visit from North Carolina and we long to see them. God is better than Good!

All in all (aside for a few minor irritants), I am well and so in awe of how, with the trials, God not only makes a way out but a way up. It seems that for every hardship, God has been providing a deeper, fuller, higher view of HIMSELF. So how could this be bad? In the eternal and the temporal there is more to what HE HIMSELF IS, and IS doing, in and through this time than I can fully express. Suffice it to say that I am living on another plane and perhaps even looking down from the heavenlies AND THE VIEW IS PHENOMENAL!

Bless you all; know how much you are loved.
Pat

From Bradley to Jefferson

October 26, 2011

Bless you all! Well, yesterday was an interesting day... but a very good one. We started at Bradley Hospital with my regular weekly blood test. Then we proceeded to Jefferson Diagnostic to get approval for the port. All in all things went well, and I am scheduled for the port installation on Thursday morning around 8 AM. Please pray all goes well.

This morning I was reading Acts 16, about the jailer who was present when God caused an earthquake and opened the prison cell doors where Paul was imprisoned. The wonder-filled revelation that came to me is the fact that when the jailer realized it was God who opened the prison doors, he became a believer and chose immediately afterward to "wash the wounds" of his prisoners! What powerful evidence of a changed life! The prison guard washed the wounds of his prisoners.

So, too, I see all of you. You are all illustrations of a changed life. I have seen you give and serve me in ways that continually touch my heart. So be encouraged today knowing that you are doing what you are...HIS child, serving by HIS Spirit and looking very much like HIM.

THANK YOU, THANK YOU, THANK YOU!
Pat

October 26, 2011 (continued)

Later...Same day

Here is one part of the story I forgot to mention. AND the good thing is that it was the hard part of yesterday... and I forgot it.

But here it is. When we were <u>through</u> (my favorite word these days) at Jefferson, we returned to Hartford to see my doctor, because I had developed itchy blisters on my head and felt terrible pressure when my wig was on, which would give me a headache. She said they were my body's attempt to grow hair while the chemo was killing the hair-growing function so as a result infection can occur. I am now on an antibiotic, and again I see how God created a body that wants always to restore itself.

Everything is in such perfect balance that when one function is suspended, it affects many other functions. God is amazing. In this situation, for one week the hair follicles are called to stop growing hair, and then for the next two weeks normal hair-building functions return. (The good thing is, there is real promise in hair re-growth.)

Can you imagine how miraculous it is that I am doing well during all this??? Well, with HIM, "It is well with my soul!"

Thanks for reading my sometimes choppy communication.
Pat

Power Outage

November 6, 2011

Well... I guess we are all inhaling and exhaling at this point. God has been good during the power outage. Last Thursday, Oct. 27th, Kristin and John, Tori and Levi came to visit. We so enjoyed them, and it was the right time in my treatment cycle for visitors. They left on Sunday morning after much deliberation regarding road conditions but were able to make it to Laurie Ann's house in Virginia and then home the next morning.

God seems to have known our needs (seems???...of course He knows) and blessed us through Carl's friendly personality. Our power went out on Sunday (10/30) at 2AM, and we pondered on what we should do. I was a little panicky and thought that without heat or a generator we should try to get a room at the Comfort Inn®. So at 6AM on Sunday morning (while Kristin was still here) we booked a room. Later we found out that just 15 minutes later all the rooms had been reserved.

So back to Carl and his friendly personality. As Carl was coming back from the Comfort Inn (where he went to charge our phones), he noticed a new neighbor in the second phase of our development shoveling snow and having his garage door go up and down "by itself". (Also right around this time I began to feel I could not go to the hotel. I just couldn't deal with all the decisions that had to be made.) Carl wondered how that could be

November 6, 2011 (continued)

happening without power and discovered that the newer phase of our community had power. But more than having power, this neighbor had a generator he was not using. Carl talked to this newest neighbor of three months and, yes, he offered it to us. The generator had enough power to keep our refrigerator and separate freezer going, along with protecting a few local neighbors' special frozen items for them. God is so good even in the frozen areas of life.

On Monday night I asked a lady friend who lives in the same Phase 2 housing (having power) if I could bring our frozen dinner and if we could eat together at her house. She was so appreciative of our company, as she lives alone, and her husband has been in an Alzheimer facility for two years. When we returned to our dark, cold house, I again had to ask for God's help. At 2 AM Tuesday morning the power returned. My response was 1000 Thank You's and 1000 Hallelujahs.

So this past week was my chemo week, and I am just beginning (Sunday morn) to come out of the extreme weakness and susceptibility to infection. These past two

days are the worst. Often I will take denauseating medication which makes me weaker and dizzier. Fortunately, this time around I have not had intestinal issues. (It is amazing how thankful I am for "normal" body function...it is so critical at these times.)

God has blessed me with friends and family who have come alongside me to drive me to treatment, stay with me, and take me home. What a joy it is to have them with me as I am persevering **through** the battle. We also were able to receive help in our own home by good friends who had no power and could be here two nights with and for us when our power had returned.

The last seven days (with the storm and chemo) have been disorienting to say the least, and yet we have come **through**. I am not considering how much there is to go, just that God is a daily deliverer. I have missed your responses to e-mails as we just got our phone and internet back yesterday. You are all so precious to me, and as you walk along this trial with me, I am empowered to do what I never thought I would be able to do.

As we were reading our devotion this morning based on Revelation Chapter 1, I began to ponder on what John experienced as he was exiled to the Island of Patmos. He must have been desperately lonely, without human comforts and wondering what would eventually happen to him. YET he was the one who saw Christ in a way no one else saw HIM, and he was the one who was told to write the

November 6, 2011 (continued)

"Revelation" that we still read today. The question is, "Was it worth it?" So, too, I ask, "Is it worth it?" Is this trial worth it? I have to say that, based on Scripture, *it is!* "Nothing you do for the Lord is in vain." (I Cor. 15:58) And as I choose to allow HIM to use my trial for HIS Glory...HE WILL! He can and will use trials if we *let* HIM.

Romans 8:28 tells us that "*ALL things work together for the good of those who love HIM.*" So is this part of "ALL things"? Do we really believe that this is the heritage for the children of God... namely you? If so....Let HIM use yours as well.

Love, blessings and prayers,

Pat

Amazed

November 9, 2011

Here's the song that I woke up with at 4:20 this morning:

*Wonderful, wonderful, Jesus is to me
Counselor, Prince of Peace,
Mighty God is He.
Saving me, keeping me,
From all sin and shame (PAIN)
Jesus is my Savior and
I'll praise HIS holy name!*

So what does that translate to???? NO REACTION TO THE *NEULASTA* MEDICATION GIVEN MORE THAN 80 HOURS AGO! THAT IS NO, NOTHING, NUDA, NIENTE, NIL! (This is the drug that often makes people feel like their marrow is being torn out of their bones.)

"*We were sailing along on Moonlight Bay. We could hear the voices ringing. They seemed to say...*". I think that's how the song goes.

I guess you can tell that I stand amazed. My doctor has been amazed as well and was concerned that I was not taking my pain medications. Well, no pain, no need for meds AND at this point I am pretty much off of EVERYTHING!!

November 9, 2011 (continued)

I was instructed not to take my vitamins during this treatment time, and there is nothing else I have taken in a couple of days when the pain _should_ be the worst.

How free I feel and, could it be that GOD ALONE can take care of ALL my needs??? Seems like HE'S done it!

So, how are you all? I do pray that in the "every days" of life, you are experiencing the songs, the answers to prayer, and the powerful results of your intimate relationship with our Savior, Jesus.

Love to hug each one of you!

Pat

DOING WELL

NOVEMBER 15, 2011

Hi Fellow Sojourners,

It has been a while since I have written, and you are assuming correctly if you believe that I am well. It seems that every day brings a new friend or family member into my life who helps me with errands or medical appointments or just company (in person or via phone), and I am grateful. I have written a Christmas letter and many notes to individuals, but I have not given you all an update.

What does *doing well* look like these days? I have more energy than in the past and this is my best week of my cycle. I am still careful about possible infection but have gone to malls and individual stores at non-peak times and have always washed or sanitized my hands as soon as possible. So far, so very good. My weight has been fluctuating these days, and it is either my digital scale or food or fluid. I will ask on Friday when I get my pretreatment exam and blood test.

The port incision is healing as is my surgery site. Naturally, this internal heal will take longer, but everyone who sees me comments about how good I look, and that encourages me to persist as I wait for the rest of my healing to catch up. I take a walk as often as possible and, for the most part, feel pretty "normal" these days. My next treatment cycle will be Thanksgiving week. I will not be in treatment on Thursday but will be all the other

November 15, 2011 (continued)

days. Both our children's families have been up to visit recently, so Carl and I will relax and recover on Thanksgiving Day.

One new awareness came to me last night which is wonderful and very life-changing and which I believe has caused healing in my body as well. I realize that I have never "**owned**" this disease. Yes, I have heard the diagnosis and have felt the pain associated with the surgery and treatments, but there is a way that I am outside of the process. It is something that I am going **through** but does not permanently affect me. It does not determine my destiny or my identity. It is like I am in it and yet above it. It is like I am going through it but am still outside of it. It is difficult to explain, yet is very real for me.

The courage and positive attitude I have is because of this sense that this thing does not own or dictate my future, and I have been given the "grace through faith" not to accept it as a permanent or future part of me. So I live with expectant hope, and that hope heals and encourages me as I walk this time out.

There was also another wonderful truth that came to me these past few days. It is the truth that God is healing me by HIS LOVE. As I was reading Romans 8:31-39, I was struck by the fact that one of the specific ways that God persists in HIS love for us is that even when we

worry, that worry cannot stop the flow of God's love to us. So even when we worry HE loves us.

As I continued to ponder, I asked how it was that God was healing me. What was the power that made it happen? The thought that came to mind was HIS LOVE. When I looked at the commentary on this section of scripture in my Bible it said "God heals by HIS LOVE." So the more we accept and live in the truth of HIS LOVE for us the more HIS power to heal is available to us. This sounds so simple, but as it becomes REALITY it empowers great blessing and overwhelms us with the mighty supernatural power and love HE gives us.

The other facet of this powerful love is that it comes through you. Each time you give because you love HIM and for HIS glory, HE takes your act of service and changes that into healing for me. HIS LOVE extended through your hands is HIS power to heal and change me. What a remarkable truth!. You are actually Jesus to me in all HIS power and grace as you give as directed and in tune with what and who HE is. I do pray these words minister to your heart so that Jesus becomes more than you ever imagined.

Love,
Pat

Peace

November 19, 2011

Morning

"Peace is not the absence of trouble. Peace is the presence of Christ." I was told that Sheila Walsh shared this at the Women of Faith Conference this year. Well, as I picked up my eyes from the computer, I looked up at the sunrise and saw beautiful pinks and blues painted across the sky. The pinks were more like magenta, and the blues were a delicate baby blue. The trees are mostly bare and their shadows are like filigree against the sky as their backdrop. Why is this significant???? Because when I see all this and acknowledge that God made everything good, I know that HE is *in* this moment to speak and to bless and to raise our perspective to one of wonder.

Specifically, I can sense HIM saying "I am here and there is nothing that lies before you that I am not able to take total care of...lean on ME, I am here." So today do some leaning and HE'LL do some lifting of your perspective and all those things in your life you think you have to carry....I will choose to do the same.

For those of you who do not know my treatment schedule; I will be in treatment next week, off for Thanksgiving, and finished with my treatment cycles in the beginning of January 2012.

I will be excited to celebrate the new year because for me it will bring documented verification of my healing!!

Love you all,
Pat

AFTERNOON

Wanted to add some thoughts to this morning's message. They revolve around the story of Jonah and his unwillingness to obey God when HE asked Jonah to go to Nineveh to preach HIS saving grace to those people. As I reflected on Jonah's unwillingness to go to Nineveh as God had instructed, I realized there are areas where I will not go to my "Nineveh"...the place where I am doubtful that God can change me. The area that came to mind this morning was that of patience.

November 19, 2011 (continued)

Often I will react in a very impatient and almost demanding my way. It is a real battle for me to listen thoroughly, ponder, and see what is being said before I react or respond with an appropriate up-building word. As I asked the Lord why this happens, what came to mind was the way I functioned as a young girl. It seemed that the faster I did things, the more praise I got from my parents... whether it was washing the dishes, finishing my homework or doing a sewing project...**fast = success**.

So...I translated that into a belief system which says that if you do it fast, you do it well, then you are a success and of value. Of course this is a LIE, but when you have functioned in it for so long, it *looks* like the truth.

So today I am asking Jesus to help me recognize my impatience when it rises up so I can surrender it again to HIM and ask for HIS help to conquer the LIE with the TRUTH. When I think about Nineveh, its location in Assyria and the heinous battle strategies it had, I wonder if **I** would be willing to help them find God. Yet God in His abundant mercy sent Jonah to do just that.

Some other scriptures came to mind:
"*Mercy triumphs over judgment...*". (James 2:13)

If "mercy triumphs over judgment", then we are to be merciful as HE is merciful. As it says in the Sermon on the Mount, "*The merciful shall be shown mercy.*"

(Matthew 5:7) "*Vengeance is MINE, I will repay, saith the LORD*"... (Deut.32:35) So if "vengeance is HIS", then it is <u>HIS</u> hand, and <u>not ours</u>, that exacts the punishment, and HE promises to judge in HIS time and in HIS way.

There were some other stories in scripture that came to my mind that speak of mercy. The story of the man who

owed a great debt, who was released because of his master's mercy, and then angrily tried to get a small debt owed him from his fellow servant. And the story about the laborers and how at the end of the day they were all paid the same wage and many believed it was unfair. This story really stumps us at times, because it seems so unfair for a laborer who worked only one hour to get the same wage as one who worked all day. We seem to deem fairness as greater than mercy. Yet, if God was only fair to us and not merciful... where would we be?

Mercy is so very hard to grasp at times, because it is part of the true nature of God and we have to purposely put away our rights to see mercy as the higher calling and indeed the wonderful nature of God. God's plan for me is to be merciful like HIMSELF. This means patience and willingness to wait for others, to deny my "fast" approach and consider where others may be, <u>and</u> to think more highly of them than myself-even if they don't work on my schedule.

Thank God that HE shows us where we have gone astray and where we are hindering ourselves from being free and more like HIM.

Be blessed,

Pat

HAPPY THANKSGIVING!!!

NOVEMBER 24, 2011

And it truly is a happy one for us. To know that all of you have invested, given, prayed, and served us makes our cup overflow. Carl and I will take a quiet restful day to regain my strength after my three long days of chemo. Our joy is not diminished by our absence from family, because you are all with us, and we so appreciate you. And so our thanksgiving overflows in too many directions to count.

Bless you all, as HE opens our eyes to see ALL HE has given. I thank HIM especially for what HE has given us through each one of you.

HAPPY, HAPPY THANKSGIVING!!

Pat and Carl

Coming Back

NOVEMBER 26, 2011

Yes, I am coming back, and what a celebration it is to know I will *feel* like I am in the land of the living. These past two days have been harder physically and emotionally than my past cycles. It seems that as they are completed I should be feeling more energized and encouraged that they are coming to an end (only 2 cycles to go). Yet the debilitating weakness is not something I am getting used to. However, I have learned that whether it is being thankful **in** or **for** all things, HE is the power without whom I cannot.

During these past two days I fell into trying to make myself better and I could not. Because I tried to accelerate the healing process, I was very frustrated.

Thank God for this morning. As I awoke, I was reminded that HE is my strength and song, my hope and my health. Am I saying that energy and health are not to be desired?? NO, rather, that my attitude is more important than even my aptitude or, in my case, energy.

So, again I joyfully surrender to the process, and I am thanking GOD for how wonderfully HE is working to heal me. I accept that "no energy" and a great attitude of hope and faith can buoy me up in spirit, and the flesh WILL follow. "This is the Day" was the song I heard playing in my mind when I awoke, and the scripture for today was Ps. 118:24 (same as song). I praise God that HE is still speaking and yearns for me to know that "*HE sings over me.*" (Zeph. 3:17) All of HIS personal intimate word to me creates in me a new joy and uplifted hope...Psalm 24 showed me again who my Savior is, and I am rejoicing.

Bless you and may your hearts be ever thankful.

Pat

UPDATE FROM CARL

NOVEMBER 27, 2011

Pat has slept and been groggy all day yesterday and most of today. Each day forward she should get a little stronger and back to her happy self. We went up to Hartford early this morning to get her Neulasta shot to replace the white blood cells in her bone marrow which were killed off by the chemo drugs. We are rejoicing also for the good reports that show her numbers decreasing and having little or no side effects (other than exhaustion).

Keep praying that Pat's immune system can handle this fatigue, as it seems to be increasing with each additional cycle. I understand now why there are only six of these treatments. The drugs are powerful and nasty, but they seem to be doing the job on the "nasty" cancer cells. For that we are thankful to God. Thank you, too, for being our friends, praying with us and for us as we go through this trial.

Do you know that Chip D. just started on the same chemo drug (Ifosamide®) that Pat has been on? What a strong man and committed sacrificer he is. All these years, all these trials he has been on testing drugs for future data results to help people, even like Pat. He is my hero.

Carl

BELIEVE

NOVEMBER 28, 2011

On Saturday I wrote about allowing God to be my strength and accepting that I could not do, in and of myself, what I physically wanted to do. So this morning I'm thinking about *how* to let HIM be my strength, my song, my hope...The first thought that comes to mind is in the familiar scripture..."*Be still and know that I AM GOD.*" (Psalm 46) Yet how do we do that??? As I pondered, I sensed that *we do it until we believe it* (or always). At this time of year Macy's has the same theme, *BELIEVE!* And of course *BELIEVE* means rely on, trust in, depend totally on, (or even as I picture, sit down in it).

OK, so HIS help comes when we *BELIEVE*. How do we access that belief?? What physically helps us do that??? For me it is getting to a place of quiet rest, with song or HIS WORD becoming my sole focus and waiting in faith that HE will come and help me. We do live by faith, but unfortunately our world lives by sight, and sight just does not work when we have trials, nor does it work when we force our own destiny. At best we come up attaining what we want and lose the deep sense of fulfillment that we thought would be a part of the goal.

So having "faith in God" really **is** what is required. That means living each moment *BELIEVING* that HE is with us (Emmanuel), HE cares (...*casting all your cares upon HIM,*

November 28, 2011 (continued)

for HE cares for you), and KNOWING that all this is based on the love that sent HIM ultimately to the cross and brought HIM down to earth for Christmas. It's just that simple, but, OH, will we take time to surrender to this great truth???

The "season" is upon us. What do you think HE wants for Christmas??? Maybe just **us** in a more surrendered **BELIEVING** way than ever before. And if we choose this sweet fellowship, HE will be our most wonderful Christmas present. *"God so loved the world that HE gave..."* (John 3:16) First and foremost let us, "come let us adore HIM". HE is the one, the LORD, WHO will be everything we need if we **BELIEVE!**

Bless you as you continue your preparations for this HOLY season. May HE be at the core of all you do.

Pat

BELIEVING

DECEMBER 3, 2011

Just another quick insight about *believing*. As I was pondering about how to *believe,* which I wrote about in my last message, a wonderful thought came to mind regarding God's gracious nature. HE does not condemn us for seeking and needing HIM... so when we lack *belief* or are unbelieving and we say, "I *believe,* help my *unbelief,"* HE says "Yes" and "I am pleased."

Now I wouldn't want to put words into God's mouth, but based on my understanding of scripture and HIS nature, it seems so like HIM to respond to any of our honest cries for help with "I AM here, my child, I will help you...It is my joy to do so."

Love you all,

Pat

REST

December 9, 2011

What an awesome word...REST...And do we do much of it this season??? I guess I should not be so quick to ask, since I have a forced limitation on my going and coming. Our choice to have only one car at this time, coupled with Carl's choice to drive himself to work instead of using the carpool (so that he can go and come as needs arise) and, of course, one week out of three at the treatment center has surely clipped my wings. This will all end in January when my treatments end. This too shall pass!!!

Now for the REST...This morning as Carl and I were praying (we had just read I Kings, Chapter 3, where Solomon was given an opportunity to ask for what he wanted and chose wisdom to lead God's people), we had a sense that even in our prayers we are looking for the next step and, like Solomon, we needed more of who God is than an answer or next step.

Oh yes, we need wisdom for the next step; however, we also need to fully REST until the next step comes. And the focus has to be on RESTING in HIM, not on making something happen and being consumed with "Is this the next step?"

REST is the state of faithful waiting, knowing that God has it all in HIS hands for HIS perfect time and plan. It seemed that we became aware that we spend so much

time focusing on the next step that we miss the most important part of our life in Christ. That part is that our life is hidden WITH HIM and IN HIM. It is a life of quiet assurance and deep peace and REST and joy. It is a place where there are NO concerns and HE is everything we need.

Now does that mean we do nothing??? Of course not, BUT all we do is an out-working of that REST which provides direction and confirmation and overwhelming assurance that HE is in control of all the outcomes. Now who wouldn't want to be focused on this kind of REST?? We all settle for so much less than HE has. Will we **choose** to REST? HE is waiting for us to so completely REST in HIM that all else is of no consequence, because it is hidden in HIS wonderful plan for us...today, tomorrow and forever.

Do we have emotions?? Yes. Do they say other things than REST?? Yes. Can we choose to believe God and seek HIS REST more than all we feel or think? Yes...So, will we seek for what HE would so graciously offer...and at no cost?

May this Christmas be filled with more REST than you ever thought possible, even if that REST comes in the midst of your busiest moments. Yet may we find the time to reflect on what it truly means to have Christ come at Christmas in those quiet times when all we see is HIM.

December 9, 2011 (continued)

"O, come let us adore HIM...Christ the LORD."

Have a blessed Christmas, filled with Christ HIMSELF.

Pat

P.S. Next week is my chemo week...Thanks for your sustaining prayer for me.

MINOR SURGERY

DECEMBER 14, 2011

Hi All,

Just wanted to send you a short update and prayer request. At 10AM I will be having minor surgery to re-adjust my placement port which seems to have rotated causing an inability to be accessed by the nurses for infusion. Please pray for hands guided by God, for me to remember that HE is holding my hand, and that all the procedures would be done correctly and with foresight as to how the positioning of this port can be stabilized.

If you don't get this e-mail this morning, I believe in retroactive prayer, especially since all time is in HIS hands.

Be blessed and full of faith today.

Love you all so much,
Pat

ADDENDUM:

Hi Everyone,

Just got home and did not have to have surgery. The doctor was able to manually turn the port. Praise God, and thanks for your faithful prayers.
Pat

"Bearable" Mountains

December 15, 2011

It's 3:30 AM. I am awake and feeling so blessed at yesterday's reprieve from another surgery. The port <u>manual repositioning</u> was grace to me. I asked the doctor what would cause the port to turn around, and after many questions, I got the real answer. The doctor said that he always stitches the port in place, and that really confused me, so I asked some more questions and found out that the stitches dissolve after three weeks and then the port can turn. Of course, my nurse told me that this usually happens in obese people.

So here we are on the other side of the mountain. Yet I am often reminded of the old Girl Scout song..."The **bear**

went over the mountain...and what do you think he saw... he saw another mountain"... and that's how I feel at times. This weekend usually is my weakest time, yet God reminds me to remember that at the beginning of this journey HE told me HE would never let go of my hand. So it is with HIM that I **bear** all things.

I feel a bit like a runner may feel as she is approaching the end of the race...just a little bit to go but it's the hardest part. Even after the Israelites saw all the deliverances from Egypt they still saw their journey as an uphill one. So I again go back to the Rock of my salvation.

Let me also ask for prayer regarding my hands. As I write this e-mail I began with no pain in the fingers of my left hand. Now both my left and right hands are beginning to be painfully numb. I have had some carpal tunnel issues in the past, and I believe God wants me to write. Would you pray for HIS direction in healing?

Thank you all and bless you,
Pat

December 15, 2011 (continued)

Same Day (Morning)

Just wanted to share a good Word from God. The first verses Carl read to me this morning were from Romans 8:23-25. It gave me great encouragement knowing that our yearning is to be out of our bodies and with the Lord. This is how HE made us and on some days our yearning is greater. Hebrews 6:18-20 talks about HIS sure promise, not an abstract, but a real tangible guaranteed hope.

Do hope these verses encourage you today.

Love,

Pat

SURRENDER

DECEMBER 18, 2011

Sometimes I wonder why I share so many details of my journey with you but it seems the journey is more real when I do. Yesterday was a washout. Washout…let's see…that means moving from one recliner to another and wobbling on the way. It also means emotional weakness. I find myself crying even though I am not depressed. It is so difficult to focus at these times, and I cannot read or even hold a book. It even takes great effort to listen to someone read to me. This past week was more difficult because of the readjustment of my port and the concern over needing it to be surgically re-implanted in my chest. Praise God that was done manually and no surgery was needed. However, the pain and discomfort because of the manipulation caused me to wonder if it was stable, but with

December 18, 2011 (continued)

some input from medical personnel, I gave up that concern.

Surrender is a word we use often, but doing it is difficult. Not doing the teeny little things you've always done is a definite challenge. Yet I am on the other side now. I am getting stronger as evidenced by my writing to you again. A few days ago I shared with you the old Girl Scout song, "The bear went over the mountain...and what do you think he saw?...he saw another mountain."

Well, after I wrote that e-mail I was reminded of yet another song...this one says, "HE IS BIGGER THAN ANY MOUNTAIN I CAN OR CANNOT SEE." It has been my sustaining theme these past days.

Our son-in-law John is with us and has been since last Saturday and his visit is good for me. He is working up in East Windsor at Lincoln Technical Institute as an instructor, and we are thankful we can help with this transitional time. God has blessed him with wonderful new staff members who have made John feel so at home.

We are so thankful after many years of financial struggle down in North Carolina due to changes in our economy.

My left hand is getting numb, but I have discovered that a more upright position keeps it going longer. My right hand seems to be OK.

We are nearly on to the last cycle and pray that the port does not need any more adjustment. The LAST cycle begins on January 3rd-6th. Can't wait, but I will by God's amazing grace. Was it easy?... NO. Did it accomplish what HE had in mind?...I pray so and as I continue to persevere and walk, even more will be revealed.

So, as Christmas Day draws near, with our daughter Laurie Ann and family arriving on the 22nd, I am looking forward and upward. I choose to ponder on the birth of One who came to die for me, and as I do, all my painful experiences pale in comparison. What a Savior, what a friend HE is to me these days.

I pray HIS presence and peace come into the deepest part of your hearts.

Love you all!

Pat

TIMING

DECEMBER 18, 2011 (CONTINUED)

So often I begin writing in the wee hours and later have wonderful scriptures that confirm and encourage our chats.

Isaiah 30:20-21 speaks of the Lord giving us adversity and the food of affliction but also HIS hand that teaches and shows us HIMSELF.

II Corinthians 4:17 tells us that our present troubles pale in comparison to Jesus' gift to us at Christmas from sooo far away and in comparison to the immeasurably great Glory that will last forever.

Galatians 4 talks about the FULLNESS of time, the absolute perfect timing of God
for these things to be, and
for them to end.

I am so encouraged that the
Celebration is coming. It will
be God's perfect time for
this to end soon. I CAN'T
WAIT!!!! BUT I WILL, BY
GRACE, AND WE WILL ALL SEE WHAT HE HAS DONE!!

Love and great HOPE!
Pat

NEW BEGINNINGS

JANUARY 1, 2012

HAPPY NEW YEAR...and may it be one of great expectations, for we have a great God. Thanks to each and every one of you for your help and encouragement. Without you and your prayer support I am not sure I could walk this road. I am so thankful that God put you in my path and that you have also been encouraged by my trial.

Our daughter Laurie Ann and her family left Wednesday morning, and our son-in-law John will be here today, January 1st. It was a good Christmas. God sustained me by HIS grace, and there were no real challenges. We are awaiting some final arrangements for John and Kristin and their move to Connecticut. God has been gracious to them, and we expect that by HIS nature HE will continue to be.

As for me...this morning Carl noticed that I had one eyelash hair on my right eyelid and three eyelash hairs on my left eyelid. As I read Habakkuk, I was struck by a verse that seems to speak to me regarding this and has been one of my favorites. It says: "*Though there are no cattle in the barn...or grapes on the vine...*". I could say, "Though there be only one eyelash hair on one eye and only three on the other..." and, as Habakkuk continues, "<u>*still I will rejoice in God my Savior*</u>."

January 1, 2012 (continued)

There have been other minor issues, but I also remember that "in this life we will have momentary light afflictions that will work for eternal glory." So it would be best not to even mention them. They are light and momentary **BUT HIS** glory and our share in it will be eternal. Here's what the amplified version in the Bible says:

> *"For our light, momentary affliction (this slight distress of the passing hour) is ever more and more abundantly preparing and producing and achieving for us an everlasting weight of glory--beyond all measure, excessively surpassing all comparisons and all calculations, a vast and transcendent glory and blessedness never to cease!"*
> (II Cor. 4:17)

My last week of chemo starts on Tuesday, January 3, 2012. It seems to have been a long haul at times and sometimes straight up hill. But this I know...God has been with me! HE has sustained me with health to finish the treatment on schedule, emotional strength, and a positive faith through all the pain and all the changes that have occurred. *So this coming week will be the last cycle.* HALLELUJAH!!! I still have to go through it, and

do ask you to pray that my port will function properly, also that I will have peace in trusting God about it.

May you become more and more aware of HIS sustaining grace and love for you as you walk into this new year with confidence that in and through HIM you can truly do all things.

Love and joy,
Pat

TODAY'S THOUGHTS

JANUARY 3, 2012

Today is the beginning of the end...YEA!! The last week, the last cycle...THIS IS VERY, VERY GOOD! And as I write this, my left hand is already beginning to hurt and go numb. Last night when I went to bed, and for two days, I have felt pain in my left foot. The pain was like a nail being driven into the heel of my foot. I also felt a protrusion and tightening in my chest that restricted me from stretching my right arm and lying on my right side. I know you are all praying for me.

So...This is what came to mind to help me with maintaining the right attitude **through** the pain and discomfort (am now writing with only my right hand because of intolerable pain in my left hand).

The nail...I began to imagine what the nails in Jesus' feet were like. Now, I do not fully know what that pain was like, nor can I know. But somehow I had an understanding of HIS pain that had to be many times more than mine, and mine was barely tolerable. The comparison brought me to a place of humble thanksgiving for HIS sacrifice for me/us. My pain seemed to be insignificant compared to HIS love as HE suffered in such an incomprehensible way for me/us.

As I pondered on all my other symptoms, I began thinking about your prayers...rising as incense to our FATHER'S THRONE. It was like seeing many, many hands lifted as they presented my needs and pain up to our Father in heaven. (And even as I write this many of your faces come before me.) There was a sense of reality that I had never experienced before. It seems that God opens my spiritual eyes when I am in pain, in need, and look to HIM for help.

He is so gracious...I get to a place where I cannot help myself, and HE shows me what it is REALLY like in a world where I have never been before. HE shows me how real HIS word and promises are and actually shows me that they are working on my behalf, because of HIS love alone. What an awesome, incomprehensibly loving GOD we serve.

I pray that as you take time with HIM today, you will wait on HIM till HE makes HIMSELF known to you in ways you have never imagined before.

In HIS Amazing Love and unending grace,

Pat

Praise Report

JANUARY 4, 2012

Just wanted to let you all know how God is answering prayer. My port was in the perfect position this morning to be accessed. And my foot pain was gone. Yes, I was off my feet for most of the day. I am thankful even if tired. Had a friend with me and was served and blessed and encouraged and loved.

God is Good ALL the time.

Love you all.

Thanks for praying,

Pat

Appreciation

January 5, 2012

Hello,

Pat just came home (5 pm) after completing her last day of her 6th and final round of treatments at the HH Grey Center in Hartford. I know she will write her message of joy and thanksgiving to you soon. However, I would like to say my own special **Thank You** for being there with her these last five months with your prayers, e-mails, dinners, cards, phone calls, words of encouragement, hugs, and assistance in driving her to appointments. Because you have helped out in so many areas, you have given me the ability to keep working, albeit at a reduced level, instead of taking many days off to meet Pat's need.

Your friendship is a gift: I value you highly. Your listening ear, hugs, and tears back in August showed me you care and would be there for us no matter what. Well, today we can say Pat is finished with chemo. PTL, Hallelujah. God has answered our prayers! I look forward to seeing you very soon and giving a grateful hug. Thank you for being there for me as you have cared for my precious and wonderful, fearless and faithful wife. We look forward to New Beginnings in 2012 with you. Keep on praying, keep on believing. Hope!

Pat will write soon, I promise.

Carl

DISORIENTATION

JANUARY 7, 2012

So today is Saturday--it's a strange time. I am relieved that my six cycles are over but feeling emotionally spent. Tears come to my eyes without me sensing they are coming. I began reading a part of a book where a woman was dying of stomach cancer in the 1960's. Oh, how thankful I am that medical science has improved so much since then and that all my tests are good.

Still, there is disorientation--I am not sure where I am--I know I am "finished", but the infusion port needs to come out, then the doctor's visit, then the CT Scan--<u>Am I finished</u>? Then, too, there is the hair loss, the long time for it to grow in again, the daily dealing with 25 extra pounds of weight, and the clothes and the head coverings. I want it to be over NOW. Yet this is the transition phase. This, too, will take determination and faith. Maybe this is the harder time, for it is, and yet, it is not.

Everyone prays and loves and blesses and cares, and I'm thankful, but I am here, and I don't know if anyone else knows where that is.

Maybe it is a REALITY CHECK, and I'm still not sure what that is. The song comes to mind "I Know That My Redeemer Lives" even if I don't feel that... then another song "It is finished, the battle is over.... and Jesus is LORD." Yes, and I can celebrate... that HE lives forever more. And most of all, it is "THROUGH IT ALL, I've learned to trust in Jesus, learned to depend upon HIS Word." So...I am here in another **THROUGH**. I know HE WILL be with me, and HE will help me, and HE WILL be what I need. HE is the only one who can interpret this time to my heart and keep me going forward and upward to where HE has a place for me. Actually, I am already in that place. As I rest in HIM, HE keeps me, trains me, and is satisfied with me.

Waiting gives unique peace--it is where HE takes over and we surrender. It is where we have peace and rest and HE does the work. It is stress-less and timeless, and all is in HIS HANDS. I choose again to trust, to wait, to let HIM love me and take me through to the place of peace in HIM that HE has set for me.

Tomorrow will be a better day.

Pat

HOPE GIVING SCRIPTURES

JANUARY 8, 2012

Some scriptures came to my attention today, and they blessed my heart and are encouraging me. I also read "Jesus Calling" (a wonderful devotion that seems to have Jesus speaking directly to us). The intent of the devotion for me was that in times of weakness, God is closer than ever and it can be our access point to HIM. HE does not reprimand us for weakness; instead, "*He will not crush a bruised reed.*" (Isaiah 42:3) When we feel lost or hopeless or self-pity or discouragement, HE is closer than ever. HE weeps for our pain and is an ever present help in trouble. So I will not fear and I look for the light ahead.

These scriptures gave me hope:

> Psalm 46:1 - *God is our refuge and strength, ALWAYS ready to help in times of trouble.*
> Romans 12:12—*Be glad for all God is planning for you. Be patient in trouble, and always be prayerful.*
> Romans 15:13 - *So I pray that God, who gives you hope, will keep you happy and full of peace as you believe in HIM. May you overflow with hope through the power of the Holy Spirit.*

And, lastly, a song... "Don't grow weary in the fight, don't surrender... keep on doing what you know is right... there will be seasons of testing and there will be... in the night... but soon you'll be reaping the blessings... "So today is bright. HIS grace has again been extended (has really always been there), and I am hopeful and  encouraged waiting and trusting HIM for the power to continue to go *through*.

Bless you all, and may HIS hand of love encompass every part of your being.

Love,

Pat

CHOOSING THE BETTER WAY

JANUARY 11, 2012

Hello my Friends and Family,

Wrote to you two days ago and accidently hit the delete key instead of the backspace key and oops! Lost it all before sending, so I will review what I typed as I remember. Most of my writing that day was in the complaining mode, but the end was hope and surrender and wait. It was a little like a psalm where David pours  out his complaint *before* the Lord and then gets to the place where he decides that his only hope is *in* the Lord.

My complaints were again about the transition period that I am in and the impatience I was sensing because of discomfort. I was a little angry with my doctor and was going to lay before her my demands to fix various things that bothered me. Of course, I realized that she is not God and that healing may take longer than I would like. (We are not machines that just get a new part and then work perfectly...in fact, some new parts take breaking

in.) Then, too, I realized that my complaints were not going to be taken care of today...and if not today, then a day at a time is all I really have to concern myself with... Didn't Jesus say that *each day has enough concern of its own?*

So the end of the struggle left me again with the choice for peace...for HIM, for trust and for Rest. And so I chose the better way and I am moving forward. I did call a follow-up counselor and had a good conversation with her about some of my frustration. She had a listening ear, sympathetic understanding, and good input regarding my state in the healing process. All in all, I am glad that God brought me through and that HIS perspective and grace are sufficient for the place HE is leading me.

My daughter sent me a scripture that encouraged me (Psalm 34:17-18). "*The righteous cry out and the Lord hears them. He delivers them from all their troubles. The Lord is close to the brokenhearted and saves those who are crushed in spirit.*"

May you be encouraged today...*HE's got it!*

Love,
Pat

THE LITTLE THINGS

JANUARY 12, 2012

Today as I was taking a shower...I thanked God for the little things: My soap dispenser, the refreshing sense of clean, the energy to take a shower, the clean-smelling soap. Then there was a teeny bit of weight loss...maybe six pounds...since all my chemo fluids are leaving. The heat in my bathroom, the cream for my dry skin, even the mascara that sticks to my eye lid and makes me look like I have lashes. And then there are those fuzzy things growing on my head...I guess I know how a youth feels when he is getting ready for his first shave. The ability to make oatmeal for my new family (including John). The energy to plan and cook dinner. Then there was a 15-minute rest period between my activities. Cleaning up the kitchen sink, wiping off the kitchen table, walking slowly to the mailbox, and enjoying the sun on my face and the crisp air in my nostrils.

Wow, was all this here before and I didn't notice???
I'm sure I could go on and on and, of course, I am most thankful for the ONE who made me conscious of what has been given to me. But let this suffice to say...It is a good life-giving place to be. Perhaps today we could live a bit more in thanksgiving and less in complaint.

Bless you as you thank our Gracious God whose character is wrapped up in giving to HIS children.

Pat

The Night is Past

JANUARY 14, 2012

It is 7 AM, and that's a bit late for me. But, lest you think I missed the wee hours of the morning, I did not. It seems that every night I wake up with profuse sweating, especially on my head. I often explain it like this: Before surgery I had a broken thermostat, after surgery I had no thermostat, and now after chemo I have heat generation. So when I wake up I usually stay up awhile so that I will be able to cool off, and I do go back to bed after an hour or so and am usually able to go back to sleep. Thank God!

So, what's <u>new</u> is the next phase. Monday I will be going to a follow-up counselor who will give me some information regarding my next steps. I do know that I will be having a CT scan on the 26th and a doctor visit and blood tests on the 30th. Then I will be going to a LIVESTRONG® program at the YMCA® for cancer survivors on February 1st. So it seems the path is prepared for me.

The Scripture that comes to my heart this morning is Isaiah 40:31: *"But they who trust in the Lord will find new strength. They will soar high on wings like eagles. They will not grow weary. They will walk and not faint."*
For me today I see rest and yet growing activity at a slow pace. The verse says *"walk and not faint"*...and that's where I am. I am going to stores (at non-peak

times), taking short walks, cooking, and even visiting restaurants with friends and family for whom I am very grateful.

On Monday I will take my first solo "flight" into Hartford for my follow-up visit. I am walking and not getting too weary and am choosing patience. Jesus continues to hold my hand through this part of the journey.

Bless you all, and may you find HIS peace for your life journey as well.

Pat

Elephant Feet

JANUARY 16, 2012

This morning at 4 AM I awoke in serious pain. It felt as if there was an elephant foot on each hip. Then I began to feel a tearing and pulling in my thighs. I wondered about the Neulasta shot which I got on January 5th. It didn't seem like I should be having a reaction 11 days later.

I did not want to take the high-powered drugs that were given for these reactions. Then I sensed I should just take two Tylenol®. Within an hour the pain was gone. Was it the Tylenol®, God???

I am so grateful that the pain left so quickly and that God gave me the confidence to wait. HE is a wonderful God.

The song that came to my heart during the time says, "I will survive, I am alive, I stand beside the crucified One." Bless you all.

Love,
Pat

THE RECOVERY PROCESS

JANUARY 24, 2012

Hi Friends and Family,

Just thought I'd let you know where I am in the recovery process. Yes, it is a process, and even as I look for an end, I know that every part of our lives goes from one step to another, and it is indeed a process. The process ends when we die. So it makes sense, and indeed is wisdom, to enjoy the process and at times to walk through what we must.

We can rejoice as Paul did in his prison cell and bring salvation to the jailer and his family, or we can complain and live in depression and despair. It is always our choice, and although one choice seems easier than the other, the results are dramatically different. One is the declaration of victory by faith, and the other an agreement with our enemy that there is no hope. Our God is the God of HOPE. Romans 15:13 tells us to *"abound in hope"*, 8:25 tells us to *"persevere in hope when we do not see"*, and 5:5 says that *"hope never disappoints"*.

So, for me, I am confessing these truths as I go through a number of tests this week. I will be having a CT scan on Thursday and a biopsy on Friday. I was instructed to do nothing after the biopsy and am trusting for good results in each test. Then next week I will be going to a

January 24, 2012 (continued)

dermatologist and a therapist to massage my hands and feet so as to reverse the neuropathy.

Today I went to the LIVESTRONG® program at the YMCA® for cancer survivors. It is a program that will help me get back to the activity level that I've been used to or, perhaps more accurately, help me become more active than I have been. I am encouraged but, like David, I often want to say "make me wings so I might fly away". This will be the case for all of us...in time.

Bless you all, and thanks for your prayers.

Love,

Pat

APPOINTMENTS

JANUARY 27, 2012

Thanks for your prayers. My CT scan went very well. It was the fastest in history. They used my port and, because I knew what the procedure would be like, it went really fast. I was in at 8:40 AM in Glastonbury and home by 10 AM.

This morning I will be going for a breast biopsy at 10:10 AM. **Through** is still the theme, and although I am unfamiliar with this procedure, with my history it can't be that difficult...AND, as I say much these days, "This, too, shall pass."

Coming up is a visit with a nutritionist on Monday as well as a re-evaluation visit with my surgeon. On Tuesday I have an appointment for hand massage. The sensation in my left hand is becoming more painful. Thanks for your prayers. Home stretch can't be far away. I won't know the results for a few days, but I can't imagine they would be anything but good based on all my other test results.

"*This is the day that the Lord has made; we will rejoice and be glad in it.*" (By the way, this is part of Psalm 118 and is said to be the song that Jesus and HIS disciples shared before He was crucified.)

Love you all. Keep the faith.

Pat

It Is Finished!

January 30, 2012

Well...HALLELUJAH AND AMEN!!!! My doctor's visit and my tests were normal!! She said that few ever do as well as I did during treatment. The drug I was on is usually very toxic, but I seemed to be protected from its negative effects.

Bottom line is that I am cancer free. I will be going for checkups now and then but no more Chemo.

We serve a Mighty God and your prayers in conjunction with His will have brought wonderful victory.

Bless you all...this journey you have been on with me is your victory too!

Love,
Pat

THE RECOVERY - PHASE I

FEBRUARY 13, 2012

Hello Dear Ones,

It has been a while, but aren't you all glad that I am not writing at 2 AM and sleeping instead?

Do you remember when the kids constantly asked, "Are we there yet?" That's somewhat how I feel these days. I was so thankful I could return to church and that Carl could take me to "Love in the Afternoon" at Elim Park. The operatic program featured familiar arias from my most beloved operas. Then there was a wonderful lunch of lobster and shrimp in a wonderful cream sauce, and at the end of the performance all the ladies were given beautiful long-stem roses. How blessed I was to be treated so royally and to see so many who had been praying for me and have a chance to hug each one of them.

This time is one of wonderful celebration and re-entry into a world I have become accustomed to living without. God has a new phase for me, and the re-entry is not without adjustment. As I look back I can see that HE has changed me. Now activity is not as important as it was, and rest in both the spiritual and physical realms make me so content. I am so acquainted with that rest that I almost resist coming out of it. Perhaps God wants me to remain in it even when I do venture out. My

FEBRUARY 13, 2012 (CONTINUED)

appreciation of the WORD and HIS voice through it all has made me want to wait, and watch for what HE wants to do in and eventually through me.

This morning a series of phrases came to mind:

> ♪ I did it my way....(Frank Sinatra's song)
> Have it your way....at Burger King®
> And
> Runnin' on Dunkin....Dunkin Donuts®

What came to my heart is God's admonition to:

Do it HIS way...
Giving up my way....

And living on every word that comes from the mouth of God.

Walking and not being weary; running and not fainting. Teach us Lord to wait...upon YOU!

Bless you today,

Pat

"Testing"

February 15, 2012

Yesterday I went to see a hand therapist. She was very thorough and she shared some things with me. One of the things she told me was that she had just read a scientific article which stated that there was no clear understanding of why chemo causes neuropathy. So it is difficult to treat something whose cause you do not know.

When I returned home and during the night, I did not sense any real relief from the pain, tingling or numbness in my left hand. I also realized that God knows what is going on in my body, and HE knows how and when to heal it. The wonderful insight HE gave me was that the one who ministers to us is not the one who heals us. It is *always* the Lord who heals us. I am so thankful that HE chooses whom we come in contact with for HIS purposes. No one has the power to heal, only God. And HE has already given me a sense of what to say to my therapist the next time I see her.

So today as I wait for HIM, I know HE will release HIS power through his loving hand of mercy, and HE will be with me as I wait expectantly for HIM.

Love you all,
Pat

Healthy Thoughts

February 20, 2012

Yesterday as I was reading I Samuel, I began to think about what cuts off our communication with God. At that time I was angry. I'm not sure at whom or whether it was frustration, rejection, or offense.

I know that the text in Chapter 3 talks about how Eli could not hear God (due to his negligence in disciplining his sons who were defiling the temple) and Samuel could.

The feelings that surfaced were ugly, and yet there was in me a push or compulsion to nurse those feelings. As I pondered and prayed, the revelation came to me that all these feelings were accomplishing was bondage.

I began to realize that these kinds of feelings can begin to build so that they are out of control as James tells us in Chapter 1. They entrap us. The anger feeds bondage. Yet how easy it is for us to want to hold on to our hurt feelings and blame someone else for making us feel this way.

The enemy deceives us into believing that it is good to get even and that, since we are right, we are entitled to our feelings. We mistakenly think we are justified in feeling the way we do and do not seek or surrender to the truth that bondage is on the way.

So, my dear friends, when you experience the push or urge to give in to those feelings and ponder on them, remember you are choosing to listen to them instead of the LORD and without HIM we walk in darkness. Don't be deceived...God is not mocked...Open your heart and be humble. Ask for HIS light and HE will reveal the truth that will set us all free.

Bless you today,

Pat

CLOSING A CHAPTER OF LIFE

MARCH 15, 2012

And so it seems we have come to the end of this chapter of my life. I do pray that it has enriched your life and that your outlook on God has changed. I pray that you are more in tune with HIS voice and even more aware of HIS presence and power to take you through whatever you may have to go through in this life.

I think about what John 16:33 says: "In this life you will have tribulation, but take heart, I have overcome the world."

As to my present condition, I am still a work in progress. My fingers on my left hand are still numb, tingling, and with use become very painful. My upper thighs are numb and sore, and my back often feels like there are two elephants sitting on my hips. I am not able to exercise and want so

much to lose the 25 pounds I have put on during this season. YET, as Job said, "I know that my redeemer liveth..." and that is enough for me. In HIS time HE will restore all things. I am looking forward to the completion HE has for us all.

And, to end with a song:

> *When we all get to heaven*
> *What a day of rejoicing*
> *That will be!*
> *When we all see Jesus*
> *We'll sing and shout the victory!!*

Looking forward to seeing you there.

Pat

Editor's Note: *Excerpt from Pat's personal journal.*

3/16/12

Feeling a little low - YET am searching ... for more of GOD -
Found words from J. Newton -
"GOD often takes a course for accomplishing His purposes directly contrary to what our narrow views would prescribe. He brings a death upon our feelings, wishes and prospects when He is about to give us the desire of our hearts."
So even this mrng - Sarah - a merry heart - brings healing - ^{Pv} 17:22, 15:13, 15 —

It's not *too* hard to believe God vs. my feelings - even (J.N.) and Sarah - abundant life is not nec. health + wealth - instead relax where you are ...
Life is in choosing life - in finding Him even in the circumstances (Pvbs 15:15 AMP). Life is HIM all else is background

How great is the love the Father has lavished on us, ✱
that we should be called children of God!
1 JOHN 3:1 NIV

noise. - Focus instead on 1 Jn 3:1 *
Remembering HE sings over us —
Yet it makes no sense to be in
pain w Him watching YET HE
lives to help me to live above it
and be bound by no-thing.
The conquering power of Jesus <u>in</u>
<u>me</u> is accomplished by sur-
render and confident, positive,
expectation of HIS good reward
but mostly HIM as my reward.
The desire of my heart has to
always be first and foremost
HIM - Hearing HIM. Knowing
HE is here w me to go <u>though</u>
this dark time is more
light than "success - health -
wealth" and a shallow
relationship w Him. And the
rewards··· they always have to
be an overflow of HIM — never
an end in themselves for
they then become empty.
Momentary "light" afflictions"?"
How is it light — It is as we see it:

through the eye of eternity and His constant presence now OR through the eye of pain, inconvenience, and impatience — HE is more & more my source and my goal. He is my comforter and even the one who calls me to comfort as I have been comforted. He has wonderful plans, fulfilling plans for me and in it all He will be glorified!
* He is my satisfaction — even the provider of all my needs as I walk on this earth — ever looking & longing for Him and my home on the streets of GOD — forever!

*Praise the Lord, O my soul, and forget not all His benefits...
who satisfies your desires with good things.
PSALM 103:2, 5 NIV

TRANSLATED: Feeling a little low this morning, YET am searching . . . for more of GOD. Quoting words from John N., "God often takes a course for accomplishing His purposes directly contrary to what our narrow views would prescribe. He brings a death upon our feelings, wishes, and prospects when He is about to give us the desire of our hearts." So, even this morning, Sarah, "*A merry heart brings healing*". (Proverbs 7:22, 15:13-13)

It's not too hard to believe God vs. my feelings. Abundant life is not necessarily health and wealth. Instead, relax where you are. Life is in CHOOSING LIFE, in finding HIM even in the circumstances. <u>LIFE IS HIM</u>! All else is background noise. Focus instead on 1 John, 3:1 remembering <u>HE sings over us</u>. Yes, I know it makes no sense to be in pain with HIM watching, YET HE lives to help me live above the pain and be bound by NO thing. The conquering power of Jesus <u>in me</u> is accomplished by surrender and confident, positive expectation of HIS good reward. The desire of my heart must always be, first and foremost, HIM: Hearing HIM. Knowing HE is here with me to go <u>through</u> this dark time is *more light* than "success-health-wealth" and a shallow relationship with HIM. And the rewards? They always have to be an overflow of HIM, never an end in themselves, for they then become empty. Momentary "*light*" fixation? How is it light? It is as we see it: either through the eye of eternity and HIS constant presence now, or through the eye of pain, inconvenience, and impatience.

HE is more and more my source and my goal. HE is my comforter--and even the one who calls me to comfort as I have been comforted. HE has wonderful plans, fulfilling plans for me, and in it all HE will be glorified! HE is my satisfaction, the provider of all my needs, as I walk this earth ever looking and longing for HIM and my eternal home on the streets of GOLD forever!

Deep, Deep, Thoughts

MARCH 20, 2012

Dear Brothers and Sisters,

Just felt I wanted to communicate with you all in a deeper way. (These past few weeks I have had serious back pain and also continued pain in my left hand. I am going for physical therapy and will be seeing a neurologist on Friday.) So here goes...

If God is faithful, and if HE has remembered HIS promises to us, and if we are HIS beloved, why do we suffer so much??? And do we really suffer *so* much? There are many who are suffering more than we can imagine and for the cause of Christ. Why do we even ask why? One of my friends says that pain sidetracks us. So maybe our battle is to praise God and believe HIM when nothing looks like HE is with us. Why do we even think HE is not with us? Maybe because we

interpret pain as a withdrawal of HIS presence and blessing. Is HE far away? No. Do we function by our feelings so that we think HE is? Yes. Our greatest weapon is praise <u>in</u> and <u>through</u> the pain.

A friend of mine asked if I was in pain during chemo, and for the most part I have to say "no" (unless of course my memory is selective). I know that at that time I truly sensed God had put me in a bubble of HIS protection and HIS presence. So why all the pain now??? Again, why am I even asking? Perhaps the day in and day out pain cycle and the expectation that I would be beginning the up and out phase of recovery, is my idea and not God's. Then again, is God in the pain business? Of course not! Yet HIS view of my circumstances is definitely different than mine. Shall I ask what HE wants me to learn? Maybe...and maybe HE just wants me to be still waiting in faith, in positive expectation, knowing HIS plan and will is good.

Am I the first to suffer? Will I be the last? How foolish of me to even ask. This is my "tour of duty" and HIS school of refining. When we sing "refiner's fire, my heart's desire", do we know what we are asking? And yet we do not choose what HE has chosen to allow into our lives. One thing is sure: He loves us with an everlasting love.

Bless you all,
Pat

Sketch inspired by Carden's Design Photography, CardensDesign.com

NEW MESSAGE FROM CARL

MARCH 25, 2012

Hello All,

Pat has been experiencing <u>low</u> back pain, gripping or knifing <u>low</u> abdominal cramps, and thigh pain for the last 3-4 days. We thought it might be in response to her starting and having PT, but the pain has been increasing even after taking round-the-clock 1000mg Tylenol alternating with 800mg Motrin.

The nights are worse--shades of where she was seven months ago. She hasn't been able to find a comfortable position while either sitting or standing up, so tonight at 7PM I called Dr. B's ER office. The on-call doctor's advice was to take a stronger pain med through the night and see Dr. B. tomorrow in her office at 8AM in HH.

Pat has been finished with Chemo since 1/6/12 and has been feeling relatively good. Her beautiful silver hair is returning (3/8 of an inch so far), yet she has had numbness in her fingers and was being treated with Neurontin® for post-chemo neuropathy. Friday her neurologist indicated, after testing, that her numbness/tingling is due more to Carpal Tunnel Syndrome than chemo related.

It's now 10:30 PM and Pat has been sleeping for the last hour and a half for which I'm grateful.

Pray that Pat sleeps better tonight, that we can see Dr. B. tomorrow without an appointment, that whatever is going on in her body can be identified and treated, that her excess fluids and weight can be reduced, that her energy returns, that we understand what her "new normal" looks like, and <u>we thank & trust God for His healing</u>.

Let me encourage you with the words from Psalm 143:1-12.

Remember, keep on praying, keep on believing! The battle is the Lord's.

Pat sends her love as I do.

Carl

NEW BEGINNINGS OF THE OLD

MARCH 28, 2012

Hello All,

Well, after almost 48 hours of talking to many nurses, technicians, interns, supervisors, resident doctors, MDs, and their assistants, even orderlies, etc., in the ED at HH, its amazing how the whole system can function or work at all. Through many errors of omission, oversight, oops, oddities, and slip ups. **Our dear Patricia is in the hospital with the return of carcinosarcoma cancer.** Remember when we said it was **"rare, microscopic, and aggressive"** seven months ago (almost to the day)? <u>It's that way again</u>! She has a large, melon-sized mass in her abdominal cavity, along with several smaller ones that are pressing on her liver, kidneys, bladder and bowel. How did we find that out?

Well after spending another 7 hrs in the ED on Monday, 3/26, and Dr B. out of town this week, the ED doctors concluded that Pat had a UTI and were ready to release her with antibiotics. I insisted on a CT Scan; which took 2 hrs to schedule and another 2 hrs to locate a doctor covering for Dr. B. to interpret the results. During this time Pat started vomiting for no apparent reason as she had not eaten anything in 24 hrs. The covering physician noticed a blockage (tumor) on Pat's left kidney causing the dry heaves and vomiting and recommended a minor by-pass to relieve this pressure. Pat agreed to this

procedure yesterday. The Dr. concluded by telling us Pat's empty abdominal cavity is filled with a new larger tumor. <u>Carcinosarcoma</u>! Pat and I looked lovingly at each other across the room like Maria and Tony did in *West Side Story*. It was a moment in time I will always remember as Pat held up her right index finger. I knew what she meant. **One time!** Back in August when she had to choose one of four treatment plans, Pat chose the chemo with the best results but worst side effects. Pat said then, "I will give it **one** shot. For God will see me through." Now with the cancer back, she was saying, "No more treatments. I'm ready for Jesus. Keep me comfortable." Pat was admitted once again into HH.

The by-pass procedure was done this morning. The vomiting has ceased. PTL!! She is more comfortable now with a pain level of 5, but that is with several high-level drugs through her button control of dosage. Her prayer request is that God will deliver her from the pain and vomiting, that she gets out of the hospital quickly, and that I learn how to cook.

March 28, 2012 (continued)

Seriously, this journey has taught me many things besides waiting and trusting in God. One of them is to not long for the absence of problems in my life. That is an unrealistic goal, since in this world we will have troubles. But we have an <u>eternity</u> of problem-free living reserved for us in heaven. Let us rejoice in that inheritance if you can receive it. Remember, it's how we respond to the trials in our lives that define us as Christians and people.

As Pat has been holding onto the hand of Him who gives her peace in the storm of <u>her</u> life, my prayer is that I practice the presence and peace of knowing GOD better. He will be there for you also. Thanks for being our family and friend. Our love for you grows stronger and deeper with each new day of experiences as you have reached out to us in our test of faith.

Pat has asked that you refrain from visiting her right now; e-mails and text messages will be great. She or I will respond when we can. Keep on praying.

With our love overflowing for you,
Pat & Carl

Editor's Note: *Pat is in HH 3/26-4/2*

Palm Sunday

April 1, 2012

From Carl (written at night from HH, the day before Pat was released to Elim Park under Hospice care)

Wave the Palms, Spread the Branches —
Jesus is Coming into Jerusalem!

Clap your Hands,
All ye Saints —
Jesus is Calling.

Jesus is Calling Patricia,
maybe Today, maybe
Tomorrow, someday Soon.

Jesus is Calling her Home,
Patricia is going Home, Alleluia!

He is Holding her Hand, He will See her Through. Alleluia!

Thanks for praying, thanks for believing, pray now for a quick release.

Love from the entire Jahrstorfer family

ELIM PARK

APRIL 3, 2012

A quick update--

Pat left HH at 3pm and was settled in at Elim Park (EP) by 7pm tonight through an excellent and thorough EP admission team effort. However, her pain level increased dramatically through Sunday night, so she is now at 9 mg an hour of Dilaudid. It's keeping Pat comfortable but sleepy and therefore difficult to communicate with.

She is being cared for under the supervision of the VNA Hospice program of Cheshire with the outstanding nursing team of EP assisting as necessary. The week-long hospital stay was difficult for Pat. She now finds the peace and release she is ready for as she o_ver c_omes and wins the battle of this aggressive and rare carcinosarcoma cancer with her faith and acceptance of GOD's will for her life. God is sovereign, and we trust Him with our lives for what we don't see. Amen!

Pray for Pat to rest in the Lord's arms like a little lamb in the shepherd's and that we grieve well yet rejoice in her wonder, wisdom and wit—as is Patricia Ann Dorothy Concetta La Russa Jahrstorfer.

Your friend and brother,
Carl

A Note from Carl at Elim Park

APRIL 4, 2012

Loved Ones,

Pat is heavily sedated now. She is unable to communicate in any form. I ache with pain and gripping sobs of emotion when I look at what the enemy of our flesh has done with the shell/tent of my beloved wife of almost 47 years. But, praise GOD that her soul will be released soon to be free singing with the angels and soaring with the eagles.

Pat is quiet and locked into the body that is contaminated, but I know to believe that "the tiger in her tank", her very soul, is being ready to be released like a butterfly bursting out of its cocoon...like the power of Jesus' resurrection that we will celebrate this Sunday. Perhaps there will be a double celebration on Easter.

Elim Park and Hospice have been exactly what I hoped and expected to provide for Pat. We have caring and

April 4, 2012 (continued)

compassionate, well-trained nurses and aides to serve the needs of the terminally ill. Pat is comfortable for half a day, and then doctors need to increase the dosage of the pain meds as the cancer tumors keeps growing and forcing her body to push out more fluids and work over time. Her heart rate is beating rapidly at 125 b.p.m. She is getting weaker looking, yet internally she is a very strong woman of character, unfailing faith, and everlasting love for us.

Let us continue to pray for a quick release and peace. Thank you as she leads the way for us as we face our own trials still left behind on this dying planet. Let us have hope, knowledge, and believe that Sunday is coming!

Alleluia.

Carl

EASTER IS COMING

APRIL 6, 2012

GOOD FRIDAY MORNING

Hello Precious Family and Friends,

Yes, you are precious in His sight as well as ours. Pat is very weak and close to being called out of her earthly veil of pain and tears by God, and He is wrapping her spirit in a new heavenly gown waiting for Jesus to embrace her. She no longer needs His hand, for she will be in His presence forever.

Pat's last few thoughts and words communicated from her life to mine:

> *Cry a little, but then mourn no more. For some, it will take longer, I know. But rejoice in the LORD and let me go. I'm where I want to be.*

Wouldn't it be a <u>celebration</u> if Pat waited till Sunday for His touch?! Thanks for being supportive and praying.

Your brother and friend in Christ,

Carl

A Bittersweet Passage

April 7, 2012

Dear Family and Friends,

It is with a heavy heart but a joy in my spirit to tell you that our little but brave Patricia has left this earth of pain and tears (April 6, 10:30 PM) to be with her Lord and Savior, Jesus Christ.

The little girl who had been talking about holding Jesus' hand while riding her 3 wheeler as a 4 year old is now complete. She is free to sing with all the angels of heaven. Jesus has carried her **through**.

Pat was a miracle, surviving major 5 hour surgery, enduring six cycles of chemo, and severe pain from newly formed cancer. She never complained or questioned why? She endured the trial of her life by envisioning herself in a bubble holding the hand of Jesus, the author and finisher of our faith.

I believe Pat Over Came Ovarian Cancer.

She faced the enemy of our souls, she fought the good fight, and she won the victory. She cried out in her soul (like Jesus in the garden and on the cross) in the middle of the night. It was a Good Friday! Jesus called her to Himself last night at 10:30 PM. She now joins the saints of heaven singing the Hallelujah Chorus the way she

always wanted-- with trumpets, drums and cymbals!
The life she lived, seeker of truth, a laugh and smile that radiated wholeness, peace, and joy; yet a personality and character that was a challenge to behold. Pat's constitution was strong: She was direct, even blunt sometimes causing hurt, but her forgiveness was real. She loved to laugh, read, talk, write, and she loved to encourage us to grow in our faith to find the TRUTH, for the truth will set you free.

Some of her last words spoken and communicated through me before she went under heavy sedation last Sunday (4/1/2012):

> *Cry a little, but then mourn no more.*
> *For some it will take longer, I know.*
> *But please let me go.*

> *Remember, trust God, leave all the consequences to Him.*
>
> *Rejoice in the Lord always, again, I say rejoice in the Lord!*
>
> *Yes, I suffered and died, some will question why?*
>
> *But, the bigger question is what will you do when Jesus knocks on the door of your heart?*
>
> *Do what I did. Look up to God and grasp the hand of His son, Jesus.*
>
> *He will give you peace and hope in a dying world.*
>
> *I know...for I am in His embrace right now!*

CPSIA information can be obtained at www.ICGtesting.com
Printed in the USA
LVOW13s0719030414

380151LV00001B/140/P